GW00457002

GAME OVER

WHITHALL UNIVERSITY

LISA HELEN GRAY

Copyrights reserved © Lisa Helen Gray

Edited by Stephanie Farrant at Bookworm Editing Services
Cover Design by Cassy Roop at Pink Ink Designs
Paperback Interior Format by Abigail Davies at Pink Elephant Designs

No part of this publication may be reproduced or transmitted in any form or by any means, electronic or mechanical, including photocopy, recording, or any information storage and retrieval system without the prior written consent from the publisher, except in the instance of quotes for reviews. No part of this book may be scanned, uploaded, or distributed via the Internet without the publisher's permission and is a violation of the international copyright law, which subjects the violator to severe fines and imprisonment.

This book is licensed for your enjoyment. E-book copies may not be resold or given away to other people. If you would like to share with a friend, please buy an extra copy. Thank you for respecting the author's work.

This is a work of fiction. Any names, characters, places and events are all product of the author's imagination. Any resemblance to actual persons, living or dead, business or establishments is purely coincidental.

Out of the darkness, comes light.

Prologue

My shoes beat along the paved pavement, following behind at a healthy pace. She doesn't hear me, see me, or even sense me watching.

So much had changed over the past couple of weeks; deep within me I felt something crack, until finally—deliciously—I felt that something snap.

A darkness now filled my empty soul, flooding life back into me. For so long I had felt empty, like something was wrong with me. Now, I know I was right. I hadn't been who I was meant to be, who I was born to be.

Now, I've been reborn.

And it's all because of her.

My fists clench as I think about her. She's mine. She'll always be mine. She just hasn't gotten to know me, the real me. But she will.

And he'll be gone.

When I saw them kissing—when they didn't think anyone was looking—I was enraged. The thought of her with him, with anyone, made my blood boil. The anger inside me built and built, until it was almost like I was choking on it.

Shaking my head, my thoughts go to a happier time, a time when everything was perfect.

The first time I saw her, she was walking across the quad to class. Her bronze hair shone against the summer sun, and her eyes sparkled in the light. She smiled as she walked past, unaware of what she had stirred inside me as she carried on walking with her friend.

She's the light to my dark.

And soon, she'll know just how much we belong together.

Today, I'm going to show her just how much I love her. How much she means to me. It will be like a present, of sorts.

Christie, the girl I'm following, stops outside her residential hall. She throws up in a bush and I grin, carrying on into the building to start my surprise.

You see, Christie did something, something not many know. But I do. And I'm going to make her pay.

Finding her room isn't hard. The girl sleeps around like no one's business —her room number is on the back of most toilets.

She's just that easy.

I jiggle the handle of her door, not at all surprised to find it open.

Fools, the lot of them, and incredibly weak-minded.

All except her.

I flick the lamp on when I enter, looking around for the best place to wait until she arrives. In the corner is a chair, pressed between the wall and a dresser. Grinning, I walk over and sit down, crossing my legs as I wait.

It isn't long before the door flies open and she comes staggering in. I made sure she came home alone tonight. After all, not many lads want to sleep with someone who is going to be sloppy.

I planned this down to the last second, and I'll be damned if some cheap hook-up is going to ruin it for me.

"Whoops."

She falls onto her bed, kicking off her shoes, making everything so much easier for me. It's like she wants to die tonight.

Taking a deep breath, I stand slowly, making sure I don't make a noise as I move over to her. She's grumbling about never drinking again, and I want to tell her it will no longer be a problem for her.

Because after tonight, she'll be merely a memory.

She'll just be some girl who died on campus.

My fingers wrap around the heavy torch in my trousers, and I raise it above my head. She must hear me because she turns, a startled look on her face, before I hit her. She falls down easily and I grin, catching her.

I'm going to drag this out and have plenty of fun doing it.

I make quick work of tying her to the bed and gagging her. The last thing I need is for her to alert someone of me being here. It would ruin my plans.

And I must feed the beast inside me.

Groaning, she comes to, her eyes blinking rapidly. I watch as everything comes back to her, before she starts struggling. I sit astride her, feeding on the fear radiating from her in waves. I inhale through my nose, my body humming at the intoxicating scent.

"I'd like to say this isn't personal, but we both know it is." My voice is

rough, unrecognisable in my desire to cause her pain, so I pull off my hood, revealing myself to her.

She blinks, surprise flashing across her face before she once again starts struggling, cursing under the gag. It makes me laugh, a sinister smile spreading across my face.

My fingers glide up her arms, loving the way she struggles beneath my touch. Maybe a taste of her own medicine is what she needs, but her blonde hair, green eyes, and hollow face just don't do it for me.

I sigh, tilting my head to the side.

"You need to be punished, Christie."

Her head shakes from side to side as my hands make their way up to her neck, squeezing as hard as I can. My fingers dig into her pulse, feeling it beating erratically under my touch.

It feeds the beast further, like he's coming home for the first time.

After a few minutes, her porcelain skin turns purple and her futile struggling becomes slow and weak.

I let go, needing to prolong her punishment.

She gasps, trying to catch her breath. Her eyes dilate, her pupils bloodshot, and I lean down, licking the side of her face, chin to ear. She tries to fight me, to get away, her screams muffled behind the gag.

"If I let you go, will you promise to leave Whithall University?" I ask, slowly running my fingers down her hair.

She looks at me wild-eyed, nodding her head furiously as tears fall down her cheeks.

Unable to resist, I lean down, capturing them with a lazy swipe of my tongue.

"You taste so good. Fear becomes you," I murmur in her ear. "But I'm sorry, you need to be punished."

She shakes her head, her screams getting louder and louder as her legs kick and her hips buck to get free.

I throw my head back, laughing, before looking her straight in the eye, showing her just who she's dealing with.

She must see her death in my gaze because she starts shaking her head, her eyes pleading with me to set her free.

And I will. Death will be the ultimate freedom. The price of her sins. I'm doing the world a favour. She's dirty, unclean... She deserves what is about to happen.

With a grin, I lean down, my hot breath fanning across her face before I grip her neck once again, my hold tighter, stronger.

Only this time, I won't give her the slightest bit of hope. Because now, I'm going to choke the life out of her.

Just as the blood vessels in her eyes pop, I lift the knife out of my back pocket, before plunging it into her stomach. I do it again when the warmth of her blood runs through my fingers, then once more to feel that rush.

Her movements slow down, the fight leaving her body, along with the last bit of oxygen, until finally, her body slumps to the bed lifelessly.

But my beast doesn't calm. If anything, the rage building inside me continues, wanting and needing more. I need to show her *she can't kiss other people, that she can't leave me. She's mine.*

It's only when a noise next door startles me do I let go, sitting back to admire my handywork. I wipe the knife on my leg, nodding my approval.

Her wild hair captures my attention, and yearning to tame it settles in my mind. I manoeuvre my body off hers and look around the room, before picking up the brush on the desk and moving back to the bed.

She looks peaceful, finally in a place she belongs.

I brush the front of her hair, hypnotised by how easily it combs through. I reach out, touching the strands of hair that feel nothing like hers. *They don't feel silky or soft. I growl, anger at Christie piercing my chest.*

Grabbing my backpack, I look through the contents before finding what I need.

I undo her ties and cross her hands over her chest, before moving back to her hair. I lift her head, fingers fumbling slightly as I feel around the back of her skull before snipping off a chunk of her blonde locks, needing it to remember her, to remember this moment.

I place it in a clear bag and put it in the front of my backpack, not wanting it to get spoiled by the yogurt and drink I have in there.

It needs to be cherished, to be admired, which is what I'll do.

With that done, I get up from the bed, carefully tucking the blanket up to her chin and covering the blood seeping from her wounds. A part of me wants to leave her eyes open, wishing I could be here when her roommate finds her and sees the fear in those glassy orbs, the fear she felt in the last moments of her life.

It will scare her roommate, the thought bringing a new kind of shiver to run down my spine.

Sighing, I close them, wanting her to rot here for as long as possible. If fate is on my side, her roommate will stay out all weekend and leave Christie to fester.

Now all I can do is wait for her to find out the news. She'll know I did this for her. She will. And she'll thank me for it, worship me even.

As I begin to leave, I turn back around, wanting to capture the moment to memory. An idea occurs, and I pull out my phone, snapping a picture before grinning down at it.

Yes, the beast has been tamed.

But for how long?

Chapter 1

Life at Whithall hall has changed drastically over the course of two weeks. Logan and Jamie were sent to prison, with no chance of parole, for the series of rapes they committed.

What has everyone on edge and still whispering are the events that happened the day they were sentenced.

Christie, a girl who was partly involved in incidents that happened on Halloween—when we took down Logan and Jamie—was murdered. She was found in her dorm room by her roommate, stabbed to death. It was shocking to us all.

The university closed down for a week to have new security measures installed. They made sure the university was securely shut after her murder, meaning no classes and no staying on uni grounds. Those who couldn't get home were given a place to stay at a local hotel, funded by the university.

Since me and my best friend lived in our own flats near the university, we didn't really have to leave. But much to our dismay, our parents had other ideas, since we had a week off for the holidays.

Low's mum, I could understand. Her daughter was brutally assaulted by one of her best friends and then managed to take him down, thanks to a group of us. They also had a tight relationship, something I'd never had with my mum or dad.

My dad worked a lot, and although our relationship is better now that my mother is no longer in the picture, his reasons for me to come home so urgently were puzzling. Before coming to Whithall, he spent the majority of his life in his office or at work.

What surprised me the most was that he stayed at home to spend time with me, even if it was only for an hour or two.

Mel, Willow's mum, and my dad arranged for us to have a meal a few days after we returned home. They wanted us to sit down and to talk to us about something important. Due to Low getting her night-mares again, it was cancelled.

She had them after her attack, but with time, they dwindled. Being

7

back at our parents' homes, though… She started getting them again, tenfold. I tried everything to help my friend. I stayed at hers, or her mine, and slept in the same bed to try and help soothe her tortured mind, but I think being back there was hurting her. The memories she had once fondly shared with Logan tarnished everything around her. Her mum, Mel, had thought ahead and tried to remove pictures and other things of him from their house, but there's only so much you can try to erase. Memories are harder.

After a week and a half, I couldn't take any more. Seeing my friend in emotional torment stirred the guilt I already felt and deserved. I'll never be able to apologise enough to her. My part in her attack could have been prevented, and for that, I'll always feel terrible for the pain I've caused her.

Night after night I've listened to her scream out for help, pleading with her tormentor to stop. I never spoke about what she said in her nightmares, not wanting to bring it up, but the minute she was fully conscious I only had to look in her eyes to know she knew she'd had another nightmare. She would lash out at me in her sleep, her grip tightening on me painfully.

I had nearly given in three days ago and called her boyfriend, Cole, for help. She seems to do better when she's around him. He helped her, first as a neighbour, then as a friend, and now as a boyfriend. They're relationship has blossomed into something beautiful.

She made me promise not to call him, telling me he needed the alone time with his family. I knew she felt guilty for occupying his time, but Cole doesn't mind and neither does his family. They love her. But then again, who wouldn't. Willow is the greatest friend anyone could wish for. It's me who keeps letting her down.

When we woke this morning, I told her we needed to come home, that being back at our parents', where all her memories with Logan were, wasn't helping her recovery. She declined, but the look in her eyes was answer enough. She was suffering and she needed her safe haven; she needed Cole. By dinner time, I had finally convinced her. I was no longer able to take in her tired, red-rimmed eyes. It was breaking my heart.

We planned to tell our parents together, but with both of them at work, we decided to drop in on them separately at work to say goodbye. Only, when we arrived at my house to grab my stuff, we caught the both of them together on the sofa.

Something I wish I could erase from my mind.

Which is why we hightailed it to my room, packed my bags, and got out of there, ignoring their pleas to explain.

There wasn't any explaining needed. It was obvious what they were doing.

Now we're back home, where we can take the time to forget the whole day.

I shiver, running my eyes over our brightly lit kitchen. It's late, and I didn't think Rosie and Becca would be up, but the lights in the front room are on too.

We walk in, finding them both on the sofa, Becca with her arm around a crying Rosie. We met Rosie and Becca when we were finding proof of what Logan was doing. At the time, we thought it was just him, but that day, we found Rosie badly beaten and scared after having spent the weekend in Jamie's room being abused.

I drop my bag, rushing over to the two girls who have become best friends to me. "What's wrong? What happened?"

Willow sits on the opposite side of Becca, leaning around her so she can look at Rosie's tear-streaked face.

"Hey, what's up?" she asks softly.

Becca gives us a small smile, but I can see the anger brewing behind her chocolate-brown eyes. "Rosie called her parents tonight." Her eyes drift back to her friend, pity filling them.

Before we left, both girls still hadn't told their parents about what had happened to them. We've managed to get both into a group counselling session—our friend Jordan, who runs a blog, organised it all, and even some one-on-one sessions for Rosie, who went through the most. Neither wanted their families to find out, and they never told us why.

Rosie's found the sessions hard and can only go if Becca is with her.

"What happened?" I ask, taking her cold, slim hand in mine. Rosie's lost weight since her attack, a lot of it. The photos they shared with me and Willow, showed the girl to be healthy and happy. The girl in front of me is broken and a mess. And rightly so.

Rosie looks up, wiping her cheeks. "We thought it was time to tell them what happened."

"Bringing up those memories must have been hard for you," I comment.

She shakes her head, her eyes brimming with more tears as she looses a forlorn laugh. "It was, but that's not why I'm upset. Our parents—*my* parents are..."

"What she's trying to tell you is that our parents are religious. Rosie's are catholic and have strong beliefs when it comes to what they think is right or wrong. My parent's only attend church every Sunday, but Rosie's... they preach it. They think what happened to her is God's will and He's punishing her for her sins." Becca's last words come out with a bite, her face stormy and red with anger. I don't blame her, my own anger is rising and I don't get mad, like, ever.

How could her parents believe that? You only have to look at Rosie to know she's everything that is good in the world. She wouldn't hurt a fly.

"Why on earth would they say such a thing?" Willow grits her teeth, looking away so she doesn't show her anger.

"You know what they are saying isn't true, don't you?" I ask Rosie, squeezing her hand.

Rosie nods. "I do, but hearing it still hurts. It's why we decided to move so far away to attend university. Becca's parents aren't like mine; they're kind and understanding. They know I'm gay and don't see me any differently. They didn't try to make me change or lock me in a basement until God himself saw me cleansed."

"Your parents are arseholes," Willow tells her, not ashamed to call them out. It's why I love her so much. She's always had my back. Seeing the fight in her eyes reminds me of the old Willow, before she was attacked, and it brings tears to my eyes. She was always feisty and carefree. She said what she thought and didn't care who heard. Now, she's wary of who she speaks to and is constantly looking over her shoulder, even if she doesn't realise she's doing it.

Rosie lets out a watery laugh. "They are. They blamed what happened to me on me being gay. I don't know why I thought telling them would make them feel any different towards me. I guess I was hoping they'd hear how badly I was hurt and would come running."

Understanding dawns on me. "You thought they would break their beliefs after knowing you were hurt and become the loving parents you wished them to be?"

She eyes me gratefully. "You understand?"

I nod solemnly. "I do. My mother isn't a nice person. When I was younger, I would do everything I could to gain her love and respect. But it never happened. When... well, you know who, tried to do what he did, she didn't even care. She just saw a payday. I wanted to get back at her for putting me in the position she did, and told her I was going to tell Low," I whisper, remembering her fingers digging into my bicep. They bruised my skin, marking me for weeks. "She manipulated me. She told me Dad would hate me if he lost all his money and his job. She said we'd lose our house and everything."

"You didn't tell me that," Willow whispers.

I glance at her, shrugging. "It doesn't excuse lying to you. I knew it was wrong."

She leans over, giving me a one-armed hug.

"We have screwed-up parents," Rosie comments, making me laugh. "We do."

"We really do." Willow groans, falling back on the sofa.

Becca and Rosie turn to her with a sceptical eye. "What do you mean? Your mum is wonderful. She loves seeing you."

Low opens one eye, staring at them. "I saw more of my mum tonight than I ever wanted to. Trust me."

Becca grins, turning to look at me. I hold my hands up. "She's right, only I saw my father's backside, and trust me, I'll be having nightmares for weeks."

Willow groans, covering her face with her hands before turning to glare at me, as if to say, *Really?*

Rosie blushes. "Wait… your parents…"

"Hooked up? Yes." Willow nods solemnly, looking a little pale. I don't blame her; my stomach is still a little queasy.

Becca laughs before sobering. "Wait, is that what they wanted you both to go home to talk about?" She looks excited, and I want to snap at her that this isn't funny, but knowing Becca, she would take it to heart. It would be like kicking a puppy. I couldn't do it.

"Yes," I tell her, wanting to moan.

"You'll be step-sisters," Rosie says, her tears now gone.

"I'm glad my dad bumping uglies with my best friend's mum, cheers you up." I pause, what she said registering, and my eyes snap to Willow's, a grin forming. "Holy moly, we will be like real sisters."

She rolls her eyes. "We didn't need our parents doing *that* for us to know we're sisters. We've always been sisters."

"Sister from another mister," I laugh.

She laughs too, shaking her head at me before turning to the girls. "We haven't eaten. We felt too sick to stop and eat after what we witnessed. Do you fancy sharing pizza?"

Rosie's belly rumbles and we all laugh. "I'll go order."

There's a knock on the door before I make it to my bag to grab my phone, so I stop to answer it, forgetting to use the peephole.

I don't even have chance to open the door all the way before I'm lifted into the air and swung around by strong, muscled arms.

"Put me down, you oversized ape," I squeal, smacking CJ's back. And although I sound pissed, I'm far from it. I've missed him so much since we've been away. Talking to him over the phone hasn't been the same.

Since Willow's attack, he's stayed with me. He's slept on the sofa, on the floor, and once, even outside my room—unbeknownst to me at the time. It was the night Willow found out about me knowing about Logan. It wasn't all night; my dad woke him to go back to his flat.

Before I left, he started to sleep in my bed, doing nothing but hold me all night, and I've missed his touch. I've missed being in his arms.

I've missed him.

I try to hide my smile as he puts me down, but it's useless when I see his boyishly charming grin spread across his face.

"Cupcake!" he yells, making sure everyone knows he's arrived. I inwardly groan at the nickname he's christened me with. "I've missed you."

Before I can answer, he pulls me against him and kisses me. His hot lips pressed against mine taste sweet—my favourite flavour—and I can't help but moan in delight.

"Woah, keep it PG. There's eyes in the room," Willow calls out, before dissolving into a fit of giggles.

I pull away, my gaze never leaving CJ's as I stare into his mesmerising mocha-coloured eyes. "Hi," I greet breathlessly.

He grins, kissing the tip of my nose. "Cupcake, I've missed you. Aren't you going to tell me you've missed me, too?"

Instead of greeting me like a normal, sane boyfriend would, he has to outmatch everyone. Hell, I haven't even heard Cole utter a word to Willow, but then again, his eyes communicate everything he wants to say. He's dark and broody most of the time, but there's no denying he loves her with his whole heart.

"I don't know yet. I'm still kind of pissed at you," I lie, having gotten over my tantrum before I'd even left to go back home.

He rolls his eyes as he leans down to kiss my nose once again, something he does often. "I told you I was sorry. You can't be still mad at me over that?"

I want to kick his shin because although I'm no longer mad, it still riles me up. Everyone knows to leave my stash alone.

"It was my last Sherbet Fountain, CJ. I have to special order them from Amazon."

His face drops. "You knew about the Sherbet Fountain?"

My eyes narrow dangerously as I tap my foot on the carpeted floor, giving him a pointed look. "Why else would I yell at you for stealing my sweets, CJ?"

He rubs the back of his neck, looking to the ceiling for a second before giving me a sheepish smile. "I thought it was over the Frosties."

His admission has my fists clenching. "CJ!" I scream. "They are even harder to get. It took me a month to find another website that had them in stock."

"Shit!"

Cole and Willow laugh, and when I turn to throw them my glare, they shut up. I take my sweets seriously. Everyone, and I mean *everyone*, down to the teachers at university, know not to touch my sweets. But CJ? He just can't get the message through that head of his. He sees it, wants it, then takes it. It's how he got me to agree to be his girlfriend. I didn't even know what I was agreeing to until it was too late.

Not that I'd change it for a second.

I'd never had a boyfriend before. Crushed, yes, but I was never brave enough to take a chance. It didn't help I wasn't myself. I didn't trust boys, either.

"You do know it's a break up offence?"

He looks taken aback, and fear fills his eyes. "No. It's not. Go to your room; I have a surprise for you." I blush, knowing Cole and Willow are still here, and go to tell him what for, when he gives me that bloody heart-melting grin of his. "Allie, Allie, Allie. Are you thinking naughty things?"

He waggles his eyebrows and I slap his chest. "Shut up. I wasn't."

He laughs. "You so were. It's okay, my little cupcake. I won't tell anyone how naughty you are."

Or how I'm going to wring your bloody neck.

"CJ, I swear to—"

He puts a hand over my mouth, stopping my threat of castration, his eyes twinkling with mischief. "As much as I love where your dirty mind is going, I only told you to go into your room because I left a surprise on your bed." He winks and I scrunch my face up in revulsion, hoping he's not implying what I think he is. His laugh echoes in the tiny flat. "My, my, what a little time away can do to my good little cupcake. But get your mind out of the gutter and go look on your bed. Mum helped me."

Hearing his mum helped him, I take a step back, letting his hand drop to his side as I bounce excitedly. I know he's told her about us, and she's looking forward to meeting me, but if I'm honest, I'm nervous as hell; I've never met the rents before. But I'm more nervous over the fact that if it goes terribly wrong, CJ will dump me. He loves his mum and wouldn't do anything to upset her. I'm just glad he hasn't mentioned seeing her again since. "Can you order pizza for us while I go look? We were going to veg out on the sofas with the girls."

He nods, pulling his phone out of his pocket. "Good idea, I'm starving."

"You just had a bucket of chicken from KFC," Cole states dryly.

CJ's shoulders lift as he taps his belly. "I'm a growing boy."

We roll our eyes at him because his stomach is an endless pit.

I turn, heading for my room, which is the first door on the left. I'm sharing the flat now with Becca and Rosie since they don't feel safe enough to go back to their rooms at the university. They're sharing Willow's room for the time being, until something in a private, secure building comes along. It's just until Becca's parents can find somewhere else for them to live.

Stepping into my room, my shoulders sag and my heart melts at the sight on my bed. A wooden wicca basket is filled with various sweets, with a bow wrapped around it.

All of my favourites.

I also notice some boxes peeking out from under my bed. The first to catch my eyes are Cola Frosties. I giggle, walking over to the hamper he put together so thoughtfully. This is better than any present I could receive.

It's hard to stay mad at CJ on a good day; he's always so bubbly and outgoing. But when he does something like this, it's impossible. It just makes me open my heart up to him more and more.

"Do you like it?" he whispers, coming up behind me and startling me.

I turn, leaning up on my toes to wrap my arms around his neck. "I love it. Thank you."

His eyes fill with warmth. I love it when he looks at me like that, it makes me go weak at the knees. "You're more than welcome. I even put some extra boxes at the bottom of your wardrobe and under your bed, so we can share."

Hold up!

I don't think so.

I raise my hand, narrowing my eyes. "No. They're mine."

He chuckles deeply. "Cupcake, I bought those for me, too, so I can stop taking yours."

I shake my head. "Nope. You should have hidden them in *your* room, because they're mine now." I grin at his crestfallen expression and kiss his lips before skipping out of the room.

One should know, never, and I mean ever, think you can share sweets with Allie Davis. It just isn't going to happen.

Chapter 2

When it comes to uni, I'm the biggest nerd there is. Early mornings, on the other hand, suck and make me rethink the whole liking going to uni thing.

"Come on, Cupcake, you have to wake up. You have to be at the library in a few hours."

I smack CJ's hand away from my hair and face plant into my pillow. "Go away."

"You've got to get up."

"No!"

He chuckles, his fingers running down my back, causing me to shiver. "Cupcake, do you really want to miss your first day back at work?"

"Wake me up five minutes before I have to leave."

When he doesn't go away, I scream in frustration. I need sleep. A lot of it. Sleep, sweets, sleep, sweets, and books is my life. They're my life goals. I could survive on the three of them.

"You'll be late. I'll buy you a white chocolate mocha."

That gets my attention, so I turn my head to glare up at the man determined to get me out of bed. "I'm listening."

His smile blinds me. "And whatever you wish for breakfast. Now get your arse up. I want to spend some time with you before you have to work."

I pout, wondering if there is any way I can get out of it. "Can't I just call in sick?"

"You said not to let you when you warned me you would ask last night, remember? Plus, Alex texted to see if you can work through lunch because Martina called in sick or something. I don't know; he was stuttering a lot."

Alex was the first friend I made here at Whithall University and the only one I've got, besides Willow, that I'm close to.

We hit it off on my first day working at the library and have been close ever since. He makes some of the long days bearable.

17

I grunt, sitting up and wiping the hair out of my face. "I bet *she's* having a good sleep. And don't be mean about Alex."

He laughs before lifting the blanket off me. "Sorry."

When I notice he's fully clothed and freshly showered, I narrow my eyes. "Why are you already showered and dressed?"

He taps my nose. "Because, Cupcake, I had practice this morning. Some of us don't sleep until noon."

I frown, narrowing my eyes. "It's eight in the morning. Why would they possibly want you practicing at that time? And you owe me two white chocolate mochas for being so chirpy."

"Early bird catches the worm and all that. Now, get ready. I'll meet you in the living room when you're ready."

"Oh, all right, bossy."

"Just call me master," he tells me, winking over his shoulder.

I roll my eyes, giggling, and drop back down on the pillow. A few more minutes to wake myself up won't hurt anyone.

Work sucks. Over the half term, someone had come in and trashed the back of the library where we keep some of the older books. Instead of having someone come in at the time of the break in, they decided to wait until we were back to give us the grunt work.

Go figure.

Alex walks up to me, his lanky frame struggling to hold the pile of books in his fragile arms. "You could help carry these, you know."

I give him my sweetest smile. "But then who would sort them out into piles?"

He rolls his eyes as he puts down another pile on the table. I don't think any more are going to fit on this one, and I've already started piles on the floor.

"You could at least pretend to want to help, you know."

I shrug, shoving a lollipop in my mouth. I go back to the task at hand, when the door to the library opens. Alex and I look to each other warily before I get up off the floor to see who has come in. It's been closed for the day, until we can get some of the books in order.

When Jordan comes into view, I break out in a wide smile and rush over to greet her. "Jordan, hey. How are you? Did you have a good break?"

She smiles back, waving. Jordan is beautiful, even with all her piercings and tattoos. They add to her feminine, badass sex appeal. She has it all going on.

Her hair has grown since I last saw her and is now in a short bob, the left side shaved in some sort of pattern. The ends of her black hair are florescent pink. I like it; it suits her.

"Hey, Allie. It's been good—I'm good." She glances over my shoulder, smiling. "Hey, Alex, how's it going?"

"I'm doing all the shit work," he gripes.

I turn around and roll my eyes at him. "Stop complaining already."

Jordan laughs. "She getting you to work all those muscles?"

He laughs at her teasing, not taking what she said to heart. "Something like that. It's good to see you, but I need to get these books out here. There isn't enough room back there for us to sort them back into order."

She nods and waits for him to leave before turning to me. When her expression turns serious, I know she's found something.

When we took down Logan and his friend, it felt good, really good. Not only that, but when it was announced they had been arrested, I noticed a difference in Rosie, Becca and Willow. Something had flashed in their eyes, and I knew I wanted to do it again. I wanted to help people find justice.

And if I'm honest, all the planning, the secrecy, and getting justice lit something inside me. When Christie was announced murdered on the news, that same spark lit inside me and I knew I had to find out who did it. I'm also shit at waiting for the ending of a story, so I want to find it out myself.

It gave me the idea to write a book on a true murder, and what better way of writing it than finding out who the killer is and why they killed her.

Jordan was already working on the case, reporting what happened on her blog, so I asked if she could share any information she finds. I also wanted to know if this happened to Christie because of Logan. It just seemed weird it happened so soon after their arrest.

"What did you find?"

She nods towards the empty table near the front desk, and I follow. She grabs a folder and a memory stick before looking at me.

"I found out a lot and none of it is pretty. A friend of mine hacked into the police database. I didn't ask how or why he did it, but he did. The memory card has the crime scene photos. He took out the gruesome ones of her wounds, but other than them, that's everything they have. The only things that stand out are the way she was positioned, almost like he took care of her, and the cause of death... She didn't die from the stab wounds; she died of strangulation. Evidence, however..." she says, opening the folder. "Her hair was cut. From what I've read on true murders before, a killer will do this when he or she wants a keepsake, a memento. It's the only explanation I have on the hair thing."

Jordan tugs on her lip ring for a second before taking a deep breath. "You could have been on to something when you said Logan was somehow involved. If his parents are as high up as you say they are, then he could have easily gotten them to hire someone. Sounds very Chicago Mob, I know."

I stop her from turning the page, holding her arm. "So, he could have done it?"

I didn't like Christie, but she didn't deserve to die. I'm not going to cry over her death, but I'm also not going to rejoice in the fact she's gone, either. She was bitch and made Willow's life hard after she'd been raped.

She sighs, dropping the page she was about to turn. "I don't know. It doesn't make any sense. Christie got away with a warning because she testified against them in court. But both Jamie and Logan had been sentenced before her murder. It still pisses me off that she got away with drugging some of the victims."

"He could have done it for revenge."

20

"But for what gain?"

I bite the lollipop I had been sucking in the side of my mouth, thinking over her theory. "Okay, so let's put him aside. I don't want to rule that theory out just yet though. I asked my dad some questions about Logan's dad, and according to him, his dad has lost his job, along with several judges, and is fighting a prison sentence in court himself."

Her eyes light up with excitement. I don't blame her either. Logan's dad had paid off the judge to dismiss Jordan's sister's case. "Really?"

I smile at her expression. "Yep. Well-deserved too."

She nods, and I bet she's dying to inform her sister. "What else did you find out?"

"I'm going to talk to her roommate. She went back home for break, so I don't know when she'll be back. I also got a list of friends who were close with Christie. I faked an account on Facebook and added them. I think Christie's page was opened publicly by her family because I was able to get on hers too. A lot of them had nice things to say, but I also noticed a few trolls commenting with nasty remarks. I want to check those people out, suss whether they're involved or not. But now you have how she was murdered and the other little details, I can see if any other murders have happened with the same MO."

A look of pride flashes across her face. "Look at you. We'll make a Nancy Drew out of you yet."

I laugh, taking the files from her and putting them in my bag behind the desk. "Thank you for doing this."

"It's fine. Just don't let anyone know you've got them, and when this is all done, burn them. I don't need to warn you to not mention me if you're caught with them, do I?"

I giggle at her stern look. "No. Oh, and before I forget, we're going to the cinema later with everyone, if you want to come. Rosie had a bad phone call with her parents the other day and she's been a little more down than usual. We want to cheer her up and take her mind off things."

Her eyes fill with concern. She really cares about Rosie, and I know the two spend a lot of time together. Rosie still isn't up to going out on her own just yet, not without Becca or Jordan. "What happened?"

Not sure if I should say something or not, I decide to shrug, keeping my answer evasive. "You'll have to speak to her about it. I'm not sure how much I can share. I don't want to betray her trust. I'm sorry."

She gives me a small smile, but her attention is elsewhere as she takes her phone out of her pocket. "Let me know what time you're going. I have to show a new girl around the English building, but I'm free afterwards."

"Okay."

Another small smile as she lifts her phone. "I'm going to call her. I've got a feeling I know what her parents have done. She said she was going to talk to them the other week about what happened to her, but I got the gist she didn't want to. She looked scared. From what little I do know about them, they aren't good people."

I scoff. "That's putting it nicely."

"I'll talk to you later. Good luck with all that," she tells me, pointing towards the folder she gave me.

I watch her go for a second before taking the folder and memory stick and putting them in my bag.

"What you got there?"

I jump, turning to face Alex. "Oh, my God, you scared the hell out of me. Don't sneak up on me."

He grins sheepishly. "Sorry. Thought you heard me. What's that?"

I bite my lip as I consider what I should tell him. CJ wasn't happy when I announced I was going to look into it, so I told him I'd just read the newspapers and stuff to get the information I needed. He doesn't need to know how far into the case I'm looking.

"Just some stuff I asked Jordan to get."

He looks at me closely, suspiciously. "What kind of stuff?"

Shifting restlessly on my feet, I run my fingers through my hair. "It's about Christie's killer."

"What?" Alex pales, stepping forwards to grab my biceps, his nails biting into my skin. "Why are you looking into her murder, Allie? You need to stay away from that stuff. The newspapers are saying to be on alert."

I yank my arms from his grip. "I just asked for some details on the case. I need it for my English paper, and if I want to write a book about this, then I need to know the facts."

He scrubs a hand across his face. "It could be dangerous. I don't want you to get hurt."

"I'm not going to get hurt. For all we know, this has to do with Logan. He could have been getting revenge."

"That's what I thought when we first heard about the murder. She wasn't exactly a nice person, but still, you don't know *why* she was killed. There's a sick fuck out there walking free. It's not safe until he's caught."

I sigh, leaning back against the counter. "I know, I know. Can we keep this bit of information between us? I don't want CJ to find out, or Willow, for that matter. She'll only get upset."

He looks torn, but after a few painfully slow seconds, he nods. "Just be careful. Don't go looking for trouble."

"I will be."

The sound of the door opening gains my attention. Turning, I notice a guy who's in my English Lit class and possibly another, though I can't think what one it might be—outside my circle of friends, I don't really know anyone.

"Sorry, we're not open today," Alex calls out over my shoulder.

As the guy's gaze nervously flicks between me and Alex, I try to remember his name, but it's evading me. "I'm here to see Allie."

I sense Alex turning to me for answers but keep my focus on the guy in front of me. I don't know what he could possibly want with me. We've never spoken to each other.

"Can I help you?"

He takes a hesitant step forward. "I'm Ian. I'm in the same English class as you. I was wondering if we could talk for a moment?"

"Sure." I glance over my shoulder to where he's looking and notice Alex still standing there, watching him with the same interest.

"I'll come help in a minute," I tell Alex, wondering why he seems so tense.

He nods, walking into the back. When he's gone, I gesture for Ian to sit down at the table. As I take a seat opposite him, watching as he continues to look around nervously, my mind tries to figure out what he could want from me. The only thing I can come up with is he needs some tutoring for our English class. I can help him; I don't mind. But he might have to come into the library when I'm working because I don't think I'll have the time otherwise.

"What can I help you with?"

He jumps, like he forgot I was sitting here. Weird.

"Our teacher said I need to get at least a B on our next assignment. I need to pass this course this year if I want to finish my degree. She mentioned partnering up with someone. I remembered you from class and was wondering if you wanted to—team up, that is."

Okay, not what I was expecting, and really, he shouldn't have started by saying he needs to pass this course. It tells me he's not applying himself, or he's struggling, and teaming up with me, a straight A student, is a sure way to pass.

"I'm sorry, I already have my assignment planned out and am in the middle of writing it."

"Already? We have six months to complete it."

"I like to get a head start on everything. But if you want some tutoring, I'd be happy to help."

He looks around the room again, when there's a noise at the door. I glance over my shoulder, not finding a reason for the source of the noise.

"Would you?"

"Yeah." I smile at the relief in his expression.

"Would you like to meet up tonight to work out a plan? We can meet up at Perk Inn on the corner of Green Street."

"I actually have plans tonight, and if you really want my help, I'll only be able to meet you here when I'm working."

I hate letting him down—letting anyone down really. I see his shoulders sag and want to take back what I said, but I know I can't.

Since dating CJ and standing up to Logan, I've felt a new-found confidence, something that wasn't there before. I'm more social and have started to speak up instead of being spoken down to.

He keeps crossing and uncrossing his arms. "Cool, cool. What about—"

"Cupcake! I've come to offer you my services. And in case you're wondering, that's my extremely well-endowed muscles."

I turn, a smile breaking across my face as CJ walks in. He frowns when he sees Ian, giving him a look that has the poor guy getting to his feet. He nearly trips over himself to get past me and CJ.

"I'll, um, talk to you, um, later," he stutters over his shoulder, before rushing through the doors.

CJ raises his eyebrow at me. "What's his deal? And are those his friends outside giggling like little kids?"

There are people out there?

"I didn't know anyone was out there. He wanted to work together for our English Lit project."

He looks taken aback. "What? But you wouldn't work with me!"

I laugh at his expression. "I'm not working with him, either, but... I did offer to help him with it. And I said no to working with you because you wanted to write about real life BDSM experiences."

He scoffs, straddling the chair Ian vacated. "It's a valid lifestyle, but is it classed as domestic or just kink?"

I feel my cheeks heat—no doubt they are bright red. "It's BDSM."

"Yes, but with that porn movie out, there's a lot of controversy over the subject."

"What? You're still going to work on it?" I squeak. I thought he had been joking when he brought it up in class.

He looks puzzled for a moment. "Um, yeah. I told you: it would be a good thing to look up. Are you still going with the murder at the university?"

I look away, my mind going to the folder in my bag, before turning back to him. "Yeah, I think so. I do have a backup plan if all else fails though." I give him a coy grin, which sparks his interest.

"Oh yeah, and what would that be?"

"I'm going to put my name on yours."

I start laughing at his shocked expression.

"Miss goody two shoes is going to cheat?"

I smack his arm lightly. "I'm kidding. I was going to write a piece on the effects of dirty water in Africa."

He grins, tipping the chair forward so he can kiss me. I kiss him back, loving the feel of his soft lips. When his tongue flicks against mine, I moan at the taste of peppermint.

He pulls back, his eyes filled with heat. "I missed you."

I giggle, leaning into his touch. "You saw me four hours ago."

He sighs, like it's a hardship. "I know. We should make sure we see each other every hour."

"Yes, because we wouldn't want you to miss me," I tease.

"No, we wouldn't want to do anything to upset me." He pouts, winking at me before looking around the room. "Are you trying to see how many books you can fit on the table before it collapses?"

I look over his shoulder to the table in question and giggle. "Yep. We're up to four hundred."

He snaps his head back to me. "No shit?"

Laughing, I shake my head, watching him slump over with resignation.

"Are you going to help—Oh, hey, CJ. I didn't know you were here," Alex says, coming to a stop.

CJ gives him a bored look, leaning back in his chair. "Yeah, I missed my girl. I thought I'd come help out since she said there was loads to do. I can see she was right," he says, giving the pile of books a distasteful expression.

Alex chuckles. "Only because she refuses to help me carry the books back here."

CJ jumps up from the chair, kissing me on the nose before turning to Alex. "Lead the way, my man. Let's put these beasts to work."

I stifle a giggle and a roll of my eyes when he flexes his biceps. I watch him leave with Alex and admire his arse the entire way.

It should be a crime to have an arse like that. It's perfectly round and plump, and even though I've not seen him naked, I have seen him in boxers, and boy... he has a nice arse.

He turns to face me before he rounds the corner, winking at me. "I'll send you a picture, babe, that way you won't miss staring at my arse."

With flaming hot cheeks, I narrow my eyes at him. "Do some work, would ya."

He laughs, and it echoes around the library as he leaves with Alex. I shake my head. I should have learnt my lesson by now to not stare for more than five seconds. Anything longer and it's like he can feel it. And instead of being the good boyfriend and ignoring it, he makes sure to call me out on it.

With a huff, I get up from the table and walk over to the mounds of books waiting to be sorted into their piles. If I want to get back home today and have time to look over what Jordan brought me, then I need to get a move on.

Chapter 3

It's Saturday, a day I promised myself I would sleep in and enjoy not going to work or class. CJ, on the other hand, hates me. He must do, because once again I wake up to him determined to be slaughtered like a pig.

"If you don't remove your hands from my arse, I will knee you in the balls."

I feel rather than see him grin against my neck. "Cupcake, you love my balls. They're special cargo; you can't go mishandling them. Unless... If that's what you're really into, then—"

I elbow him in the stomach, smiling when I hear him grunt. "Enough about your balls. Let me sleep."

"Nope."

I scream into my pillow before rolling over to glare at him. "Why? What could you possibly want me up for? I don't have work or class."

He waggles his eyebrows as he slips him arm over my waist, tugging me closer, so I'm pressed against his front. "Because, Cupcake, I promised my mum we would go see her."

I must still be asleep because I'm pretty sure he just said we were going to see his mum. A mum he dotes on, adores, and loves more than his food. A mother who loves her son more than anything.

"I'm sorry, what?"

He rolls his eyes at me. "I told her we'd be over today for lunch. It's already eleven."

My eyes narrow because there's no way in hell it's eleven. I don't feel rested enough to have slept in late.

And he wakes me up with the news of meeting his mum for the first time.

"I can't meet your mum," I blurt out.

A flash of hurt passes through his eyes. "Why?"

Hearing the doubt and hurt in his voice, I place my hand on his broad shoulder. "Because I haven't had time to get an outfit ready or figure out what to say to make her like me." A growing panic burns inside me. There's no way I can meet his mum. I just can't.

What if she hates me?

He laughs, kissing the tip of my nose. "She's going to love you. Trust me. She doesn't have a nasty bone in her body."

"I didn't say she was nasty, but she is a mother. You're her only son, so of course she's going to hate me. She's not going to want you to have another woman in your life."

"And what made you come to this conclusion?"

When he starts laughing at my reaction, I slap his chest lightly. "It's a fact. I swear, you guys don't have to worry about this stuff. You had Willow's mum wrapped around your finger the second you met her. You had it easy."

With a cocky grin, he leans forward. "That's because I'm fucking awesome. And I was nervous about meeting your dad, you know."

"We weren't dating when you met my dad, though."

"No, but I knew we were going to."

I rear back a little, raising my eyebrows. "Did you now?"

He grins, showing his pearly whites. "Fuck yeah, I did. I knew the minute you stood staring at me awkwardly in the hallway that you were going to fall in love me."

That earns him another eye roll. "Your ego is amazing."

"I know."

"I was being sarcastic," I mutter dryly.

"I know that too. Now, get up. I really did promise Mum I'd bring you over. She wants to meet you. She felt bad she couldn't come over before now."

I bite my lip nervously. "What if she really doesn't like me, CJ? It will come between us and I don't want to lose you."

His face turns serious, the joking side of him gone as he runs his fingers across my cheek. "Cupcake, she isn't going to hate you. She'll love you. I was even going to warn you about her being touchy feely. She loves to hug people, so be prepared. And nothing will ever come between us, ever. I've been in relationships before, and not once have I brought a girl home to meet her. You mean something to me, Cupcake. What we have I don't take lightly, and I'd fight to keep you. You're pretty fucking special."

My eyes burn with threatening tears. Sometimes I wonder if he has a serious bone in his body, but then he has these moments where he drops the cool boy act he loves to play and speaks from his heart. He did it the night Willow learned about my past with Logan. He found out what happened, and he was here. He stayed with me until I told him he had to go. The next morning, he came barging in, demanding I tell him everything that Logan did.

I'd never seen anger like he showed that day. I didn't think he possessed the emotion; he's so laid back. It was scary, but behind that anger I saw pain, turmoil. I knew he wasn't just feeding off what happened to me, but something that had happened to him. That's when I told him everything, and before I knew it, he was telling me everything about himself: how his mum was raped, and he was the product of it.

To me, his mum is the bravest and strongest person I've ever heard of, and I've never even met her. It didn't matter how she conceived him; she loved him anyway. And loveable he is.

"You really do say the sweetest things," I tell him, before kissing him. He runs his tongue across my bottom lip and I grant him access, opening my mouth. Even with the horror of morning breath, I let him deepen the kiss, running my fingers through his hair.

His hand glides down my side, causing shivers to break out all over. When he pulls back, I want to moan in protest.

His eyes are heated as he stares down at me. "Maybe we should stay in bed and do this all day."

I can feel his erection pressing against my hip, and although the thought of staying in bed with him all day excites me, I know I'll cave under his touch.

I've been wanting to go further in our relationship for a while, but something inside me has wanted to pull back and make sure he really does have the same feelings I have for him. He could fuck me, then finish with me in a blink of an eye. I'd rather know for sure how he feels, hear him say it before going further, but I'll not push those feelings onto him by telling him that. I want to know that when he tells me, it's true and honest, not something he knows I want to hear.

I kiss him once more before pulling back. "Let's get ready. I don't want my first impression to be bad if we're doing this."

He grins down at me like I'm nuts. "You're such a goof."

I slap his shoulder. "Stop it. Let's go and do this."

The minute we pull into the drive of an extravagant home, I know I'm completely out of my element. My dad comes from money and our house is pretty big, with one cook and a housekeeper, but this house is something else entirely. It's big enough to fit the entire student population at Whithall and still have rooms free.

Okay, I might be exaggerating, but still, it's *huge*.

I look down at my clothes once again, feeling like I should have put something nicer on. Instead, I opted for my white T-shirt with black pinafore dress. I made sure to put my black pumps on with my thigh-high socks and a black jacket to match. I even accessorized with a black bow choker.

I left my hair down to dry, and now it's a mass of loose waves. I wish CJ had given me more time to sort it out, as it looks a little frizzy.

I'm slow in the mornings as it is, but with so little time, I did the best I could. I just wish CJ would have given me a fifth cup of coffee; I'd probably be a little more productive.

"You ready?" CJ asks, pulling me from my thoughts as he parks in front of a four-door garage.

I nibble on my bottom lip, nervously looking from the house to CJ. "I think so."

He pulls my lip from between my teeth. "Stop biting that lip, it's tempting me."

A blush rises in my cheeks, and even though I'm a nervous wreck, my body sways towards him. When he's blunt and talking dirty, it's like I lose every train of thought.

Before I can stop myself, I lean over, pull his head towards me and kiss him. When I taste the sweetness of his tongue, my head snaps back and I narrow my eyes at him.

"You've been eating my sweets—again!"

He rolls his eyes at me, unbuckling his seatbelt. "I had to have something while I was waiting for you to get ready. I was going to die of starvation."

"You were eating a massive bowl of cereal when I left to jump in the shower. I've told you too many times about my sweets, CJ. I take them very seriously."

He laughs and opens his car door, before quickly turning back and kissing me. "Yeah, but if I didn't, I wouldn't witness how cute and sexy you look when you're mad."

I want to growl, but the heated look in his eyes stops me, and before I know it he's walking around the car and opening my door. I'm just stepping out of the car when the front door opens. A woman who looks to be in her twenties, but I know is in her late-thirties, is standing in the doorway. When her eyes land on CJ, they light up, and a smile, just like her son's, spreads across her face.

She looks so much like him. I didn't know what to expect, but I'm glad he has more of her looks than his dad's. The thought of her having to see him every time she looked at CJ kind of troubled me. I don't know what I would have done or how I would have reacted had I been in her shoes.

She's got a dark tan, like CJ, and the same dark brown eyes and glossy black hair. She's beautiful—very exotic-looking.

She rushes towards us and we meet her halfway. As soon as she's close enough, CJ drops my hand and wraps his arms around his mum's tiny waist. She leans up on her toes, clinging to his neck.

"CJ, I've missed you so much."

She pulls back and kisses both of his cheeks. He blushes, and I notice he doesn't look at me. I'm grinning, all too happy to see him squirm. "I was here last week, Mum."

"Too long." She swats his shoulder lightly before her beautiful dark eyes turn to me. I shift nervously under her appraisal, feeling my breathing pick up. I open my mouth to greet her, but no sound escapes. Before I know what's happening, I'm wrapped up in her arms, engulfed in a hug.

Not wanting to be rude, I hug her back, feeling warmth from the woman in front of me. She's so much the opposite of my own mum, and it's then I realise there was another reason for my nervousness: deep down, I was afraid she would be just like her. No matter how much I tried to get my mum to love me, she just wouldn't—or couldn't.

"You are so beautiful," she tells me, before sending a disapproving frown at CJ. "CJ, you never said she was this beautiful." Her bright eyes and smile turn to me. "I'm Milly, by the way."

I smile, feeling my cheeks heat at her calling me beautiful. "I'm Allie."

"Um, yeah I did. I said she was hot as fuck and smart as hell," CJ adds, interrupting us.

She tuts at her son before wrapping her arm over my shoulder and guiding me into their home. "Ignore my son. Come, let's eat so I can get to know you."

"Thank you. It's lovely to finally meet you, Milly."

She beams at me as we step inside her kitchen. There's a table placed by the windows that look out over her garden, and she gestures for me to take a seat. I'm too anxious to take a real nose, so I pay attention to Milly.

"You too, Allie. My son talks about you a lot."

He does?

"I'm starving. Is the food ready?" CJ asks as he takes a seat at the table. His mum sits across from us, eyeing her son with love as she feigns annoyance.

She looks at me, rolling her eyes. "I don't think he's ever not hungry."

I give her a mischievous smile. "About that... Have you ever gotten him checked for worms? He doesn't stop eating, and I'm not sure where it's going. It's kind of worrying."

CJ opens his mouth but his mum holds her hand up, stopping him. "Do not use crude words in this house, CJ. I know what your explanation is going to be."

"But it's true," he boasts.

Confused, I glance over at him. "What are you talking about?"

He looks down at his lap, wiggling his eyebrows. "That's where it goes, Cupcake."

My mouth drops open and he begins to laugh. "I can't even—"

"CJ!" His mum narrows her eyes at him, but they soften when they turn their way back to me. "And, Allie, to answer your question, I have. The school even called social services a few times because they were afraid I wasn't feeding him. He'd eat not only his school lunch, but other students' lunch too."

My eyes widen in shock. Slowly, I face CJ. "You didn't?"

He shrugs, looking a little embarrassed. "I was a growing boy."

"They did say it was normal."

I smile when I address his mum. "Well, he hasn't changed. When was the last time you took him?"

"Mum!" CJ whines, covering his face.

I smile at the awkwardness in his voice, practically bouncing in my seat. "When?"

"Allie!" CJ groans.

Milly ignores her son, winking at me. "A few weeks ago. He'd come home and eaten all the food. I thought he'd outgrown it, but no; he just learnt how to hide it."

"I really am hungry," CJ comments, pretending we aren't talking about him. He's seriously cute when he pouts.

"I'll get the food ready."

While we eat, I listen to all of Milly's stories about CJ growing up. I even asked what his initials stand for, but she laughed, saying she'd promised CJ she wouldn't tell anyone. I tried my hardest to find out, but it was no use—not with him sitting across from his mum, glaring at her in warning.

I'll have to make sure I get her alone.

As the hours pass, I begin to kick myself for worrying over nothing. Milly is nothing like my mother, or like the mothers I heard stories from who have met the parents. She's kind, funny, and so much like her son it's uncanny.

She also loves him as much as he loves her, and it warmed my heart to see their interactions. It allowed me to see another side to him. He was so careful with his mum, always offering to help with something, like the dishes, or to do something while he was there. He was interested in how she was doing or how her week at work had been. It was a relationship I never had with either of my parents, and it made me crave it more as I witnessed the bond they shared. It was like nothing I'd ever seen before.

I must have spaced out because CJ elbows me in the ribs. "Sorry, what?"

He chuckles. "Sorry, are we boring you?"

My cheeks burn. "No, sorry. I was just thinking."

His mum laughs, tapping the top of my hand affectionately. "Not to worry. We all do it."

"What did you say?" I ask, glancing at CJ.

"Mum asked how the councillor was getting on with the victims. She knows about everything that happened with Logan and Jamie, and I told her about Jordan's company that works with young victims and how she helped the girls."

My eyes widen in surprise, shocked he would tell his mum about the mess Logan caused. But as I think about it further, it makes sense that he would talk to her about it. They have an open and honest relationship, and he doesn't hold much back from her.

I turn to Milly and give her a small smile. "It's going really good for some of the girls. Some are able to find closure, from what they've told me. I keep in touch with a lot of them, but some are still struggling to go to their appointments. We booked one-to-one sessions for those who needed them, but I don't know if it's helping."

Milly's eyes draw together as she thinks something over. "We have a program for young victims. It's an intense course, but it's helped a lot of young women. If you want to refer anyone, I can give you a bunch of leaflets before you leave. I'm sorry about what happened to you and your friends. CJ filled me in. How are your friends coping?"

CJ squeezes my hand under the table, and I'm grateful for the support. "Willow was doing okay until we went home for our term break. I think being back in a space where she spent so much time with him brought back all those memories for her. It's why we came back a few days early."

She nods in understanding. "She has a lot to get through. If you want, I can meet up with her personally. I run sessions Mondays and Thursdays for people who just want to get out. It doesn't have to involve anything about what happened. A few of my girls just want the company, and some aren't ready to get back to work or school, so I help them focus on other stuff."

An idea occurs to me, and I don't know why I didn't think about it before. CJ had told me what his mum does, how she works with others who have lived through similar circumstances to her. She helps them build a new life. I didn't know just how personally involved she got, but from the way she describes it, it's just like two friends getting together to catch up. Rosie would benefit immensely from something like that.

"Actually, there might be something you could do for me."

Surprise flickers in her eyes. "Of course—anything."

I smile with gratitude. "Our new roommate, Rosie, the girl who wasn't drugged, has been struggling with what happened to her. We organised group sessions for her, but she would return from them even more withdrawn. She confided in me how she hated that the other girls were torn over not remembering what happened to them, when all she wished was that she didn't. When we realised the group therapy wasn't working, we got her one-on-one sessions. She was doing loads better, but then, a few days ago, she told her parents what happened. It didn't go well; they basically said it was God's will—that she deserved to be punished for her sins."

"Her sins?" Milly asks, and I can see the spark of anger behind her eyes.

"She's gay. I don't want to go into too much detail because it's not my story to tell, but since then, she hasn't wanted to leave the house. We tried taking her to the cinema the other day, but she panicked and shut down on us. I hate seeing her hurting so much."

My eyes water as I think about that night. We'd planned to cheer her up, but all we did was break her apart. She had a panic attack and we ended up taking her home. She hasn't even been to her one-on-one session since that phone call, or class.

"I understand. I can come over to see her myself, if you'd like?"

My eyes light up. "You would?"

Her expression softens as she gazes at me. "Of course. I'll do my best to help her. I promise."

"Thank you. Thank you so much."

"Okay, let's talk about me for a bit," CJ says, lightening the mood.

I laugh, dropping my head on his shoulder. "We're always talking about you."

"Yeah, cause I'm awesome."

"That you are, dear, that you are," his mother snickers.

He rolls his eyes and gets up from his chair. "I'm going to find some dessert."

We watch him go, and for the first time since arriving, I'm alone with his mum. I'm not as nervous as I thought I would be; she's easy to talk to. CJ was right about her.

"How is school? CJ says you work at the library?"

"I do. I love it there. It's become a second home. And school is great. I actually take English Lit with CJ."

She giggles, and on any other woman her age, she'd have looked stupid, but Milly doesn't. "He told me. I remember when he called me not long after you moved in. He told me an angel who would be his future wife had moved in across the hall and smelled like cupcakes.

Then he told me how he argued with her about literature, just to see her eyes light up."

I blush because I really did smell like cupcakes. I had eaten twelve on the car ride from home to Whithall. And I remember the argument well. I'd been so surprised to see him enter the class with Cole— neither seemed like the sort to study English Lit—and then he argued some good, valid points over some of the books we were going to be reading. Because of my crush, and the way he infuriated me constantly, I argued back.

"He didn't?"

Her gaze turns to her son looking through the cupboards before coming back to me, her eyes alight with something. "I've never heard him speak so fondly about a girl before. He's had girlfriends, but none he's ever told me about or introduced me to. Ever since he met you, every phone call has been a surprise, because he always has a new story to tell me about you."

I chuckle at that. "Did he tell you I wouldn't write my English paper on him?"

She throws her head back, laughing. "Yes, he did. Five times, if I remember correctly."

"He really was devastated I wouldn't do it."

"I'm glad you keep him on his toes."

"He's a lot to handle at times. I've never met anyone like him, but I wouldn't change a thing. I'd never admit it to him, but he's nearly kind of perfect."

Her grin is wide.

"Nearly?" CJ scoffs from somewhere, but I don't look away from Milly.

I sigh, my shoulders slumping. I should have known his big ears would hear me. I swear, they have their own satellite frequency.

"He eats all my sweets; it's kind a deal-breaker for me. If he were anyone else, I'd have unfriended him."

From the corner of my eye, I notice CJ's head pop up from the freezer he was looking through. "You love me, and secretly, you like that I eat your sweets. Plus, sharing is caring."

"You didn't get the sweet packages he got for you?"

I turn back to Milly, hearing CJ's grunt. "I did. I've already gone through three boxes. But CJ owes me more because he still keeps eating them."

She grins before looking over at her son. "You should get your own."

He groans, throwing his hands up in the air. "I did, and she claimed those, too."

Milly looks at me, raising her eyebrow.

"I did. He left them in my room, so I claimed them."

She giggles, shaking her head. Just when she's about to speak, her house phone rings. I'm a little startled as I've not heard a house phone in so long. I'd begun to think they were myths.

"If you'll excuse me a moment."

She gets up and walks over to the cordless phone hanging on the wall, before answering it. As she steps out, CJ walks back over, taking a seat next to me after shoving something into his mouth.

He's eating—again?

"Your mum is amazing."

His eyes warm at my compliment and he leans forward. "I told you she was. I can tell she loves you already. She's going to invite you to go shopping, by the way. I know you hate surprises like this and I didn't want you to feel put on the spot. She's always trying to get me to go, and as much as I love my mum, I don't do shopping. If you don't want to, say now, and I'll offer to go instead."

I laugh at his horrified expression. "I don't mind going shopping with her. I never did any of that with my mum, so it'll be nice, and I can get to know her more. Maybe she'll let slip about your real name."

He chuckles. "Cupcake, I told you: she won't reveal my secret. Not even Cole would. And he only knows it because when my great-grandparents were alive, they called me by my given name."

"Chris, wasn't it?"

He shakes his head. "No, it's—" His eyes widen. "You nearly had me then."

39

I giggle. "I'll find out eventually, you know. I'm like a little Nancy Drew."

His lips twitch as he leans forward, pressing them against mine.

A throat clears and we break apart. I blush at being caught, but turn to greet his mum, smiling.

"Sorry, that was work."

"Everything okay?" CJ asks.

"Yes. They want me to go in shortly to look around some new woman shelters." She gives him an apologetic smile.

"We need to get going soon, anyway, Mum. I've got to start my paper that's due in a few weeks."

"You're such a good boy," she tells him, giving him a soft smile. Then her eyes widen as she turns to me. "CJ told me it's your birthday in a few weeks. Would you like to go shopping with me? I can treat you. It would be nice to have some girl time. I understand if you'd rather not. You probably have loads of girlfriends you can go with." Her rambling is endearing.

CJ playfully nudges my knee under the table, as if to remind me he told me so. I nod at Milly, thrilled with the idea. "Yes, I'd love to. But I have to warn you, I'm more into buying books than shoes. My friend Willow, however, has a million pairs of the things, some of which I'm sure she's never even tried on."

Milly laughs. "If you want your friend to tag along, the more the merrier. With CJ, it was a case of running to the shops, grabbing what he needed and getting out of there. Any longer and he'd have a meltdown."

"It's for girls," CJ mutters dryly.

She looks at me as if to say, *you see.* "Let CJ know what days and times you're working or have class, and I can work around it. We could go for lunch while we're there."

"Sounds really good. I'm looking forward to it."

And I am.

Before, whenever Willow would even mention shopping, I'd have a cardiac arrest. The thought of spending countless hours in a shop, trying on clothes, would be enough for me to fake a deadly illness. I hated it. But because she was my friend, I'd go.

We would compromise, and she'd come to a book shop with me. The idea of going with Milly and Willow is actually something I'm looking forward to. It may not be the same as my mum taking me, but it's close. I'm also thrilled she asked me. I feel honoured.

Maybe when we go, I can get her to spill CJ's real name.

With that in mind, we hug Milly goodbye and leave. And for the first time since I can remember, I'm truly excited about something.

Chapter 4

"Linda Cooper was reported missing by her parents on Monday 23rd. Seven-teen-year-old Linda was last seen heading out for her run Sunday morning. Police are asking for anyone who may have seen this girl or witnessed anyone who seemed out of place around Whithall River at roughly nine a.m. to please come forward.

"An inside source says: "The parents are completely devastated and beside themselves with grief. Linda is a bright young girl who is training for the August Charity Marathon in London to raise money for Leukaemia. They're positive something has happened to their daughter. She's never had problems at school or at home. What happened has come as a huge shock to them, and they are pleading with anyone who may know something to come forward."

The picture of a young girl stares back at me from the television. She has light brown hair, hazel eyes, and a blinding smile. I can't look away from the screen, even when they show a picture of her parents walking out of the police station, their eyes swollen and red. They go on to describe how they've been searching for her nonstop since Sunday afternoon.

My heart pummels to my throat as I watch it. They look distraught. The husband does his best to console his wife, but the grief and sorrow on his face is crippling.

When we applied for university, we checked to make sure the area was safe. We didn't want to end up in a town where crime was at its highest, especially since we were moving here without our parents. Even though there is no place on Earth where someone isn't doing something illegal, we didn't want to be in the centre of a gang war.

A town an hour away has two gang rivals constantly at war, but other than that, Whithall seemed like your normal place. In fact, when we researched Whithall, there hadn't been anything other than petty arrests for fighting or theft.

So we moved here, and since then, we've had a serial rapist, a murder, and now a missing girl. It just seems like a lot has happened for what was known as a relatively quiet town.

If my father sees this on the news, I'll be expecting a phone call and demands to move back home.

The television draws my attention once again. The Cooper's had gone to the police station to file a missing person's report on Sunday night after they still hadn't heard from her, but the police couldn't do anything for twenty-four hours because she was classed as an adult. It's now Wednesday; four days of the Cooper's not knowing what happened to their daughter, and it must be killing them.

From what I'm hearing on the news, Linda Cooper isn't someone who would go somewhere without telling her parents. She's never been in trouble, not at school or with the police. She even has a few charities she helps raise money for. And according to her Facebook account, she was well liked. There wasn't one person on there who was arguing and saying she just ran away.

The news reporter had her old high school headteacher give a statement, as well as some of her friends. They've also been showing Facebook posts from all her friends on the bottom of the screen and with the twitter caption, #FindLindaCooper.

The clock mounted on the wall catches my eye and I hiss out a breath. I'm going to be late for class if I don't get a move on. I'd been so consumed with what was happening on the television and reading the kind words from her friends that I'd forgotten about my Historical Literature class.

I've been dreading this class since I returned to school. When I first applied, I thought the class would be a breeze, but I had been wrong. I've been struggling a little on the archaeology of Greece and the historical development of literature from the medieval period to the 17th century. Both are a requirement to pass my course.

It's hard to enjoy the class when I'm struggling so much, and the only student study group is held on the nights I work. I asked a few people if they wanted to meet up on different days, but they declined.

With one last look at the news playing on the television, showing a picture of Linda Cooper smiling, I grab my bags and keys, and rush out the door. It's only when I'm half way to class that I realise I didn't say goodbye to Rosie or let her know I'll be going out to lunch with CJ, so won't be back.

I'm late.

I slow my run to a walk when I reach the door, and take a deep breath, preparing myself for all the stares that will come—like they always do when someone disrupts their class.

I quietly open the door, hoping I can sneak in unnoticed, and as I reach the back of the classroom, where my chair is located, I think I've gotten away with it.

"Nice of you to join us, Miss Davis."

I inwardly groan, feeling my face heat as I pull out my chair and take a seat. My gaze turns to our teacher, Geoffrey Flint. "I'm sorry."

He gives me a disapproving gaze before focusing back on the class. Quietly, I take out my notepad and pens and listen to what he is teaching. I try my hardest to follow but somewhere along the way my mind drifts back to the girl plastered all over the news.

She's out there somewhere. She could be scared, alone, hurt. She could be happy and feeling guilty about scaring her parents and family. It is a mystery that only Linda Cooper can answer. That thought alone is horrible, because if something bad happens, only she will have the answers to give her parents the peace of mind they'll need.

I guess it's another reason why I'm so determined to write about Christie's murder. Only she and the killer know what happened to her that night.

Her parents have pleaded and even offered a reward for any help that leads to an arrest of the person who killed her. They will do anything to know why their daughter was taken away from them so cruelly. I want to find them justice, but in order to do that, I need to get into the mind of the killer, and to do that, I need to figure out *why* Christie. Why did he kill her? Was it something she had done, said or saw? There's a trillion and one ideas that come to mind, making me more determined than ever to find out.

I'm so lost in my own thoughts that I don't notice Mr. Flint standing beside me. He kneels down next to me, and like clockwork, leans forward —too close for my liking—and rests his arm along the back of my chair.

"Is everything okay?"

I try to scoot away without it looking too obvious. Mr. Flint has a way of making me feel uncomfortable. Whenever he comes to see me about something, he always gets far too close. My personal space is just that: personal.

"Um, yeah."

"Good. I'd like to see you after class today. Make sure you wait behind, okay?"

I nod, wringing my hands together in my lap, scared I'm going to be in trouble. It's the first time I've ever been late, and although I'm struggling in class, I still do my work to the best of my ability. "Okay."

He stands up, his fingers running across my neck, causing me to stiffen. He doesn't seem to notice or care as he squeezes my shoulder and goes back to his desk.

I watch him closely as he takes a seat, not wanting to take my eyes off him. When he picks up his coffee cup, our gazes meet. He smiles and I look away, a shiver running down my spine.

I glance around the room to see if anyone else had seen what happened, but they're all looking down at the worksheets in front of them. When I look at my desk, I notice my own one on the wooden surface and inwardly kick myself. How did I miss this being handed out to me?

Not wanting to give Mr. Flint another reason to keep me longer, I get to work. Every so often I feel his eyes on me, and when I look up, he's staring at me, and a sense of foreboding creeps through me. It's creepy and, in my eyes, utterly unprofessional.

By the time class is over, my nerves have got me sweating. Everyone is piling out of the room, not giving me a second glance as I pack my stuff away.

"Come take a seat, Allie."

I grab my bag and make my way down to the front of the classroom. Mr. Flint sits back on his desk, his legs crossed at the ankles and his arms gripping the edge of the dark wood. The way he gazes at me—the slow appraisal as his eyes rake up and down my body—has me itching to bolt.

I've never been in trouble before, so this is all new for me. I swallow hard when he gestures to the chair he's put in front of his desk.

"I'd like to talk to you about your coursework."

Okay, this isn't about being late, then?

"Okay."

I clasp my hands together in my lap, watching him closely as he pulls another chair up next to mine and takes a seat.

"I've noticed you've been struggling and was wondering why you weren't attending the study group I arranged for everyone."

"I work during the times you allocated. I did ask if there was any way one of them was willing to meet me when I was free, but they've got too much schoolwork."

He hums in the back of his throat. "I have night classes Tuesday, Wednesday and Thursday, but if you're free Friday, I can help you catch up. You don't have to struggle alone," he tells me softly.

I jump at the feel of his hand landing on my thigh, my body instantly freezing at the bold, unwanted move. I try to move away, but his fingers tighten a little; not enough to hurt, but enough to make me take notice. I stop moving and pick up my bag.

"I…well… I'm busy on Friday nights. I'll be fine. I promise to catch up, and come to think of it, I just remembered a friend of mine took this class last year. She said she wouldn't mind tutoring me."

His thumb rubs slow circles on my thigh. My throat closes, and with adrenaline pumping through my veins, I jump up to my feet. His hand slips free from my leg as he stands with me, standing close enough that if I were to move he would be touching me.

"If you ever change your mind, you know where to find me. We could meet up here, or somewhere more… private."

My eyes widen at the way he says 'private': slowly, deliberately. "Okay. Thank you. I have to go; my boyfriend is waiting for me."

Something flashes in his eyes but it's gone when the door to the classroom is pushed open.

"Cupcake, there you are. Did you forget we were meeting for lunch?"

Relieved to see CJ, I step around Mr. Flint and walk over to him. I force a smile, but CJ being CJ sees through it and eyes me more closely.

"See you in next class. I shouldn't have to remind you to be on time."

I quickly turn around after taking CJ's hand and nod. "I won't be. Thank you."

Mr. Flint grunts something under his breath that I don't hear. CJ notices and pauses. Not wanting anything to happen, I take his hand and pull him out the door.

The air leaves my lungs the second we're out of the classroom. Even with the room being one of the biggest lecture halls, it felt claustrophobic in there.

"You okay?" CJ asks, once we're outside. It's raining, so I pull my hood over my head, hoping to cover my facial expression from him. He'll be able to tell that I'm lying. He always does.

"Yeah."

"What was all that about in there, then? You seemed uncomfortable."

I sigh, moving closer to him to get warm. "He wanted to talk about my work. I've been struggling a little with the subject so he offered to help me. I was also late for class."

He chuckles. "You, late?"

I gently nudge his shoulder with mine, grateful he believed my half lie. CJ has a tendency to act first, think later when it comes to someone being hurt. I don't want him to get into trouble over something that is probably nothing.

"Yes, late. I got distracted watching the news."

"And I can help you if you're struggling, but I'm pretty sure they do study groups you can attend."

I shake my head when I notice he's watching me. "I can't. They meet up on the day I'm working at the library. I've asked them if they would consider having it there, but they said there would be too many interruptions with people coming and going. Honestly, I think they just didn't want to add one more student to their list."

He scoffs. "Sounds about right. But I can help you."

I look at him dubiously. "How? You aren't in that class."

Sending me a smug smile, he pulls me into the dining hall. "No, but I got bored last year so I did some online classes in my spare time. Historic Literature was actually one of my favourites."

Why doesn't that surprise me?

Here is the thing about CJ. He may look like some careless, easy-going, kind of clueless student, but he's not. Not only does he ace every subject, but he also has a high IQ that he doesn't put to any use. He loves sports and wants to get a degree in sport news. He'd be good at it. He'd be good at anything he wanted to do.

"If you don't mind, I could really use the help. I'd rather not be called to stay after class again."

We step into line and he turns to face me, pulling my hood down, grinning. He kisses me, pulling me against him, before his hands roam my back and backside.

"My little rebel," he whispers as he pulls away.

I can't help but smile. "Shut up."

I jump when Jordan steps up beside us, looking a little upset.

"Are you okay?"

"No, did you see the news?"

"I did. It's terrible."

"What is?" CJ asks, after ordering us enough food to feed an army.

Jordan turns to CJ, startled, as if she didn't notice him standing there. "Oh, hey, CJ. A girl is missing. She went for a run and never returned home."

CJ seems unfazed as he shrugs. "Probably a runaway, or she's out partying with friends."

As much as his answer pisses me off, he's entitled to think that. It's what anyone would think, given the circumstances. She's a teenage girl.

Jordan shakes her head at him. "No, it's not like that. Her parents did a press conference this afternoon and explained this is out of character for their daughter. She's never run away before, she doesn't party with friends, and also lets them know when she does go out. Plus, she was dressed for a run, not to go clubbing. She had leukaemia as a child, so she doesn't do anything that could risk her health again. She's been training to do a charity run to raise money for the cause."

We take a table in the back by the window. We're barely seated when Willow and Cole join us.

"What are you all looking so serious about?" Willow asks as she opens her water.

I answer, watching her closely. She looks so much happier now that we're back here. "A girl went missing whilst out on a run Sunday. Her parents are worried because it's unlike her. It's been all over the news today. I'm surprised you haven't seen or heard about it. She lives five minutes away."

Her eyes widen in shock. "Oh, my gosh. What do you think happened to her? What on earth is going on with this place. We can't seem to catch a break!"

"They don't know. But it's unlike her, according to her parents and everyone the news reporters have spoken to. Even her friends have spoken up about this being out of character for her, and they're worried. The police are finally taking it seriously since they found her phone earlier this morning down by the river. I think it's why they got on the news so quickly. Seeing her parents so distraught on the television, begging for anyone who knows something to come forward, was really upsetting," Jordan says, her eyes a little distant.

"They did? I didn't hear about the phone on the news earlier. What a shame. Hope they find her. And I agree: seeing her parents like that got me all choked up," I tell her.

Jordan turns her attention to me. "It's not public knowledge. My mum asked me to take her lunch to work and I overheard a few offi-cers talking about it at the police station."

My stomach turns at what that could mean. It definitely isn't good, that's for sure.

"I hope they find her," Willow whispers quietly. Without a word, Cole lifts her out of her chair and into his lap, kissing the side of her head.

"All we can do is pray for a safe return," he tells her.

All of us are silent, not voicing our thoughts out loud. We all know the chances of Linda Cooper being okay is low.

I just hope they find out what's happened to her and pray that she does turn up—in one piece.

Chapter 5

Over the past week, everything has dragged. With work, classes, and catching up with homework, I've barely had time to myself or for CJ.

I felt bad when I spent the one day I did have off with CJ's mum and Willow, shopping. He still stays with me every night, even if I'm working late. It's nice—having those moments with him. I just wish I could have more. We've settled into a nice routine, though, since getting together. Sometimes it feels like we've been together a lot longer. I already know all the important stuff, so getting to know all the little things about him is a bonus I don't take for granted. He was there for me when he barely knew me. He got to me in ways not even my own family got to see, and he cared about everything I said and did.

Today is my birthday and waking up to sweet kisses across my neck is something I could definitely get used to for every birthday. I've not even opened my eyes and already I can tell you it's the best birthday ever.

I hum lightly, still rousing from sleep, and tilt my neck to give him more access. He chuckles, licking the tender spot below my ear. I hum again deep in my throat, burying myself closer to him.

"Happy Birthday, Cupcake."

Hearing 'Cupcake' used to drive me nuts. I hated it. Hated any pet name given to anyone. It made me want to scream at them to use our proper names.

Secretly though, I'd long to hear him say it to me. I had heard him call other girls 'babe', not out of endearment, but out of habit. So, when I hear him call me Cupcake, it means something to me, it makes my heart soar. And now, just like any other time he says it, I lock it away for safekeeping.

"Morning." I open my eyes to find him staring down at me, his filled with light and lust. CJ, when he first wakes up, gets these cute little crinkles at the side of his eyes. Seeing them, I know he's not been

51

awake long. They make him look hotter, and I didn't think that was possible. The man is every young girl's heartthrob.

My head rests back against the pillow, my hand wrapping around his neck to play with the back of his hair. It's soft, like silk. It's one of my favourite things to do. CJ seems to like it too. His eyes close, a blissful expression on his face.

I move closer, wanting him to kiss me. Figuring out what I want, he moves between my legs. He's already hard, causing me to squirm.

We may not have had sex yet, and I may still be waiting for the right moment, but my body? My body is screaming for a release I know only he can give me. I've wanted to explore more than our heated kisses for a while, but I've never had the courage to bring up the topic.

Now, I'm twenty, and for the first time since I was a teenager and knew what sex was, I feel like I'm missing out, wasting time waiting for something that will eventually happen. I might not want sex right now, but I do want to go further in our relationship.

"Touch me," I whisper against his mouth, before kissing him, making sure he can't say anything to ruin the moment.

His body stiffens under my touch, but the second I run my tongue over his bottom lip, he relaxes, deepening the kiss.

If I had given him chance to talk, he would have asked me to explain, and explaining is something I really don't want to do when I can show him. And he'll only make me embarrassed, calling me out when I begin to blush.

My fingers glide down from his neck to his back, feeling his muscles clench under my touch as I go. His narrow waist is next, and I feel myself gripping him when he gasps, kissing the edge of my jaw.

I almost forget what I'm trying to accomplish when he grinds himself against my core, causing me to moan. He's done this a few times while we've been kissing heatedly. I knew then, though, that it wouldn't go any further, whereas now, it will. I want it to. I'm ready for it to.

My fingers dig into his arse as I pull him against me, showing him how much I'm into this. He would usually stop before it got this far before, so I'm hoping he doesn't this time.

I see stars when he slides the thin strap of my camisole off my shoulder, kissing me on my collar bone.

He flicks his tongue, and like he flipped a switch, my hips buckle beneath him, rubbing me against his hardness.

My eyes close when he pulls my top down further, baring one of my breasts. Goose bumps travel over my skin and a bolt of pleasure shoots through my lower stomach.

My body comes to life when his lips close around my tight bud, and a strangled cry erupts from within me. He tugs at my nipple with his soft, full lips, and something begins to build inside me.

God, nothing has ever felt this good, this freeing.

I cry with protest when he lets my nipple fall from his lips with a pop. He eyes are glazed over as he gazes at me.

"What do you want, Cupcake?"

"I want you," I rasp out, moving my hands to run my fingers through the sides of his hair.

"But how far? I don't want to push you past what you're ready for, and believe me, when I have you screaming my name, you'll begging me to fuck you."

Wetness pools between my legs at his crude words. "No sex, everything else but sex."

"So, no penetration?"

I shake my head, still in a daze of sheer pleasure to ask what he means. "Please."

He leans up on his knees, his fingers hooking in the waistband of my knickers before rolling them down my legs. I shiver, my eyes never leaving his. The sheer determination and lust rolling off him is enough to make me want to cry out.

His touch, his eyes, his lips… it's enough to make any girl want to come.

He bends down, his face inches away from my sex, and I try to close my legs, embarrassed. I thought for sure there would be touching, but I didn't expect that. Not yet.

He pulls my thighs apart, kissing the inside of one, and I flop down on my back, gasping at the sensation travelling through my body.

He keeps going, reaching ever closer to my sex, and I want nothing more than to let him, but the urge to touch him is overwhelming. I want to make him feel good too.

"I want to touch you, too," I gasp out, breathing heavily.

His head pops ups, looking almost comical with his wide eyes and open mouth. "What?"

"I want to touch you, too. I want to do it together."

He nods, but he looks a little nervous as he moves up the bed, lying down by my side. He pulls his boxers off, and although this isn't the first time I've seen him naked—since he doesn't have a problem with being nude—I'm shocked to see how big and hard he is. The tip of his dick looks ready to burst, and has a large, thick vein running down the side, pulsing.

Timidly, I reach out, grasping his thick length. It twitches in my hand, causing another roll of pleasure to course through me. It's turning me on to touch him like this, and when he groans, it nearly undoes me.

He shoves his face into the side of my neck, moving closer and wrapping his hand around mine, stoking up and down his length, showing me without telling me what to do.

"Fuck, your hand feels like silk wrapped around my dick."

I don't know what to say, so I stay quiet, moving my hand up and down at the speed he showed me. When pre-come leaks out the tip, I get curious, swiping my thumb over it before bringing it to my mouth.

CJ, in a daze, watches me, his eyes dilating further as a growl escapes his throat. He moves as soon as I suck the salty liquid from my thumb, slamming his lips down on mine. I moan, taking him back in my hand.

Tossing CJ off has just become one of my new favourite things to do, and we'll definitely be doing this again. He can be sure of it.

When I imagine giving him a blowjob, I nearly squeeze him too tight, but he doesn't seem to care as he pulls back from the kiss, his fingers moving down body. My hand traps him, so I swap, using my left to grip him. His eyes close, his hips rocking into my touch.

When his fingers softly touch my pubic hair, my hips buck off the bed. He growls, his fingers sliding through my slippery sex coated with wetness.

"Fuck, you feel so good," he tells me, swirling his fingers over my clit. I moan, loving the feel of him touching me, which causes me to forget about the pleasure I'm giving CJ.

Just when I'm about to apologise for stopping, CJ grabs me around the hips and manoeuvres me so I'm lying on top of him. His hand reaches between us, lifting his cock so its settled between my sex. The sensation is almost too much, and already my wetness is coating his erection, along with his own juices.

"W-what are you doing?" I ask nervously. I'm seconds away of begging him just to have sex with me. Nothing has ever felt like this. Every touch, movement, or twitch sets my body alight.

"I want you to slide your pussy over my cock. This way, I get to play with your tits," he tells me, his voice raspy and filled with desire.

His large hands on my hips begin my movements. My body is tense, but the minute I realise he won't go inside me, I relax, overcome by the feel of him sliding over my sensitive clit.

"Oh, God," I cry out, moving on my own.

With my eyes closed, I don't see him move, but I do feel him when he reaches for my top, and in one rough movement, he has it around my waist, leaving me completely bare, with just a piece of material around my stomach. I cry out when I feel his hands cup my breasts.

The sound of us together is almost my undoing. It feels naughty. I'm getting wetter by the second, especially when his head touches my clit.

My stomach swirls as my hips move faster, rocking back and forth without abandon. It feels so good.

"CJ," I cry, arching my chest into his hands.

"Fuck," he growls, and I watch as he closes his eyes, panting heavily. "I don't think I'm going last, Cupcake."

Suddenly, it's like my soul leaves my body as my stomach tenses, and I arch my back, screaming his name in ecstasy.

His hands abandon my chest and grip my hips, keeping them moving faster as each tidal wave of pleasure shoots through me.

He groans, his fingers tightening to the point I know they'll leave bruises, just as warm liquid squirts all over my sex and his stomach. I'm already sensitive from my orgasm, but the second I grind myself over him, rubbing our come together, I shatter into a thousand pieces once more, before I fall against his chest.

I'm breathing heavily, my head lying on his hard pec, when he starts to laugh. Embarrassed, I tiredly look him in the eye and glare. "What?"

"It's supposed to be your birthday, not mine." He grins, running his fingers through my now messy hair.

I giggle, falling back onto his chest. "Best birthday ever."

"I can't wait to see what you have planned for mine," he tells me in a hoarse voice, and I begin to laugh harder.

I scream, jumping up and down in my living room filled with people.

CJ and I managed to leave my room this morning after we had showered together, which involved orgasms—two for me, one for him —and got dressed. I wanted to stay in bed, but I'm glad I didn't.

The second we made it out of my room, the front door had opened and Willow and Cole walked in, carrying bags of breakfast from Mc Donald's.

Rosie and Becca joined us, and that's when presents were handed out.

Willow got me a frame with a dozen photos of us, Cole and CJ in. There were also a few with Rosie, Becca and Jordan. I loved it. I also loved the red blouse with black bow tie and black skirt she got me. It was perfect and I loved it.

Cole said he helped glue the pictures in and shrugged. It made me smile, so I hugged them both and thanked them.

Rosie and Becca got me an Amazon gift card worth fifty pounds. My eyes had watered as I thought of how many books I could buy with it. I was in heaven.

But it was CJ who had surprised me the most.

He got me the pair of black Converse I had seen in town when I went shopping with his mum. I loved them the minute I saw them, but I knew I couldn't afford them with the allowance my dad was giving me. He'd give me more if I let him, but I wanted to be responsible and not rely on him. So, I walked away with a sad heart. His mum must have told him because they were now on my feet, the red, glittery rose on the side giving them colour. I also loved the red laces that went with them.

Then he handed me another bag, and my eyes watered as I opened it to reveal a cupcake-shaped pillow with the word *mine* written on it. I know he must have had someone make it personally for me, because I've never seen a pillow like this before. They were, without a doubt, the most thoughtful gifts I've ever received.

He also got me my favourite perfume, sweets, and a new pair of pink suspenders.

But what has me screaming like a banshee and jumping around the room, waving a piece of paper around, are the tickets he got me to the biggest book signing they do in the UK. It's called Brits on Tour, and when I had tried to purchase the tickets for myself, they'd sold out. I was gutted and sad for days, because I knew this one was close by. All the others had been too far away, and I hated travelling, especially on my own.

"Oh, my God, thank you, thank you, thank you, thank you." I jump into his arms, wrapping my legs around his waist, and kiss him. We've never been into PDA—well, not me at least—but knowing he went to all this trouble to get me the things I liked and would use, made me warm all over. I felt truly blessed and spoiled.

Only Willow has ever gotten me a gift so thoughtful, and with that, I burst into tears, shoving my face into his neck.

He clears his throat, rubbing a hand down my back. "Why are you crying? I thought you loved them," he asks, sounding panicked.

I lift my head, looking at him through my tears. "You got me tickets to go to Brits on Tour," I wail, taking his face in my hands. "This has to be the best gift anyone has ever given me, CJ."

I love him.

I truly love him.

I can feel it in my chest, how tight it's gotten, and how much I crave the man holding me. Any doubts I had before are washed out the window because now I know, without a doubt, he would never do this for another girl, not even one he really liked.

"I love you," I blurt out.

He freezes, staring at me intently and not speaking. I'm about to take it back, hurt and embarrassed he didn't reciprocate, but then he kisses me. He kisses me so hard I whimper.

"Um, maybe get a room?" Cole mutters dryly.

I giggle against CJ's mouth, pulling back a little. His eyes look misty, like he's fighting back tears. My chest aches at seeing the love shining back at me.

"I love you, too, Cupcake. I've been waiting for you to tell me for weeks."

"Weeks?" I ask, and he nods. My eyebrows scrunch up in confusion, wondering why he never said anything. "Why didn't you tell me?"

He raises an eyebrow, looking incredibly sexy. "And have my ego bruised by you rejecting me again? No, thank you."

"I wouldn't have done that."

He gives me a dry look. "Do you realise how hard I worked just to get you to go out with me?"

I shake my head, laughing at his absurd statement. To anyone else, it might sound like he was joking, but unfortunately, he isn't.

"Well, I love you, doofus."

"I love you, too, Cupcake."

"Thank you for my presents. I love every single one of them."

His eyes fill with warmth. "Anything for you."

I kiss him again, when another throat clears. "Like, seriously, get a room."

CJ looks over my shoulder at Willow, grinning. "We're in one. It's not our fault you've chosen to watch us rather than leave, you dirty minx."

I roll my eyes and slap his shoulder, indicating for him to put me down. He does, but keeps me close, moving us back to the sofa where I continue to look in awe at my presents. I've never felt so spoiled before.

And the best part... The tickets and hotel are for two people, meaning CJ is coming with me.

The man really does love me.

Willow smiles as she walks over to me, before pulling me into her arms and out of CJ's. "I'm so happy for you. We should all go for dinner later to celebrate your birthday and the little moment you just had."

CJ pulls me out of her embrace after a few seconds, playfully narrowing his eyes. "She's mine now."

I roll my eyes at him before glancing at Willow. "Thank you. And sounds good. It will have to be after six, though; Dad is going to Face-time me later."

"What did he get you?" she asks, moving back to stand next to Cole.

I duck my head, feeling a like a spoiled rich kid when I say, "A new car. It won't arrive for another month or so as they're waiting for it to be put on sale. He has it reserved."

Her face lights up. "No shit?"

Relaxing because no one has called me out on being a 'daddy's girl', I tell her, "Yep, and he's going to put the car in your name. It will be yours."

She squeals, jumping in Cole's arms. "Oh, my God. This is amazing. My mum is going to lose her shit when I tell her."

I laugh at her enthusiasm. "Which reminds me... He asked if we were okay with them being together."

She scrunches her face up. "Yeah, Mum did too. I'm okay as long as she's happy, though I never want to witness what we did again, and I do have a few reservations about their relationship. But she assures me it's fine and she's happy, so I'm happy."

I nod, agreeing. "I told him pretty much the same thing. I told him I was worried he would ruin our friendship if he treated her the way he treated Mum."

"What did he say?" she asks, looking eager for the answer.

"He promised it was different, that things with Mum were complicated. He wouldn't have treated her so badly if they were in love with each other. He said he'd explain things the next time he pops down."

She relaxes. "I'm glad you told me. It was what I was worried about."

"You two really should communicate more," CJ blurts out, and we all look to him. He holds his hands up. "Sorry. Just saying. Couple goals and all that."

We all laugh, shaking our heads at him.

"Come on. Let's go out for coffee before he starts telling us what it entails to keep the relationship blissful," Cole states dryly.

He grins. "That's easy—"

I slap my hand over his mouth, muffling the rest of what he was going to say. "Nope. Let's go."

Still laughing, I grab my bag and coat and head out with the others, ready to spend the rest of my birthday with them.

Chapter 6

I've never been more excited in my life than I am right now, travelling to London to meet some of my favourite authors.

Yesterday, I called Milly, and together, we went shopping for a new trolley crate to put my books in, so I won't have to carry them around. The plan is to take the books I have and get them signed by their authors at the event, and maybe buy a few new ones while I'm there. I'm so hyped up about it I can barely keep still in my seat.

"You really are excited, aren't you?"

I turn to CJ, whose eyes are still on the road, and he's smiling wide. "I am. *Alanea Alder* is going to be there. She's from America, I think— I'm not sure. But her books are freaking amazing. Her one character, Meryn, is a massive *Doctor Who* fan and is hilarious. In this one book, she flies a drone into a detention cell which has a spell cast to it. They let the spell go inside the room with him. The next day, any time he tries to say his name, douchebag comes out instead. It was so funny I had to keep re-reading it over and over. She does loads of funny stuff like that in her books though. Her writing is really amazing. And *KC Lynn* is going to be there, too. She's lovely. I follow her posts on Facebook and she has the most adorable family ever. Oh, and *E. A. Western*, *Kirsty Mosely*, and *Nicola C. Priest* is signing there, too. I can't wait to meet them. Did you know…" I stop when I realise I'm rambling, but in my peripheral vision, CJ's smiling big.

Hearing I've stopped, he turns to me, a twinkle in his eye. "You really love this shit, don't you?"

I sigh, falling back in my seat. "I do. I love reading. I love how authors can take something so ordinary and make it extraordinary. I like how they can create their own world and make it thrive. I love books. I'm just excited about meeting them tomorrow. It's going to be awesome. I've only been to a small book signing before. This one is going to be huge, with thousands of guests."

"Thousands?" he asks, looking at me from the corner of his eye.

"Oh, yeah. Not only will authors from all over the world be there, but people also travel from across the globe to attend. It's incredible."

"No shit?"

I laugh at his shocked expression. "Yep. It'll be like being in a room full of celebrities, because to us book nerds, authors are like our famous actors and actresses."

"I never thought of it like that. Are you going to go all squealy again when you meet them? You got all crazy-eyed when I mentioned some of the authors attending."

"I did not go crazy-eyed," I defend.

"Cupcake, you did. Even Cole took a step back, and Willow already had the incentive to give you room. You nearly took out my balls."

I pout because I hadn't meant to get that excited. I'd started jumping around again, flapping my arms like a lunatic, and nearly hit CJ in the balls. Luckily for him, I only hit his lower stomach.

"I said I was sorry."

He begins to laugh. "Ten minutes later—after we finally got you to calm down."

"When are we going to get there?" I ask, changing the subject.

He chuckles deeply. "Not long. We need to check in at the hotel, then we can go get something to eat. You do realise the signing isn't until the morning, though, right?"

"Yes," I say dryly. "I just want to check, one more time, that I have everything ready. We need to be up early so we aren't waiting around in a queue to get in."

"That's fine. We can grab breakfast around seven, then finish getting ready before heading over. It's only a five-minute drive according to Google, and the doors don't open until nine."

"Sounds like a plan."

We're stepping over the threshold of our room and I'm about to dive onto the bed, when CJ snags me around the waist, stopping me.

"What are you doing?" I ask, looking over my shoulder at CJ.

He smirks, taking his phone out of his back pocket. "Snapping a picture for my mum. She asked me to send her a picture of the room."

"And you're stopping me from going in because…?"

"And… I don't want you messing the bed up and throwing your shit everywhere. At least let her *think* we're clean and tidy."

I roll my eyes but watch as he snaps a few pictures of the room. The second he lets me go, I dive onto the bed, bouncing into the middle with a huge sigh.

"This is so comfy."

He gives me an amused chuckle. "Looks it. I'm starving; do you want to go eat downstairs or go look somewhere else for food?"

I look around, not really in the mood for a long trek to find somewhere to eat. I just want to relax. Anything involving any kind of exercise and I stay away from it. It's why I hate our apartment so badly. The lift is always breaking down, and I swear it hates me because it always does it when I have something to lug up the stairs.

It kills me every time.

"Downstairs. Then we can come up and find a movie to watch. I want an early night."

"It's five," he states, looking at me like I'm an alien.

"And we have to be up at the crack arse of dawn. I'm going to have to get up at six so I have time to wake up properly before getting ready. I need to make sure I have enough time to do my hair and shit because there is no way I'm looking like a slouch in front of a bunch of authors. No way."

He chuckles, grabbing my hands and pulling me off the bed. "You really do amaze me sometimes. I still don't know how people confuse you to be this shy, timid girl. You're batshit crazy."

"I am not!" I pout but then tilt my head to the side, sagging my shoulders. "Okay, maybe a little, but I'm one of those people who hates meeting new people. It makes me uncomfortable so I stay quiet. If I don't, I ramble and blurt out stuff I shouldn't. But the minute I'm your friend, you're out of luck. I'll end up telling you my life story."

"I know. When we first met you wouldn't even look at me. You'd blush and start stuttering."

"That's because you were hot."

His chest puffs out as his eyes light up. "I knew it. You had the hots for me." He winks, pulling me against his hard chest. "It doesn't matter either way. I love all sides to you, and there's definitely more than one. I'm just lucky I get to see all of them."

He says the sweetest things.

I did have the hots for him. How could I not? He was everything I normally stayed away from because of how intimidatingly sexy he looked. People who are overly confident weren't who I hung around with at all. In fact, Willow had been my only real friend for a long time, until we arrived at Whithall. It was hard to be heard, being who I was, let alone being around someone who demanded attention without even asking for it.

People always spoke over me at school. I'd be in the middle of saying something and they'd start something up, and everyone would pay attention to them. It hurt, so after so much of it, I learnt to keep quiet. After, it became a habit. It's only ever Willow who let me be me. She was outgoing, friendly, and sometimes loud, but she always listened, asked for my opinion, and never left me out.

CJ, however, is not who I thought he was when I first met him. I was completely wrong about him from the beginning. Yes, he is confident and has an ego the size of the Titanic, but he is more than a pretty face. He's incredibly smart, even though he prefers for people to think he's dumb; he's good-looking, yes, but he doesn't exploit it to get attention or what he wants; he listens to people, no matter what they're talking about; he's never been selfish, not in the time I've known him; and he's the most selfless person I know; he'd give the shirt off his back, if you needed it.

With a heart full of love, and an empty stomach, I squeeze his hand. "Let's go get something to eat. Maybe if you're good, I'll let you have one of my sweets when we get back."

His eyes widen in mock shock, and he rests a hand over his heart. "I'm... I'm speechless, Cupcake. I'd be honoured to eat your sweets."

Giggling, I pull him toward the door, grabbing my bag from where I dropped it on the floor.

The restaurant is busy when we arrive, but we manage to get a table without waiting. The place is beautiful and expensive-looking. I would have been happy with a Travel Lodge or a bed and breakfast. Instead, the place looks like something you'd see in a magazine.

The floor is black-glittered marble, shiny enough you can see a little of your reflection. Extravagant art lines the inside walls of the building, while the outside wall is glass.

The decor is dark wood. It's warm and inviting, especially with the light shining through the window.

You can even watch as the chef cooks, flipping steaks and other stuff on the hot stove. Waiters and waitresses are dressed to impress too. The girls are wearing black skirts that end below the knees, white shirts and black ties. The guys are wearing the same but with trousers.

Fresh flowers in little vases are on every table, and as we arrive at ours, we have fresh bread and cold water waiting for us.

"Do you think all these people are here for the signing?" he asks, looking around the busy restaurant as we sit down. I do have to admit, when my eyes scan the room, I do notice more women than men here.

"Probably, but there's also a Comic-Con convention going on nearby, so they could be here for that."

"No wonder I had to get my mum to find us a room. Everywhere I looked said they were fully booked."

"You asked your mum?" I smile.

"Yeah. She also found me the tickets. I told her how badly you wanted to go, but there weren't any tickets left. She told me to wait a few days to see what she could do. Apparently, she knew one of the organisers and managed to snag a couple of tickets. They keep a few spares for raffles or something. I paid the money to get them, and then she helped find this place. She has to come here a lot for business trips so she has a standing reservation."

"That is awesome. She didn't mind doing it?"

He chuckles, taking a sip of his water. "Are you kidding me? She loves this shit. She called me after our first visit with her and said she nearly blurted out my surprise a few times. It was killing her not being able to talk about it."

"No?" I laugh. "Is that how she knew about my birthday?"

"Yeah."

"Your mum is amazing. You're really lucky to have her."

His expression softens, and he takes my hand. "I am. She's the best. She's been through so much, and her family aren't really the supportive kind. We avoid them at all costs now."

"What do you mean?" I ask, happy he's opening up more. He told me about his mum, but when it comes to his other family, he shuts down, getting a hard look in his eyes. I never brought them up again. I didn't like seeing him so upset.

"They disowned her after she decided to keep me." He scoffs, looking disgusted. "They didn't understand why she would keep me after what happened to her. According to them, she should have aborted me when she had the chance."

I gulp, rubbing my thumb over the top of his hand.

"I know it's a hard question to ask, but… *why* did she? Not that I'm not happy she did, because I am—I wouldn't have met you if she hadn't. But you have to admit, it's not something you hear happening every day." When his gaze darkens, I immediately feel bad. "Sorry, that was rude of me."

He pulls my hand closer, kissing my knuckles. "No, it's fine. A lot of people ask the same thing when they find out. You'd be surprised at how many women my mum helps who are in the same position she once was. It's more common than people think. It's just not something people broadcast to others."

"I guess."

"Anyway, after she was raped, she had all the tests they do at the beginning and took the morning after pill they gave her. That night, though, she said she was violently ill, throwing up, which was caused by bad memories. The after pill never had chance to get into her system, so it didn't work. Three months later, she found out she was pregnant with me. She admitted to me about being torn, not wanting anything to do with the monster who hurt her, but the second she had her scan, she fell in love. She wasn't repulsed, she didn't have any reservations about keeping me, she just knew it didn't matter how I came to be. What was important was that I was there, and I was hers."

"What did she do next?" I ask. His mum is more incredible than I first believed. The amount of strength she must have possessed is inspiring.

"As far as I know, she kept it from her parents for as long as she could—they already looked at her differently after the attack—but when they found out, they went ballistic. They couldn't comprehend why she would keep me."

I rub my chest, the ache there hurting for both CJ and his mum. "So, what did her parents do?"

"They kicked her out." He shrugs, but I can see their actions hurt him more than he's letting on. "Her grandparents took her in. They weren't like her parents; they were kind and loving. It's how she ended up inheriting everything they owned after they died."

"What were they like—your great-grandparents?"

Light fills his eyes when he speaks. "They were the best people in my life, apart from my mum. They loved me unconditionally and weren't afraid to show it. They didn't treat me any differently. We lived with them until they passed away. Mum didn't want to leave them as they were getting on a bit, so we never moved out of their house. And it was nice to have them around all the time. My granddad taught me everything I know."

"What about her parents, though, surely after seeing how you turned out, they changed their beliefs. Did they not contact you once? Or your mum?"

His eyes harden again, and I wish I didn't bring it up. He scoffs. "They hated me. They couldn't stand the sight of me and I knew it from an early age. They always seemed repulsed at the mention of my name."

"That sounds awful," I whisper, feeling the back of my eyes burn.

"Not as bad as my cousins. My mum's brother and sister obviously didn't mind what they spoke about in front of their kids. They're a lot older than mum. When I was nine, they made sure I knew how I was conceived. They'd call me a monster, a rapist, a sicko... whatever they could come up with. We were all the same age, near enough. Even my uncle and granddad would tell me I would end up just like my dad."

I gasp, putting my hand over my mouth, before looking at him dead in the eye. "You are nothing like *that* man. You even *look* like your mother, CJ. And you don't have a vicious bone in your body. Argh, I could kill your grandparents. Who do they think they are? And your cousins?" I grunt, getting really good and angry now. "Bet none of them have a high IQ like you do. Bet they're working in McDonald's for minimum wage."

He places a hand over mine, stopping me from going further and drawing attention to us, and chuckles. "Cupcake," he says, a small grin lighting his face. "It's sexy when you get mad, but it's fine. I'm over it, and since my great-grandparents passed away, we don't go to any family gatherings. I have my family; my mum and Cole, and now you and Low. I'm good, really good."

"It's still not okay, though. That's a horrible way to be treated. That could have been one of their stories."

He kisses my knuckles again, and I relax into my seat, even if I am still sickened he had to listen to them spout venomous lies. "It is, but if I'm honest, seeing my mum hurt by their accusations is what hurt me more. I'm glad they told me though. That night, it brought me and my mum even closer. I never understood why people distanced them-selves from us until then. Knowing what she went through, yet still choosing to have me and loving me with her whole heart... it made me realise just how lucky I was to have her. After that, I made sure I didn't get into trouble," he says, but I give him a look that says 'yeah right', making him chuckle. "Okay, I tried to stay out of trouble, but I still did all my school work, even took extra lessons and made sure I got all the best grades. I was polite to my elders and respected any and every girl I went out with. Not many people know about what happened to my mum, but there were a few times when girls, who knew one of my cousins, would avoid me, looking at me like *I* was the rapist."

It saddens me that he went through this. I shake my head glumly, feeling tears gather behind my eyelids. "It's still not fair. I'm glad you have your mum, and now us. And those girls? They missed out big time." I wipe my cheeks, feeling more tears building behind my eyes.

There's so much devastation already in this world. We don't need people making life harder, especially family; the people who are supposed to protect and love you.

"Don't cry, Cupcake, this is supposed to be a happy day. I didn't tell you this to make you sad. It was a long time ago; I'm over it. And my mum is better off now that they aren't in her life."

I sniffle, wiping my running nose. "I know, but it's horrible. And it doesn't seem right that someone as bright as you had to be around a place so dark. And your mum had to grow up around that too. It's just so hard to get my head around. You've been through so much."

"Mum always said I was bright," he says, puffing his chest out, lighting the conversation.

I giggle, taking another sip of my water. "That you are. That. You. Are."

"That's better. I don't like seeing you cry," he tells me, absently rubbing his chest. He truly is the most caring person I know. He feels everything deeply.

"Want to get double dessert after and ask if we can take it to our room?" I ask, wanting to be alone with him and away from the noise in the restaurant.

He grins wickedly. "Of course."

A plan in action, we quickly order our food and dessert, explaining we want to take it upstairs and to charge it to our room.

Even though he changes the subject, it's hard not to think about what he went through. I knew his start in life was bad, but to find out how bad... It's killing me. No one should have to go through that. And for him to turn out as brilliant as he has, is nothing short of amazing.

Everyone deserves to be surrounded by love, especially an innocent baby.

Chapter 7

The day has finally arrived, and I've never been more excited in my life. I'm so nervous, my stomach is doing somersaults.

From the road trip, till this very second, it has all been a dream come true for me. I never imagined I would ever get to meet my favourite authors of all time, or get my books signed.

Now the day is starting and I'm charged with pure joy and excitement.

I'm glad I decided to wear tights with the new outfit Willow got me. The red blouse with its cute black bow tie matched well with the black glittered suspenders and black cardigan. It's one of my favourites outfits yet. Even the black Converse CJ bought me go really well with it. It took me a while to stop staring at the glittered rose on the side when I first put them on this morning. They're truly beautiful, and the most comfortable shoes I've ever worn. And at the end of the day, I'll be grateful for that. My outfit is the bomb, too. Willow knows my tastes so well.

I love funky outfits like this. Don't get me wrong, a good pair of leggings or jeans and a T-shirt go a long way, but these clothes… they make me feel like me. I don't care if people stare at my whacky choice of clothes, or if they think they don't fit into societal standards. It's me.

The day didn't really start off as planned. I was worried about my outfit choice when I looked out our room's window and noticed it had snowed overnight—was still snowing—but it wasn't enough to stop us from getting to the venue the signing was held at.

I hate snow. Especially when I'm standing in it for just under an hour. Snow should only come out at Christmas, but since I live in Great Britain, the weather never sticks to its four seasons. It's frustrating as hell. I have a right mind to get the Christmas tree back out.

Thankfully, as we stepped inside, the heating was on and warmed us up in no time.

The place was packed. Not only was there a signing that had thousands of women waiting excitedly to meet their favourite authors, but also a Comic-Con going on in the same building. You couldn't move without bumping into someone else. It was great. I didn't even care I was still a little chilled from waiting in the line outside, or that my legs were already beginning to feel the burn of standing for so long. It would all be worth it when I left at the end of the day with all my pretties signed.

Already I had made some new friends and promised to add them on Facebook once I got signal. There was nothing I loved more than raving about my favourite book to someone else who loved it also. I could rattle on for hours about the latest book I just read, or one of my all-time favourites.

The feeling was bliss.

Willow, even though she was my best friend, was into shoes like I was into books. Half of them she didn't even wear, but my books… I read each and every one of them. The only thing we have in common when it comes to the two is that we both zone out when the other is talking about it. It's not like I don't care about her interests; I do, but I don't care about what new shoe is out or how her sparkly ones light up. I love my boots, Converse, and sometimes dolly shoes. Anything with a heel is a no go for me.

I still love her though, and one day, I know I'll be able to win her over and not only get her to start reading but enjoy it too. It's only of a matter of time.

"I'm still getting stared at," CJ grumbles from beside me, leaning in closer.

Since arriving, every woman, young or old, has stared at my boyfriend openly. At first, it was a little annoying; I mean, he's here with his girlfriend. Thankfully, none have come over and flirted with him. I wouldn't know what to do if that happened. I don't know if I'd get jealous or not. I guess it depends on who the person is and if it's teasing or actually trying to get his attention. I've never been in a situation like it, so I have no clue. I'm not like most girls who would attack. I'd probably stand there looking special. Would I say something? Ignore it? I don't know.

He'd smiled at first, loving the attention, but then things became a little awkward when a group of girls slyly took photos, giggling to each other. I have to admit, seeing his taken aback look was worth it. He's usually all for it. I was surprised he didn't start posing. He only has to see someone at Whithall taking a photo or selfie and he's in it, grinning wide.

He pushes my trolley forward in the line, glancing around the room warily. We're in a small lobby that leads to the main room, and its filled with women with suitcases, trolleys, crates like mine, and other fun things to cart their goods around.

He looks comical standing next to mine with his tall frame and bulging muscles. He seems so out of his comfort zone it's hilarious.

I may or may not have gone a tad overboard on books, so he's lucky I didn't buy two crates. I didn't realise I had so many until I unpacked them and stacked them in the trolley, making sure they were in order to grab for the first authors I see.

"They're probably imagining you as their latest book boyfriend."

We move up further, getting closer to the registration desk to grab our wristbands. "Book boyfriend?"

I glance at him, smiling as another woman slyly takes a photo of him. "Yeah. It's what us bookworms call our favourite male characters."

He seems to think that over, looking deep in thought "Do *you* have one?" I blush, ducking my head a little. He chuckles, titling my head up to meet his gaze. He kisses me softly, and a loud sigh come from behind us. "Do you?"

I drop my head to his shoulder before glancing back up at him. "I do. I have loads. It's hard to choose when th8ey're just that perfect," I tell him adamantly. My focus wavers a little, thinking of my latest… Chase. God, who knew mafia men who shoot people for fun could be so hot.

An irritated expression flashes through his eyes. "*I'm* fucking perfect."

Chuckles come from the lady standing in front of us. "You sure are."

He grins at her, his chest puffing out. "Thanks."

I roll my eyes, tapping on his shoulder to get his attention. The guy loves being flattered. He gets withdrawal if he doesn't hear how good-looking he is after so long. "They're from books. And in the unlikely event that I do ever meet a replica of a book boyfriend, I'd still love you more."

He looks taken aback. "But you'd still love them?"

I giggle at the wounded expression on his face. "They aren't real!"

A lady behind gasps. "Don't kill my dream!"

I wince, looking behind me. "Sorry," I tell her, before turning back to CJ. "Stop being a pain in the arse and move forward. We're next."

He kisses me again before pushing the trolley forward. CJ orders our wristbands, while I chat the ear off one of the volunteers, explaining how excited I am. She chuckles, giving me a name badge and a free tote bag.

"Thank you so much," I tell her, taking it from her. This is so cool. It has the signing logo on it and everything.

"Jesus, come on, you nerd." CJ chuckles, taking my hand. He goes to lead me to the right of the room, but I gasp, stopping him.

"No, we have to start over there. I want to make sure I see my favourite authors before I see anyone else."

"How do you know where they are?" he asks, dodging a woman pulling a pushchair piled high with books. He looks down at it with wide eyes. "Where's the baby?"

I giggle at his expression. "Not there. It's hard to lug books around, you know. I didn't think of a pushchair." Maybe next time. It does look big enough to hold everything I want to get. "And I downloaded a seating plan last night, whilst you were snoring. I figured it would be good to know where to go."

He smirks, shaking his head at me. "Lead the way then, Cupcake. Oh, and I don't snore; I'm far too pretty."

I roll my eyes, giggling. "Trust me, you do. It's a wonder Cole hasn't smothered you in your sleep."

I don't bother telling him I find the sound comforting. He'd only

73

tease me. The expression on his face is another reason. He looks truly confused and a little embarrassed.

"I don't."

"You really do," I tell him, getting in line.

I bite my lip to stop myself from laughing when he begins to pout. "I don't," he grumbles under his breath.

An hour passes and I've only managed to see six authors. Finally, the line to see Alanea Alder has died down enough for me to see her. We had to stop by the bar a few times just so CJ could grab a beer. Apparently, there was only so many photos he could pose for.

At first, he enjoyed the compliments he got for being mistaken for a cover model. But the touchier the women got, the more he didn't like it. I found it amusing and made sure to snap a few myself to send to Cole and Willow.

Juggling three gift bags full of swag, my trolley, a few books that won't fit into the trolley, and a beer, he moves forward for us to take our turn.

I chat animatedly with Alanea, telling her how much I love her books whilst buying the remainders of the series that I need. I relentlessly ask her questions about what we should expect, while picking everything and anything I can get my hands on that she is giving away on her table.

"Who's your favourite characters?" she asks, grabbing another book to sign.

I don't even have to think about it. "Meryn. She's hilarious; no other character can compete with her. She's incredible. Although, second is Kendrick Ashwood, then Colton. Although, now they're in Noctum Falls, I kind of love the twins."

She looks up, smiling wide. "I'm so glad you like it."

"I'm pretty sure she just named every single one your characters," CJ mutters, looking at me in bewilderment.

I roll my eyes. "Trust me, they come nowhere near as close to all of her characters. You're lucky I love one more than the others, otherwise we would have been here all day with me naming every single one and giving reasons as to why I like them."

"She has a point." Alanea giggles, handing over the last of the books.

"This is crazy. It's just a book."

A few gasps echo mine. "No, they are not."

He holds his full hands up, stepping back. "Sorry. I know, it's life. Your life. Please don't bust my balls."

Shaking my head, I turn to Alanea. "Men." She nods, agreeing, her smile infectious. "Can I have a photo?"

"Of course." She smiles, standing up.

Her accent is incredible. She sounds like she could lull a baby to sleep by reading a bedtime story with a voice like hers.

I throw my phone in CJ's direction, and with his hands full, he drops most of the items on the floor before catching it. Just as I'm about to step forward, I trip over my own feet, nearly falling over her table.

Well, crap.

"Are you okay?" she asks, looking concerned. Probably for my mental stability.

My face is no doubt beet red because it feels like it's on fire. "Yep, I'm good," I tell her, shaking it off.

"Come on, let's take a few funny photos and then a nice one."

I beam, loving this woman even more. She's amazing and really flipping sweet.

CJ is still pouting over the mess on the floor, the camera ready in his hand. We start goofing around, both of us laughing at his expression as we take the last of our photos.

"Thank you for coming to see me," she tells me in that accent of hers, giving me one last hug.

"It's my pleasure. Thank you for being awesome. I'm looking forward to your next release."

I grab my pretties before moving over to CJ, helping him pick up my stuff before getting out of the way of the line.

"Can we sit down? My feet are killing."

I give him an 'are you kidding' look. "We only get five hours, CJ.

Every second is precious. We can't waste time sitting down. Sitting down is for quitters."

He takes a step back from my outburst before nodding. "Okay, it was only a suggestion."

We move on to the next table and the author starts laughing. "Are you enjoying yourself?"

I look up from my browsing to see that her question isn't directed at me but at CJ.

He chuckles, struggling to manoeuvre the bags into a more comfortable position. "Apparently I'm only here to carry the goods. She won't even let me take a break. I'm starving."

The woman looks flabbergasted but doesn't look at me disapprovingly. If anything, she looks amused.

I growl under my breath and turn to CJ. "You have a stash of stuff in my trolley, which is why you're carrying four of my books. And you ate a Burger King half an hour ago when you left to 'take a phone call'."

"I'm a growing boy." His reply is always the same. I swear, he uses the excuse for everything.

The author laughs. "I have some spare room under my table if you'd like to store some of it until you leave?"

CJ is about to accept, but I hold my hand up to stop him. "That's really kind of you, but he'll only annoy me if he has nothing to do."

She laughs, understanding dawning in her eyes. "Enjoy the rest of your visit."

"I will." I smile, handing her the money for a book that caught my eye. The cover is pink with sparkly writing all over it. I don't even know what it's about, but I can't wait to see what it looks like on my shelf.

As we move away, CJ sidles up close to me, leaning down to whisper in my ear, "I didn't know you get this heated over books. It's like you're a different person."

"I'm not," I lie. I totally am. I'm like a kangaroo on speed, wanting to jump from one table to the next. I can't help it; I want to make sure I get to see everyone. And then there's the people I talk to in the lines.

I can't exactly blank them. We're like family in the book community; we share everything and anything.

"Cupcake, you nearly took out that woman who was browsing over the table. She wasn't even waiting to see the author and you got all crazy-eyed."

"I did not."

"You did," he argues, silently laughing at me. "She looked seconds away from either pissing herself or ramming her cart into your legs."

I scoff. "She shouldn't have pushed in. We were in that queue ten minutes."

"She picked up a pen. I noticed she had a bagful, so she must have been collecting from each author."

"Whatever."

"And don't get me started on how many times you've spoken so fast no one has understood a word you've said. That one author just nodded and smiled," he says, laughing.

"I was nervous," I tell him, blushing a little. I tend to get carried away when I speak about something that means so much to me.

"And the nearly falling over your feet to get to authors?"

I send him a mock glare, but I can't really be mad when he's one hundred percent right. I have tripped more than once. At one author's table, I knocked over her display. It was embarrassing. She took it like a champ, though. Even offered me a chair and a bottle of water.

Bless her heart.

"We've got half an hour to go and I don't have much money left."

He snorts, smiling at me. "That's because you've bought at least one book from every author you've seen."

"I might not ever see them again."

He laughs while looking around the room. "I'm going to head back to the bar for a drink. I'm getting thirsty. I swear, people have done nothing but talk my ear off since we walked in. My throat is parched. If I wasn't so fond of the sound of my own voice, I'd be sick of it by now."

I don't bother telling him that it was him talking to every Tom, Dick and Harry and their family. It's just who is he. Then again, I've been the same, which is unlike me. There's just something about a fellow book nerd that makes me relax enough to speak.

"Okay. I'm going to head on over there and try to make my way down the line of authors. I've seen everyone I desperately wanted to, so who I see now is a bonus."

He nods, leaning down to kiss me. "I'll take these with me. See you in a few."

I watch him go for a second, giggling when I notice a group of old ladies swooning over him. The second he's out of sight, I make my way over to the last row of authors and begin my march down the aisle. I'm determined to see every single one of them.

CJ lied when he said he would be back in a few. The place is now closing, and people have already begun filing out.

I begin to feel bad for how I've treated him today. I didn't stop to consider how bored by all of this he would be. He must have been going out of his mind. I was being selfish with my own excitement. As soon as we'd leave one table, I'd be dragging him over to the next.

I feel a little bad, like I've mistreated him or something.

Today has been the best day of my life. I've never seen so many unicorn authors in one room before, and never authors this big. And all of it is because of CJ. He was the one who went above and beyond to get me the tickets—hell, the fact he even thought of something so personal amazes me. Not that he isn't a compassionate person, but because most boyfriends would give you a bunch of flowers and a box of chocolates and be done with it. Not something like this.

I just hope he can forgive me for turning into a grizzly bear over books.

Books are something I'm truly passionate about. People have favourite TV shows, movies, or hobbies; I have books. I have the joy and escape they give me. They inspire me to be a better person, to hold out for something special. They gave me hope when I thought I had none.

And I know CJ will understand that. However, he still should have had my undivided attention today.

He might have left me here, not wanting to associate with the crazy-eyed person any longer. I wouldn't blame him, either. We were only on the third author when I snapped at him for putting the book in the trolley on its side. The pages were bending and it was ruining the book. In my world, that is a serious crime. It's like people who put books on their shelves without the covers facing outward. It just shouldn't happen.

From there, I only got worse. If I wasn't being territorial over my books, then I was acting like a girl who never got let out for a day in her life.

The day has been awesome though. I just wish I'd thought to have brought more money with me because there was so much more I wanted to buy. In my race to get on the road here, I left my bankcard on my bed at home.

One author had these cute little owl earrings, another had a bunch of beautiful dreamcatchers, and others had T-shirts, tote bags, and more cool stuff to buy.

I wanted it all. Even if I never got to use it, they would be great mementos for my time here.

My eyes search the almost empty hall once again, this time finding CJ walking toward me a few tables over. He's carrying a big cardboard box with a few things overflowing from the top and is struggling to push my trolley.

I giggle at the sight and take a quick photo before rushing over to help him.

"What the hell is all this?" I ask, dropping my purchases down on the pile in the trolley. I don't even know how we're going to get this out to the car without something falling out. It makes me nauseous to think of one of my beauties getting ruined in the dreaded white stuff.

"I got a little carried away," he says sheepishly, before dropping the box down on the table. Luckily, the author has already packed up and left, otherwise we'd be using the floor like a lot of others are, and I don't think my back could take it. I'd never be able to get back up again.

"What do you mean?" I ask, leaning up on my tiptoes to see what's in the box.

He laughs, pushing me away a little with a sparkle in his eyes. "Well, when we first got here you completely missed the raffle table they had going on—"

"What?" I ask, outraged I never saw it. I look around, my eyes not finding the table in question. I freaking love entering raffles. I can't believe I never saw it.

He laughs at my expense, putting the box down. "Anyhow, I went ahead and got a bunch of tickets. You won, which is what is in here," he tells me, pointing at the box. "There's three hampers with books and other stuff in it, a few signed books, a couple of amazon gift cards, and you won a purple HD Kindle Fire."

"No," I breath, staring at him in awe. "Really?"

He nods, then bursts out laughing when I jump into his arms, kissing him. He pulls back, grinning at me. "And I got you some things I noticed you eyeing earlier, when you didn't think I was paying attention."

"What?" I breathe, too in shock to say anything else.

He shrugs like it's no big deal, but it is. I've been acting like a crazy bitch on speed all day. "I'll show you when we get back. Oh, and we're totally ordering room service. My feet can't take another step at this point."

I smile at him, kissing him quickly before pulling away. "You are amazing, CJ. I love you so much. And I'm sorry for acting so crazy today."

He laughs again, kissing the tip of my nose. "Cupcake, I'll take you any way I can get you; crazy and all. I'm just glad you've had a nice time."

"I've had the best," I tell him sincerely. It's been one day I'll never forget, and I can't wait to go over all my goodies when we get back, and post pictures on Facebook.

Not being able to keep my hands or lips away, I press forward, deepening the kiss until we're forced to pull away by the catcalls and whistles.

"Come on, let's get back and order room service."

I glance up at the huskiness in his voice that causes my stomach to tighten. His eyes are filled with desire, catching my breath.

"I love you," I tell him softly, my gaze never wavering.

I love him so much it hurts. I love him when he drives me crazy, when he eats my sweets, and when he wakes me up too goddamn early. I love him fiercely, irrevocably. I love him more than my heart can take. But I'll try, because I can't imagine being in a world where I don't.

His gaze softens, and he brings his hands up to cup my cheeks. He kisses the tip of my nose, his lips spreading into a warm smile when he pulls back to look at me. "Not as much as I love you, Cupcake."

"I do."

"Impossible," he breathes, before kissing me once more, taking my breath away.

Chapter 8

A chocked cry crawls its way up my throat when I hear a door in the near distance click shut. That sound can only mean one thing:

He's here and he's close.

Fat tear drops fall down my cheeks, splashing against my knees that are pressed against my chest.

It still feels like I'm living in a nightmare. I've been pinching the inside of my arms, willing myself to wake up. But I can't.

It's real, every single second of it.

Sunday, I went for my morning run. My trainer, who is helping me prep for my marathon, demanded I train every morning. Most of the time I do track at our local sports club, but every Sunday morning, I like to go out, breathe in the fresh air.

It started off as a normal day; nothing seemed out of the ordinary. I had been running for twenty minutes when I reached the crossing where one path leads to the park and the other to the train station. That's where I had been hit from behind.

I woke up here.

In Hell.

I still don't understand why I am here.

I've asked the man who took me so many times why he wants me, what I did to deserve being stolen. I've begged him to free me, but he talks over me, like he doesn't hear me speak.

On the second day of waking up here—and I'm only guessing the days as I'm going by the one meal he brings me each day—I panicked, screaming and shouting for him to free me. He lost his patience, and before me, in a fit of rage, I met the demon nightmares are made of.

He was a monster when he hit me, cutting my lip open in a deep gash. That day I was humiliated.

Being scared out of my mind, not knowing what was going to happen to me, I soiled myself. I wept, begged, and fought for him to let me go home, but to no avail.

I wanted my mum and dad.

Instead, he stripped me of my running clothes, then put me in the shower to scrub me clean. My skin was red raw, parts still sensitive on my weak, frail body. I tried to do everything I could to get away but was forced to endure it, tied up. I had no say, no argument, as he washed me, touching parts of my body he had no right to touch.

He's done this every day for twelve days.

Twelve days of nothing but gut-wrenching fear.

That first day I not only lost a part of my soul, but my dignity.

Each day he would wake me up. I'd be groggy, having fought sleep, too scared he would come when I was at my most vulnerable. He's everywhere; in my nightmares and reality.

I've had no choice but to let him take me to the toilet, where he watches me, and then cleans me afterwards.

The second time he comes in a day, he brings me food. He feeds me like I'm a baby, sitting down with me to watch television and act like we're friends. All the while I cry, pleading with him to let me go.

It's what he is here to do now: bring me food and make me endure his company. At least, I think he is. Time... it's long forgotten. Hours, minutes, seconds have passed, but I couldn't tell you how many. I can only go by my guess.

I know what I'm about to endure. He'll ignore my cries, my demands to go home. He'll shower me, brush my teeth, then dress me in another nightgown. All of them are the same: old-fashioned, but thankfully they cover me from head to toe. After, he will sit me down on a stool in front of a mirror and brush my hair, telling me how perfect I am and how much I belong to him.

He may have touched me inappropriately, but none of it has been sexual. It doesn't mean I don't fear that one day that is what will happen. I do.

I've been living in a constant state of fear since I woke up here and realised I had been kidnapped, torn away from my friends and family.

He won't even tell me if they're okay.

I wipe my cheeks once again, not wanting him to see me cry. *Even a speck of dirt or tears and he will use it as an excuse to shower me.*

I'm weak. Twelve days of eating nothing but ham sandwiches and drinking little bits of water when he visits is all I've been allowed. I asked him to leave me water, but he yelled, telling me he already gives me water and I shouldn't ask for more.

I've lost any hope of being set free, but it doesn't mean I'll stop pleading. I've prayed he will begin to see that what he's doing is wrong, that he will grow a conscience.

No one is coming to get me.

No one is going to save me.

My last days on Earth will be spent tortured, broken and afraid. It's inevitable. In the deepest part of my heart, I know death is how this will end.

The chains on the second door, before the one leading to my cell, rattle. My breathing picks up, my body breaking out in a cold sweat. I rub the palm of my hands down the white nightgown, my eyes watching the door like a hawk.

The key in the lock causes a whimper to escape. I'm terrified about being in his company for however long he decides to stay this time.

Trembling, I sit up against the headboard, hugging my knees as tight to my chest as the chains around my wrists and ankles allow. I cringe as they chink against the bedposts they're tied to. I wince at the sting where the rough metal has rubbed my skin raw.

I jump when my door opens and he walks in, looking intimidating and scary. Under normal circumstances, I wouldn't have found anything harmful about him.

But under the intelligence and knowledge he holds close, he is soulless. There is nothing but darkness when I look into his eyes, nothing but anger, hatred and rage. He seems calm and collected on the outside, but he's not. He's a ticking time bomb, and no matter what you try to do to defuse it, he will blow.

"Please, I want to go home. I want my mum and dad," I beg, my voice scratchy from lack of water. The tears I willed to stop begin to fall helplessly.

He storms over to the TV and switches it on, before pacing in front of it.

Instantly, I know something is wrong. A shiver runs along my spine.

One, he isn't carrying the tray of food he normally brings, and two, he hasn't even looked at me, not once.

"I'm good enough, dammit!" he yells, his voice filled with anger.

The hairs on the back of my neck bristle, and I try to bury further into the headboard of the bed.

He throws all his anger towards me when he turns, his eyes blood-red, his fists shaking violently by his side.

"Why do you always moan?"

"I want to go home," I whisper. Something in the tone of his voice stops me from my usual pleading.

"You're just like her!"

"Her?"

He glares at me, stomping over to my bed. He pulls roughly at the cuffs, grabbing the small key to unlock me.

"Why can't you be her?"

I know from the look in his eyes he's not even hearing me. I don't even think he is truly seeing me as he unlocks my feet.

He hauls me roughly off the bed and my knees hit the floor. I cry out in pain, looking up at him with wide eyes, my heart pounding as dread seeps in like poison.

This is it.

He doesn't bother to wait for me to get up. Instead, he drags me across the floor to the shower he must have had installed recently.

I don't know exactly where I am, if I'm in a warehouse, an old house, building or what have you. All I know is what I see. And that's one room, no windows, a bed, a chest of drawers filled with nightgowns, and a dressing table with a mirror. The shower and toilet are right next to each other, the shower looking newer than everything else in the room, including the toilet that looks to be years old and never used or cleaned until I arrived.

On the dressing table is one brush, one hand-held mirror, and a bobble.

The only other furniture is in the corner, where the TV, two-seater sofa and coffee table are.

I grab the leg of the bed, stopping him from taking me further. He pulls harder, but when I don't budge, he turns, his anger directed at me. He looks through me, his expression thunderous as he kicks me in the ribs.

"Move it, now! You need to be better. You need to be! I'm the one who cares."

"Let me go! I want to go home!" I scream, kicking his legs.

He grunts, grabbing my hair, and had I not let go of the bed, a chunk would have surely been ripped out by the force of his pull.

I scream. Even though my throat is raw, I scream for help, for my parents, for anyone to come save me. I pray and plead, but my prayers go unheard as he shoves me against the shower stall. My head smacks the tiled wall with a thud, and my vision blurs.

Too weak and a little disorientated, I don't fight when he pulls me up, turning the shower on with both of us under the cold spray.

"Please, let me go. I'm not who you think I am. I've never even met you," I cry, although he does remind me of a science teacher.

"You aren't her! I need her!" he yells, his fingers digging into my biceps.

"Please, my name is Linda Cooper. I live with my parents, who I love and miss. Please, let me go."

He shakes his head, and when his eyes meet mine, I flinch, taking a small step back until my spine is against the tiles.

His lips curls in a snarl as he takes a step forward, slamming his fists against the tiles on either side of my head.

I cry out, my eyes closing in fear. "Please, don't hurt me. Please. Just let me go. I won't tell anyone."

Cold fingers grab the hem of my dress, and in one swift movement, I'm standing naked in front of my captor.

My eyes snap open as I try in vain to cover myself, more tears falling down my face and blurring my vision.

"I've given you everything. Why can't you be happy?" he screams in my face, spit splattering across me.

"Please, I want to go home. I didn't ask for this."

"You aren't her. You were supposed to be her. You were supposed to be happy. But you're not. You're just a silly, ungrateful, whore. I need her."

A strangled sob tears from my throat as I bend a little to cover myself. He moves closer, closer than he's ever been, and cold dread swarms through me.

"Please, don't do this."

Is he going to rape me?

My heart races, and as each horrendous thought passes through my mind, warmth trickles between my legs.

I hear the disgusted hiss from his lips, and before I know what is happen-

ing, he's slamming my shoulders back against the tiles, knocking the air out of me.

"Why can't you be thankful?"

Nothing could have prepared me for the feel of fingers wrapping around my neck. My eyes bulge when I realise he isn't doing this to scare me into submission.

He's going to kill me.

I wheeze through the little air I have left, using my gaze to try and plead with him to let me go. "Please!"

It only fuels his anger, tightening his grip on my neck. He lifts me off the cold, tiled floor, my legs dangling uselessly as I cling to the last bit of oxygen I have left inside me.

My eyes close, and I picture my parents in my mind. I remember the morning I left for my run, saying goodbye to them and kissing them on the cheek. A lone tear falls from under my closed eyelid as I think of how I will never feel the warmth of their embrace again, never get to tell them how much I love them and how great they were as parents. I think about all the things we did together, as well as the things we will never get to experience.

I think of my friends and family, the people I'll never get to see again.

And then nothing.

Just darkness.

Like the light that was once blazing inside me has been snuffed out.

Chapter 9

Damn flipping stairs.

Damn exercise.

I huff and puff, taking another step up. Whoever invented stairs needs to be held accountable for the people they're trying to kill. Surely it has to be a crime.

"Why, oh why, do we pay our building maintenance fees when they don't bloody fix anything," I growl, stopping at the bottom of another flight of stairs. The instant I look up, I want to give up. My legs are burning, my feet are already throbbing, and I'm wheezing like I smoke forty a day.

I hate exercise with a passion.

And thanks to our lift being out of order once again, I'm now sweating, not prettily either.

Then there's CJ standing next to me, looking amused as hell. He doesn't even look effected and he's carrying my crate that's filled with books and two bags of luggage. It would have been one, but we needed to go out and buy something to put my goodies in, otherwise we would never have gotten them into the car.

I think the only time I've seen him sweaty is when he's playing rugby. And he doesn't even look like a drowned rat whilst sweating, no, he looks goddamn edible.

It's unfair.

I whimper, wanting to cry.

CJ, the traitor, laughs. "You're exaggerating, Cupcake."

I wheeze again, one arm on the stairwell banister and one on my bent knee. I glare up at him. "They do this shit on purpose, I swear. It was broken before we left for break, and before we left, I told them it better be fixed by the time I got back—well, I got Jordan to do it, but the message was clear! I wanted it fixed. I was fed up of walking up seven flights of stairs."

He throws the bags over one shoulder whilst stalking toward me. I stand up, wary. When he bends down, shoving his shoulder into my belly, I grunt, the air whooshing out of my lungs as he throws me over his shoulder before bending down to pick up the crate.

"CJ," I squeal, gripping the back of his jeans with all my might.

He slaps my arse, so I slap his back, laughing when I feel his teeth graze the skin that is showing near my hip.

"Come on, I'm starving and you're taking your sweet-arse time."

My eyes narrow. "They're freaking steep and exhausting, you know. They should install those moving platforms they have at the airport. They'd be great."

"The stairs aren't straight," he chuckles, carrying me up the last two flights.

"So, who cares? Make little mini ones on each flight of stairs. I can't keep doing this exercise stuff. It's killing me, CJ. Killing me. I feel like I'm about to have a heart attack."

He laughs uproariously, not caring that it's a little insulting. I'm in real health danger here. My heart can't take the rate it's going.

He puts me down on the floor, moving the bags over to the other shoulder. "Let's go show Willow what you've won and order those pictures to be developed."

Distracted and excited once again, I nod, rushing to the door that leads to our hall. "I can't wait. I'm going to give her my old kindle, and then set up my new one. Can you believe it's purple?"

He chuckles, shaking his head at me before dropping the stuff in front of my door. He pulls me into his arms, looking down at me lovingly. "I'm glad you've had a good weekend. I've really enjoyed myself too."

I beam up at him. "I've had the best. Thank you again, CJ."

We move together, our lips meeting in a heated kiss.

My thoughts drift to his hands touching me, then to my hands touching him. There's something I've been wanting to do since I read it in a book a few weeks ago.

All the stories I read have sex scenes. Some make me glad I'm a virgin, some make me want more, and some... they intrigue me. And the one that got my attention was a scene where the female lead is giving her man a blowjob, but she does this thing with her tongue, her hand, and a finger. It made me curious as to whether it's as pleasurable as it sounded.

I'm about to suggest we sneak off to his flat, when a throat clearing behind me has us pulling apart.

I turn, finding my other best friend, Alex, looking red and embarrassed at catching us kissing. "Alex, hey. You are never going to believe who I met over the weekend and all the stuff I got. And most of it was free," I tell him, my excitement building once again.

I want to tell everyone and anyone what I got up to. I want the world to know what an amazing weekend I had. And Alex loves reading as much as me; he just doesn't read the same genre I do. He's more into sci-fi and paranormal.

"Just don't ask questions, it will take her longer to finish telling you," CJ laughs. "I was there and she still replayed everything that happened. Twice."

Alex laughs, looking down at my bags. "You just got back?"

"Yeah, we got stuck in traffic. It was lined up for hours."

"Looks like you had fun. Is that all the books you bought?" he asks in bewilderment.

I look down at my bags, frowning. "Um, not all of it."

CJ laughs, grabbing his key for my flat and opening the door. "Dude, don't listen to her. It's all fucking books. I had to chuck my T and jeans just so she could fit more in."

I pout. "Hey, I couldn't leave without the T-shirts you bought me."

He kicks the crate with his foot, sliding it across the floor toward the entrance of the kitchen, before bending down and picking up our bags.

"Allie, is that you?" Willow calls.

"Yeah! You are never going to believe what an amazing time I've had."

She comes running into the hallway, her face pale and her body trembling. "You need to see this. They found a body. It's all over the news."

"What?" CJ and I ask at the same time.

"Come on," she urges, before heading back into the front room.

We follow as Willow goes straight to Cole. Jordan and Becca are here, sitting in front of the television, the sound louder than we normally have it.

"It's been playing on repeat for an hour," Cole says, and I look to find him watching CJ.

CJ rubs the back of his neck. "Fuck!"

I ignore the two and step closer to Jordan and Becca, sitting between them on the sofa. Alex moves to sit on the floor at the end, tucking his knees to his chest as he, too, watches on as a reporter standing outside a blue tent starts talking.

"Whithall Police department were called down to Rally River when a passer-by found a young woman, dead. Police have confirmed the young woman is Linda Cooper, who was reported missing on Monday 23rd January by her parents, Caroline and Antony Cooper.

"There are no witnesses at this time, but police are urgently asking anyone to come forward if they have any information or were around Rally River from five a.m. this morning.

"Whithall police will also be investigating local areas for any footage that could help lead them to the killer.

"Whithall University has issued a message to all students to be vigilant of their surroundings. The police believe the murder is connected to the murder that happened at Whithall University in December.

"Melissa Atwood gives her statement about her ordeal this morning. Over to you, Doug."

The screen switches to the other cameraman's view, where a younger man stands next to a middle-aged woman outside a house. In the background, there are tons of people watching, some weeping quietly as they listen to what she has to say.

My stomach turns as I think of what Linda Cooper must have through, what the girl's mum and dad are going through. It's devastating.

"Can you tell us what happened this morning?" the news reporter asks.

The woman nods, wiping under her eyes. "I take my dogs out every morning along the river. The dogs started barking, so I ran over to see what was happening, and saw the young girl. At first, I thought she was just passed *out—I've walked that trail for years and have encountered more than one passed out drunk, since it's close to some of the local clubs. But something didn't feel right when the dogs started whimpering. I just didn't imagine it to be what it was. When I touched her, she was so cold..."* She pauses, more tears sliding down her face. *"I didn't know. She looked so peaceful, her hands resting under her cheek, like she was praying. The hair at the back of her head had been cut off. I called for the police straight away. I'm still in shock. I don't think I'll ever be able to walk down that path again after this morning. My heart goes out to the family."*

"Were there any wounds on the victim?"

I gasp at the audacity of his question. How heartless could he be?

The woman narrows her eyes, wiping her nose with a tissue. *"No, but I'd like you to respect the young woman who was killed, and her parents who are grieving the loss of their only child."*

The man looks shocked to be answered back to on live television, but nods, looking back to the camera with a guilty expression. *"Back to the studio."*

The news reporter at the studio swings his head back to the screen. *"Thank you, Doug."* He puts his finger to his ear, like he's listening in. *"We just had a statement come in from the Cooper's."* The screen once again changes to show Linda's parents. They both look incredibly tired.

"Our beautiful daughter is gone. Words cannot describe the grief and shock of what we are going through. Linda was loved by many. She will be missed, she will be remembered, and she will be loved. We are asking for privacy during this difficult time. Nobody wants answers more than we do right now, but at this moment in time, we would like to grieve the loss of our daughter alone."

Cole mutes the television, leaning back against the chair he's in, pulling Willow against him. The room is quiet as we soak in what has happened. Those poor parents. That poor girl.

"I know everyone will say this would never happen to them, but this just proves it can happen; it could be you. I know you girls love your independence, but from now on, you aren't to walk out alone. This girl was taken in the morning, in broad daylight. This person isn't scared about being seen," CJ says, sitting across from me, next to the television.

He doesn't even need to push this. I agree wholeheartedly. "I agree."

"I can't believe this is happening," Willow whispers, still watching the screen where messages from Linda's friends run across the bottom.

"How do they know it's connected to Christie's murder?" Cole asks.

Me and Jordan share a look. Both of us know more than we should since we got those files. I haven't told CJ and telling him now will make it look like I lied to him. I didn't; I just withheld the information.

"What was that look for?" CJ asks, looking between me and Jordan.

Jordan clears her throat, sitting forward. "I know how it's connect-ed," she tells him, then looks at me.

I nod, sitting forward and clasping my hands together. "When we got back, Jordan brought me all the information she got on Christie's murder."

"What?" CJ explodes, standing up. He runs his fingers through his hair, pulling at it and looking ashen.

I stand, meeting him in the middle of the floor and taking his hands in mine. "I didn't go looking myself. I promised you that much. But I needed to know, CJ. I needed to know this had nothing to do with Logan. I couldn't risk putting Willow in danger again. I couldn't," I tell him, my eyes watering.

He runs his fingers through my hair. "Why didn't you tell me?"

I sniffle, wiping my nose with the sleeve of my shirt. "You made it clear where you stood on the matter, but I needed to do this."

"Why didn't you tell me?" Willow asks, her voice shaky. She never saw the connection between Logan and Christie. She presumed, like the rest of them, that Christie just pissed off the wrong person. She wasn't exactly known for being nice.

I turn to look at my best friend. "I failed you once, Willow; I wasn't going to do it again. If it turned out not to be related to Logan then I would have scared you for nothing. You weren't sleeping back home. You had nightmares every night and it killed me inside because I did that to you," I tell her, putting my hand up to stop her when she goes to interrupt me. "I know what happened wasn't my fault. I get that. But I'm still partly to blame for the pain you all suffer. No matter what you say, that much is true."

CJ pulls me into his arms and I go willingly, resting my head against his pec and wrapping my arm around his waist. "Cupcake, you should have come to me. If I knew it meant this much to you I would have helped. And you have to stop blaming yourself. You can't be responsible for what others do. They have their own minds."

I look up at him and smile. "I didn't want you to be mad."

He looks like I slapped him, and it hurts. "I'd never be mad at you, Allie, ever. I may raise my voice, but only in worry, in concern, and that's because I love you. I don't want anything to happen to you."

"I'm sorry for not talking to you about it."

He kisses me lightly before pulling away, shifting us so we're facing the room.

"What did you find out?" Cole asks, his expression blank.

I shrug. "Not a lot. Nothing really ties Christie's murder to Logan. He had no reason to kill her, other than for revenge, which seems petty and a little farfetched since he's in prison. If it had happened before she testified, then I would have understood. I'm going to keep researching, but after this second murder, I might need to take a step back. I can still do my piece on Christie's murder or on something else."

"What makes you think these two murders are connected?" Cole asks, cuddling Willow to his chest.

"The hair," I whisper, feeling sick.

"What?" both he and CJ ask.

Sensing my reluctance to answer, Jordan speaks up. "I got the files on Christie's murder. In it, it says a chunk of hair was cut and taken from her head. She was also placed peacefully in bed, similar to the position Linda was in when she was found. It's like he feels remorse for killing them. I don't know. He could be a complete psychopath.

The only thing that doesn't make sense is that Christie was stabbed, and this girl wasn't."

Alex clears his throat. "It does seem strange. Why do you think he's taking their hair?"

Jordan looks to a pale Alex and shrugs. "I'm not sure. A memento?"

He looks away, staring down at his phone. "I've got to go. My nan needs me to mow the grass."

He gets up, leaving with a goodbye. When the front door shuts, CJ pulls me over to the sofa, sitting me down on his lap. "He's mowing his grass in January?"

Cole chuckles. "He is a little weird."

"Leave him alone. He's my friend."

"He did look a little pale before he left," Jordan mentions. "Hope he's okay. I know how sensitive he is. I bet you he's worried about all of this."

"True," I murmur. "The other week he did say he wished the police would do more to keep us safe. He even complained to the university about the drug dealings he keeps witnessing at the back of the library. They put a camera up, but it was destroyed when they broke into the library. He probably doesn't feel safe here anymore, and he has reason to believe that. I've tried to keep his mind off things, but he can be a little closed off at times."

CJ looks at me with love in his eyes. "You're a good friend to him."

"He doesn't really have anyone else. People aren't nice to him because of the way he dresses and looks."

He looks at me guiltily. "I'm sorry. I'll try harder, but I can't promise anything. We have nothing in common with each other. I can deal with weird—I am going out with you, after all—but he doesn't like letting people in," he says. I slap his arm over the comment about me being weird, even though I know he's joking.

"He has you there," Willow giggles.

"Nah, I can see what CJ is saying. Every time we've tried to get to know him, to make friends, he's acted withdrawn and weird. The only time I see him comfortable is when he is with you girls and no one else is around. He acts himself then," Cole adds.

"How would you know that?" Willow asks, voicing my thoughts.

"You guys didn't hear us come in once when you were all watching movies. We were getting a beer out of the kitchen and watched how is with you. He seems like a good lad, just a little weird. I don't think he's had great past with other males."

I never really noticed. He's a little shy, but now they've mentioned it, he does seem more comfortable when it's just us girls.

"Maybe you all intimidate him."

"Probably, but he has to know we'd never hurt him," CJ says.

"He does, but I'll talk to him again. He did get bullied a lot at school, so it could be because of that."

"I'm going to see if Rosie is a wake," Jordan says, and that's when I notice she isn't here.

"Is she okay?" I ask softly, looking at Jordan and Becca.

Becca's expression is sad. "She didn't sleep again last night. Me and Jordan sat with her this morning to try and distract her. She fell asleep while Jordan bored her to death by explaining the Game of Thrones family trees."

I giggle, looking at Jordan's annoyed expression. "I didn't bore her. She was just relaxed enough to sleep in my presence."

"Lord, I was falling asleep. My brain hurt trying to keep up with who was related to who, and a little disgusted over siblings sleeping together. And I heard they kill horses. I don't get why people rave about this show."

Jordan rolls her eyes before getting up. "When Rosie's better, I'll watch it with her. I'll have to skip parts, but other than that, it's the shit. The girl has dragons, Becca. *Dragons*. I want to be Daenerys Targaryen when I grow up."

"You are grown up," CJ mutters. He taps his chin, smirking. "But I wouldn't have minded doing Daenerys Targaryen when she walked out of that flaming hut in Vaes Dothrak."

"Really?" I drawl dryly.

He smiles now, pulling me close. "Cupcake, you're all I'll ever need, but maybe we should have a rule for one person. Yours could be your book boyfriends and mine could be her or Blake Lively."

I just roll my eyes and turn back to the others. "Men."

"Well, after that important information, CJ, I'll defo sleep tonight," Jordan says sarcastically, before getting up and leaving the room.

We all laugh, watching her go.

"I swear, even with her horrible taste in TV shows, I don't know what I would do without her. She's been so good to Rosie, and I know if she didn't keep her on her toes, Rosie wouldn't be Rosie anymore. Sometimes I think it's only Jordan keeping that last part of her intact," Becca says, a faraway look in her eyes.

"It's going to take time, but I promise we'll help her," Cole says.

"I know. I'm so grateful for you all, too. And for letting us stay here. You'll never understand how much it means to us. The generosity and friendship you've shown us is remarkable and humbling."

"It's fine. It's one room that wouldn't get used. I can't really sleep well without Cole," Willow admits softly.

Becca's face relaxes. "It's still kind of you to let us stay here. My mum is trying to get the flat four floors down. The woman's son graduated last year and they've been renting it out ever since, but they're fed up of dealing with noise complaints and paying for the damages."

That gets my attention. "Four floors down?"

CJ starts laughing at me, but I ignore him, still staring at Becca who looks taken aback by my outburst.

"Um, yeah. The woman hasn't made it official or anything yet. My mum was asking the building manager about places and he mentioned it, but she's unsure if she can afford it. She was hoping to talk the lady into renting it to her."

My eyes nearly bug out. "Oh, my God. Move in here and pay rent, if that's what you want to do. I want that flat. I want it now. Oh, my God. I'm going to call my dad."

I try to get off CJ's lap, but he pulls me back down, laughing. "Cupcake."

"Don't 'Cupcake' me," I snap.

Becca seems puzzled when she says, "Um, hate to state the obvious, but you live here."

"On the seventh floor," I tell her, nodding. "That flat is on the third floor."

"What about us?" Willow says, pouting. "We won't be living across from each other anymore."

I turn to my best friend, torn for just a second. "But it's only three flights, Willow. I'd give up sweets if it meant not walking up those death traps. Ever since we moved here I've been experiencing shortness of breath, rapid heartbeat, and aches and pains."

Willow giggles. "You would really give up sweets?"

I tilt my head, pouting. "No! But it's not really the issue. The issue is I won't have to walk up those goddamn stairs."

"Just think of it as your daily exercise," Becca adds, shrugging.

I gasp, swinging my head in her direction. "How could you?"

She looks confused. "Sorry?"

"You should be."

Willow, still giggling, pauses to explain. "Allie hates anything to do with exercise."

"Not all exercise," I defend. "I don't mind walking, as long as it's not up hills or too strenuous."

Willow gives me a dry look before looking at Becca. "She doesn't like any exercise."

Becca's shocked eyes come to me. "But you're so skinny."

"And I'd be healthy if I didn't have to walk up the stairs every time the lift breaks down."

CJ chuckles against my neck. "I'll carry you, Cupcake."

I smile at his sweetness. "You love me," I sing.

He chuckles. "I do."

"Ya know, come to think of it, did you even do one PE lesson?"

I turn to Willow, smiling. "No. I had a doctor's note. I sweat profusely and had to have special deodorant that burnt my sweat glands. And I had anxiety over sweating. It's not like I sweat like a normal person; I look like I've been swimming, so the school understood my anxiety over it."

CJ, looking a little pale, looks up at me. "Um, what about when we have sex? Because I can tell you now, it's going to be fucking strenuous. You won't walk for weeks."

My breathing picks up, a tingle shooting between my legs. I ignore the others laughing and lean in to whisper in his ear. "Oh, trust me, sex will not be included in the same category as exercise because I fully intend to enjoy it."

His eyes spark, and without warning, he lifts me in the air and over his shoulder.

"Nice seeing you guys, but we're wiped. We're going to take a little nap."

The laughter that follows has me blushing, but I can't find the thought to care. Some more time alone with CJ is worth everyone knowing we're about to do something naughty.

Even if it isn't sex.

At least, not today.

For that, I plan for it to be just us two with no interruptions or chances of one of our roommates walking in.

Or when the moment takes us there.

Chapter 10

Since finding out about the second murder a few days ago, I've not been able to get Linda Cooper out of my mind.

What she must have gone through is something I can't bear to think about yet can't help but do it. The press have, thankfully, left her parents alone, but it hasn't stopped them from running the story and interviewing her friends.

How someone could do this to another human being is beyond me. Nobody deserves to die like that. He or she has made an innocent family suffer for their sick enjoyment, and knowing we're walking around with that monster out there doesn't bear thinking about. He could be someone we've walked past, someone we go to class with or are friends with. It scares the crap out of me.

I promised CJ and the others that I would take a step back from it all, but I can't. It's a dangerous situation to be in, I know. No one knows what this person is capable of, what he would do if he ever found out I was looking into the murders.

All I've been able to find out is he's targeting girls, cuts their hair, and rests them peacefully after he kills them. I can't determine a pattern in the women other than the colour of their hair. Linda didn't go to Whithall University; she was still attending a local college closer to her home, and from my research online, she has no ties to Christie.

I texted Jordan last night to meet up with me at the library, since no one we knew was working there today. Alex has classes all day, so he won't be there to see what we're up to. I have to get to my Historical English class right after, so I can't be long with her.

When I walk in, she's already sitting down at our table. I sit next to her and grab the file I made from my bag. "Hey, I'm glad you could meet me." When I open it, I pull out the newspaper clippings I found last night and hand one to her. "A murder similar to Christie's and Linda's happened not far from here fifteen years ago. A wife found her husband cheating and decided to get revenge."

She takes the paper from me, her eyebrows drawn together. I wait a few minutes for her to read over the first one before handing her another.

"Oh, my God," she murmurs, her eyes flicking over the sentences quickly.

"I know. The details are limited due to the nature of the murder, but from what this one reporter wrote, the wife had killed the mistress in front of her husband. She shaved off her hair so he wouldn't be attracted to her anymore. In an interview they did with her, when she was admitted, she explained how her husband had a ton of pictures of his mistress hidden in a shoebox and on his phone. In the photos, he would always be touching her hair, sniffing it, or running his fingers through it."

"This is insane," Jordan tells me, looking up from the article. "How did I not find this?"

I shrug, not sure either, as it was on the second page when I searched. I did a basic Google search and found the newspaper articles online. "I'm not sure. It's not really much to go on, but for some reason, I feel like these are related."

"How? It says in this article she killed herself in a psychiatric prison four months later."

I sag into my chair. This is where I come to a dead end. "I know. That's why I called you here to meet me. We need to see if the couple had any other members of family, or maybe children. The reports don't say anything, but I only found those three that covered the murder after she was convicted. I can't find anything about before, or where or when the bodies were found."

She quickly scans over them again. "I'll look into it, but this was fifteen years ago, Allie. We might not find anything. I do agree it's too much of a coincidence not to be related. And she was diagnosed with schizophrenia. If she had a child or a sibling with the same disorder, they could be repeating the pattern. Maybe Christie betrayed whoever the killer is, and it's somehow set something off inside him, which made him kill another girl?"

"That's what I was thinking. I looked it up and it does say schizophrenia has a component to be hereditary. I think we should ask some more questions to Christie's friends, see if she had any ex-boyfriends that ended on a bad term."

"I'm actually meeting with her close friend later. I've got to tutor her for an exam she has coming up. I'll see if I can fit it into the conversation."

"That would be amazing."

"I still can't believe another body has been found," she tells me, rubbing her hands across her face.

I shudder. "I know. My phone has been ringing off the hook. My dad is worried about us being here. He doesn't think it's safe so keeps begging us to take a term off."

"What are you going to do? Honestly, with this happening, it sounds like a good idea. We don't know who he will target next, or if he will."

"As much as it scares me that there's a killer wandering the streets, I can't. I already waited a few years to attend university with Willow. We had the grades to attend once we finished our year at college, but we wanted to work so we could pay for uni ourselves before attending. I did it more for Willow, as her mum couldn't afford the fees by herself."

"She did mention you waited to attend college so you could both come together."

"If it does get any worse, and I feel unsafe, I'll take a week or two off. But if everyone went home because of this killer, we'd lose our grades."

"I graduate this year and I'd rather keep it that way, so I can see where you're coming from."

I smile, happy for her. "Any ideas on what you will do after?"

A frustrated look appears over her expression. "Nope. My parents want me to work for my uncle at the local news station, but it's not what I want to do. I love my blog. I love reporting that way and I'll probably keep doing it. I love it. I've applied for a few jobs that are looking for columnists. I'm just waiting to hear back. I've also looked into teaching."

"Teaching?" I ask, surprised. She's never mentioned it before now.

"Yeah." She blushes, looking up through her eyelashes. "It's been on my mind for over a year, since I started tutoring. I really enjoy doing it. I know I'll miss it which is why I decided on teaching."

I smile, squeezing her hand, before pulling back. "Then do it. You can teach with your degree, and I think you'll be good at it."

"You think?"

"I know."

"Thank you."

"It's my pleasure," I tell her, then look at the time. "Shit, I'd better getting going. I was late to Mr. Flint's class a few weeks ago and it didn't end well. He kinda creeped me out."

Jordan grabs my arm, stopping me from getting my things. I look up, then groan when I realise what I just revealed.

"What do you mean he creeped you out?"

"It's nothing. He just doesn't understand personal space is all. I'm sure it's just me. I've always hated people being close to me, it's why I'm not a crowd person."

"You need to report him," she says, a look in her eyes, like she knows something.

"What? Why? I was probably overreacting."

She shakes her head, looking deep in thought. "No. Can you remember a while ago when I had to show a new student around for her night classes?"

I think back and nod, because I do remember. She came to meet us after to take Rosie out, which didn't end up going as planned. "Why?"

"Well, the girl, Emma, is really skittish. She jumps at every noise and any time I've asked to meet up in the day, she said she's busy. I feel there's more to her story. I don't think she liked being around people, which I was why I think she's taking night classes. I've only ever met her twice, so I'm not sure what her story is. Anyway, when I checked in with her a week ago to see how she was settling in, I asked her about Mr. Flint's class. She froze on me. She went white as a sheet and started visibly shaking. She didn't answer me and avoided it entirely by bringing something else up, so I didn't mention again. I've got a bad feeling about it."

"He is a little touchy feely. If she doesn't like large crowds then she probably doesn't like him being close. I plan to not draw any more attention to myself."

She seems to think that over. "It could be. Just be careful. Something doesn't feel right with him. I've not had a class with him, but even when I introduced her to him, he seemed kind of sleazy, which is weird for an impeccably dressed English teacher. I'm actually meeting up with her again soon."

"That's kind of you. Does she have anyone she can talk to around here?"

"She lives with her cousin and his boyfriend. They're actually pretty cool. I can't see anyone messing with her with those two around. One is big as hell and the other looks intimidating with all his tattoos. She also has a friend called Banner, who I think she has a crush on. She's not really open."

I smile at that. "Ah, maybe you should see if they'll meet up with you and Rosie. Rosie and Emma seem to be in the same position with not liking large crowds. They could get along and become friends. Rosie needs that right now."

Her eyes light up. "That's a great idea. I don't know why I didn't think of it before. I'll see if they're up for it. Right, you'd better go before you're late."

I laugh, grabbing the file and newspaper clippings, and start stuffing them into my bag. "I'll see you later. Are you meeting us at the café for lunch?"

"If I can make it, yeah. I have to meet up with another student beforehand, and he's a little slow."

"Okay, I'll see you later—if you can."

I grab my bag, waving goodbye, before leaving the library. The air outside is chilly, which means we're in for another coat of snow.

Great.

～

Class is coming to an end, and I'm watching the clock. I've been counting down the minutes since I arrived.

Jordan's warning about Mr. Flint keeps surfacing to the front of my mind, especially when he leans over me to look at my work. Instead of standing to the side, he looms behind me, peering over my shoulder with his hands resting on the desk on either side of me. He's so close I can feel his breath on my cheek, the warmth of his chest on my back.

"That's really good, Allie. If you'd like, we can go over your coursework later, make sure you're on schedule?"

Palms sweaty, and a little shaky, I answer, my voice full of nerves and anxiety. "Thank you for the offer, but I'll be fine, Mr. Flint."

"Please, call me Geoff," he tells me, squeezing my shoulder.

The lesson comes to an end and I relax as he steps back. I quickly grab my books, bag, coat, and scarf, not bothering to put anything away before standing. "See you next class, Mr. Flint."

I hear an unpleasant sound from behind me, and it has me hurrying toward the exit. I leave the room, my breaths coming in short pants.

The guy creeps me out. He's getting bolder and bolder with each lesson. There's nothing I can do, apart from report him. If he exhibits the same behaviour during our next lesson together, I'll have to say something to someone.

I step outside into the freezing cold and walk over to the vacant bench. I rest my bag on it and start putting my books away. After, I waste no time in pulling my coat on and wrapping my scarf around my neck. Once I have everything on, my bag back over my shoulder, I slide my hands into my gloves.

God, it's cold.

I cannot wait for summer. After exercise, being cold is the second most thing I hate. I'm one of those awkward people who are never happy. I moan if it's too cold, but then moan if it's too hot. Why can there never be an in between? All year round.

Hearing my name being shouted grabs my attention. I turn around and face the person calling me. It takes me a few seconds to register who it is. When it comes to me, I smile. "Hey, Ian, how are you doing? You sorted your English Lit assignment?"

"It's going good. Me and Nathan," he starts, pointing to a boy next to him. He's lanky and a little dorky-looking but seems smart and sophisticated. It's the clothes and posture, I think, that makes him seem that way. "We're working on it together now. You might see us in the library a lot."

"That's great. Sorry I couldn't be of more help."

He shrugs, looking to his friend, who seems overly quiet. "We were wondering if you wanted to hang out."

Flattered and a little embarrassed, I give him a small smile. "I'm so sorry; I can't. I'm actually on my way to meet my boyfriend but thank you for the offer."

His smile gets wider. "That's fine. Maybe next time you could both meet us."

"Yeah, maybe. I've got to go, but it was nice seeing you again."

"You too," he says, before walking off with his friend.

I watch them for a moment longer before heading toward the café I planned to meet CJ and the rest of them at.

It takes me ten minutes to get there, and when I do, everyone is already seated. They've pulled four tables together so we can all sit as one large group.

"There's my cupcake," CJ booms, getting up from his chair and walking over to me. He hands me a bag and I frown, puzzled as to why he's buying me more gifts. "I got you something."

"You got me something? But it's already been my birthday."

He chuckles, bringing me in for a kiss before pulling away. "Open it."

I smile, opening the bag to find a rectangular gift box. I pull it out, handing him the bag so I can open it. I do, gasping. I pull my glove off using my teeth, so I can touch the silver beauty.

A silver linked charmed bracelet glitters before me. On it, rests a book charm, a bow tie, and a pair of Converse. It's beautiful, meaningful.

It's me.

"Oh, CJ, it's beautiful."

He bounces on his feet, taking it out of the box and wrapping it around my wrist. The charms sparkle under the light when I raise my arm up to see it better. It's truly beautiful.

I lean up on my toes, placing my arms around his neck. He wastes no time in wrapping his arms around me, resting his hands on the top of my arse, pulling me further against him as he leans down for a kiss.

My body hums with delight from the feel of his mouth on mine, the taste of his tongue. Butterflies erupt in my stomach like they do every single time we kiss or touch.

"You get him, girl," Willow shouts.

I laugh against CJ's mouth, pulling back a little. I didn't hear everyone cat-calling or whistling before, too lost in our kiss.

CJ grins smugly, wrapping his arm around my shoulder and steering me over to the seats he saved for us.

"Hey, has Jordan texted anyone? She said she might be able to make it."

Just as the words leave my mouth, the door opens and Jordan walks in with four other people. My eyes widen at the lad at the back. CJ is still by far the best-looking person I've ever met, but my connection to him makes me kind of biased—and the fact I don't just love him for his looks.

This lad, however, is really something. Something book covers are made of, with his short brown spiked hair, chiselled jaw, and chocolate brown eyes. He's got an athletic build, and wide thick shoulders. He's clearly strong. The girl tucked under his arm is just as beautiful with her slim frame and sharp blue eyes. Her hair, though... her hair is beautiful, falling in loose waves down her back and reaching her waist.

The girl walking behind with another bloke makes me pause. Something in her eyes resembles what I see in Rosie's every day. She looks sad, but happy about the girl in front of her being there, if the longing looks she's sending her way are any indication.

She's beautiful.

The lad next to her, talking quietly into her ear, looks familiar. I've probably seen him around the university. He's athletic, like the lad in front of him, only he has a smaller frame. He's covered in tattoos, black and white, and some are colourful. He's a pretty boy, though, through and through, even with his rough-shaven jaw.

Jordan waves before heading over to us and sits in front of me, next to Rosie. "Who was that?" Willow asks, voicing my question.

"I know the girl, Emma. She's the small one next to the guy with tatts."

"Is that the girl you mentioned earlier?" I ask, double-checking.

"Yeah. I saw them outside and said hi. Her friend and her boyfriend have come from out of town to visit and see how she's getting on. I sense more of a story there, but don't want to pry. That Max guy is a hoot. Kind of reminds me of you, CJ."

CJ chokes on his hot chocolate, narrowing his eyes. "There's only one me. I'm limited edition."

Jordan's lips twitch in amusement. "Yep, definitely reminds me of you. He said something similar out in the carpark."

CJ scoffs, looking across the room at the table the two couples have sat down at. "Nope, only one me. I'm fucking awesome."

I tap his leg, placating him. "Okay, we get it. Did you eat?"

He groans, rubbing his stomach. "I'm starving actually."

Willow leans over Cole to glance at us. "You ate a sub not fifteen minutes ago because the waiting was making you hungry."

CJ grins. "That was fifteen minutes ago, now is now," he tells her, before turning to me. "What would you like to eat?"

"Just a sandwich—if they have cheese. And a double chocolate chip muffin, if they have that, too."

He licks his lips. "I'm sure they do. Want any chips? I'm going to get the lasagne."

In other words, he wants me to order chips so he doesn't look like a pig in front of the others. I giggle and nod. "Sure, but I probably won't eat them."

"That's okay; I'm sure I can finish what you don't eat."

Meaning all of them, I muse.

The boys leave the table to go order, leaving Becca, Willow, Jordan, Rosie and me at the table.

Willow turns to me, smiling. "The lads were telling us how their coach has organised a last-minute game this Saturday to raise money for the children's hospital. Are you working?"

"I'm not this Saturday. The manager has someone from the local high school doing work experience, so she doesn't need all of us."

Willow claps her hands excitedly. "That's great. We'll all be able to go. I don't think I could stomach watching that again on my own."

I giggle at her pale face. "True. It was brutal. Maybe we can bring some snacks this time. I know I'm bringing sweets."

"Something warm 'cause we're meant to have three inches of snow over the weekend," Jordan adds.

"Will they still do the game if it snows?" Rosie asks.

"Who knows. This is England; we only have to get a sheet of snow and everyone goes crazy. I only went for bread the other day and the shop had sold out. Same at the next three shops I went to. You'd think we were having a zombie apocalypse."

I start laughing at Jordan's expression. She looks so torn up over bread, so annoyed people went and bought it all. It's hysterical.

"What you all laughing at?" CJ asks, sitting down.

I lean into him, smiling. "Zombies."

He shudders, looking around warily. "Fucking zombies. I'd beat that shit hands down. Fuckers would never get near me."

I begin to laugh, hoping he doesn't start off on his list of shit to do if we were to ever have an outbreak. He has it down to where he would go, what he would do, and who he would take with him. I thought I was crazy loving The Walking Dead, but then I met CJ and realised I was sane compared to him.

I space out when they start talking about zombies, Willow begging them to shut up. My eyes drift back over to the table Emma is sitting at, my mind wondering why she holds so much pain.

I'm glad she has Jordan because I know if anyone can help her, she can. She looks so fragile and broken. It hurts to watch her.

Chapter 11

I look out of our flat window, wincing at the amount of rain pouring. Instead of the snow the weatherman predicted, we got rain. I guess it's better than snow. But still rain.

Today's the day of the charity rugby match, and if I weren't all about supporting my boyfriend and desperately wanting to see him in his uniform again, I'd totally ditch to snuggle in bed and read.

But what kind of girlfriend would I be if I didn't turn up, especially after he took me to a book signing.

"What time do we have to be there?" I ask Willow, who is finishing filling our flasks with hot drinks.

"We've still got thirty minutes."

I nod, my attention turning to the TV when I hear the news reporter mention Whithall University.

"Oh, my God," I gasp. The girls look to the TV, and I hear their horrified gasps follow mine.

Marie Fleet, age nineteen, was reported missing this morning. An inside source says Miss Fleet was taken from her shared house sometime last night between ten p.m. and seven a.m. Roommates returned home this morning and found signs of a struggle, before calling the police. Whithall police department aren't giving a statement at this time.

"If anyone knows anything related to the abduction of Marie Fleet, police are asking them to step forward."

I mute the TV, my arse hitting the sofa with a thud. "I can't believe this is happening."

Jordan looks as white as a ghost. "This is bad. Really bad. This guy just became a serial killer. There's no telling when this will end."

"Do they have any leads?" I ask her, hands shaking.

She stares blankly in space for a second before meeting my eyes. "No."

"We were friends," Rosie admits from the sofa, looking as pale as the rest of us. "We both took our required English course together at the beginning of term. She has a twin sister who is a few years ahead of her on the course. Marie was recovering from cancer at the time, which is why both went into medicine. She wanted to find a cure."

Tears gather in my eyes. "I'm so sorry, Rosie. Do you still speak to her sister? Maybe you can take her a gift basket, let her know you're thinking of her."

She nods, taking out her phone. "Kate has probably got her phone turned off. She loves her sister. It's why she wants to be a doctor. She hated the way her sister suffered, so she wanted to do something that could help others."

She quickly types out a text while we stay quiet, feeling remorse on behalf of our friend. She's been through so much already; she doesn't need this.

Her phone beeps and she looks down, her face scrunching up in pain, before she starts sobbing. We all move to crowd around her. I rest my hands on her knees, rubbing my thumbs across her skin.

"It will be okay, Rosie," Becca whispers, pulling her friend into her arms.

"She—she said—" She chokes up and Jordan takes her phone.

Her eyes fill with tears as she stares down at Rosie's screen. "She said: Thank you, Rosie. I appreciate it. But there's no point in praying. She's gone. I can feel it in my soul. I don't feel her with me."

I start crying, dropping my head into Rosie's lap. My heart hurts for Kate. I sit up, wiping furiously at my tears.

"The police need to find out who is doing this. How could they do this to innocent people?"

Willow reaches over and squeezes my shoulder. "He's a monster. Hopefully the police find him before he hurts her. There's still a chance she's okay. Linda Cooper was found two weeks after she disappeared. You've got to keep praying. You can't give up."

"She's her twin," Rosie whispers, lifting her head out of her hands. Her eyes are swollen and red. She wipes her nose with the sleeve of her T-shirt, looking at Willow helplessly. "If anyone would know, it would be her. They were close, as close as any siblings I've ever seen."

Willow takes her hand. "The closest thing I have to a sibling is Allie, so I can only imagine the pain she's going through right now.

But at the moment, she's grieving. Her sister has been taken and she's scared. She's letting her grief drive her emotions. Just be there for her, support her. That is all you can do. Remind her she's not alone."

Rosie nods, wiping her eyes. "You're right. I'd feel the same if I lost Becca. She's like my sister."

Willow leans forward and kisses her cheek. "It's all you can do."

"If it's okay, I'm going to stay here instead of going to the game. I'm going to order some stuff for Katie."

"That's a great idea. We can put a movie on," I offer.

She shakes her head. "No, you guys go. CJ and Cole will only be grumpy if you don't. And I don't want them giving me the stink eye. It makes me nervous," she giggles, teasing.

A month ago, I would have taken that comment seriously. She was scared to be in the same room as them. But since she moved in, she's gotten used to them. She doesn't even flinch when they're being loud and boisterous. She's come a long way, but she still has a long road ahead of her.

I frown. "Yeah, you're probably right."

She laughs, shooing us away. "Seriously, go. I'll be fine."

"I'll stay with her. I need to get some homework done, anyway. I just didn't want to be rude when CJ demanded I go and root for him."

I laugh, remembering CJ's reaction to Jordan telling him that watching boys running around sweating wasn't her thing. He told her he was everyone's thing.

"Are you sure?" I ask, looking at Rosie.

She blushes a little, no doubt over being alone with Jordan, but nods. "Yeah, I'm sure."

"Okay, well, we best get going. We want to get a place at the front before their little fan club get there," Willow says, looking torn about leaving, like the rest of us.

I scoff, rolling my eyes as I walk over to my coat, gloves and hat. "Hopefully they stay in."

"Did you want me to stay?" I hear Becca ask Rosie quietly.

"I promise, I'm fine. You go. I know you've been dying to see a certain player in action," Rosie teases.

Becca slaps her arm lightly, glaring. "Shush."

"What's this about a player?" I ask, smiling.

She gets up from the sofa, pulling her coat on. "Nope, not telling."

Rosie and Jordan laugh. "Come on, tell us," Willow and I call when she starts walking out the door.

"Nope," she shouts.

Willow and I grin at each other before racing out of the door after her.

Umbrella in one hand, cup of hot chocolate in the other, we wait for the boys to come out of the changing area.

There are more girls than families coming to watch them play. I thought the rain would at least keep some of them at bay.

I was wrong.

"Who is this mystery boy, then?" I ask Becca, smirking when a blush covers her cheeks and neck.

She bites her bottom lip, looking around. "Are you going to keep hounding me until I tell you?"

Me and Willow turn to face her, standing side by side, and nod. "Yes," we say simultaneously.

She sighs, handing Willow her umbrella. "Let me throw my hair up."

We wait for her to pull her hair up, watching her impatiently. Becca is nearly as closed off as Rosie. For her to be interested in a boy is miraculous. Willow, bless her soul, got lucky when she began to move forward with Cole. They built a connection, a kindred friendship.

Becca, however, hardly socialises. Hearing this is a huge deal, and I'm not about to let it go. I'm also going to treat it like any other girl-friend would: by teasing the hell out of her.

"Stop stalling," Willow pouts.

With a grimace, Becca takes the umbrella back and faces us, her cheeks as red as ever. "I don't know if you know him. His name is

Dylan Ford. Please, don't say anything to anyone, especially Cole and CJ. God, I'd never hear the end of it," she groans.

"We won't. I promise."

Taking a deep breath, she continues. "I met him in the cafeteria. I bumped into him and spilled his Coke all over him." She pauses, frowning when we start laughing. "Shut up! It's not funny, it was humiliating."

Willow pats her shoulder. "Sorry, but you gotta admit, that's pretty darn funny."

She covers her face with one hand before removing it, shoving it into her coat pocket. "Trust me, it wasn't. He was with a group of girls who started throwing insults and making fun of me."

Our laughter subsides. Willow and I turn to each other, both with matching frowns, before turning back to Becca. "Why didn't you tell us?"

She shrugs. "It wasn't a big deal. He told them to shut up, told me it was fine, before walking away. I thought that was the end of it. Then I saw him..." She pauses, biting her lip again and glancing over the field.

"You saw him...?" I start, wondering where this is going. If she says she bumped into him again, I won't be able to hold my laughter in.

Gulping, she straightens her back. "I saw him at the group victim meeting Jordan organised. He was dropping his sister off. I wasn't sure about going in, so I was standing outside the front of the building, just out of sight. Rosie wasn't with me and I didn't feel comfortable walking in by myself. I started crying, and he must have heard me sniffle."

While she takes a deep breath, I melt. She never told us any of this, and it occurs to me that she probably didn't because of Rosie, wanting to be there for her friend more.

"What happened then?" Willow asks.

She looks up, her eyes watering but a smile on her face. "He walked over, took one look at me, and pulled me in for a hug. I froze, scared because I'd only had that one encounter with him. But then he pulled away just as quickly, looking down at me with understanding shining in his eyes. He asked if I was going inside, and I told him no; I couldn't do it without my friend. He then asked if I wanted to get a drink and wait in the coffee shop until the meeting was over. He said that if I wanted to talk, he'd listen. It's how I found out about his sister. He told me all about her."

My eyes are completely wide with shock. "And you spoke to him about what happened to you?"

Blushing further, she nods. "Yeah—I couldn't help it. He was so kind, so understanding, and easy to talk to. Once he opened up about why he was there, I couldn't shut my mouth."

Willow is now smiling. "Cole is like that. He made me feel safe." She pauses, eyeing the field for a second before turning back to Becca. "Have you seen him again since?"

She nods. "I keep seeing him around the university. He'll give me a chin lift or say hello, but he's always with his friends, and I get nervous and rush off. It's how Rosie knows about him: she caught the way I was staring at him."

"Why don't you ask him to come to ours next weekend for a movie night?"

Doubt clouds her expression. "No. He probably felt sorry for me the day he saw me outside. I don't want to put him in a position where he feels like he can't let me down in case I break or something."

I shake my head. "You worry too much. Just ask him."

"I'll see," she says, clearly lying. She looks over to the field where the coach and two other men wearing similar uniforms come stepping out of the changing room building.

"What in the hell is she wearing?" Willow asks out of nowhere, a low growl rumbling from her chest.

I glance around her, looking in the direction she's glaring at, and my lips tighten disapprovingly.

A group of girls I remember being here the last time we came to watch are loitering near the front of the field, wearing similar shirts as to what the lads wear on the field.

One of the girls has the number fifteen on her back, with Everhert printed above it—CJ's last name.

My eyes are still narrowed into tiny slits when I become aware of a body standing next to me. I turn, smiling wide when Milly, CJ's mum, reveals herself from under her umbrella.

"Hey."

"Hello, sweets, hope you don't mind me joining you. CJ mentioned you'd all be here. As much as I love and support my son, coming here on my own is kind of boring. It wasn't like I had someone to sit with me and explain what was happening to keep me entertained. The big matches I always attend. Just don't tell CJ I bring my kindle."

I laugh, knowing the stick she'd get if he ever found out. "Your secret's safe with us. But you're gonna be disappointed with us, because we have no idea either. The last time we came to watch, I spent the majority of the game with my eyes tightly closed," I tell her. We both laugh.

"Hey, Milly, I didn't know you were coming," Willow says, looking around me. I forgot she met her when Milly had dinner with Cole's parent's.

"Hey." She smiles, but it falls when she looks behind Willow. "Why are they not wearing a coat in this weather? Do they not understand they could get pneumonia?"

Willow and I start laughing. "Milly, if you think that's bad, the last time we came here they were wearing shorts and skirts with skimpy tops."

She shakes her head and then notices Becca standing next to Willow. "You must be Becca?"

Becca looks taken aback, never having met CJ's mum before. "Um, yes. Can you read minds?" she blurts out, causing us to giggle.

Milly's eyes soften. "Thankfully, no. I met up with Rosie earlier this week for our first session. She spoke about you a lot, so I kind of had you pictured in my head." She pauses, looking around for the first time. "Speaking of, where is she? She said she was attending today."

We all lose our easy banter as I address her. "Did you watch the news today?"

Pain and worry fill her eyes. "I did. It's horrifying to see what the world is coming to. Those poor parents."

I nod, my own sympathy for their parents rising. "I know. It's a terrible tragedy. The girl who was reported missing today, Marie, was friends with Rosie. She took the news pretty hard. Marie has a twin sister who Rosie spoke with before we came out. After hearing what she had to say, she just wanted to stay in. She's taken the news pretty bad."

"That poor child. She really is going through too much." She seems lost in thought before pulling keys out of her pocket, turning towards me. "Can you tell CJ I was here but had to leave? I'm going to go check in on Rosie, see if there's anything I can do."

"Okay." I reach over, pulling her in for a hug. She's kind-hearted, attentive, and devoted to everyone, not just the girls who walk into her life seeking comfort from the traumatic ordeals they've been through.

She kisses my cheek before pulling back. "See you soon, darling."

I watch her go before turning back to the girls, who look in awe of the woman who has just left.

"She's really amazing," Willow says, still staring in the direction Milly just went.

"She is. Rosie adores and trusts her. She doesn't make her feel like a victim or like she's being pushed into talking. I really like her; she's good for Rosie," Becca adds.

"I believe if anyone can help Rosie, it's Milly."

They nod, agreeing, before turning their heads in the direction the loud howls are coming from. I grin, my own head turning towards the changing rooms, where both teams come piling out from different exits.

My eyes scan for CJ, finding his hulking body almost immediately. The second my eyes land on him, I sag, cocking my hip as I take him in.

He's beautiful, inside and out. But in that kit, he's a god. A hulking, gorgeous, seriously hot god.

His tanned skin looks darker against his red T-shirt and shorts, his thighs looking intimidatingly strong with their muscles bulging with each step he takes as he walks towards us.

His grin spreads when he notices me checking him out. I roll my eyes. However, I'm not ashamed to be caught ogling him.

My man is sexy as hell.

I take a step forward, ready to launch myself into his arms, but before my foot reaches the ground, some blonde bounces to a stop in front of him, blocking off our connection.

I growl, wanting to rip her hair out. I'd never act upon it though. Nope. Just picture it in my head over and over before I go to sleep tonight.

Willow leans over, whispering in my ear, "Did you just growl?"

My eyes narrow into slits, never leaving the back of the girl who is now on my shit list—and I don't even know her.

"Why is he not excusing himself and walking away?" I ask no one, hurt when his laughter booms across the field.

"He's just being polite," Cole adds, making me jump.

I put my cup to my chest, glancing over at him. "Jesus, a little warning. You scared the shit out of me."

He chuckles, his eyes crinkled with amusement. "I've been here for a good few minutes, Allie."

"Well, at least *you're* a good boyfriend."

I know I'm being irrational, but she's touching him, her hand squeezing his bicep, and he doesn't seem to care. He hasn't even looked in my direction once.

So much for giving him a good luck kiss. The whistle blows, indicating the game is about to start.

My pride is hurt, but so are my feelings. Since we've been together, I've never felt a shred of jealously. He's teased girls, mostly friends, but it's never done flirtatiously. Only in good fun. And most of the time, I've been there to witness it.

I listen to Cole finish kissing Willow before whispering something in her ear that makes her giggle. It makes me envious.

Since finding out another girl was found missing, I've craved a hug from him, to feel safe and loved.

As Cole rushes out onto the field, meeting his coach in their huddle, my eyes turn back to CJ, watching in horror as the girl wraps her arms around his neck.

A girl who is wearing his damn name and number.

The hug doesn't last long, but it's long enough for our eyes to meet over her shoulder. His face scrunches up with confusion as he watches me. Even when he pulls back slowly from her embrace, he doesn't look away.

I shake my head, hoping he can see the hurt his actions have caused. I don't know this girl. She could be an ex or someone he slept with before me. If the roles were reversed, I know he wouldn't be happy.

Tears sting the back of my eyes, but I don't let him see them, instead turning back to my friend, ignoring the howls coming from his teammates, gearing up to start.

"I'm sorry, but I need to go. I'm not feeling very well."

"Are you sure?" Willow asks, pity filling her eyes.

I look away. "Yeah, I'm going to call my dad, see what he's up to."

"Want me to come with you?"

"No, I'll be fine. Enjoy the game, you two." I'm about to pick up my bag from the little huddle we made under a bench behind us, when I remember Becca's crush. "Hey, Becca, where's the guy you were telling us about?"

She blushes, looking away from the field. "Um, he's number twenty-two."

I glance around the field until I spot his number, my eyes widening when I see the size of him.

Shit, he makes CJ and Cole look like midgets.

I whistle through my teeth. "Holy shit! He's fine."

"He looks like he could crush buildings with his pinky finger," Willow states, her eyes round.

Becca giggles, ducking her face into her scarf. I grin, looking back at my best friend in the whole world.

"I'll see you at home. After I've called Dad, I'm gonna finish my homework."

"Okay, I'll see you in a bit. Do you want me to tell CJ anything?" Her voice is hesitant, quiet.

Pain fills my chest as I look back to the field, wincing when I see one of the opposing players rush him and take him to the ground with a loud thud. The girl from earlier starts shouting abuse, defending CJ, like she has the right, and that hurt grows a little more.

"No. He probably won't even notice I've gone," I whisper, before picking my bag up and leaving, ignoring her calls to wait.

Chapter 12

By the time I make it back to our block of flats, I'm soaked, sweating, and wishing Willow and I wasn't still sharing a car. When we have our own, it will save us a lot of hassle when we need to be in two different places.

I'm no longer hurt by CJ's actions; I'm angry. I should have walked over and said something. I've seen how all the girls react around him. They have no boundaries, and CJ, ever the gentlemen, would never embarrass them by calling them out. It's another thing I love about him, but sometimes, I wish he could let them down gently or just remove himself from the situation completely.

When we're together and a girl goes too far, he'll put his arm around me and kiss me, showing her he isn't interested. Most get the picture, others… not so much.

It's all that dark tanned skin and muscles. You can't say no. It would be like me saying no to sweets, which would happen… never.

My thighs burn as I take the steps up to our building, my hand aching from the tight grip I've had on my umbrella. I couldn't let the wind win by taking away my only shelter from the rain. Not that it's done much good. My leggings are soaked through.

I don't even want to look at the state of my boots. My black, biker ankle boots. I'd managed to save them from the mud puddles over at the field, but there was no saving them on the way home. I thought I'd be clever by taking a shortcut, but it turned out to be flooded, thanks to a blocked drain. I inwardly gag at the thought of what I walked through to get home. The smell was bad enough.

So lost in my thoughts, I don't see anyone coming down the stairs until my umbrella smacks them in the face, knocking me back a step. "I'm so sorry," I stress, moving the umbrella to reveal my victim. "Alex!" I call, surprised.

He rubs his head, wincing. "Hey. I came by to see if you wanted to hang out. They said you weren't in."

I pause for a moment, certain I told him we were watching the boys play today, and instantly feel bad if I didn't. He's not really social, and I do try to get him out more. But Alex likes to keep to himself, I've noticed.

"I'm so sorry. We were watching the lads play rugby. It's the charity game today. I thought I told you about it."

He removes his glasses, wiping them on the sleeve of his jacket before putting them back on. "I must have forgotten. My nan hasn't been well."

I gasp, feeling like a terrible friend. "Alex, why didn't you say something? I could have come around to help you out. Is she okay?"

I've yet to meet his nan, but he has offered for me to go meet her a few times. It's just always been when I'm busy, so it's been hard to find a time that suits both of us. But still, if she's sick, I would have dropped everything to help him. It's what friends do.

He waves me off. "It's only the flu. I've got it handled. She's doing loads better now, just a sore throat."

"I'm glad. You should have said something though. I would have made her some soup."

His eyes twinkle. "I've eaten your soup. It tastes like water."

I narrow my eyes because I'm a damn good cook. I had to be; my mother wasn't really the kind of person to lay food on the table. If you wanted to be fed, you fed yourself. She ate out at fancy restaurants, but I got sick of the food pretty quickly.

"I'm a good cook," I defend, placing one hand on my hip.

He laughs. "Yeah, but everyone has their kryptonite. Yours is soup."

I giggle, shaking my head. "At least I know what to make CJ later."

He frowns, taking a step forward and placing his hand on my shoulder. "Hey, are you okay? What's happened? Did he eat your sweets again?"

I scoff. "I wish. It's nothing. I'm probably just being stupid."

"Tell me," he urges, removing his hand to tuck it in his pocket.

"Some girl was flirting with him at the field and it looked like he was enjoying it. He didn't even excuse himself to come see me before the game started. It hurt a lot more than I thought it would."

Anger flashes in his eyes. "Want me to have a word with him?"

I'd laugh, but I don't want to hurt his feelings. He wouldn't stand a chance against CJ and we both know it, but the fact he's willing to… it's admirable and kind of cute.

"It's fine. I'm being dramatic."

"Just be careful. He has a reputation around here, you know. I heard stories about him before you showed up. Most girls would jump at the chance to be with him. Do you think he can keep turning them down? He's a male after all."

I glance at him, hurt, my heart full of sorrow and anguish at his harsh words.

Why would he say that?

"I'm going to go. I don't feel all that well," I snap, my voice full of hurt.

His face softens, but guilt lingers in his eyes. "Sorry! That came out wrong, Allie," he says, grabbing my arm to stop me when I walk past him.

I spin around, careful not to hit him with my umbrella again. "It's fine. I know how you feel about CJ; I do. But he's not like that, not with me. I'm not some stupid girl who is willing to put up with shit just to be with someone. If I truly thought he would cheat on me, or had cheated on me, I'd be gone in a flash. I might be hurt he flirted back with some girl, but I know, in my heart, that is all it will ever be. But I'm still allowed to have a snit about it. I'm still a girl after all."

It wasn't until hearing him accuse CJ that I realised he would never do anything intentionally to hurt me. I may be hurt and angry right now, but that much I do know.

He rubs a hand over his head, looking remorseful. "I'm sorry. I shouldn't have said that." He pauses, looking out into the carpark before back to me. "Do you want to grab something to eat?"

I wasn't lying earlier when I said I feel sick. I've had an upset stomach since the field, and it's only gotten worse since leaving. It's the anxiety and stress over the situation, knowing I probably reacted worse than I should have.

"It's fine. Just, please, give him a chance. If he does step out of line, you can say whatever you want about him. I promise." I return the relieved smile he gives me. "As for food, I couldn't eat even if I wanted to. I'm really not feeling all that great. I'm gonna go lie down. Maybe tomorrow?"

His shoulders slump, his entire expression crumbling. "Yeah, sounds good."

I feel bad for letting him down. I hate that look on his face, the one that makes me feel like I just killed his puppy.

Needing him to know I'm not mad, I move forward, pulling him into my arms and squeezing him to death. "You're one of my best friends. You know that, right?" I pull back when I feel him nod against my shoulder. Looking into his eyes, I beam at him. "I'm lucky to have a friend like you."

He smiles at that. "Good, so you won't kill me when I tell you that the lift is out again?"

I glance at the building behind me, narrowing my eyes with hate. "I really hate this building."

He chuckles. "I'll let you get started on your mission. Message me tomorrow when you're free."

I nod, waving goodbye before facing my enemy. With one deep breath, I move forward, taking it one step at a time. By the time I open the door to the stair access, I can already feel sweat running down my spine. And I haven't even walked the first flight yet.

"Please, God, if you can hear me, don't let me have a heart attack on these stairs."

With each flight, the worse I feel—and no doubt, look. I'm wheezing and clinging to the banister like my life depends on it.

With the rate I'm going, the others will be back from the game before I reach our floor.

With one more flight to go, I pull my shit together, wiping away the sweat from my forehead and hair that clings to my skin.

When I reach our floor, I'm too exhausted to even cheer for another success in reaching the top. I'd probably collapse if I even showed enthusiasm.

When I burst into the flat, everyone in the kitchen turns to me.

"Oh my," Milly says, her hand covering her mouth.

I can picture what I look like: a hairy cat that's soaking wet. Attractive, I know.

I wheeze, putting my hand up to stop her from coming to help me. "I'm fine."

Rosie giggles, but bless her heart, she does try to cover it. Jordan, however, laughs outright, slapping her thigh.

"She hates exercise," Rosie informs Milly.

Milly still looks unsure, her feet twitching to come to me. I'd laugh, but unfortunately, I've seen pictures of me in this state. It's not a good look at all.

"But she's so fit and skinny."

Jordan scoffs, handing me a bottle of water. "Don't remind us. If she wasn't so sweet, I'd hate her."

Getting my breath back, I glare at my friend. "No, you wouldn't."

She laughs, shaking her head at me. "Why aren't you at the game."

I point at Milly whilst taking long gulp of water.

"Me?" she asks, sounding confused.

I nod, twisting the lid back on. "Your son. I was mad about him ignoring me and flirting with another girl. Now, I'm too pissed at the maintenance guy. If I wrote fiction novels, I'd totally kill him off in my book."

The girls laugh, and I'm about to defend myself and explain my reasons, but my ringtone starts playing.

I grab my phone out of my coat pocket. The first mistake I make is not checking to see who it is. The second, is not putting the phone down when I realise who it is.

"Hello?"

"Alison, darling, it's your mother." I wince as soon as I hear her voice. Her words sound kind, almost loving, but it's the bite in her tone that tells me someone is on the other end with her, listening in, and she doesn't like it.

Probably the new husband who she doesn't want to let see her true colours until he says, 'I do'.

The woman in me wants to rebel and pray she has her phone on loudspeaker so he can hear me give her a piece of my mind. The other part is still a scared little girl, who only wants her mother to love her.

"Mum," I whisper, not looking at the others in the room as I excuse myself, stepping into my bedroom for privacy.

"You haven't called or visited. And I heard from Mrs. Dailey that you visited your father not long ago."

I notice she doesn't say she misses me, like most parents would. Even my father messages me to say he misses me. I get nothing from my so-called mother.

I roll my eyes. "Because that's my home." I pause, then smile, grinning wickedly. "And he wanted to introduce me to his new girlfriend."

"Girlfriend?" she screeches, and I have to remove the phone from my ear a little, wincing.

I hear someone mumbling something to her, but then her voice carries clearer across the line. "It's nothing, honey. Why don't you go and get your suit ready for the party tonight and I'll be up shortly?" I smile at her haste to assure her soon-to-be husband and get rid of him. It also doesn't escape my notice that she leaves out what she meant.

"Mum, I have schoolwork to do. Was there something you wanted?"

"That is no way to speak to your mother," she snaps, showing her true colours. *Ah, this is the mother I know.* "And what is this about a girlfriend?"

"He's dating Low's mum, Mel."

"What?" she yells, before cursing up a storm. "That low life? He's too good for someone like her. She's probably after his money. It won't last long. Your father will never get over me."

He moved on ages ago, I want to say.

Her snotty attitude is beginning to get to me, so I move the conversation on.

"Mum, I really do have work to do. Is there something you want?"

She snorts. "Yes. Benjamin and I, as you know but have somewhat chosen to ignore, are getting married in a few weeks. For you not to attend would look embarrassing on my behalf, and I can't have that. I have ordered you a dress that should be delivered to your *flat* in the next few days," she says, disgust in her tone at the word 'flat'. She's never liked the fact I moved here. If it were up to her, I would have gone to a 'better' school, one where I belonged. "I can't have you turning up to our wedding dressed... unseemly. It will not be done."

I roll my eyes, glad she can't see me. I'd never hear the end of it. It still hurts that she regards and treats me the way she does. It took a long time to realise I'll never win her love or affection. I don't think she even knows *how* to love. I give up even trying. As much as it pains me, I don't want anything to do with her anymore. I'll always love her; she's my mum. But it's not the same love Willow shares with her mum. Or the love CJ shares with his.

With a sigh, I answer, prepared for the tongue-lashing I'm going to receive. "Mum, you don't need me there. *I* don't want to be there. I thought you would have realised that when I didn't return your calls or messages."

Hearing her cluck her tongue causes me to wince.

Here is goes.

"You will listen to me, young lady. You will not disrespect your mother this way. I gave birth to you, gave you life. You will attend this wedding. Benjamin won't marry me if he thinks my own daughter hates me enough not to attend our wedding. I always knew you were good for nothing, but this is a new low, Alison."

The hairs on my neck stand on end. I stand a little straighter, looking out the window. All my life I've put up with her snide remarks. I had to stand and listen to her tell me to lose weight, to wear the new range in fashion, to stand up taller, to smile more. I had to listen to her put me down, to verbally abuse me, until she found a way to psychically abuse me. Nothing that bruised, just a slap here and there. It was enough to scare me, to make me pause.

But now... enough is enough.

Even with all the bad things that have happened here at Whithall University, I've managed to come out of my shell. No longer do I live in my books or only socialise with Willow. I have friends, a life, a voice. Not my mum, or anyone else, will take that away from me.

"No, Mum, *you* listen to *me* for a change. Listen! I won't be attending your wedding. You may have given birth to me, but you didn't give me life. Life is friends, family, love. Life is the air I breathe when I step outside each day without having something squeezing the life out of me. Life is what I have now that you're no longer part of it. I don't have to listen to you anymore, and I certainly don't want to see you. I'm a grown adult in control of my own life. If your fiancé doesn't want to marry you because of me, then that is his prerogative. Don't bring me into it. But then, if it's taken him this long to realise you have no one other than him in your life, and the friends you've made through him, then he's coming to his senses. Better he cut his losses now."

I can feel the anger radiating through the phone. Her breathing is heavy, and no doubt, if I could see her, her face would be pinched tight, veins bulging to the point they look ready to burst.

Three, two, one...

"You will regret this, young lady. Mark my words. Your father will hear of this, too. If he knows what's good for him, he will get you to listen. I can make both of your lives a living hell. How long do you think Melissa will stick around once I tell her how your father cheated repeatedly on me?" She pauses when I suck in a sharp breath. She laughs when she hears it, the sound manic and smug. "Oh, you didn't know? All those long nights at the office? They weren't for working, dear. They were for boning the secretary."

My mind only pauses to feel the pain of my dad's disappearance all those years. All those years I needed him at home, needed to feel some sort of love from a parent, and instead he was having an affair. It cuts deep to hear such a betrayal.

But when I put my mum into the equation, can I really be mad at him?

I remember all those days and nights where I would sit in my room and pray for something to come up so I could leave the house and the company of my mum. I jumped at the chance to stay out at Willow's, when I was allowed. I joined every after-school club there was and then some, because I knew my mum wouldn't argue over my schooling. I even worked extra shifts at the restaurant Willow and I worked at, much to her disappointment. She even tried to get me fired a few times, but thankfully, the manager had served my mum when she worked at a higher-established restaurant and felt pity for me.

Mum threatening us now is just another way for her to control us. She knows my dad doesn't want her, and I know she doesn't love him. She isn't capable of it. She's cold-hearted enough to find pleasure in causing trouble.

As for me, I'm pretty sure I wouldn't be hearing from her had her husband not questioned my absence.

I won't let her ruin what Dad and I have built.

"Leave Dad and Mel alone. He's finally happy, and so am I. I never want to hear from you or see you again."

I end the call, throwing my phone to the bed and running my hands through my hair. Tears burn the back of my eyes, but I promised myself I'd never let her make me cry again.

A creaking sound has me turning to my door. CJ, covered in mud and dripping with sweat and rain, stands there, panting hard. He eyes me warily, stepping further into the room. I'm frozen to the spot, breathing hard, still angry I let her get to me.

"Low told me you ran off. I swear, it wasn't what you thought. She's actually gay. She doesn't want her friends to find out so she acts like they do when it comes to lads. We had a project together last year, and I found out. On my life, Allie, I would never, ever hurt you like that."

A sob I had been holding back bursts free and I run into his arms, not caring about all the mud getting over me.

"I hate my mum," I wail, crying into his shoulder.

He picks me up, carrying me over to the bed and sitting us down. "You don't hate me?" he asks, sounding confused. "And your mum? I thought you left because of my fuck up."

I look up, wiping my tears, and shake my head. "I did, but I was being stupid and immature. It hurt when you didn't brush her off and come over to say hi, but it was stupid to overreact the way I did. You've never done anything for me to not trust you."

He pushes my hair behind my ears, cupping my face. "Why all the tears, then? And I thought we already hated your mum?"

We.

I chuckle and sob at the same time, my face crumbling. "She called me not long after I got back. She demanded I attend her wedding because of her husband. He's cottoning on that I've not once visited. When I refused, she threatened to ruin what Dad has with Mel. Apparently, he cheated on Mum a lot when they were together."

He gives me a dry look. "Not that I don't blame him, 'cause your mum is a bitch, but he should have just left her. If it causes trouble for him and Mel, then that's something he'll have to deal with. He can handle it, Cupcake. That said, your mum is marrying another dude; she needs to let sleeping dogs lie."

I nod, leaning my forehead against his. "I don't understand why she had me, CJ. She doesn't love me. I don't think she ever loved my dad, either. Yet, she's still out to make my life hell. She still has a way of tearing a hole through my heart with her cruel words."

He kisses the tip of my nose before gazing into my eyes, his expression determined. "Cupcake, don't listen to her. Don't let her words hurt you, because you *are* loveable. *I* love you." He pauses, kissing me briefly. "And that hole? Every time she does manage to get in there and crack it open a little, I'll make sure to fill it back up. Because if anyone in this world is worthy of love, it's you."

I literally sag against his chest. He always knows what to say, what to do. His words though... I'll cherish them forever.

I glance into his eyes, and the love and yearning I see makes me pause to catch my breath.

He's perfect.

This moment is perfect.

"Make love to me," I demand gently.

Chapter 13

My steps are light as I walk out of my room with a smile on my face. I'm sore, tired, and well and truly happy.

"Well, don't you look chipper this afternoon," Willow sings, her hip resting against the counter, a cup of tea in her hand.

"Who's here?" I ask, leaning around the kitchen doorway to the front room, but my reach isn't far enough to see anyone.

She eyes me with suspicion. "Um… just us. The guys had practice this morning and the girls are out. Why?"

"Good," I sigh, before stepping up to her and pushing her shoulder lightly.

"Hey!" she yells, rubbing her shoulder. "What was that for?"

I point to her shoulder. "That was for lying to me."

Her brows scrunch up. "Lying to you? I've not lied to you. Did you bang your head or something?"

"When you lost your virginity, you said it didn't hurt, that it was a pinch which went away after a few minutes."

Her entire face lights up when she catches on, and she starts squealing. "Oh, my God, you slept with CJ?"

She jumps up and down, her hands on my shoulders, shaking me in the process. I put my hands on her arms, shaking her a little whilst smiling. "Stop!"

"You have to tell me everything," she squeals, pulling me into the front room and basically shoving me down onto the sofa.

My entire face and neck heat. "I am not telling you what we did."

She frowns, waving me off. "You can't tell me I lied then not explain what you meant. Tell me what happened? Didn't you enjoy it?"

My lips pull into a light smile, remembering the night before, how gentle and caring CJ was.

"Are you sure?" CJ asks.

We're both naked, CJ above me, already sheathed. His expression is soft, filled with so much love it nearly brings tears to my eyes. I've never been surer of anything, that much I know. I want him, desperately.

131

"Kiss me," I whisper.

"As you wish," he whispers back, leaning down to capture my lips.

"Ah, you totally did," Willow says, beaming at me and snapping me out of my memory. "You've got such a dopey look on your face right now. It's adorable."

I blush further. "I wouldn't change last night for the world, but you could have warned me about the pain."

She seems concerned at that, her hand reaching for mine. "Did he hurt you? Was he too rough? I swear, I will kill him." I give her a dry look and she shakes her head, still frowning at me. "Okay, I'll have Cole do it."

I stifle a giggle. I cannot believe we're actually going to talk about this, but I can't have her thinking CJ hurt me.

Here goes nothing.

"He was perfect, Low. But the pain... I was expecting a little pinch, maybe a sting, but it burned the whole way through. It felt like I was having a doctor's exam at one point."

"What do you mean?" she asks, getting more comfortable, bringing her legs under her.

I sigh. "When, you know, he..."

"Put his dick into you?"

I groan, covering my face. It's not that I'm embarrassed about the act but talking about it seems so... so crude. She giggles at my expression, cooing at me. I slap her hand away from mine, glaring at her, but then end up giggling with her.

"Yes. It really fucking hurt, Low. Like, mega. Why do people not make a big deal out of it, not warn us other girls that it really flipping hurts?"

"Allie, it didn't hurt for me. I told you, when he first entered me, it felt like a pinch, a slight burn. I guess it's different for everyone."

"What do you mean?" I ask, sitting forward.

She grins. "Well, for the girl it's her size, and for the lad, it's his *size.*" She wiggles her eyebrows at me. "Did it get better?"

I grin at her, remembering how good it got.

"I'm so sorry, Cupcake. So fucking sorry," CJ groans, his voice pained as

he moves to get off me. I lock my legs around him, stopping him. There is no way I went through that for him to stop now.

No way.

I just lost my virginity.

And it's really fucking painful.

"It's fine. It's just a little tender. Go slow?"

He looks torn, ready to bolt, but when I move my hips, biting through the pain, he groans, giving in.

"I love you. I don't want to hurt you."

I palm his cheek. "You'll never hurt me."

He pulls out until only the tip is left inside, before pushing back in slowly. His eyes close like he's in pain. "God, you're so fucking tight."

"Am I hurting you?"

Sweat beads on his forehead as he glances down at me. "No, Cupcake, you're just really tight."

It doesn't help that he's really big. Like, seriously big.

I've seen dicks before—maybe not in person, but I'm not that sheltered or naïve. His is above average, that much I do know from the things we've done before.

"At first, I felt dry because of the pain. It was like my body completely shut down for a second, so I wasn't as turned on as before," I admit, blushing.

"But you got into it?" she asks, thankfully not making me feel uncomfortable. I nod, smiling.

I got really into it.

"You feel so good," *CJ moans, thrusting inside me.*

The girth of his cock stretches me wide, filling me in a way I'll never forget. Somehow, I feel closer to him than I've ever felt before, and I don't mean distance wise, but connection wise.

"I love you," *I murmur against his mouth, feeling an orgasm building inside me. I didn't think I'd have another one, not when he gave me one before we started having sex.*

At my words, his thrusts become more frantic, his lips kissing me briefly before he pulls away, breathing heavily.

I grip onto him, my hips moving with his, ignoring the burn and stinging sensation. The more he moves, hitting the spot inside me that sends tingles all the way to my core, the easier it has become to bear with.

"Fuck, I love you," he growls, right before he changes my life.

A light slap to the cheek shakes me out of the best part of my memory, and I glare at my best friend.

"You really need to stop spacing out, it's freaking me out."

"Sorry, I can't help it. It's all I've been able to think about since it happened. It doesn't seem real, but the burn between my legs proves otherwise. I never want to forget it, Low. It was amazing."

"I'm so happy for you, Allie." She reaches over, pulling me in for a hug before pulling back and smirking at me. "It explains now why CJ was extra chirpy this morning. He could have walked into oncoming traffic and probably not even cared. He was on cloud nine."

I giggle, falling back on the sofa. "He didn't want to leave me this morning. After I took a bath last night, we spent most the night kissing and just touching each other. It was then I felt mortified. I thought his mum and you guys were still out in the living room. Thankfully he said you all went across the hall to give us some privacy." She grins, her eyes shining with happiness for me. "I feel different. I can't really explain it. I feel closer to him, too. I never knew relationships were like this; I only had my parents to go on. But he's incredible. I know I'm young, but I can't picture my life without him. I don't know whether that makes me stupid or what."

"Different as in good, then?" she asks, still smiling at me.

"Yep, definitely good."

"The joys of being in love. And I understand where you're coming from. Cole owns half of my soul. It sounds corny, but he does. He gets me. But it's more than that; I get this feeling inside me whenever I think of him. When I try to feel the true depths of the love I have for him, it actually hurts. My chest tightens and the thought of losing him is enough to break me."

I sigh, closing my eyes for a second before glancing over at her and taking her hand. "What are we like, huh?"

She giggles, hugging me. "We wouldn't change it for the world, though."

I nod, agreeing, but then remember what I wanted to talk to her about. "Um, so the pain, this burning feeling… It goes, right?"

She stares for a few moments before bursting into laughter. "Yes, it does. You do realise he's probably just big? When Mum sat me down for the sex talk, she told me her first time was uncomfortable at first, and disappointing."

"Like yours?" I tease, remembering her coming to mine angry at the world. Her boyfriend was experienced, and according to gossip, slept with his fair share of girls, but when it came to actually perform-ing, he only cared enough to get himself off. She was disappointed.

"Yeah," she laughs, but then stops, going quiet. I look at her again, noticing the serious expression she has.

"What has you thinking so hard?"

She turns to look at me, tears in her eyes. "Do you think it's wrong for me to be this happy after everything I've been through? Did I rush into things with Cole?"

I shuffle in next to her, wrapping my arm around her shoulder. "Low, you've been through so much, but you need to remember there isn't a time limit for grieving, for getting over a traumatic event. Do you feel it's right with Cole?"

She looks at me with shock plastered across her face. "Of course, it's right. I love him."

I smile, squeezing her shoulder. "That's all there is to it, then. No one has the right to judge you for moving forward. They haven't walked in your shoes. What's really brought this on?"

A tear slips down her cheek and my heart clenches. "At the game, I went back to the car to grab some gloves for Becca, when I heard those girls whispering."

"What were they saying?" I ask, yet again feeling like a shit friend for not being there for her.

"That I was lying about what happened to me because I didn't look or act like someone who had been raped."

I gasp, horrified, and get to my feet. "I'm going to—"

"They said fucking what?" Cole growls, making me jump.

I spin around to find him fuming in the door way, his face filled with rage. CJ looks just as angry as he walks over to me, pulling me into his arms. He kisses me quickly before turning to Cole, who is kneeling in front of Willow.

"Who said that about you?"

She wipes under her eyes, forcing a smile. "It's fine."

"No, it's not. They don't know a thing about you or what you've been through."

She smiles at him, this one real. "No, but you do. Allie and I were just talking, and for a moment, I felt like I was going to explode from happiness. Everything is perfect, as perfect as our lives can be. Then their words came to me and it made me feel wrong somehow."

He runs his hand down the side of her face before cupping her jaw. "I love you."

"I love you too," she says, before pushing herself up to kiss him.

I look away, smiling, and face the light of my life. My mouth goes dry at the mere sight of him, suddenly forgetting what we were talking about.

Sheesh, he's magnificent.

"Hey."

Gaining my senses, I melt into a puddle at the sound of his voice. "Hey."

He smirks down at me, pulling me against him. I relax against him, then gasp when I feel his bulge pressing against my stomach. "CJ," I hiss quietly, but can't hide the fact my body reacts.

"How are you feeling?" he asks, and I look away for a second, blushing.

Willow giggles before speaking up, "She's really sore, big guy."

"Big guy?" Cole growls, looking at Willow, then CJ, his brows scrunched together.

CJ booms out a laugh, slapping his thigh, before looking down at me. "Ah, Cupcake, you've been bragging about me." He turns to Cole, grinning smugly. "Shucks, but your girl knows I'm bigger than you now."

Cole goes to get up off the floor, but a laughing Willow stops him. "Stop teasing him, CJ."

136

Still looking smug, he shakes his head. "I can't help it. It's so easy."

The door to our flat flies open, banging against the wall with a loud thud. I jump, turning towards the door, finding Becca and Rosie clutching arms, breathing heavily.

"Are you okay?" I ask, pushing out of CJ's arms.

Rosie bursts into tears, and in a second, both CJ and I are by her side.

"What's wrong?"

"I—it was... Oh, God, I'm going to be sick," Becca announces, before rushing down the hall to the bathroom.

I glance at CJ, biting my lip worriedly. He shrugs, pulling Rosie tighter to his chest. "What happened, Rosie? Can you talk about it?"

She must be in shock because she's letting CJ hold her. I give him a look to point it out, and he nods, looking worried himself.

She wipes under her cheeks, looking up at me with sad, sky-blue eyes. "We were walking down Alton Avenue when we heard a couple start screaming for help. We rushed over and... and a girl was lying there, bruised and beaten, in a bush. She was only half covered." She pauses, her skin as pale as snow. "It was horrible. I've never seen anything like it," she whispers.

She starts to sob again, and I gasp. "Are you okay?"

It's a stupid question, but I don't know what to say. I'm stunned and a little shocked that another body has been found so quickly. It was only yesterday Marie Fleet was found. This is out of character for the killer. And if she was beaten, it's another thing to add to the list that doesn't add up.

"Do they know who it was?" Cole asks, pulling Willow against his chest.

She shakes her head. "She was pretty badly beaten; she was barely recognisable. The police questioned us, but there wasn't anything we could really say to help. We heard the couple scream and ran over. Everything from there seemed to happen quickly."

"I'm sorry you had to see that," I tell her, just as Becca comes out of the bathroom.

"I swear, I'm looking into a new school. This place is hell."

Tears run down her face and Willow moves to her friend, wrapping her arm around her shoulder. "Hey, everything will be okay."

"Not for those girls it won't, or their families," she cries.

She's right, it won't. When someone is killed so tragically, there isn't just one victim, there are two. One is the victim who is killed, the other are the family and loved ones who are left behind to grieve. This killer is doing that, and he doesn't even care. It makes me wonder if he's even human.

"We'll get through this, Becca. Don't make any rash decisions just yet, okay? You've worked hard to be here. Hopefully, the police will have some suspects soon and can stop whoever is doing this."

"And what about the next thing that happens? Did you know, before we arrived there was an explosion at the city hall? No one was killed, but twelve people were seriously injured. Then there was Logan and Jamie, and now this. How much more could happen? And why do we keep finding ourselves right in the middle of it? I don't know how much more I can deal with. My heart can't take it."

Willow steers her over to the sofa, sitting a hysterical Becca on the sofa. CJ pulls Rosie with him, sitting her next to Becca and taking the free seat next to her.

"We stay together. We're stronger together," CJ tells her, squeezing Rosie a little tighter against his chest. She looks pale, and still in shock. "I promise we will do everything in our power to keep you girls safe. It's horrific—the things that are happening around Whithall, but sadly, it's the world we live in. It won't matter if you move across the county, or to another country all together, bad things will happen wherever you go. We're a United Kingdom for a reason, though. Together, we will prevail. Together, we will get through this. Together, we are united."

"Dude, that's deep," Cole whispers, his eyes wide with shock.

"I'm a deep, emotional person. But I stand by what I said. We will make sure nothing else happens to you. I know it's hard to see with everything that is going on, but things will start to get better, safer."

"It's just so hard. How could someone do this? These girls are innocents, victims, and he's killing them for no reason other than enjoyment. I can't wrap my mind around his reasoning. Someone doesn't get up one day and decide to start killing people."

"I don't know what to say. But we have to trust that the police will find this person."

"My uncle mentioned to my dad that they had police investigators coming in. He's a serial killer, not someone the local police can catch on their own. They aren't adapted to this kind of thing. But he did say they are working around the clock to find the guy."

Becca wipes under her eyes, nodding at Cole. "I just want this to be over."

"Guys," Jordan rushes out, walking inside the living room.

I look around her, noticing the door is still wide open, and move over to shut it before Tom, Dick and Harry let themselves in, too.

"What's wrong?" I ask when I reach her.

She looks away from Rosie and Becca, her face pinched. "I came to tell you another body has been found and—"

I put my hand up to stop her when Becca gags. "We know. These two were walking down Alton Avenue when the couple found her. They saw her."

Her face pales as she turns to Rosie. "Are you okay?"

"I'm fine. Just shaken up," Rosie whispers, and whether she realises she's doing it or not, she rests her head on CJ. He smiles softly down at her, leaning back and getting comfy. His chest puffs out, proud he's a part of a miracle.

It doesn't even bother me because this is the progress we've been waiting for. CJ has hated it every single time she's flinched at his presence or avoided him all together. He might say he knows he's nothing like he's father, but I think, deep down, he's worked hard to prove to others he isn't. Seeing how Rosie reacted to him every day must have been killing him.

Jordan gives me the same wide-eyed, surprised look I gave CJ earlier. I nod, giving her a small smile and a thumbs up.

"I may or may not have been listening to the police scanner. I heard them ask for officers to go collect CCTV footage from the university."

CJ seems in thought, before looking up. "Do you think it was Marie Fleet? The girl who was reported missing yesterday?"

"No, her hair is longer than the girl's we saw today, but I can't be sure; she was barely recognisable."

I'm a little confused at first because Alton Avenue, which is near the English Building, doesn't have any cameras. It's a dead-end street that used to house the old university's dormitories.

I want to jump with joy when I realise the meaning of what she's said. Over our holiday, the university had cameras and other safety measures put into place to keep students safe. That street, since it's still used to get from the English building to the science building, had cameras put in.

"Oh, my God. It will be on camera. They'll know who the killer is."

She smiles, looking as excited as me. "Yeah, if he doesn't know they're there. But it looks like they might find this person. They need to lock him up and throw away the key."

"Hey, have they said who it was? My mate from our rugby team called me this morning. His sister was supposed to be at the game yesterday but didn't show up, and they haven't been able to get in touch with her."

Becca glances at Cole, looking green. "What friend?"

Oh, shit. She said her crush has a sister.

"Leroy. He's pretty worried. This isn't like her at all. We've met her a few times. She's a good girl."

Becca's shoulders relax somewhat when she hears it isn't who she thinks it is.

"What's his sister's name?" Jordan asks.

He pulls his phone out of his back pocket, and a few seconds later, he looks up, answering, "Kate Morrison."

Jordan pales, sitting down on the edge of the arm chair. "I'd go be there for him. I heard the name Morrison over the scanner but didn't hear what they said before." She pauses, looking to Rosie and Becca, trying to figure something out. She seems to come to some conclusion because she continues. "When I was on my way here, I was walking down Layton road. The police have taped the end of the road off, so everyone is milling around, waiting to see what's happening. There was a couple crying next to an ambulance. I was about to leave when the girls in front of me started talking. They mentioned someone called Kate. I hope I'm wrong, but I don't think I am."

Rosie looks at Becca, lifting her head off CJ's shoulder. "That's who was crying," she says to her, before turning back to the room. "We asked to leave, not wanting to be there any longer, when a couple turned up. They ran straight over to the ambulance. It wasn't even seconds before we heard the mum screaming and crying."

Oh gosh, that's terrible. That poor family.

"Fuck!" Cole groans.

I'm about to tell CJ to go, to make sure his friend is okay, when Rosie suddenly sits up, her eyes wide and cheeks pink. She glances at CJ. "Oh, no. I'm so sorry. I'm lying all over you." She pauses, looking at me. "I—I'm... I didn't mean—"

I cut her off. "It's fine. He gives great cuddles," I tell her, trying to lighten the situation.

She relaxes but doesn't move back into her position. CJ grins, tapping her on the shoulder and making her jump. I see a flash of hurt across his expression before he masks it.

"If you ever need to cuddle, I'm always here." He pauses before leaning in and whispering, "And I didn't smell *that* bad, did I?"

She giggles, shaking her head. "No, you don't smell."

He fakes relaxing against the sofa, doing it with such dramatic flair it makes me smile. "Good. Now that you're comfortable with dribbling all over me, I expect some Rosie and CJ cuddles in the future. I was starting to wonder if I had something wrong with me."

She just stares, shock written over her expression, before she surprises us by bursting into laughter. "You are terrible."

He just grins before turning to Cole. "Shall we go see if he's been told?"

Cole nods, looking down at his phone. "Yeah. Dylan is meeting us downstairs."

"Downstairs?" CJ asks.

Absently, Cole nods. "Yeah, he's moved into a spare room on the third floor."

"The third floor?" I ask, wondering why I didn't hear of any free places available.

CJ shakes his head at me, grinning. He gets up, pulling me into his arms. "No, Cupcake. Just… no."

"But—"

He kisses me, silencing me, before pulling back, grinning. "No. I'll be back in a few hours. We'll go grab a DVD to watch."

"Something funny?" Becca pipes in.

CJ grins. "I want to see that Mike and Dave Need Wedding Dates, so I'll grab that."

"Okay. I'm going to go lie down for a bit. Can you wake me up when it's dinner?" she asks, looking over at me.

I nod, agreeing. "Promise."

She leaves, moving to the room she's sharing with Rosie. I turn back to CJ. "Pick up pizza, too?"

He grins at me. "Anything for you, Cupcake."

"You two are so sickeningly sweet," Jordan groans, before sitting down next to Rosie.

"The sweetest," CJ sings, before kissing me. "Be back soon." He winks, tapping my nose, before turning to Cole.

With that, he and Cole go, leaving me and the girls alone. "So," I start, rolling on the balls of my feet. "What you want to do?"

"Um, why are you grinning? It's kind of freaking me out since we've just found out another girl has been killed."

I lose my grin instantly, feeling heartless. I didn't even realise I was smiling until she mentioned it.

Damn CJ.

"Oh, Missy here lost her virginity."

Jordan and Rosie gasp, their heads turning slowly my way, smiles on their faces.

"So, what was it like?" Jordan asks.

"You lost your virginity?" Becca asks, poking her head round the door frame, a glass of water in her hand.

I groan, covering my face with the palms of my hands. The girls giggle, making me groan louder before dropping myself down in the arm chair.

"Come on, spill."

I uncover my face and open my eyes at Jordan's request, feeling myself go all dreamy before I start telling them everything. Well, not *everything*.

Chapter 14

The university has been on edge for two weeks since the announcement of Katie's death was spread. Dylan, her brother, after hearing the news, dropped out for a term, needing the time to grieve his younger sister.

The day Becca and Rosie found her, Cole and CJ didn't come home until the next morning. They, and their team mates, stayed with Dylan and got drunk.

Really drunk if CJ's breath and swagger was to go on.

I was glad he was there for his friend. I just wish there was something we could do to help. None of my research on the murders has revealed anything.

The family from the newspaper clippings I found online is another dead end, but not one I've given up on. I've tried to find other living relatives, or to see if they had a child together. Nothing is coming up. Jordan has asked around too, but so far, nothing. I'm not giving up though. In my gut, I feel like this is the lead we should follow. The murders are too similar.

We did find out the woman was a sociopath. Jordan, ever the regular Nancy Drew, somehow managed to get her hands on a few pages of her medical history. She's still trying to locate the rest. I didn't ask questions, but she seemed a little flustered when I asked her how she got them

Her reply: 'It's better not to know'.

The few pages we had were from ages sixteen to nineteen, when she was seen regularly by a psychiatrist. The doctor had written down that Claire Laney had shown signs of a mental disorder. Claire admitted to having bad thoughts about her younger sister before she died. It went on to explain Claire didn't feel any empathy towards her sister's death. She even blamed her sister for being weak, just like their brother said she was.

A few other bits were written, but nothing that could help us figure out just who she was. It doesn't even mention the sister's name or how she died. I tried going in that direction with my research, but again, it's like the girl didn't exit. There aren't even any newspaper clippings that announce another death with Claire's last name.

Even Claire's maiden name is a no go. Jordan tried doing a background check on it, but all it led to were her medical files again.

What has us all on edge, though, is the fact that the killer hasn't taken another girl since Marie.

I'd like to think that there not being another kidnapping is a good thing, but in my gut, I feel like it's the calm before the storm.

"What has you thinking so hard?" CJ whispers, pulling my back against his front.

I smile and roll my eyes, even though he can't see me. "How do you know I was thinking?"

His fingers run up my naked side, his breath fanning my neck. "Cupcake, you woke me up you were thinking that hard. And you are tense as fuck."

"I'm just worried about everything that is going on. I wish I could do something."

His body stills behind me. "You aren't still looking into it, are you?"

I bite my lip, looking up at him through my lashes. "I—"

"Cupcake, you said you wouldn't look into it anymore," he growls, his fingers tensing on my hip before he moves away. He jumps out of bed, grabbing his joggers he threw on the floor last night, and puts them on, covering his magnificent arse.

I sigh, disappointed when the show is over. "CJ, I did stop. Then another body turned up. I'm not sure, it's a gut-feeling, but I think we have something that could identify who is doing this, or maybe point us in the right direction."

He swivels so fast on his feet I'm surprised he doesn't fall over. "Did you find anything?"

"No," I admit, curling further into my pillow.

He groans, running his fingers through his hair, his abs and arms flexing as he does.

Sigh.

"So, you're basically saying you put yourself in danger for no fucking reason?"

My eyes go up at that. "Are you trying to say if I did find something it would be a different story?"

He glares at me. "No! That's not the point. I just hate the thought of you being hurt. Fuck, it kills me every time you watch that lion advert."

I sit up, clutching the sheet to my chest. "People hunt them, CJ. It's barbaric. They need safe places to live."

He chuckles, walking back over and sitting next to me on the bed. He runs his fingers over my cheeks, brushing hair out of my face. "I love you, Allie. I don't want to see you get caught in the middle of this. At least tell me your being safe?"

Wanting to lighten up the tone, I glance down at his crotch. "Oh, I've been *really* safe."

He chuckles, his eyes dilating. "I've created a monster."

As he moves forward, the door crashes open with a thud and Willow's scream of joy enters the room.

I let out a low chuckle when CJ growls something under his breath. "Why aren't you ready? We're going to the beach." She pauses, so I look behind CJ to find her blushing, covering her eyes. "Sorry, didn't realise you were in the middle of something."

"But, Low, we don't mind the audience," he tells her, looking over his shoulder.

"Bro, you need to stop," Cole growls.

CJ laughs as he rises off me, sitting up to face the newcomers. "She's so easy to tease." Pausing, he looks at her attire, the bag in her arms, and frowns. "Since when are we going to the beach?"

I clear my throat and his eyes come to me. I slip my hand out of the blanket, raising it. "Me. It's my first weekend off in weeks, so I thought we could do something different. When I Googled stuff to do, I found this place on West Coast beach."

"What cool thing? It's a bit cold for the beach."

I roll my eyes. "We're not going to sunbathe. They have this laser quest place there that you can kill zombies in."

"Like The Walking Dead zombies?" he asks, excited.

I laugh, nodding. "Yeah. It's new, but the reviews so far say it's life-like and they had fun."

He jumps up, bouncing on the balls of his feet. "I get to practice killing zombies?"

I nod again, laughing harder.

"You do realise zombies aren't real, don't you?" Willow asks, frowning at my overexcited boyfriend.

He turns to her with a mock glare. "You do realise you'll be the first to die when we have a zombie apocalypse, right?"

"Hey," Cole snaps.

"Right," she drawls, cocking her hip to the side. "I'm really worried."

He turns to me. "Cupcake, I want you to know that even if you didn't know all the basic surviving skills, I'd have your back. I won't let you get eaten like Willow will be."

"Why will I?"

He looks at her with a condescending smile. "Because, little grasshopper, you wouldn't even know the first thing to do. My first guess: you'd probably stay at home and lock yourself in. Second guess: you'd go to the nearest police station, and we all know how well that turns out. Me and Cupcake have everything planned out. Now I get to practice shooting them."

"I have Cole to protect me," she states smugly. Cole looks at her a little wide-eyed and green in the face.

"U-uh, u-um—" he stutters, but CJ laughs, cutting him off.

"Cole will most likely die before you. His odds aren't good. The guy can't even watch a zombie show without feeling sick."

Willow looks surprised by that. "But you watched The Walking Dead with them once, remember, when I was sick?"

He rubs the back of his neck. "Yeah, I did, but—"

"He closed his eyes through most of it, but he left early to go throw up when they sliced a zombie in half and its intestines were hanging out of its belly."

She covers her mouth to hide her chuckles, but it's useless, 'cause when Cole narrows his eyes at his friend, she begins to laugh hysterically.

"Fuck you," he snaps at CJ. "And if you want to go kill some zombies, you need to get moving. We don't want to be stuck in traffic."

He storms out of the room, and seconds later, we hear banging coming from the kitchen. I giggle, looking at my best friend. "He's such a baby sometimes."

She laughs, but adoration and love fill her eyes and expression. "Yeah, but he's mine."

CJ walks over to her, gently ushering her out of the room. "Go, we need to get ready."

He closes the door behind her before turning to me, a huge grin on his face. "Cupcake, you are the best girlfriend, *ever*." He leaps onto the bed, landing on me—thankfully not using all his weight. "Do you think they have dummies there we could chop heads off?"

I roll my eyes and push him off me. "Let's go."

"Holy shit!" CJ yells, looking up at the big 'Zombie Apocalypse' sign above the entrance that looks like it's written in blood.

The place is located a five-minute walk away from the end of the beach. This side of the beach is closed off to the public. One too many deaths have happened due to the rocks, and with the tide always reaching the wall, it just isn't safe. Further down the road is where more warehouses are located. From what I read, this one we're going in used to house fishing boats and whatnot. Since then, it's been bought and refurnished and made into this.

I grab the tickets I printed off last night out of my bag, then follow the others inside.

The lad at the front desk greets us. "Hey, can I help you?"

"We're here to kill zombies," CJ tells him. I giggle at the sheer excitement in his voice. He really does act like a kid sometimes, but I love him nonetheless.

"You got a booking? We aren't taking walk-ins at the moment. The times are all booked up."

"I've got tickets," I tell him quickly, handing them to him.

It was the one time I didn't mind spending my savings, knowing I'll probably have to ask my dad for some money if things get tight. He already bought our flat and pays our utility bills, but with the extra text books I've had to buy this month, and all of our out of school activities I've done, it's been adding up.

Seeing CJ's face today was worth every penny, though. He's always doing something kind and thoughtful for me. I wanted to return the gesture, to let him know I think of him, too.

He takes the paper from me before turning to his computer, doing God knows what. CJ's arms come around me from behind and I smile, sighing when he kisses my neck, just below my ear.

"Thank you for this, Cupcake, but I could have given you money to get the tickets."

I turn around, wrapping my arms around his neck. "Nope. This was my treat. I wanted us to do something different and something you'd enjoy. If I hadn't of seen this, I probably would have gotten paintballing tickets. I just didn't want to have to go that route; I bruise easily."

He smiles, showing me those pearly whites. "Ah, it's a shame I don't want to see my girl hurt, otherwise we could have dressed Cole and Willow up as zombies and shot them with paintballs." He kisses the tip of my nose before pulling back. "I love that you did this. Thank you."

"My pleasure."

His lips meet mine, and as we're getting into it, the guy behind the counter clears his throat. We pull apart, CJ smirking down at me before looking over my shoulder at the guy.

"Here are your bands. You're up next. If you go through those doors and down the hall, a colleague will meet you for you to get suited up. There's another six people joining you. I hope you enjoy your visit."

CJ nods, before his face turns serious. "Any tips?"

"Yeah, don't die," he laughs.

"Unless it's to save me," I mutter as we head for the doors.

"Cupcake, you should know me by now," CJ says.

I beam up at him. "I know; you'd totally save me."

He frowns, but his eyes are full of mischief. "Um, no, I meant I'll avenge you if you die."

I gasp, placing my hand over my heart. "You'd let me die?"

He gives me an exaggerated eye roll, puffing his chest out. "If you're bitten, Cupcake, there's no saving you."

"You wouldn't even try?" I ask, wanting to laugh but holding it in.

He points his finger down his body, giving me a little dance of the hips. "And risk all this? No. The earth will need to be repopulated once I've killed all the zombies. They'll need good genes."

At that, I burst out laughing, linking my arm through his. "At least I won't feel guilty for letting you die now."

He stops suddenly, and I nearly trip over my own feet. "You would let me die?"

I turn to him, smiling sweetly. "Well, of course. The world will need repopulating once I've killed all the zombies. Can't let my good genes go to waste."

"You two are so weird," Cole rumbles.

"What he said," Willow says, followed by a giggle.

"Don't worry, we already planned for the two of you. If we're in a situation where we're surrounded by zombies, we're going to sacrifice you both to get away."

"Are you serious?" Cole mutters, while Willow glares.

I nod, because we did indeed discuss this before we left the bedroom this morning. "We are."

"But we're your best friends." Willow eyes me warily, before groaning. "Oh, my God, you have me talking about zombies killing me, like this is going to happen in real life. I don't even know why I feed your obsession."

I giggle at her expression, just as another worker joins us.

"But we'd make such pretty babies," I whisper.

"I'm so going to feed you to them now," she hisses back.

CJ pops his head between us. "That's treason. When we're inside, you're on your own, little one."

She rolls her eyes before facing the bloke, listening to his instructions with rapt attention.

"You'll be given body armour and a gun when we go through. The first course is the zombie apocalypse; there, you will have to kill the zombies to survive. Shots to the head, stomach, and back will take them out of the game. If you're tagged, which they'll be able to do by pressing various buttons on your gear, you are automatically out of the game and will be sent on to the next course. The next course is called Doom; inside that room is where you and the other members of your team are to team up to take out infected zombies. These zombies can only be killed with head shots. They are also sneakier and can shoot back. If you are tagged or shot, your body suit will vibrate, indicating to move on to the next level until that game is finished. The last level is called Survival; in there, you and your teammates will be against each other. There can only be one winner. Inside that room, you'll be faced with death by zombies and humans. May the best warrior win."

I feel Willow take a step back and I grin at her. She glares at me, moving closer to Cole.

"Does anyone have any questions?"

"Do you need the numbers of their next of kin?" CJ asks, pointing at the three of us.

The bloke chuckles, shaking his head. "Won't be necessary. Come on, you can meet the other group playing with you today. Remember, when you're in there, have fun. And girls, as hard as it is, try not to knee any of my workers in the nuts. They aren't really going to hurt you."

Willow and I look to each other with wide eyes before looking back at him with raised eyebrows. "Why us? You should be saying that to these two. We can control ourselves, thank you very much."

Cole scoffs. "You went all ninja over a spider web and kneed CJ in the nuts."

I feel my face turn bright red. "There was a spider on there, I saw it. And in all fairness, I was startled when he touched me. I thought it was a spider and reacted. Badly."

CJ winces next to me before facing the bloke. "Yeah, I'd tell them beforehand not to get within a few feet of them."

I glare at CJ. "Hey! And you're one to talk. You had a hissy fit over our waitress once, all because she had dark eyebrows."

CJ takes a step back, looking appalled. "They looked like caterpillars on her fucking face. They were huge...and black. And excuse me for pointing out that God gave us two eyebrows."

"CJ, you wiped at her eyebrows," I state dryly.

"They were freaking me out and it was a reflex thing. I couldn't stop myself."

"You made her cry."

"I didn't know they were drawn on," he shouts defensively.

I roll my eyes and turn back to the guy waiting for us. "You were saying we needed to be suited up?"

"Follow me," he says, trying to bite back his laughter. He probably thinks we're crazy. No, I know he does. It's written all over his face and the way his eyes drift between us all with amusement.

"You two are too funny sometimes," Willow whispers as we step into a dimly lit room.

A group of six await us, already suited and ready to go. There are three girls and three boys. The boys look they just came out of a SYFY convention, their makeup grim, with blood and gore all over them.

CJ suddenly stops, pointing at the group unashamedly. "You do know you're not the zombies and this isn't Halloween, right?"

I smack his arm. "CJ!"

He looks at me, puzzled. "What?"

I shake my head at him and address the group. "I'm sorry, he has no filter. You guys look great."

The tallest of the three boys looks at me distastefully, but the one in the middle steps forward, a creepy grin on his face, not helped by all his makeup.

"Allie?"

I'm taken aback when he pulls me in for a hug, and startled he knows my name. I pull back, feeling a little stiff from a stranger hugging me. I glance at him closer, trying to see if I recognise him. I don't. "I'm sorry, do I know you?"

"Here are your suits. Just pull them over your head," the guy from before says, passing us each our own, and then a helmet.

"It's me—Ian. We share two classes together. You remember Nathan," he says, pointing to the other guy beside him. Then he gestures to the other, still looking at me with that creepy smile. "This is my cousin from home. He's come to visit."

"Oh, hi, Ian. I didn't recognise you with all your makeup."

He smiles at me, bouncing on the balls of his feet. "This is so cool. It's great you're here."

"You know him?" CJ asks, his arm coming around me when I've finished suiting up.

I glance at him, trying to read his mood, but can't. His face is blank, giving me no clue as to what he is thinking.

"Yeah, he's in my Historical Literature and English Lit class," I tell him, then face Ian and his friends. The three girls wait behind somewhat, staring admiringly at Cole and CJ. "This is my boyfriend, CJ. CJ, this is Ian."

Ian, still smiling, reaches out to shake CJ's hand, but CJ stands there, unmoving.

Ian clears his throat, dropping his hand to his side. "Well, it's cool seeing you. Guess we should get started," he says, rubbing his hands together before turning back to the group.

I turn to CJ sharply. "What was that about?"

He doesn't even look at me when he answers. "Don't know what you're talking about."

"You were being rude. You're never rude. Not so obviously anyway."

He laughs, throwing his head back. "Cupcake, the dude has a crush on you. I knew who he was when he mentioned sharing English classes with you. Alex mentioned he was flirting with you at the library."

I don't know if I'm more shocked that he spoke to Alex, or that

Alex shared something really unnecessary.

It's bizarre, and if I'm honest, I'm a little pissed Alex would twist something around that he knew was innocent.

"Um, no, he didn't. He asked to work with me on my project, but I said no, that I already had one sorted. I offered to help him, but he said he'd be able to do it. Or something like that. That was the first time I had ever spoken him. And he wasn't flirting. I may be new to all of this, but I would have told you if some lad was flirting with me."

He holds his hands up, grinning at me. "Retract the claws, otherwise I may have to change your nickname to kitten. I'm fonder of my cupcake."

I shake my head at him but can't help but feel relief that he's not mad. "What was that about, then?"

He wraps his arm around my shoulders. "Me showing him who's boss, so if he does think about making a move, he knows I won't stand for it. And before you claw my eyes out, I know you'd never do anything. Not only do I trust you when it comes to us, but I know you wouldn't do that to anyone. And you love me."

I giggle because there's just something about his charm. "Yes, I do. But be nice. That was awkward."

"Come on, let's hope I get to kill him in the end. It will teach him for putting his arms around my cupcake."

Chapter 15

We're put into a dark room, just a set of glow lights illuminating various parts of the set up. A burnt-out car is in the centre, and all around there are made up walls for cover. There are hallways and crates and other things filling the room to give you chance to sneak up on your opponent. It's filled to the max with different things. Even the ceiling has stuff dangling from it, along with cobwebs and smoke to mist the room.

Zombie noises immediately blare from the speakers. However, I've yet to see any actual zombies. It doesn't mean they aren't there.

I find Cole and Willow still standing by the door we just entered, the light from the exit sign shining down on them. They look ready to bolt, and just before I turn to find somewhere to go and hide, I notice something slow walking towards them, arms out in front of it. I'd have warned them, but Willow's reaction when she turns to look is priceless. She screams, shoving Cole towards said zombie, before heading off into the dark.

I laugh. "Did you see her face?" I ask, turning to CJ, but he's gone, and instead, I find a zombie walking towards me.

I roll my eyes. I shouldn't be surprised that he ditched me the first chance he got.

My heart beats a little faster as I crouch down a little, shooting my gun in its direction, hoping to make a hit. I keep shooting till I reach a corridor to the right of me. I swipe at the cobwebs as I follow the small lights down the hall towards a crossroad. I look left first, the glow lights showing there are a few boxes down there, littered rubbish, and a few holes in the wall.

Next, I look right, but not before checking behind me for zombies. Turning back to the hallway to the right of me, I can make out it's a dead end, blocked off by bars that a few zombies are trying to get through. On the far-right wall, just before you reach the bars, there's another corridor, camouflaged in cobwebs.

With my mind split, I take another look to the left corridor, which is clear, knowing it must be a trap. No way would they make it that easy for us.

Would they?

And I'm right in my guess when I see another player walk out of the darkness at the other end of the hallway. They move down the hall slowly, keeping their back to the wall. I watch as arms come out from the wall, making me jump, and swipe across the big button on the person's vest.

When the second bloke we spoke to said we would have buttons the zombies would press, I presumed they would have to get close and personal. They don't. All they have to do is swipe a hand in front of where the big sensor buttons are and our vests vibrate, indicating we're out.

I'm actually kind of glad, because even though I protested at the beginning that I would have more control, I lied. I'd totally kick out if one got near me. I don't think there's a person alive who wouldn't. It's human instincts.

I laugh when the screams of a girl reach me, even over the music. I keep laughing as I turn right, running down the corridor I noticed hidden earlier, next to the zombies behind bars. I wave at the zombies, a smile stretching across my face.

"You're doing an amazing job."

I hear one of them laugh, but I don't stick around for a reply as I make my way down the corridor. Cold mist hits me in the face again, startling me.

I keep moving, checking the wall for any hidey holes and looking behind me. I hear another scream above the sound system playing the zombie noises and giggle to myself.

I'm back in the open, but now on the other side of the room. There are more boxes this side and some crates that are stacked high above my head. I keep moving.

As I turn the corner, a zombie jumps out at me. I point and shoot, screaming my head off, before running back in the other direction, nearly colliding with another zombie. I shoot—thankfully, not missing—before moving forward, stepping around the fallen zombie.

I creep around another box, noticing a group of zombies are crowding around the burnt-out car. Willow is standing on the roof, screaming bloody murder.

I roll my eyes whilst laughing. She isn't even shooting at them. I aim my gun their way, helping her out a little since she is doing this whole day for me. Three light up, indicating they're out.

I keep shooting when the buzzer of a fallen zombie sounds right behind me. I turn around, finding a zombie on the floor, right by my feet.

What the hell?

I look around, not finding the person who saved me. I keep looking, growing frustrated, but movement from above the makeshift walls catches my attention.

CJ is crouched down as he walks across it, shooting at the zombies crowding around Willow, who runs the first chance she gets. I laugh at his antics.

He must feel my eyes on him because he turns towards me and gives me a salute. I giggle, moving forward towards the larger stacked boxes but trip over something hard before I reach them.

What the fuck?

"Shit, sorry," I hear hissed.

"Ian?"

"Yes," he laughs. "I'm trying to blend in. Didn't think I'd be trampled on."

I laugh before helping him up. "Where are your friends?"

"Only Nathan is left I think. Well, he was the last time I saw him. He's around here somewhere," he tells me, before shooting his gun down the corridor to the left of us, which is filled with zombies. When one of them press his button, he groans, looking disappointed.

"All players move on to the next level," is announced over the speaker.

I look to Ian and grin. That means I'm one of the last three to stay alive. The next course only needs two to remain alive for us to move forward. I'm hoping I'm one of them.

157

We make our way over to the sign with a glowing red 'Doom' blazing at us. I meet up with CJ and hug him.

"My hero," I gush.

He grins at me, kissing my nose. "Couldn't let my cupcake die."

I melt. "You're so romantic."

He grins bigger as we step inside the next room. "I know."

My chest bubbles with excitement when I see little tunnels scattered around. There are stairs leading to various platforms and other rooms. Cobwebs and those flaps you'd find in a butcher shop are all over the place, separating the rooms and covering the corridor entrances.

It's also darker, and lightning flashing gives it an eerie effect. The noise of rain and thunder roars through the speakers, before the groaning and shuffling sound of zombies join them.

Knowing this level will be harder, I waste no time in moving away from CJ, hearing his laugh trail behind me as I run up the first lot of stairs. I move along the metal flooring, laughing the whole way. I've not had this much fun in a while, or laughed for this long.

I move towards another group of steps. There's only four, but I run up them, moving along the railing. Hands reach out of the holes in the wall, making me scream and laugh at the same time.

I jog down the next flight of stairs, reaching a darkened corridor, and stopping just short of the entrance. There's a lot of boxes—places for zombies to jump out and get me—but there's no way I'm going back up those stairs to those hands reaching out for me. One was close to getting me.

Slowly, I move down the hall, stepping around some of the boxes, careful not to knock any over. I turn left down the next one, bumping into a hard body.

"Shit, sorry," I whisper-yell over the noise.

His face lights up through the lightning, and I recognise Nathan, Ian's friend. He laughs when he sees me but doesn't stop, choosing instead to keep going.

I've not seen Willow since the car incident, and I haven't seen Cole since Willow left him to defend himself at the entrance.

When I reach the end of the hall, I come out into a maze of crates and boxes. My heart is still racing from the adrenaline, but I keep going, excited and scared at the same time.

I peek around the first stack of boxes, only to scream in fright when two arms wrap around my stomach, lifting me off the ground.

Laughter rumbles against my ear, vibrating against my neck.

I twist out of CJ's hold, turn around and slap his chest. "Don't scare me like that when there are zombies around. Are you trying to get me killed?"

He laughs as he pulls me against him, before walking us into a secluded spot between some crates and boxes, hiding us from anyone walking by.

He kisses me, his hands gripping the globes of my arse cheeks. I moan into his mouth, my fingers digging into his shoulders for support.

He pulls back, and through the flash of light, I see his eyes are heated. "God, you're so fucking hot when you're shooting shit," he whispers against my ear, so I can hear him.

"You're getting turned on by zombies?" I whisper, but there's no denying the heat in my voice. He's turning me on, especially when he grinds his hips against me.

A soft kiss on the base of my neck causes a shiver to run down my spine. "No, Cupcake, *you* turn me on. Seeing your arse run through the mazes, your cheeks flushed from the chase and the excitement in your eyes... *that* turns me on."

I cup his face, bringing my lips to his, swiping my tongue against his. His fingers dig into my arse, lifting me higher up his body. Instantly, I wrap my legs around him, rubbing myself against him, moaning.

He groans against my mouth, pressing his lips harder against mine. My fingers run through his hair, wanting him, needing him.

"Please enter your next mission. It's a game of survival, may the best warrior win."

I pull away from CJ, looking into his dilated eyes, pouting. "I didn't get to kill any zombies."

He chuckles, letting me fall down his body. "I got a few on my way to find you."

I tap his chest, kissing him quickly on the lips. "You're the best boyfriend, but when we walk into that room, you're on your own."

He lifts an eyebrow, smirking at me.

Ah, those dimples.

"Cupcake, are you saying you're going to kill me?"

I give him a coy look. "Yes. Yes I am."

He laughs and walks us towards the next door. I don't get a chance to look for Willow because the bloke starts talking.

"Pick a door. When you enter, remember: you're on your own. Good luck."

"He makes it sound like we're going to war," the girl next to us says, clearly not enjoying her time here. Ian and his friends, however, look high off adrenaline. They haven't stopped bouncing around since we walked up, their hands twitching on their guns.

"I'll—" I start to say, but when I turn to glance at CJ, he's gone. I shake my head when I see he's already in front of his door, gun up and ready, before he's off.

Smiling to myself, I move to my own door, also lifting my gun and moving through. All around me are walls of boxes, so from that, I take it it's a maze, one I'm going to get lost in. I know it. I went into the maze at Adventure Wonderland and got so lost I had to ask kids half my age for directions.

It was a defining moment.

A few seconds in, and zombies come in from all sides. I scream and start shooting along with them, grateful none of them managed to hit me before coming out of the hallway, before moving into another, this one narrow with other paths leading off.

I keep moving, finding it hard to breathe. I feel a little trapped, but I'm not going to let that stop me from winning this. If CJ wins I'll never hear the end of it. We're always arguing over what would be best if there was ever a zombie outbreak. I still think my idea is better.

A girl from the other group comes running around the corner, and

I shoot, hiding my laugh when her face looks up from the floor in shock. I quickly move down the next path before she can see me.

Another zombie moves around the corner, and when they see me, they lift their gun. I shoot first, giggling as I keep moving.

I hear a loud howl in the distance, sounding an awful lot like CJ. I stop and look up, since it sounded like it was coming from above. Not seeing anything, I keep going, moving down the hallway until I get to the next, shooting zombies along the way.

Another howl.

I look around as I run out of another hallway, coming to the centre of the room. In the middle is a stage, boxes, and fake bodies littered around it.

What has me pausing is CJ, who is standing on top of the walls they've used to make the maze. He's howling, shooting at everything and everyone he sees.

He looks kind of deranged. The weirdo.

His back is to me, which makes me smile as I move slowly into the circle, wanting to get to the table. If I can get to that table, I'll be able to aim my gun better to shoot him. I also need to be closer for the laser to work.

The first step up I take, he spins around, grinning when he spots me. I'd been so occupied on getting to the table that I forgot to have my gun ready. He aims, he shoots, he hits me.

I groan, covering my face at losing to him.

His boisterous laugh echoes around the room. "Am I not king?" he shouts, throwing his hands up in the air. He jumps down from the wall with such grace my eyes nearly pop out of their sockets.

That. Was. Hot.

The bloke from the front entrance walks in, laughing, clapping his hands at CJ. "I have to say, mate, watching you in here was hilarious. You didn't get hit once."

"I'm awesome," CJ tells him, bowing.

I roll my eyes and walk over to him, just as Cole walks out from a hallway, looking around. "Hey, guys, have you seen Willow?"

I look around, but don't see her, either. "I've not seen her, either," I tell him. In fact, I don't think I've seen her since the car incident.

CJ starts to say something, but then stops, before bursting into laughter.

"What?" Cole states dryly, eyeing him curiously. I have to admit, I'm curious too. He looks like he knows something.

He stops laughing, but still smiles wide. "I don't think I saw her enter the second room."

Cole's eyes widen. "Oh, my God, what if she got eaten by a zombie?"

CJ looks at him thoughtfully. "She had a good life?"

Cole rolls his eyes before turning back to the worker. "Can you take us back to the first room so we can take a look?"

He nods, pointing to the door I hadn't seen before. It's camouflaged with the wall material. "Just through there."

We all follow Cole as he runs in, shouting for her. The lights are on, bright, and I look around the room in amazement. They've done a pretty bang up job decorating the place. It looks derelict, like you see in the movies.

"Willow!" Cole shouts through his cupped hands.

"Is it over?" I hear her muffled voice, and turn in time to see her come out of hiding from the box she was in.

CJ and I burst out laughing, and as I look at Cole, I notice his lips twitch in amusement. He walks over, plucks her out of the box, and pulls her close.

"Why were you hiding?"

She sighs, leaning into him. "It was scary as hell. It was dark and there were zombies walking around with guts hanging out, cuts on their faces, and I'm pretty sure one of them had an eye hanging out of its socket. They didn't look fucking fake to me."

He laughs, kissing her forehead. "It wasn't real."

"So, you chickened out and hid?" CJ goads, grinning from ear to ear. "I wasted bullets for you."

She narrows her eyes at CJ. "You didn't have bullets; it was a laser."

He shrugs, looking at his fingertips. "My little grasshopper, you must learn. It was survival, and you, my friend, died."

She cocks her hip, resting her hand there. "If we're going to argue over it, then technically I won. I stayed alive and didn't get buzzed once."

"Because you hid," he tells her, throwing his hands up in the air, chuckling.

She raises her eyebrows at him. "It's survival, *my little grasshopper,* you should learn."

CJ laughs as he pulls me against his chest, kissing my cheek. "Thank you so much for bringing us. We're going to have to come again."

"On your own," Willow mutters.

CJ chuckles, kissing my cheek once more before facing her. "Chicken."

"I'll find your weakness one day, CJ, and you'll be sorry."

He gives her a knowing smirk. "No need to look, she's standing in my arms."

I turn away from her shocked expression and face the love of my life. He says the sweetest things. But when I see his expression, I can tell he's dead serious. I melt against him, overwhelmed by how that makes me feel.

"CJ," I whisper, pressing further against him.

He looks down at me, shrugging. "It's true."

"Ah damn. It's hard to be mad at you when you're all cute and romantic," Willow says, groaning.

He turns to her, grinning now. "Want me to give Cole a few pointers?"

I giggle. Cole glares and Willow rolls her eyes. "No, he's got the romantic thing down to a T."

"Yo, mate, you beat the score." We all turn to the worker who met us to put our gear on and eye him with puzzlement.

What is he going on about?

"What are you talking about?" Cole asks, pulling Willow against his front.

The worker grins big, holding a sheet of paper, something laminated, and a little trophy. "You beat the killing score. You shot forty-seven zombies. No one has gotten higher than a six since we opened."

CJ grins, taking the sheets handed to him. I look over, smiling when I see the scoreboard, the number of his vest at the top.

"Fucking ace. This is so cool," he says, his chest puffing out. I giggle at his childlike expression. He really has enjoyed himself.

"Yeah, we need ya name, if you don't mind—to put it on the scoreboard out front. It gives people something to work for, but I gotta tell ya, not even we've been able to kill that many, and we work here."

"There are forty-seven zombies working for you?" Willow asks, her face a shade of green.

He looks to her, shaking his head. "No, there's actually only twelve of us. We just send them back in to make it look like there's loads."

"What about the hands coming from the holes in the wall?" I ask, curious because there seemed like more.

"Machines. There's a few of them. If they are in distance range of the sensor button then they can buzz you out. We also have dummies we leave hanging next to a few other workers to make it look like there's a bunch of them."

"Well, it will suck if you guys ever caught the flu," CJ chuckles, still looking at his certificate with pride.

"Anyway, give your name to Lou at the front desk, man. Hope you guys had fun, but I need to get the stuff ready for the next group."

We nod and watch him go before walking back to the changing room to collect our things. We hang up our helmets and suits, before heading out.

CJ gives his name to Lou, and even adds the guys who were waiting at the front desk to congratulate him, on Facebook.

"See ya later," he shouts over his shoulder as he meets us outside. He looks at us, a wide grin spreading across his handsome face. "What do you want to do next?"

"Can we go get something to eat? Maybe we could sit on the beach for a bit before we head back?" Willow asks.

"And get sand in my food? No," CJ mutters. "Let's go somewhere to eat. We can walk on the beach later."

She nods, not arguing with him, since it's impossible to do. You'll never win; he takes his food seriously.

Out of nowhere, he picks me up and swings me around, kissing me hard. "Cupcake, you are the best girlfriend ever. Today was fucking epic."

I smile down at him, running my fingers down his cheeks and leaning in closer. "I'm glad you had fun."

"Oh, it's gonna be even better when we get home and I get you naked. Killing things has made me horny."

"We can hear you," Cole states dryly, not sounding amused at all.

"Shouldn't eavesdrop then, you big perv," CJ mutters over my shoulder, before he glances back at me, his expression softening to the one I love most; the one where he looks at me like he's seeing me for the first time and can't believe his eyes, like I'm perfect. "I love you."

I press my forehead against his, my fingers running through his hair. "I love you more."

"Do you two want to be alone, or can we go eat?" Cole asks, making me giggle against CJ's mouth.

CJ pulls back to answer, but never takes his eyes from mine. "I'd love nothing more than to be alone with my cupcake."

So sweet.

"But?" Cole adds, knowing his best friend all too well.

"We can do that after we eat."

I start laughing, sliding down his body before we walk back to the car.

Today had been a good day—the best day. If only every day could be like this. If only we didn't have to go back to Whithall, where life was a little fucked up. At least here we didn't have to worry about a serial killer.

Alas, life goes on, and carrying on as normal is the only thing we can do.

Chapter 16

The university is buzzing with fear over the death of Marie Fleet. Her body was found a few days ago, not far from the English building at the university.

Knowing she was with the killer for twenty-four days is something I can't even think about. What that poor girl must have gone through.

Since finding out about it, Rosie has, somehow, come out of her shell. Whether that's because someone else needed her, I don't know. I just know she's been there for her friend as she mourns the loss of her sister. She's left the flat more in the past few days than she has the entire time she's lived here.

Life has been crazy since.

I knew coming to Whithall would have its challenges; I just didn't realise how hard some of the coursework would be. My English Lit assignment is starting to stress me out. I've found other topics to write about, but I'm not feeling it. None of the subjects I decided on as alternatives are giving me any inspiration. My mind keeps going back to the murders, mostly Christie's.

Although, her murder does show a few discrepancies. First, she's the only victim who was murdered that had blonde hair. All the others have mousy brown hair, or as close to that colour as you can get. She was murdered in her room and left, the others have been taken somewhere, killed there, then dumped near the university. None of it adds up.

Is it a copycat or the same person?

Nothing makes sense anymore.

I promised the others I would leave it be, but I can't. At the moment, however, I'm at a dead end, so they're getting their wishes.

I throw my paperwork onto the floor, which has CJ looking up from where he's lounging on the sofa.

It's late. We've spent the night eating junk food and watching movies. When CJ put one of his army movies on, I decided to get my coursework out.

"What's up, Cupcake?" He sits up, twisting his neck side to side.

"I'm just finding this harder than I thought I would," I admit.

He looks adorably puzzled. "Watching people shoot at each other?"

I roll my eyes. "No. My English Lit assignment. Nothing is adding up. I've tried to write about another real-life topic, but my mind wanders back to Christie."

"Why Christie?" he asks, not arguing with me about still working on it.

I sit up straighter and turn to face him head on. "Okay, so I looked for ties between the girls who have been murdered. There are none. But that's when I noticed they all looked similar, except Christie. She had blonde hair. Do you think that's weird?"

He thinks that over before shrugging. "It does sound weird, but it could just be a coincidence."

I nod. "I thought that too. But when me and Jordan were talking about it, we came up with a theory that Christie's death was premeditated. I know all of them are premeditated because it does seem like he selects his victims, but what if he killed Christie because of something she did? What if, after he killed her, it set something off inside him and he started killing other girls, girls who remind him of someone."

He frowns, his forehead crinkling. He massages his temples. "If that's true, what you're describing is some mental disorder. That could actually help the police, Allie."

I shake my head, frowning. "We don't have proof, CJ. Why would they listen to us? There's other stuff we've found that could provide more proof of our theory, but we're still looking into it."

"I think we should go to the police about this."

"Then they'll ask why we got involved."

He frowns further, ready to reply, when his phone rings from the floor. He picks it up, glancing at the screen. "It's Mum," he mutters, surprised. "Hey, Mum. What's wrong? Okay, I'll be there in a minute."

He ends the call before shooting up off the sofa. Panic bubbles up inside me at his erratic behaviour. His hands are shaking as he grabs his jeans from the floor.

"Is your mum okay?"

His face is pale when he glances up from buttoning his jeans. "I don't know. Something's wrong. She's hysterical and crying. She said she needs me."

"I'll come," I tell him, getting off the sofa.

"No, it's fine. It's late and you have classes tomorrow."

I give him a dry look. "So do you. And it's your mum; I have to go."

He throws a hoodie over his head and I get up, moving to the door where my hoodie is hanging. It's actually CJ's, but as we we're having a lazy night in, I decided to wear leggings and a T-shirt. It swamps me, falling to my knees. When I'm done, I grab my bag and phone, and take his hand.

"Hey, it's going to be okay," I tell him, giving his hand a squeeze.

He looks haunted. "She sounded pretty messed up. I've not heard her cry like that since my great-grandparents died."

Seeing him like this is breaking my heart. He looks distraught and torn up. "Let's go see what she needs. Whatever it is, she has us."

He squeezes my hand and leads us out of the flat. "Thank you for your support and coming with me."

We pull up to his mum's house in CJ's car. All the lights are blaring inside the house. It's a big house, not all of those are needed to be on. She also doesn't seem the type to waste electricity.

We've barely gotten out of the car when the front door opens and his mum comes running out. The sight of her stops me in my tracks.

Something bad has happened.

Something terrible.

Her face is streaked with tears, mascara running down her cheeks, and from the swelling of her eyes, she looks like she's been crying for days, not in the time since she called CJ for help.

"Mum," CJ calls hoarsely, running up to her. He pulls her into his arms and she collapses against his chest, holding him close, wailing.

I don't even know what to do. I feel like an outsider standing here, not knowing what to do or if I should even interrupt their moment.

CJ looks over his shoulder at me, motioning for me to follow him into the house. I nod and pop back to the car, grabbing the keys he forgot to take out of the ignition.

Once the car is shut and locked, I make my way into the house, following the sound of Milly crying in the living area.

CJ holds her close, rubbing his hand down her back. "Please, Mum. What's happened? You're scaring me."

She sniffles, looking up at her son. "I'm sorry, CJ. I thought this was all behind me."

When she doesn't continue, he rubs her back. I sit on the wooden table opposite them and take her hands in mine. "We're here. You can talk to us."

"She's right, Mum. Whatever this is, we will get through it. Has something happened to someone in the family?"

She shakes her head before taking a few deep breaths to compose herself. "The police came today—about the murder of those girls."

"What?" CJ and I yell simultaneously.

"The girl, Kate Morrison… Do you know her?"

CJ nods, swallowing. "Yes, she's my friend's sister. Why?"

More tears fill her eyes. "They said her murder was done out of anger. It wasn't premeditated, like the other girls he's taken. They're keeping it out of the media until tomorrow, but another girl was taken yesterday. They're being more aggressive with their investigation. I thought it was over."

She's in shock, so I start rubbing slow circles on the backs of her hands with my thumb, wanting to soothe her.

"Mum, you aren't making sense."

She shakes herself out of it, looking at her son. "I'm so sorry this is happening, but they want you to go into the police station tomorrow for a DNA test."

My heart starts beating wildly.

"What?" he asks, looking taken aback.

She rubs her temples, closing her eyes for a few moments, before glancing back at us. "They explained that the killer was sloppy when it came to Kate. She wasn't washed like the others," she says, shuddering. "They found some DNA under her fingernails."

CJ looks sick. "Mum, what does this have to do with me?"

She pulls one of her hands free from my grip to cup his jaw, looking him squarely in the eyes, taking another deep breath. "When I was raped twenty-two years ago, they got the DNA of the rapist from me and used it to find him."

CJ nods when she pauses. He looks on the verge of losing it. It must be hard for him to hear this. I know it is for me, and I'm not her son.

"Go on."

"When they took the DNA from Kate, it came back with a possible match…" She swallows, looking pained. "It was a one hundred and ten percent familial match with the man who raped me."

CJ sits back in his seat, rubbing his hand across his face. I'm too stunned to do or say anything. I hadn't seen this coming and have no idea what it means—or why they want to question CJ.

He swallows, looking at his mum with glassy eyes. "What does that all mean? What does it have to do with me?"

"They've confirmed the killer is male, approximately in his early or late twenties. They've also established that the match is a close relative, probably a son or nephew of some sort. It's why they need you to go down the station."

He looks broken, and my heart bleeds for him. They can't possibly think he had anything to do with the murders.

He looks to me, a few tears falling down his cheeks. "I didn't do this," he croaks hoarsely.

I sit forward, placing my hands on his knees. "No one will think you did. They probably want to confirm yours isn't a match. It's procedure. Remember, they don't know you. They don't know what a selfless, kind-hearted person you are. Once they do, they will give you the all clear."

He looks to his mum, wiping under his eyes. "I didn't do this. I'm nothing like him, Mum. Does it run in the family? Will I be a monster, just like him?"

His mum starts crying and sits forward until her knees are touching CJ's. "Son, you are nothing like him. You'd never hurt a soul. You might share his DNA, but you've also got mine, and us Everherts are a lot stronger. You weren't raised by a pack of wolves; you were raised by me. But CJ, it's your heart alone that sets you so far off from them. You'd never even think of doing something so heinous like this."

His fists clench, and he sits up, breathing heavily. "I'm not going to wait around for the police to arrest me. I'm going to get this sorted tonight. If this gets out, my life is over, Mum."

He gets up, and me and his mum follow, reaching for him to stop him. "CJ, stay. You heard your mum; she said you can go in tomorrow."

He shakes his head. "No. I'm not letting him ruin my life again."

"CJ, please, let's talk about this."

He looks at his mum, sadness filling his eyes. "I'm sorry. I won't be long."

With that, he leaves, and my heart breaks. I wipe at the tears I hadn't realised were there and glance at Milly.

"Let's go get you a cup of tea," I whisper.

She nods, still looking shocked. "Yes, that sounds amazing."

We make our way into the kitchen and I sit Milly down at the table before making work of getting us a cup of tea. Finding stuff in the large kitchen is nearly impossible, but I manage, and make my way back over to Milly.

"It will be okay," I whisper, reaching over the table and rubbing her cold hand.

She looks up, her eyes red and filled with tears. "Will it? I prayed when CJ was born that I could protect him from how he was conceived. My family ruined that the first chance they got. They made his life hell, and I hated them for it. I'll never forgive them for what they did and how they did it to my son. He was my life, my world, and they set out to ruin that." She pauses, taking a sip of her tea. "But in a way, I was thankful he knew. It brought us closer. I wish it could have come from me; I never wanted him to find out from someone else."

"Was the person who raped you arrested?" I ask, something CJ never told me.

She nods. "He was. It took them a few weeks to find him, but in the end, it went to trial and he was convicted. He tried to get out on bail, but he was declined and kept in prison. I was informed of his death on the day he died—that was a while back now."

"You don't have to talk to me about this," I tell her, feeling my throat tighten.

She looks up from her cup of tea, giving me a small smile. "It's been so long I believed I'd never have to talk or think about it again. There are odd occasions where I will divulge my past with some of the girls I see, but I focus more on CJ when I do." She takes another sip, looking lost in thought. "When I was sixteen, I thought I knew everything. I never thought something like that would ever happen, thought it only happened to other people."

She's talking about when she was raped. CJ told me she was young when it happened. I take a deep breath myself, conflicted over whether I want to hear this or not. But I don't have the heart to stop her when she clearly needs to get it off her chest.

"It's okay," I assure her, squeezing her hand.

"My girlfriends wanted to go to a concert that was happening near our home. It was a big event that went on for days and had musicians from all around the world. My parents didn't want me to go. They didn't want me to do anything involving fun. I snuck out that night.

"We were having a really good time, and because everyone was drunk or high off the music, they weren't paying attention to ID's, so we got served alcohol or we stole other people's drinks. We thought we were cool, but really, we were stupid."

"No, you weren't. You just wanted to make memories with your friends. That's not stupid. You can't control other people's actions. Isn't that what you told Rosie?"

She chuckles dryly. "We got separated some time during the night. I don't think we even noticed until our alarms on our phones, telling us to get back, started going off. I left the group of people I was talking to and started looking around for them. I texted them and was waiting for them to reply, but I thought if I looked around, I'd see them," she says, pausing to rub her eyes. "I didn't even see him coming. One minute I was walking around one of the large tents they had up, the next, I was dragged behind. I saw him—saw his eyes, his expression, and I died a little inside that night. Then CJ was born. I had doubts throughout my pregnancy, scared I wouldn't love my baby. But I didn't need to worry. The second he kicked inside me, I felt something for him, and then the moment I laid eyes on him, I fell so deeply in love I felt like I could fly. I don't know how to protect him from this," she says, before bursting into tears.

I move out of my chair to kneel beside her, rubbing my hand up and down her back. "We can protect him. I think the news he has family and they are like this..." I pause, unsure what to call his dad. He's not his dad—he doesn't have the right to be called that, and he doesn't have the right to be called a sperm donor, either. Instead, I carry on. "Once everything has sunk in, he'll be fine. You've raised a beautiful, strong man, Milly. He's perfect in every way he needs to be. Yes, he has flaws, but none that matters. They're all superficial, like snoring," I tell her, trying to lighten the mood.

It works.

She snorts, rubbing her nose with her sleeve. "And that he's like a human disposable bin."

I laugh, getting back up and sitting back down in front of her. "See, he's incredible."

She looks up at me, her expression serious. "Do you really think he'll be okay?"

I can't lie to this woman. "Eventually he will, yes. Right now, he just needs time. We know he didn't do this. For one thing, he was at a rugby match with me when Katie was murdered. He has loads of witnesses to confirm that." I pause, thinking back to Linda, the second girl who was murdered. "I'm not sure where he was the time Linda was taken. It was a Sunday, so he could have been at practice or sleeping in. Plus, she was discovered when we were away for that book signing. Marie Fleet was taken the night he was with us at home, and her body was found when he was in class. He has an alibi for all of them. I can't say for sure about Christie, but he spent every night at mine due to the court case, so I'd say he was there. In fact, I'd be willing to put money on it."

"I know he didn't do it. I'm just worried about his mental state. This must be hard for him."

"We'll get through this. He isn't alone."

Milly yawns, and I follow. She looks at me, smiling. "Why don't you take CJ's old bedroom for tonight. There's no telling what time he'll be back."

"Are you sure?" I ask, noticing it's nearly two in the morning.

She nods, getting up and taking our cups to the sink. She swills them out before leaving them in the sink. "Come on, you can wear one of CJ's shirts, they're big enough that it'll look like a nightgown on you."

"Okay, thank you. I'm gonna texted CJ and tell him that I'll be staying here and to wake me up when he gets back."

I text him quickly, my eyes stinging when I glance at my phone. Milly flicks the lights off before we walk through the house to the stairs. I follow, looking around the grand staircase and pictures that line the wall. Most of them are of CJ, but a few are of him and an older couple, who I presume are his great-grandparents.

His mum stops at a door down the hall and pushes it open. I glance inside, grinning when I see his *Walking Dead* posters.

"Thank you," I tell her, stepping inside.

"I'm in the last room, right down the hall. If you need anything at all, come and get me."

I turn back to her and pull her in for a hug. I don't know if she needs it, but I know I do. "Try to get some sleep."

She pulls back, squeezing my hands. "I'll try. Goodnight, Allie."

"Goodnight, Milly."

I shut the door to after she leaves. His room is everything I thought it would be. A double bed with blue sheets, zombie posters, computer equipment that lines the wall with a huge desk, and trophies on a shelf on the other side of the room.

I walk over, picking one up, smiling when I see it's for coming first place in a go-karting race. Another one is for winning school clown.

My boyfriend. I sigh.

I blink, my eyes tired and sore, so I grab a T-shirt from his drawers and change before getting into bed.

With my phone in hand, I text CJ.

Me: Where are you? I'm worried. Please message me back.

I stare at the screen until my eyes shut, and I fall asleep.

Light pouring into the room and the bed shifting drifts me from my restless sleep. I'm not sure what time it is, but I don't feel like I've been sleeping long.

"CJ?"

A strong arm wraps around me, pulling me against a chest. "Go back to sleep," he croaks hoarsely.

He sounds rough, distraught.

Knowing he needs me, I turn in his arms, facing him. I run my fingers through his hair. "Oh, CJ. What did you do tonight?"

He sighs, resting his forehead against mine. "I gave the police my DNA. I gave them a statement, too. I'm not sure where I was the night Christie was murdered, but all the others, I'm pretty sure I have an alibi for."

"CJ, no one will think you did this."

"It doesn't matter. I'm still somehow related to whoever is doing this. I feel sick inside. I sat outside that police station just looking down at my hands. I traced the lines of my veins, disgusted with the knowledge that his blood runs through them. I can't erase him. I can't wipe him from my mum's my memory. And now he's haunting us again. I don't know what to do to make this right."

175

I cup his cheek, feeling tears flow down my face. "CJ, the blood inside you doesn't make you who you are; your heart and soul do, and, baby, you are original. You are nothing like them. You are your own person."

"I just can't believe this is happening."

"We'll get through this. Together."

"Yeah, yeah, we will," he says, but sounds distant, detached.

I worry this is just the beginning, that we might lose the CJ we know and love through all of this.

Chapter 17

The past week and a half has been a rollercoaster of emotions. Another girl, Lilian Clarke, was taken a week ago.

CJ was taken down the police station the day after for more questioning. The media and public haven't been informed of CJ's involvement, since the police are cautious it could put him in danger. They aren't wrong, and if we don't find out who is doing this, it might come to the point he will leave.

We've hardly spent any time together since he found out about the DNA. He's been holed up in his room after getting all the information he could on his mother's rapist and her family.

The only people who know, are his mum, me, Cole and Willow. He didn't want anyone else to know. It hasn't stopped me from looking into it—anything to ease his mind. I also betrayed his wishes by telling Jordan everything, knowing I'll need her help.

But the news CJ received six days ago has caused a drift between us.

"I don't get it. What do you mean?" CJ's mum demands.

CJ sits back in his chair, looking pale. I take his hand, squeezing it.

The police officer gives her a sympathetic smile. "We ran CJ's blood work. It came back with a one-thirty-five familial match. We know the DNA belongs to a male, so we believe he is a sibling, another child your attacker fathered."

"I can't believe this is happening," Milly cries.

"Does this mean I'm in the clear?" CJ whispers hoarsely, looking rough. He hasn't slept or eaten much since everything was revealed.

"Yes, we believe so."

I shake myself out of my thoughts and watch the door to the library. I asked Jordan to meet me here, since being at home felt wrong without CJ. I've been worried sick, physically and emotionally, and needed the fresh air. My stomach has been in knots for over a week.

"Are you sure you don't want me to stay and lock up?" Alex asks, sounding concerned. I glance at him; his eyes are drawn together and he's shifting nervously. For good reason. CJ hasn't been the only one not acting themselves.

I miss him.

"I'll be fine. Jordan will be here in a second. She's gonna help me with my coursework."

"I can wait around, walk you back home? With that madman out on the loose, it's not safe."

I lift my hand, stopping him from going any further. Before I can reply, the door to the library opens. I turn, expecting Jordan, but instead I find Mr. Flint walking in, a slimy smile on his face.

"Allie, what a surprise to see you here," he greets.

I glance at Alex. He's watching Mr. Flint with rapt attention, a frown upon his face.

"I work here," I tell him—something he knows. During the last lesson we had, I told him I couldn't make his appointment due to work. He clearly knew I'd be here.

"We're actually closed," Alex tells him.

He turns his nose up at Alex before turning to me, smiling once again. "I'm sure Allie wouldn't mind waiting behind so I can look for a book I need."

"Actually, I'm going to be busy. The library opens at seven in the morning. If you want to come back then, I'm sure Janie will be more than willing to help you."

The smile falls from his face. "It's important. I won't keep you long."

I force a smile. "It's late, Mr. Flint, and I have classes in the morning. I'd like to get back."

His face looks pinched when he nods. "Very well. I'll come back tomorrow. While I'm here, I'd like to book an appointment for you to come meet with me."

As much as I'd love to decline, he is my teacher. If I keep refusing to see him he might do something about it. I can't get a bad grade or report.

"When were you thinking?"

He looks to Alex distastefully before he turns to me. "Janie informed me you had a Friday night off in a few weeks. If you can come to my office then, for about seven, we can go over your work."

My heart stops. He knew when I'd be working and when I wouldn't. He was trying to catch me out on a lie.

With a wobbly smile, I answer, "That's fine."

He nods once again. "I'll see you then."

The look he gives me sends a shiver down my spine. When he's gone, I try to hide my fear, and force a smile as I look at Alex.

"Shouldn't you be going?"

He looks torn. "I don't know. That guy gives me the creeps. I've heard girls swoon over him, but I've also heard whispers from some who have said he's not who he seems to be and they don't like him."

Hearing what others have said doesn't help the fear I already have for Mr. Flint. But I need to speak to Jordan on my own, without prying ears.

"I'll be fine, and Jordan will be here soon, so I won't be on my own."

"Everything okay?" Jordan asks, making me jump.

I turn around, my hand over heart, and gasp. "Could you not sneak up on people."

She winces. "Sorry."

Alex chuckles, grabbing his things. "Since she's here, I'll go. Make sure you walk to your cars together."

"We will," I tell him.

When he's gone, Jordan gives me a questioning look. "What did I miss?"

I wave her off. "Nothing that can't wait." I pause, looking at her pleadingly. "Please tell me you've found something."

She looks away before sitting down, and a sinking feeling hits the pit of my stomach. She's found something, and it's bad. It has to be.

"Are you sure you want to hear this?" she asks, and I feel sick again.

"Yes. I need to know. He's going out of his mind, Jordan. I've hardly seen him. He's pulling away from me. The only person he really spends time with is Cole."

"I did some digging after you told me everything."

I put my hand up, stopping her, feeling the blood drain from my face. "You haven't told anyone, have you?"

She grabs my hand and rushes out, "No, of course not."

I sag against my chair. "Thank you. Go on."

"All the girls have one thing in common: CJ," she says, her eyes filled with sadness.

I push my chair back and get up, tears running down my face. "No. He didn't do this. I asked for your help to help him, not make him look guilty."

She looks at me like I've slapped her. "Allie, calm down, please. I would never think CJ did these things. Let me explain."

I wipe my cheeks and take a seat. "I'm sorry. Everything is getting to me. I miss him so much."

She rubs the top of my hand soothingly. "He just needs time. This is big. It must have hit him hard."

"It has," I tell her, sighing. "What did you find? How do they all have CJ in common?"

She pulls her laptop out of her bag, loads it up, and clicks on a file on the homepage. Photos pop up on the screen, and I frown when I see CJ standing next to Christie. I knew he knew her but seeing them together hurts. She was evil, a bitch, and I always wondered if he slept with her. I've been too scared to ask, afraid of what the answer will be.

She clicks onto the next photo. "This is Linda Cooper. She and CJ both run Whithall Hospice Charity together. I'm not sure if they knew each other personally, but this photo is of everyone who had taken part."

I take a closer look at the photo. Linda Cooper is smiling wide, sweat pouring off her, and her arms around another young girl and a middle-aged man. Next to him stands CJ, looking just as exhausted and sweaty as the rest of them.

I look to Jordan, my eyes wide. "What does this mean?"

She points over to the screen with her eyes. This time I'm looking at a new photo. "This is Marie Fleet. It seems they were out with a group of friends. Lilian Clarke, according to her Facebook posts from a year ago, actually slept with CJ. CJ also knew Kate through her brother Dylan."

"This doesn't make sense. CJ has never once mentioned he knew these girls."

She shrugs. "Why would he? Linda was a sixteen-year-old girl when this photo was taken. CJ, no offence, wouldn't pay attention to her. And if you haven't noticed, CJ loves his photo being taken. Being in a photo with a group of people is not rare for him. Why would he remember these being taken? Plus, they aren't even friends on Facebook. I doubt they know each other personally. He isn't even tagged. From what I know of him, he probably jumped in front of the camera randomly, and most likely didn't know one person in the photo."

"What about Lilian?"

She winces, pity filling her eyes. "It's no secret CJ has a past when it comes to girls. He's never hid that from you, babe."

I wipe my cheeks, wondering what all this means. "This has to mean something, right? I mean, with the murderer being related and now this, it has to."

She nods. "I've looked into the name of the person who attacked Milly. He had no wife or kids that are on record, but that's not saying they aren't out there. He had two sisters. One died young and one died in an institution in her late thirties."

It takes a minute for my brain to catch up. "Are you saying that the news article I found could be about one of his sisters?"

When she nods, I gasp, horror-struck. I knew that story meant something.

"Yes. Claire Forest, the lady who murdered her husband and his mistress, was originally Claire Lance. She took her dad's last name, but Conrad Pearson, the man who raped Milly, took *his* father's last name."

"Oh, my god, I need to tell CJ."

She stops me from getting up. "Wait, there's more."

I feel the blood drain from my face. "More?"

She nods sadly. "Yes. It's not in the public records, but after much digging I found hospital reports in Claire's name. It said she gave birth to a boy in nineteen-ninety-six."

"Does it say who?"

"No. I've looked everywhere for a birth certificate, but it's sealed. To get it unsealed I'd have to be involved with the case. Alas, I'm just a middle-class student who blogs."

"Maybe the police can."

"It won't matter. The results of the DNA test said it was a close relation, most likely a sibling. It couldn't be her child who is doing this."

"Something doesn't add up, Jordan. It must mean something. Why would it have been bugging me ever since I found it?"

"I honestly don't know. We could go to the police with what we have, but then, how would we explain what we found?"

She has a point.

"But we found the article online."

"And Conrad? What about the hospital file? How do we explain that, Allie?"

I run my fingers through my hair. My stomach starts to turn. I know it's coming, so I rush over to the bin by the counter and empty the contents of my stomach—the little bit of lunch I managed to get down.

"Allie, are you okay?"

I gag, throwing up once more. I hold my index finger up, silently asking her to give me a minute. I hear her feet move away, but I don't look, instead throwing up once more. My stomach cramps, since there's nothing left to get up.

Jordan walks back over to me, bending down and handing me a bottle of water and some tissue. I look up from the bin, my eyes watering. "Thank you."

"Are you okay? You look really pale. Maybe tonight wasn't a good idea."

I wave her off as I take a long swig of the water. It's lukewarm, but it will have to do. "It's fine. I've been getting sick for just over a week now. I think it's the stress of everything." She doesn't look convinced. "I promise, I'm fine. It's nothing you've said, I swear."

"That wasn't where I was going," she says cryptically.

I give her a questioning look. "What are you talking about?"

"Allie, could you be pregnant?"

I laugh at her absurd question, shaking my head. "What? No—no way." She doesn't say anything, but she doesn't need to.

There's no way I'm pregnant. I've missed a few pills here and there, yes, but we've been careful. I think. There were a few times we've been careless, but... I couldn't be.

I shake my head, denial hitting me. "No. I can't be."

She sits down, moving the bin out of our way. I'm still kneeling, so I sit back on my arse next to her, a little dazed.

"When was the last time you had a period?" Jordan asks softly.

I take a deep breath, wondering when, and can't think. I haven't had one recently, that's for sure. My eyes widen when it comes to me.

"I haven't had one since a few weeks after we returned from our break. I remember because I had a bad one."

"Babe, I hate to say this, but I think you should do a test. Do you have regular periods?"

"I have one every month like clockwork. They last a few days at the most."

"Then let's go get a test."

I turn to her, my eyes filled with tears. "I can't be pregnant. Not right now."

She wraps her arm around my shoulder, pulling me into her. "It will be fine, Allie. You'll figure this out."

I pull out of her hold, glancing at her as tears fall. "CJ is barely speaking to me. I'm in school and don't even have a well paid job. I don't know the first thing about raising a baby. How am I supposed to be a mother? I'm only twenty, Jordan!"

"Hey, mums have children younger than you and make it. Some might get a helping start, but they make it, Allie."

She's right, they do, but still... Am I ready to be a mother? Is CJ ready to be a father? I can't tell him about this now; he has so much going on. But I don't know if I can do this on my own.

"What should I do?"

She gets up off the floor and holds her hand out for me. I let her pull me up. "Let's get you a test first. Let's not get ahead of ourselves. It might be that you're right and you're stressed."

I nod, still dazed by it all.

We pull up outside my flat, the paper bag clutched tightly in my hand. When someone walks out of the building, I panic, shoving the pharmacy bag inside my school bag.

"Do you want me to come up with you?" Jordan asks.

I shake my head. "No, I need to do this on my own."

"What about CJ; are you going to tell him?"

I sigh. I haven't thought about it yet. "I don't know. I want to get this done first. I don't want to add more to his plate, only for it to come up negative."

"Okay. Did you want me to pick you up after classes tomorrow, so you can get your car from the library?"

"I think I'm gonna call in sick tomorrow. I'll ask Cole and Willow to go get it, if I see them."

"Are you sure you're going to be okay?"

I force a smile and open the car door. "Yeah, I'll be fine."

"Call me later if you need me, or tomorrow. Whichever. Just know I'm here."

I shut the door behind me and lean in through the window. "Thank you. And thank you for tonight—with the files, and this."

"It's what friends do," she says softly.

I tap the top of the car and head up the stairs to our building. Everything seems to be like a cloud of smoke. I have no idea what the results of this tests will say. I have no idea what my future will hold.

When the lift lights up, I wonder if it's a sign of luck on my side. I'm still in a trance-like state as the lift takes me up to my floor.

I grab my keys, and open the door, but it's all a fog, like it's not real.

"Allie? Are you okay?" Becca asks.

I jump, looking up to find her standing in the kitchen doorway with a glass of milk. "I'm fine. Why are you up?"

She holds her glass of milk up. "Rosie had a nightmare. I'm hoping this will calm her down."

I nod, understanding. "She okay?"

"Yeah," she tells me, but pauses, looking in two minds about something.

"Are you okay?" I ask her.

She seems startled by my question, before her shoulders relax. "I know it's none of my business and you can tell me to mind it, but is everything okay with you and CJ?"

My stomach cramps at hearing his name. "What makes you ask that?"

"He hasn't been around much. In fact, I think I've only seen him in passing. And you haven't been yourself lately, either."

I force a small smile. "I'm fine. We're fine. He's just dealing with some family issues at the moment."

"Is he okay?"

"He will be."

She smiles at me. "Good. Seeing him so down has been kind of scary. Anyway, I'd better take this to Rosie before she wonders where I've been. Goodnight."

"Goodnight, Becca."

Instead of going inside my room, I move into the bathroom, taking out my purchase from earlier. My hands shake violently as I stare down at the blue box.

I can barely read the instructions through the tears filling my eyes. I contemplate whether or not to do it, but I think not knowing will only make me feel worse.

Feeling numb, I pee on the stick, set the time on my phone, wash up, and put everything back in my bag. I hide the pregnancy stick up my sleeve, not wanting to run into Rosie or Becca, holding it. I can't handle any more people knowing.

I sit down on my bed, turning the test over and staring blankly at it for three whole minutes. It feels longer, but when the alarm on my phone beeps, I know it's only been three.

I feel like I'm going to be sick again. My palms are sweaty, my breathing is erratic, and I'm scared shitless.

The moment I turn the test over my whole world explodes.

Positive.

A fury of emotions run through me. I'm scared, lost, alone… and I have no idea how I'm going to do this. I have no idea how CJ will react, or if I should wait to tell him.

All I know is a life is growing inside me, and whether I'm ready or not, it's still my responsibility. If I hadn't of been so careless, I wouldn't be sitting here, alone and afraid. I wouldn't be worried about my future, or if I can even have the one I planned.

I don't know if CJ will want to keep the baby, or what will happen to us if he doesn't.

I lay down, resting my head on my pillow, and cry silently into it so I don't wake the girls up. I'm hoping tomorrow I'll wake up and this will all be a dream.

Because tomorrow, I don't know what will happen. I could lose everything in a blink of an eye.

Chapter 18

For two days, I've locked myself away from the world and my friends. I've not answered my calls or messages, and luckily, no one has knocked on my door. Yet. It won't be long until Willow barges in, demanding what is wrong.

I can't bear to face anyone, not yet, not until I've figured out what I'm going to do or say. And then there's CJ. My head is lightly warning me not to tell him; he has enough going on in his life right now and putting this on his shoulders might be too much for him. But my heart is telling me I should just speak to him. He deserves to know.

But at what cost?

I can't lose him. He helps me grow as a person. He brings a light into my life that I've never known before. Losing him would be like losing half of my soul. I'd never survive.

All I've done is cry.

I have a life growing inside me. A life I'm scared I'll ruin. I'm twenty years old and still in school. The money I earn from the library barely covers essentials. I don't get any other money—apart from money I get from my father. My father, who is going to kill me when he finds out his only daughter is pregnant.

It's not like I can keep this from him forever. In no time, I'll have a bump that I can't cover or hide.

He's going to be so disappointed in me. I knew he wanted better for me and having a child this young, wasn't something he had in mind.

When did my life get so complicated?

A door in my flat bangs open. I hear the thud of it hitting the wall and sit up. I clutch the blanket to my heaving chest, my entire body shaking.

Two seconds later, my door flies open and I gasp, jumping in place as CJ rushes in.

He's still wearing the clothes I saw him in four days ago. His jaw has days of stubble from where he hasn't shaved, and his clothes are wrinkled. His looks awful and exhausted.

"CJ?" I call out, panicked something has happened to his mum.

He doesn't stop until he's on the bed next to me, pulling my head against his chest. His body is warm, like always, but the feel of his hands in my hair… I can feel that they're cold.

"Thank fucking Christ, you're okay. You're okay. You're okay. Thank you, God," he rants, rocking me back and forth.

I pull my hands from between us and try to push him away, but his hold tightens. "CJ?" I gasp out, struggling a little to breathe he's holding me that tight.

He pulls back, and my throat tightens as tears fall down his cheeks. *What on earth has happened for him to react like this?*

"I'm so sorry. I should be here and not locked away in my room. I thought I'd lost you."

I cup his cheeks, trying to get him to calm down so I can get some sense out of him. "CJ, what has gotten into you? Is your mum okay?"

He wipes his eyes, his Adam's apple bobbing. "Mum's fine. It's *you* I'm worried about. Alex called me a few minutes ago. He said your car has been outside the library for two nights and he can't get in touch with you."

"I—"

"I thought the killer got you, Allie. I thought you were taken because of me. I'm so fucking sorry for pushing you away. I'm just scared. I'm scared of losing you. For a split second, my life flashed before my eyes. I can't live without you—I can't. I need you. I've never loved anyone the way I love you. You were an unexpected treasure to my life, something I didn't think I ever wanted but now can't live without. You can't leave me. Ever."

"You need to explain, CJ. You're scaring me, and you aren't making sense. Why would you think the killer had taken me?"

He tucks my hair behind my ears, his eyes focusing on mine. "I know you asked Jordan to look into the killer."

I'm taken aback, startled. Jordan wasn't meant to tell him I told her. "What? Have you spoken to her?"

Had she told him about the pregnancy test?

"Shh, it's okay. I'm not mad that you told her. I'm a hacker, remember? I hacked her computer to get the files she had. When I saw what she was looking into, I put two and two together."

I sag against him, gazing up into his eyes. They look darker, not the chocolate colour they normally are. I hated keeping it from him, but it was the only way I could help at the time whilst still being able to give him space.

"So, you know about the connection we found—between you and the victims?"

He nods, his eyes dropping. "Yeah, I do." He runs his fingers through his hair. "That's why when Alex called, I panicked. I came running straight over here. Low and Cole tried saying something to me last night when they came in, but I ignored them. I was fucking stupid. I've been working around the clock trying to find this son-of-a-bitch. I'm so fucking sorry for pushing you away."

I shake my head, kissing him to ease his fears. "I understand. Just don't do that to me again, please. We're supposed to be partners. And I've missed you so much."

He starts to relax, sitting back to put some space between us. He looks at me, like, really looks at me, and I start to feel uncomfortable under his gaze. Can he tell?

"Cupcake? What's wrong? You look like you've been crying for days and had no sleep. Has something happened? Is your dad okay? God, I'm an arsehole. I've been selfish and not considered what you've been going through."

I flick my eyes over his shoulder, concentrating on my door. "My dad's fine. I'm fine. Stop fretting."

He inhales. "You're lying to me."

I glance at him, tears in my eyes. "I'm scared to tell you. I don't want you to leave me."

He sits back a little, his face turning a deathly shade of green as he swallows. "Did you cheat on me?"

Hurt, I glance at him sharply. "What, no. I'd never cheat on you. Ever. I thought you knew me better than that."

189

Guilt flashes across his face. "Then what's going on? Why do you look pale and scared?"

"I—I don't know how to tell you," I say, tears falling now.

He wipes them away with the pads of his thumbs. "Cupcake, you can tell me anything. You know that, right?"

I close my eyes, praying with my whole heart that I don't lose him. "I'm pregnant."

When he starts laughing, I open my eyes, puzzled. He calms, glancing at me. "Cupcake, I thought my life was over a few minutes ago when I thought the love of my life was dead. Now is the not the time to be joking."

I look down at my lap before staring back up at him. "CJ, I'm not joking," I whisper, then lean over to open my top drawer, and pass him the pregnancy stick.

He holds it, looking down at it with a mixture of emotions. It's hard to tell what he's thinking, so I sit, twiddling my fingers in my lap.

"Please say something," I plead, my voice hoarse.

"Please tell me I'm not holding piss in my hand right now?"

Before I can stop it, I laugh, and once I start, I can't stop. It gets worse when he drops it to the floor, his face filled with disgust as he wipes his hand on his leg.

Only CJ could make a serious matter funny.

I wipe my tears as my laughter slows into chuckles.

"You're really pregnant? With my baby?"

"No, with Jesus's baby. Of course, it's yours."

When he glances down at my stomach, his eyes light up so bright it brings a smile to my face. "We're having a baby?"

"I was hoping for an alien, but a baby is good," I tease, wiping his tears away now when he looks up.

He chuckles. "When did you find out?"

"Two days ago."

He frowns. "And you didn't tell me because I've been so distant?"

I nod, squeezing his hands. "I didn't want to add more to your plate. You're going through so much already."

"But nothing trumps our baby, Allie. I'm so fucking sorry. I should have been here for you. Is that why you were scared to tell me, because you didn't know how I'd react?"

I inhale, hoping he doesn't take offence to my reply. "Yes and no. I didn't know if you wanted a baby. We've not been together long and we're still in school. Then there's the whole mess we're going through right now—with the killer on the loose. I just kept thinking about how you reacted to his DNA being a part of you. I didn't know how you'd react."

I rub a hand over my stomach, looking down at my lap, feeling ashamed. I didn't want to throw his words back at him, but I can't lie to him. The worry was there. If we decide to go through with this, then I want him to accept him or her.

He places his hand over mine. "I don't care about any of that. You were right in what you said to me at Mum's. And our baby, it will be a part of us. They won't only be raised loved, but they were made from love. And I do—I love you, and I love our baby."

"You're not scared?" I ask, because I am. I'm so scared of what our future will hold.

"A little, I guess, but I knew we were always going to have kids someday."

I smile. "You did?"

He grins. "I did. Might not have been picturing it being now, but it just means they were ready to come earlier in our lives. But make no mistakes, Cupcake, we will be damn fucking good parents. I might be immature at times, but I'm far from stupid. This isn't a new gadget, or temporary. I understand it's for life, but I really do have faith we can do this. We have our parents—if your dad doesn't get arrested for trying to kill me—and we have our friends. We can still finish our courses and find the right jobs. We can get a house, whatever we need, because together, I believe we can do anything."

His words cause a sob to break free and I fall into his arms, wrapping my own around him. "I've been so scared. I think I needed you to tell me we could do it." I pull back, biting my bottom lip. "We're so young."

His lips pull into a smirk. "Yeah, but at least we won't be doing school runs when we're old and wrinkly."

I giggle, pushing his shoulder. "Are you sure about this? This is a huge decision to make. There's no going back once we've made it."

He shuffles forward as he pulls me closer, our knees touching on the bed. "Okay, let's put it this way: before you found out you were pregnant, where did you see us going as a couple?"

My heart melts and my cheeks heat. "Together, married, children and grandchildren."

He runs a finger down my cheek. "Exactly. So what if the timeline has been pushed forward. People younger than us do this every day and raise perfectly well-balanced individuals."

I laugh at his explanation. "You moaned at the young couple down the road from Cole's mum's because they didn't watch their kids properly."

He groans, ducking his head a little. "Let's forget about that tiny incident. Plus, those kids needed some manners knocked into them. Would it kill them to watch where they are riding their bikes and to speak politely? I swear, I thought that one little girl was going to kick me in the nuts."

"She was six," I remind him, giggling.

He rolls his eyes. "Not a prime example, I know. But we aren't them. We are going to raise our kids right. We're going to make them play in the garden, not in the middle of the road. We are going to love and adore them."

When he cups my cheek, I let my head fall to the side, grateful for his touch. "I love you, CJ. I love you so much."

"I love you too. Now scoot over, I'm knackered, and I've missed my cupcake."

I move over until there's room for him to get in and cuddle up to his shoulder. I start running my finger up and down his chest.

"Things have been so crazy around here. This news hasn't exactly come at a good time."

He plays with a strand of my hair, twirling it through his fingers. "No, but is any time a good time? We'll get through this. I promise."

"I was so scared you were going to leave me," I whisper, feeling my throat close up.

He squeezes me tighter against his chest. "I'd never leave you." He pauses when he realises he did kind of leave me. "For long anyway. I just had to get my head out of my arse. I'm so sorry you had to deal with this on your own."

"I can't believe we're going to be parents," I murmur, a smile spreading across my face.

"I hope we have a girl who looks just like you," he says, and I can hear the smile in his voice.

"Nope. I want a little boy like you. I want him to have your eyes, your skin tone, and your heart."

"He does sound perfect. Maybe a boy would be better."

I giggle, poking his belly. He laughs, pulling away a little.

"That's mean."

"I'm sorry. But seriously, I'd be in jail by the time I'm what... thirty-seven, because I've beaten her boyfriend to death."

I shove my face in his chest, laughing. His chest vibrates under me with his own laughter.

"I'm glad you're here," I tell him after a moment, looking up at him.

He glances down at me, smiling. "I shouldn't have been anywhere else. I love you."

"I love you too."

"Are you sure you should be working?" CJ asks, looking around the busy library.

I wrap my arms around his neck, smiling at his concerned expression. I feel fine. It's been two days since we found out and went to the doctors to get it confirmed. We have an appointment with the midwife booked for a week's time and will go from there. My morning sickness is still present, but if I stay away from the scent of food, I'll be fine.

"I'm fine. After my shift's over we can go home and relax, get ready for tomorrow. Tomorrow, we'll meet our parents and Willow's mum for dinner, tell them the good news, then meet everyone else at home and fill them in. Everything will be fine."

He looks doubtful. "What about the all the heavy lifting? Maybe I should stay and help out."

I raise my eyebrows at that. "We agreed last night that we were to act like nothing is different and now you want to co-work with me? People, including my boss, will ask questions. Stop worrying, CJ. And you have classes until three. You can't blow off another day. You graduate this year; you don't want to risk jeopardising that."

He still doesn't look convinced. "I just don't feel right leaving you. I want to keep you safe."

Ah, so that's what this is about. I rub his cheek, stepping further into his embrace. "I'm sorry you had a scare the other day, but as you can see, I'm fine. I'm surrounded by people, and you'll be here when I'm finished."

He inhales, his shoulders sagging. "Okay—but keep your phone on you. If you need me, ring me. Don't worry about me being in class."

"Okay," I agree.

His squeezes my hips, a smirk tugging at his lips. "Are you scared about telling the parents tomorrow?"

I relax. "Petrified," I admit. "You?" I've been putting on a brave face because he seemed so cool and collected.

But I'm terrified of my dad's reaction. It's not going to be a good one, that's for sure. When we rang them yesterday, I just told Dad I wanted him to meet Milly and for Milly to meet him and Willow's mum. He seemed pleased, but it won't last long when I tell him the news.

We didn't want to tell Willow or Cole until we had told our parents. They've been badgering us to tell them what has been going on, but we've managed to get away with vague answers.

"Honestly, I was fine until I woke up this morning. Your dad killed me in my dreams, Allie."

"My dad won't hurt you," I tell him, laughing a little.

He raises an eyebrow. "Are you serious? He's going to neuter me.

Why do you think I picked a public place to tell them rather than having dinner at my mum's house? I want witnesses. Lots of them. And I'm hoping one of them will help in my time of need."

I giggle, shaking my head at him. "You're being a drama bear, as usual. Dad said he'll be here around five. I finish at four tomorrow, so do you want me to meet you back at the flat or are you meeting me?"

He gives me a dry look. "I'll meet you after class. It's with Mr. Flint, right?"

I nod, biting my bottom lip. I still haven't told him about Mr. Flint, and before, I did it because I felt like I was being paranoid. Now, I feel like I'm lying to him.

At the moment, I want to focus on telling our parents and our friends. After, I'll find the time to tell him.

He leans down, kissing me and pulling me closer. "I love you," he whispers against my lips when he pulls back.

"I love you too."

"I'll be back after my class has finished. Don't leave without me, unless you have to. But if you do, ring me."

I shake my head at his antics. "I will. Now shoo. I've got work to do."

He thumbs my chin, kissing me, before leaving. I watch him as he walks to the door. He turns, winking at me.

"Love you, my beautiful cupcake," he shouts. I duck my head, blushing when people turn to stare. A few girls ooh and ahh, while the lads giggle, cheering him on.

I shake my head at him and blow him a kiss.

Men.

I'm nearly at the end of my shift and I feel worn out and tired. It's been a long day. It feels like everyone who's anyone has wanted to check out a book, or needed help finding one.

Tina, one of the library supervisors, walks up to me, looking at her watch. "Allie, you've got just over an hour left of your shift, right?"

"Hi, Tina, and yes. Why?"

"Can you grab the boxes of books we just got in and start adding them into the system? I need to pop out for a minute and there's only you and Alex here. He's still putting away the books from the return cart."

Biting my bottom lip, I nod. She turns and leaves, leaving me kicking myself.

CJ told me under no circumstances were I to lift anything heavy.

Now I can't avoid it. Those boxes look heavy, and there's more than one.

Shit.

I head over to the counter, grateful when I find the room has quietened down and a lot of students have left.

I look around, trying to spot Alex, and find him near the geometry section. He glances up from the book he's stamping, a wide smile spreading across his face.

"Hey, you okay? It's been pretty busy in here today, huh?"

I force a laugh, shifting nervously on my feet. "It has. Um, Alex, can I ask a huge favour?"

He looks up at the ceiling, groaning. "Please don't ask me to take an online quiz again. I don't need to know who my celebrity lookalike is."

I grin at that. Good times. "I still can't believe it came up as Harry Potter."

He looks at me sourly. "Not all of us can be Selena Gomez."

"I think I look more like Jade from Little Mix. Hell, we even have the same fashion style."

He eyes me up and down, realisation dawning on his face. "Oh, my God, you actually do. In that T-shirt and skirt, you'd only need to dye your hair purple and you'd be twins."

I roll my eyes. "I'm not dying my hair purple," I tell him, running my hand down my white T-shirt. On it, it says, Tinkerbell. I'm wearing it with my favourite purple skirt and white tennis shoes that have a Mini Mouse ears keyring attached to the shoelace. It's one of my favourite outfits.

"Whatever," he says, chuckling. "So, what did you want to ask me?"

"Can you help me with the new books we have in the back room, please?"

He stops putting the books on the shelf and turns to me. "I thought Tina asked you to do it. I still have to get these put away. My shift ends in twenty minutes."

I feel guilty for asking, but I'm not willing to risk my baby's life, and I know Alex will understand and help once I tell him.

I grab his hand and pull him into the aisle of books, heading towards the English books before stopping. I look around to make sure no one is watching, before facing him.

"I need you to help me because I can't lift those boxes."

He grins. "You brought me over here to tell me you're weak?"

I smack his arm lightly. "No. I've dragged you over here because..."

"Because?"

I shake my head before straightening, taking a deep breath. "You can't tell anyone what I'm about to tell you. I want to tell my dad first. Okay?"

He rolls his eyes. "Are you going to tell me you're pregnant?"

When he laughs, I wince, looking away. "Yes."

He stops laughing, grabbing my arms. "What? Are you serious? Does CJ know? What did he say? Are you keeping it?"

"Woah, woah, woah, woah. Calm down with the questions. Yes, I'm serious, yes CJ knows, and we're both happy about it now. We're keeping him or her. And don't call my baby an it."

"Well I couldn't say they or them, it didn't bloody sound right." He removes his glasses, running a hand across his face, looking deep in thought. He turns, pacing, before stopping in front of me, putting his glasses back on. "Wow. Didn't see this coming. Are you sure this is what you want? CJ hasn't pressured you into this? You're really young, Allie. This is a long-term commitment."

Although I knew people would have doubts, it hurts hearing it. I wasn't expecting congratulations and a party, but a little faith wouldn't have hurt.

"We've spoken about it thoroughly. We know this isn't going to be easy, but we're happy."

"You're really going to have a baby?" he asks, just as a face appears around the end of the shelves we're standing by.

I shrink back when Mr. Flint grins, a sparkle in his eye I don't like. "Well, well, well. Pregnant. Didn't think you were the type," he sneers, eyeing me up and down, making me feel guilty. "You do realise you won't be able to finish school with a new baby, Miss Davis."

I go solid at his words and the sneer in his voice. "Mr. Flint, this was a private conversation."

He looks around the shelves of books, smiling. "Not very private in a public library."

Alex looks between us, a frown marring his face. "Come on, Allie, let's get those books finished."

"I'll see you tomorrow, Miss Davis."

I glance over my shoulder and shudder when I find him leaning against the shelves, his finger tapping his chin like he's mulling over something. I don't like it. Not one single bit.

When we're out of hearing range, Alex leans in and whispers. "That guy really needs to get his arse fired. He shouldn't speak to you like that. And I'll get the books. You sit down and start adding them into the computer. I'll tell Tina I'll finish returns tomorrow morning when I come in."

I nod, still feeling a sense of foreboding. "Thank you, Alex. And please, don't tell anyone what I told you."

"I won't. I promise. Is this why you asked us to meet up tomorrow after your dad leaves?"

"Yes. We only want to tell close friends and our parents."

He rubs my arm. "Well, I promise to act surprised tomorrow," he tells me, before heading to the back room.

I sit down at the computer, and it's only when my phone beeps with a message that I realise Alex didn't congratulate me.

Is this how my other friends will react?

Chapter 19

I'm so nervous, I'm sweating profusely. I've got five minutes left of class before I have to go home and get ready to meet my father and CJ's mum. CJ and I have gone over what we're going to say, and how we're going to say it, but I still can't help but keep going over it. We didn't factor in nerves. We didn't factor in one or both of our parents cancelling or unloading something on us. It's not like we can give them the news if something else is going on.

Right?

I glance up from my work and lock eyes with Mr. Flint, who keeps his expression blank, like he has done most of the lesson. He's kept his distance the entire two hours I've been here, and I don't know whether to be happy about it or not. Because if I'm honest, it's making me kind of uncomfortable. I feel like he's up to something, but I can't figure out what.

I grab my bottle of water, not looking away from him, and take a swig. He smirks just as I take a swig, and I begin to choke.

Please no, not now.

The water drops from my hands, falling to the floor and spilling everywhere. My stomach rolls and I begin to heave from the water going down the wrong hole.

A hand lightly taps me on the back, causing me to jump. When I look up through watery eyes, I find Mr. Flint standing next to me, holding a new bottle of water.

"Here, take this. I don't want you sick in my class," he whispers.

A shiver runs down my spine at the disgusted look he gives me, but needing the water since mine is gone, I take it.

"Thank you," I croak out, opening it. I take a swig, not looking at him this time. Something about him doesn't add up. It never has.

He doesn't say anything, just nods and walks back to the front of the class, where his desk is located. He sits on the edge, clapping his hands together to get everyone's attention.

"If everyone wants to finish what they're doing, you can leave a few minutes early."

Not one to look a gift horse in the mouth, I grab my things, leaving the half bottle of water on the table.

CJ is waiting for me outside the doors. I smile, walking up to him. He envelops me in a hug.

"How was class?" he asks.

I shrug. "Boring."

"You ready for tonight?"

"Are you sure we shouldn't wait a little longer?"

He chuckles, pulling away to take my hand. We start walking towards the exit.

"We've got this, Cupcake. They're going to find out sometime, might as well be from us."

I sigh because I hate it when he's right. "Okay, but I've changed my mind; you can tell the parents."

He stops short, but I let go of his hand and keep walking, smiling to myself.

"Cupcake, you can't be serious," he yells after me.

I shrug and swing around to face him, walking backwards. "Dead serious."

I thought taking the pregnancy test was the scary part. I was so fucking wrong. It's not even close.

Telling your parent that their twenty-year-old daughter is pregnant is.

I feel like I can hardly breathe. I've got cramps from anxiety and feel like I could throw up any second, and if we want this to go as planned, throwing up at the table isn't going to help.

Dad walks into the fairly quiet restaurant we chose—hoping it will deter them from causing a scene.

"Dad." I smile, walking around the table to hug him. He hugs me back, pulling me in close.

"Hi, darlin'. You okay?"

"Yes," I lie, then turn to Melanie. She looks at me curiously before her eyes widen. I shake my head, knowing she has figured it out. She opens her mouth, looking to my father then back to me. Before she can say anything, I hug her. "Please don't say anything. We're going to tell them," I whisper.

When I pull back, she nods, smiling, but it's small. I can't tell what she's thinking.

"Hi, Mr. Davis," CJ greets, shaking my dad's hand.

"Hey, son, how's rugby going? Allie said you had a game a few weeks ago. I'm sorry I couldn't come down to watch."

CJ waves him off. "It's fine. You can come to the next one," he tells him. "I want you to meet my mum, Milly. Mum, this is Sam, Allie's dad, and Melanie, Willow's mum."

My dad steps forward, shaking Milly's hand. "It's lovely to meet you. You've got a fine son. I couldn't have picked better for my daughter."

She beams, looking proudly up at her son as she leans into him. "He is pretty incredible. And you have a beautiful daughter. CJ really needed someone like her in his life. I couldn't have wished better for him."

CJ's chest puffs out, ignoring his mum's comment. "I really am perfect."

I giggle, slapping his chest, and lean my head on his shoulder. "Stop, your head won't fit through the restaurant door when we leave."

He pouts, looking offended, before turning to Melanie. "Mel, a pleasure as always. Seems you've got yourself a catch," he says, wiggling his eyebrows.

I sigh. I can't take him anywhere.

She laughs, shaking her head. She's actually immune to his charms. Doesn't mean she still wouldn't do anything he asks. He's hard to say no to.

"CJ, lovely as ever," she says, before turning to Milly. "It's lovely to meet you. Willow has sung your praises. I want to take a moment to say how grateful I am to you for being there for my girl. You've helped her tremendously. Thank you."

Melanie steps forward, hugging Milly. Milly looks shocked but soon returns the gesture.

"Your daughter is strong. From what she's told me about you, she gets it from you."

When Melanie pulls back, she has tears in her eyes. "Yes, but since she's been speaking to you, I've heard and seen a spark in my daughter's life."

"I'm glad," Milly says, then gestures to the table. "Shall we order drinks?"

"I hope you haven't waited long," Dad asks. He kisses my temple before taking a seat next to Melanie.

"No, we've not long got here," I tell him, sitting next to CJ.

I take his hand under the table and squeeze. When we planned what to say, we decided to tell them before we eat. We—I mean, *I*, felt that waiting until we had finished would be excruciating.

It's now or never.

I kick CJ's leg under the table, glancing at him. Sweat pours down the side of his face, and his Adam's apple bobs.

I kick him again. He clears his throat, looking up from the table and facing our parents.

"Okay, so we had a reason for bringing you together this evening. First, we want you guys to know we have thought about this. We've gone over everything thoroughly." He pauses, taking a swig of water that had already been placed on our table, before looking at my dad. "Sir, I didn't take advantage of your daughter or force her into anything. I promise. This is a decision we made together. I need you to know that."

That was not in our plan of action. I glare at CJ, pinching his leg under the table.

"What's going on? You didn't get married, did you? Because you're young, Allie," Dad says, looking between us with a mixture of confusion and worry. He scrubs his jaw, looking to Melanie for answers. She looks ahead, and I feel bad for putting this on her. But I couldn't well ask her to stay home because there might be a family drama. She's part of our family now.

"CJ, honey, what is going on?" Milly asks, frowning.

"It wasn't planned," he says, and just like that, my dad turns a deathly shade of grey.

"I'm pregnant," I blurt out, sitting back and preparing myself for the outburst.

No one says anything. It's so silent, you could hear crickets. My body is tense, watching my dad's face morph from shock to worry.

"Allie, you're twenty years old. You aren't ready to have a baby. You haven't even finished school."

"Dad, women younger than me have kids all the time. We haven't taken this decision lightly. We know what's at stake."

He bangs his fist on the table. "No, Allie, I don't think you do. You aren't prepared at all. It's endless nights of feeding and changing nappies."

"Dad," I say quietly, stopping him.

"He's right. Have you two really thought this through? It's not just feeding and changing nappies. This is a big responsibility. I couldn't even leave the house to get a loaf of bread without having to pack everything but the kitchen sink. And they aren't babies forever. They grow. You have to think about finding a place to live, safeguarding your home, then stairgates, a nursery, school, funding uniforms. You two haven't seen the world yet. CJ, you've always wanted to experience South Africa. You can't do that with a baby."

My eyes water, and CJ, sensing my distress, pulls me against his chest before facing our parents. "Your listing off reasons why it's hard to have children, but you forget, we're your children. Yet, here we are. You did it. I know we're young, but we can do this. We don't see not being able to do things like go out, go on holidays, or pop to the shop whenever, as our life being over. We understand changes are going to be made, but we're ready for them. More than ready." He takes in a deep breath. "We didn't come here today to ask for your permission. We came here to ask for your support."

CJ runs a hand through my hair. His words mean everything to me, and the fact he stood up for us like that, in front of our parents, a mum who he loves and respects, is humbling.

His mum is first to clear her throat, her eyes filled with tears as she reaches out to squeeze CJ's free hand on top of the table. "I'll always support you. I just wanted to make sure you'd thought this through. Do I wish you'd waited until you were older? Yes. But if now is when it is meant to be, then so be it. I'll be here for whatever you need."

"Thanks, Mum."

I glance at my dad, noticing his eyes are watery too. I've never seen him cry, not once, and seeing him now hurts my chest.

"Dad?"

He shakes his head, his gaze focusing on me. "I'll support your decision, if this is really what you want. But it's going to take some time to get used to, sweetie. You had so much to experience before settling down like this."

"I'm happy, Dad. Really happy. I'm scared of what our future will hold now, but I know I will love our baby with my whole heart. I already love them and I've never even met them. I want this, Dad. I'm ready—well, as ready as a newbie mum can be. I just don't want you to hate me," I tell him, feeling my throat close on the last bit.

He looks like he's been slapped. He jumps from his chair and walks around to my side, kneeling on the floor and taking my hands in his.

"I could never hate you," he chokes out, a lone tear falling down his cheek. "I'll stand by you, Allie, I will. You're going to have a child now, my darlin' girl, so you'll soon understand my fears. You just want what is best for your children." He takes a deep breath. "I've not been the best father when it comes to you. I'll always regret and hate myself for that. But I promise, I will be a better granddad."

"Not grandpa?" CJ asks, leaning around me. Dad glares over my shoulder. "Too soon?"

I inwardly groan.

"You got my daughter pregnant. It will always be soon," Dad growls, before looking at me, his face softening.

"My bad," CJ whispers.

Dad gets up, leaning down to kiss my forehead before moving to take a seat.

"Does Willow know?" Melanie asks, taking my dad's hand when he sits back down.

I shake my head. "No. We wanted to tell you before anyone else. It's still early, so we're only going to tell our close friends. They'll know something is up before long, so it's easier if they know now."

"We're actually going to tell them after we leave here."

"She'll be thrilled for you. I just hope she doesn't get any ideas," she tells us, chuckling.

I laugh. "She won't. She's already got her life mapped out. Babies aren't happening until she's twenty-six."

Melanie relaxes. "Well thank goodness. I'll start saving now."

We all laugh at her expression, the table going from tense to relaxed. I'm grateful and mouth 'thank you' to her.

"Well, after that, I need a beer," CJ says, looking around for the waitress.

"You need a beer? I need a whiskey," Dad states, waving down the waitress in question.

After all that worrying, all that anxiety, it was mostly for nothing. The smile on my face has my cheeks hurting.

I don't think there has been a time in my life when I've been so blissfully happy, and that's saying something as CJ makes me extremely happy.

CJ glances down at me, winking. "I love you."

I relax into him. "Love you too."

My steps feel lighter after our visit with the parents. I'd been worked up for days over nothing. My dad still had his concerns over his daughter being pregnant, but in time, I think he will be overcome with joy and delight at the idea of becoming a granddad.

Milly seemed to have forgotten her earlier reservations and was already talking about what the baby will need. Melanie soon joined in, leaving me, Dad, and CJ pale and lost. We knew we'd have to get a lot of stuff—our baby will need a lot—but they were listing off things I'd never even heard of.

We left them talking over drinks not long after. We're grateful they gave us the chance to speak to our friends first. I know Melanie is dying to see her daughter, but she promised she was okay and would pop round in the morning.

It's toasty warm when we step inside our flat. I'm grateful for the girls thinking ahead because it's freezing outside, and when we don't have the heating on, our flat is just as bad, if not worse.

I'm surprised to find everyone here and waiting for us. We still have half an hour to go before we told them to be here.

"Hey, guys, you're early," I greet, smiling at everyone.

CJ, a little more than tipsy, flops down into the armchair.

Cole turns to his friend, an eyebrow arched. "You okay, mate?"

CJ looks up, a dopey smile on his face. "All is good in the world. I'm not dead, am I?"

Not understanding, Cole shakes his head, his forehead scrunched up. I duck my head to hide my smile. "Should you be?"

CJ nods dramatically. "Yes, yes I should. Damn dreams."

"Well, okay then," Cole mutters at him before looking at me. "Is there a reason we're all here? Does it have something to do with meeting your parents?"

"Yeah, were they trying to talk you into going home? I know it's bad here, but we have school," Willow adds.

I raise my hand in the air, stopping them. "No, we brought you here because we have something to tell you."

"Have you figured out who the killer is?" Jordan adds.

My smile falls, and I shake my head. "No. It's nothing about that."

CJ taps the back of my leg and I sit down on the arm of the sofa. "We called to share something good with you," he tells them.

"This can't be good," Cole mutters, loud enough for us all to hear. Everyone laughs, turning from Cole to us.

"I'm pregnant," I blurt out.

Just like with our parents, the room falls silent. Alex is the first to speak, standing from his place in the corner next to Becca. "Congratulations. I'm happy for you both."

I give him a soft smile, glad he acted surprised for us. "Thank you."

When I glance at Willow, she has tears in her eyes, her hands covering her mouth. She steps forward, but stops, shaking her head.

"Really?" Cole asks, looking sceptical.

I laugh. "Yes, I'm pregnant. A doctor confirmed it and everything."

Coming unstuck, Willow steps forward again so she's stood in front of me. "I'm going to be an auntie?"

I stand up and nod. "Yes, and I'm going to be a mum."

She rushes into me, wrapping her arms around my neck. "I'm so happy. I'm happy for the both of you," she tells me, then pulls back, keeping my hands in hers. "How are you feeling? How far along are you? Are you scared?"

I giggle at her rambling. "I'm feeling great—better than ever. We're not sure how far along I am yet, but I must be around four weeks. And I'm petrified, but I know we can do this."

She beams at me. "Hell yes, you can. Not sure about him, though," she says, her eyes turning down to CJ. I laugh when I find him eating their leftover Chinese.

Next, Jordan steps forward, hugging me. "Congratulations. And you can put me down for babysitting duty."

"Thank you," I reply, smiling at her.

Rosie and Becca step forward next. "Us too. We used to babysit the kids where we lived, so we're good with them," Rosie tells us.

"Well, I'm glad you two live here now. We've still got a lot to learn, so any advice will be appreciated."

"If anyone can do it, you can, Allie," Becca says gently. "A baby... I can't believe we'll have a baby in the fold in less than a year's time."

I smile at that. "I know. It still doesn't feel real. But I am happy."

"We should celebrate," Cole says.

I look over the girls' shoulders to find him standing next to CJ, who has now gotten up and is moving back from his friend's embrace.

Aw, they were hugging it out.

Willow's head pops up from her phone. "Allie can't drink. She also can't have caffeine, so no giving her fizzy pop anymore, either."

I freeze in place, glancing at my best friend in horror. "No! That can't be right. Check it again," I demand.

She chuckles, waving her phone in the air. "It says it all on here. There's a lot of stuff you can't touch, so it's just water for you."

CJ turns pale, his head snapping to me. "Wait! Didn't you have fizzy pop at the restaurant?"

I roll my eyes. "No. I actually had an orange juice."

He relaxes, leaning against Cole. "Thank fuck. I'm over the limit to drive you to the hospital."

Cole shoves his shoulder. "There are more than one of us in the room that have a driving licence, ya know."

"We'll go get some drinks for everyone," Rosie says, trying to hide her giggle.

"Yeah, but she's my responsibility," CJ argues, facing his friend.

"I'll help," Alex says somewhere close, sounding uncomfortable.

Cole clips him around the ear. "And we're family now, and family helps family. She's carrying my baby niece or nephew in there."

A lopsided smirk tugs at CJ's lips. "Oh yeah. Does that mean you'll share nappy duties with me?"

Cole rears back in disgust, and I laugh at his expression. "Um, no. I had enough of my sisters', thank you."

Someone hands me a water as I watch the two argue back and forth. I'm about to say thank you, but Willow steps up beside me so we're both watching the two in amusement.

"I can't believe you're going to be a mum," Willow whispers, resting her head on my shoulder.

I rest my head against hers, and smile. "Me neither. I'm so excited though."

She takes my hand, squeezing it in support. "You aren't alone. He may come across as a goof, but underneath all of that is someone who would walk through fire for the ones he loves. And the way he looks at you… it's like you hung the moon and invented life. He'd do anything for you, and for your baby. That little boy or girl doesn't realise how lucky they are to have parents like you two."

I lift my head, turning to face my friend with a watery smile. "You're an amazing friend, Low. I'm so glad I have you in my life. And even though you'll be an auntie to our child, I want you to be their godmother, too."

"Really?" she asks, glancing at me in awe and shock.

I giggle, wiping under my eyes. "Yes. I couldn't ask for anyone else to look after my baby."

She envelops me in a hug, shaking me from side to side. "You've made me the happiest girl alive."

I groan, stepping back. "And I've still got an upset stomach," I tell her, then take a large gulp of my water.

She winces. "Sorry."

"Hey, I thought *I* made you the happiest girl alive?" Cole says. I jump, not realising he and CJ had stopped arguing and were watching us.

She bats her eyelids at him. "You do. You do."

He shakes his head, grinning at her before pulling her into his arms. CJ does the same with me before facing the room.

"How about we order from that new dessert place that opened last week—they deliver—and watch a movie or something."

"Not zombies," Cole adds, giving everyone in the room a warning look.

I lick my lips. "Sounds like a plan. Do you have a menu?"

He rolls his eyes at me. "Do I have a menu," he scoffs, before pulling out his phone. "I downloaded the app the day it opened."

I giggle, shaking my head at him. But I wouldn't have him any other way. Like Willow said, he might act like a goofball the majority of the time, but underneath all that is one of the most organised and put together men I know. His attitude towards enjoying life is what makes me love him. His characteristics is what made him stand out from the rest of the boys and made me take notice.

And now I get to spend the rest of my life with him.

Things couldn't be more perfect.

Chapter 20

I'm startled awake by a sharp pain in my stomach and close my eyes in a grimace. I clutch my belly, sweat pouring down my face, skin clammy. The instant a new wave of pain flows through my stomach, I know something is wrong and begin to cry out.

My body is being tortured from the inside with no end or limit. It's excruciating.

I shake CJ, who is snoring loudly, choking on air as I try to breathe through it. "CJ, wake up. Something's wrong," I beg, my voice pleading and laced with pain.

He shoots up from bed, drowsily looking around the room for some kind of intrusion. "What? What's wrong?"

I cry out, curling into a ball on my side as pain shoots through my lower back and stomach. It's getting worse; I can barely breathe through it.

"Fuck," he says, and I feel his body shaking as he quickly jumps from the bed and flicks the lamp on. "We need to get you to the hospital, Cupcake."

I nod, but double over again when I try to turn in his direction. I fall helplessly to the side when the pain gets too much to bear. "CJ, it hurts so badly," I cry.

"Okay, it's okay. I've got this," he tells me and pulls back the blanket. He hisses through his teeth. I glance up at him, panting, and notice him standing there, frozen in place, his eyes no longer carrying their usual warmth. His face has turned a greyish colour, looking clammy. I glance down to find what has him looking so broken, and when my eyes land on the bed, I begin to sob.

No!

I didn't even feel it.

I'm lying in a dark patch of my own blood. I stare at it, crying helplessly as CJ runs around the room, throwing some clothes on.

"Hi, I need an ambulance," he says, before rattling off our address.

"My girlfriend—she's bleeding really bad. She's around four weeks pregnant. Yes. Okay, yes. Please hurry. She's in so much pain."

I glance up at CJ when he steps towards me. He pulls off the stained top I pinched off him last night and puts a new one on.

"Do you want me to change your knickers before the paramedics arrive?" he asks softly. Tears cloud his eyes, his body trembling as he looks down at me with so much vulnerability.

"Everything will be fine. Everything's fine. Women bleed during pregnancy. It's common," I tell him, hoping the words hold truth.

I can't lose my baby.

He nods, but deep down I know he's only doing it for my benefit. "I'm going to get Cole and Willow, so they can meet us at the hospital."

I clutch his hand, crying out as more pain erupts through my stomach. "Don't leave me. Please don't leave me."

He grabs my hand, running his other through my hair. "Never," he declares, and I feel a tear fall to my cheek. He kisses my forehead before pulling back. "I'm just going to the bedroom door. I'll shout and wake the girls up." I nod and pant through the pain, letting his hand go. "Rosie, Becca, I need you," he yells, and I can hear his voice breaking.

Seconds later the door down the hall opens and I hear Becca's voice.

"What's going on? Is everything okay?"

I don't hear CJ's response but seconds later, he's stepping back into the room, sitting by my side and taking my hand.

I try to find reasons as to why I'm in unbearable pain, why I feel like my insides are on fire, because the truth isn't something I want to accept.

Why is this happening to me? It's not fair or right. It feels like I was given a puzzle, only to have pieces missing. Why hand me such a beautiful gift, then take it away like this, so cruelly?

It's not fair.

The door, which was only shut to, opens suddenly. Willow rushes in wearing one of Cole's T-shirts that reaches her knees, with a pair of leggings. She's next to me and CJ in seconds, tears already falling down her face.

"I'm so sorry, Allie. I'm so sorry."

I shake my head at her. It's small, but it's all I can manage. "Everything's fine."

She glances up at CJ, and they share a look. I turn away. I can't bear to see the pity on her face.

"The paramedics are here," Cole whispers.

"Make it stop," I cry, clinging to CJ's hand.

CJ runs his hand over my head, watching the door for the paramedics. It's not long before they're filing into the room.

It's a blur of activity as CJ lifts me onto a gurney and the paramedics load me into the ambulance.

The whole way to the hospital I concentrate on the sound of the sirens and the flashes of blue lights. I try to ignore the pain, feeling so lost and confused the whole way there.

I'm sorry, you've lost your baby.

You've lost your baby.

Those are the words that have been repeating in my head ever since the doctors announced what I already knew but didn't want to believe.

My baby is gone.

Just gone.

There isn't a body, a foetus… Just gone.

I don't even know if our baby was a boy or a girl. It doesn't seem right that they don't have a name, something for me to call them.

"Cupcake, your dad's here with my mum," CJ croaks out, his eyes red and watery. "Do you want me to let them in, or would you like more time alone?"

I asked for Willow and Cole to stay outside. I couldn't bear to watch them grieve when I couldn't make sense of why this had happened to me.

Not seven hours ago, I was fine. We had a night of fun with our friends and were happy. We had planned for our future. We went to bed smiling, excited for what the next nine months would bring us and so on.

We were happy.

Now, we're torn apart, too lost in our grief to even think about tomorrow.

"Let them in. My dad will kick off if he doesn't get to see if I'm okay," I tell him softly.

He cups my cheek. "I think your dad will understand if you need more time."

My eyes water. I didn't think I had any more tears left, I've cried so much. "It's fine. Tell Willow and Cole they can come in after. They need to go home and rest."

Worry lines mar his forehead. "Okay, I won't be long. They're just in the hall."

He leaves the room quietly—he's done everything quietly, too scared to make a sound. I might not want to see anyone right now, but CJ needs support. I've got him here, but he doesn't have anyone. Watching him break is something I never want to see again.

My dad and Milly come walking in. They force a smile, moving to either side of my bed. CJ stays at the bottom, his hand resting on my blanket, over my feet.

"Are you okay, sweetie?"

I look up to my dad, and the sadness and grief in his eyes undoes me once again, and I burst into tears.

"I lost our baby, Dad. My baby."

"I know, darlin'. I know. It might not seem like it right now, but it will get better. I promise."

"What did I do wrong?" I ask, my voice tortured.

Milly places her hand over my bicep, mindful of all the tubes and wires.

"You did nothing, sweetheart. Nothing whatsoever. It's a tragic thing, but this happens. No one knows why or how, but it does."

My dad moves aside to let CJ stand next to me. I watch him pinch the bridge of his nose to stop himself from crying.

I wipe my tears, blinking up at CJ. It's the first time I've really spoken about it. A part of me was still in denial.

"How can I miss someone I never even got to meet, so much?" I ask him, my throat raw.

Tears fall from CJ's eyes as he takes my hand in his. "Because they were a part of you and me. Because you have a huge heart. We will get through this, Allie. She or he may never have taken a breath, but they will never be forgotten. They will always be in our hearts."

"They don't even have a name, CJ," I sob out, clutching my chest. "We didn't get to see their face, hear them laugh, or hear them cry. We don't even know if they were a boy or a girl."

"Shh, the doctor said to stay calm, it's not good for your blood pressure."

I still cry, clutching at my chest, over my heart, where it hurts. "We lost our baby."

He nods, a flood of tears falling freely down his cheeks. He doesn't even bother to hide them as he holds my hand tighter. "We did, and we could have lost you." He pauses, running a hand over his tired, worn face. When he looks at me again, the sadness in his eyes is overwhelming. He looks tormented and devastated. "How about we pick a name suitable for a girl or a boy. We can have a stone put in next my great-grandparent's graves. That way, we have a place to visit, to remember them by."

The idea makes me love him more. For him to give us a place to visit, to grieve even though there isn't a body, means everything to me.

"It's a great idea. I'll call first thing tomorrow," his mum says softly, stroking my hair.

"What time is it?" I croak out.

"It's five in the morning, darlin'," Dad tells me, rubbing my shin.

The door to my room opens and the doctor who examined me earlier steps inside. The expression on his face is unreadable, but the last time we saw him, he said he'd have another doctor check on me later.

Something is wrong.

I share a worried and concerned look with CJ but face the man standing at the end of my bed, his hands resting on the bars.

"We have the results from your bloodwork. Can we have a minute to talk privately?" he asks.

My eye flick through everyone in the room, before facing him and shaking my head. "These are our parents; they can stay."

"As you wish," he says gently, before inhaling deeply and lifting the chart from under his arm. "As you know we ran some tests earlier as procedure. We found large amounts of methotrexate, also known as amethopterin, and misoprostol in your system."

I'm genuinely confused, and I'm not the only one as CJ gives him a puzzled look. "What's that?" CJ asks, rubbing his thumb over the palm of my hand.

I notice the doctor grimace, before he recovers. "Methotrexate taken on its own isn't considerably dangerous. However, taken with misoprostol... it causes miscarriage. It's what doctors use to induce abortion."

"What?" I breathe out, feeling faint. "How? I've not taken any tablets. I didn't kill my baby!"

"How would someone even get their hands on this stuff if it's used for abortion?" Milly asks, a hard tone in her voice.

"Misoprostol is also used for the prevention of gastric ulcers, and methotrexate is common. It's a chemotology agent and immune system suppressant. Sadly, I can't tell you how you digested it, only that it's in your system."

"Somebody had to have given this to me. We only told our friends and parents last night." I gasp, turning to CJ in horror. "Oh, my God."

"What, Cupcake?" he asks, sitting forward in his chair.

I struggle to breathe, and the monitors next to me start going crazy. The doctor rushes over, sitting me forward. "Breathe in and out, nice big, deep breaths. You're having a panic attack."

I breath in and out like he ordered, my head bent but turned to CJ.

"Mr. Flint. Knew," I pant out, closing my eyes tight.

I breathe, trying to calm myself. One, two, three, in and out.

"You aren't making sense, Cupcake."

I sit up, still panting as I face him. Tears fall, and I can barely see through them as I tell him, "When I was at the library the other night, Tina asked me to unload the new textbooks from the back. I knew you didn't want me lifting anything heavy, so I had to ask Alex to help —I had to tell him about the baby. Mr. Flint overheard us."

But he didn't give me anything that day.

My eyes shoot open and I turn to the doctor. "My teacher! He gave me a bottle of water yesterday. Could they have been in that?"

He eyebrows draw together, but he nods slowly. "Yes, I suppose."

"Why would Mr. Flint want to kill our baby?" CJ asks, and me keeping secrets from him has finally caught up to me.

I turn to the doctor, feeling numb. This is all my fault. "Can we have a minute?"

He nods. "If you need anything, press the button next you and a nurse will be right in. Again, I'm sorry for your loss."

Once he's gone, the room is quiet, until Milly speaks up. "Would you like us to give you some privacy?"

"I'm not going anywhere," Dad grits out. "I want to know why this sick son of a bitch killed my grandbaby."

I wipe my tears, turning to CJ. I can barely look at him. "Mr. Flint creeps me out. He's touchy-feely with me, always leaning in too close, touching my leg and making me uncomfortable," I blurt out. When CJ shoots out of his chair, banging it into the wall behind him, I stop, reaching out for him. "I'm so sorry I didn't tell you, but I thought I was being paranoid. I didn't want to cause a scene if it was nothing."

"That doesn't sound like nothing, sweetheart," Milly says, rubbing my shoulder.

I meet her eyes. "I didn't think he'd do this. I didn't know—I didn't. I was going to go to the schoolboard if it happened again."

"Shh, this isn't your fault. But the police need to be informed."

I nod, wiping angrily at my tears. From the corner of my eye, I can see CJ breathing heavily, his hands clenched into fists at his side.

"I'm going to kill him," he growls, before storming out.

"CJ, no. Please, wait!" I yell through tears. I grab the clips on my chest, the ones monitoring my heart, and rip them off. Milly's hands immediately stop me, pinning them to my chest.

"You need to stop before you hurt yourself."

"I have to stop him," I tell her, pleading.

She looks to the door, seeming torn, before she turns to my father. I meet his eyes, seeing the same rage I saw in CJ's moments ago.

"Dad, please stop him. I can't lose him, too. I can't."

He gives me a sharp nod but doesn't make eye contact with me. "I'll go see where he is. Hopefully Cole is still out there and can help me."

I quickly grab his hand before he goes, stopping him. "Please tell him I'm sorry. I'm so, so, so sorry."

He leans in, kissing my forehead hard before pulling back and staring into my eyes. "This is not your fault. I'll call the police while I'm out there. This is a crime. Now rest; you need some sleep."

I nod, falling back onto my pillow, but the fear swimming through my veins won't let me relax, because it doesn't matter who gave me those pills; I could have prevented it, just like I could have prevented the rapes.

It seems all I'm good for is getting people hurt.

I numb myself, not wanting to let anything in right now. Not when I'm responsible for so much grief.

I wouldn't blame CJ if he can't forgive me.

I'll never be able to forgive myself.

Chapter 21

It's been days since we lost our baby. Days of mourning and regret. Mourning for the child we will never get to hold, to watch open their eyes for the first time and take their first breath. Regret for not protecting our child better, for not reporting Mr. Flint when I should have.

I've been in a zombie-like state, not really knowing who's been coming or going, or when. I've tried to keep up with what's going on, but the atmosphere in our flat has been tense, everyone walking around on eggshells.

Ever since we got an update from the police officer in charge of our case, I've locked myself away in my room. I can't bear to be around everyone and endure their sorrow and pity. I just want to mourn my baby, my loss. I want the unbearable pain inside me to go away. I want my heart to stop aching and the pain in my chest to go.

It hasn't helped that when the police officer in charge reported back, they had nothing but bad news. They tried contacting Mr. Flint to get his statement, but they've not managed to locate him. When I told them that was impossible, he had classes to teach, they informed me he had been suspended from the university for gross misconduct.

The anger I felt when he told us he couldn't be found is something I'd never experienced. I wanted revenge. I wanted him to hurt the way he hurt me. I wanted him to suffer.

He shouldn't be able to get away with this. Our baby may not have taken their first breath, but they were a living human being growing inside me. He took that away.

If there was any doubt he was innocent, Mr. Flint going missing the night we were in the hospital drove that away. It's just made him look guiltier.

He was meant to be in his classroom, teaching an early morning class, but when Cole, CJ and Dad got there, there was another teacher substituting.

From what my dad said, he had had found CJ and Cole waiting for a taxi outside the hospital, looking ready to tear the world apart. How they managed it, I don't know, but they got him to calm down enough to find an all-night café near the university. By the time the sun rose, and early morning classes were about begin, CJ had excused himself to go to the toilet. Dad hadn't realised he had snuck out the back until it was too late. But it was pointless, because, Mr. Flint wasn't even there.

I reckon if he knew Mr. Flint's address, he would have turned up there. I'm grateful he wasn't in the classroom though. As much as I want him to pay for what he's done, I don't want to lose CJ in the process.

I wasn't given details about it, but Cole did say CJ had broken down outside the English department. It's why it had taken them so long to get back to the hospital that day.

I think that time apart was good for me, in a way, because the second he walked through the door, my brave façade crumbled, and I told him everything I was feeling. I told him how sorry I was, and how he had every right to blame me. I let everything I had stored over the hours he was gone, explode.

He assured me there was nothing to be sorry for, that I didn't do this, but it's hard to believe something when that guilt is eating away at you from the inside.

I'll never get over losing my baby. I'll always remember and love them. Nothing can ever change that. I just wish I'd had a chance to hold them, to tell them I loved them and would do anything for them.

But that chance was taken away from me.

Cruelly.

There have been moments where I wonder how life can go on. How do I pretend that everything is okay, when it's not? How can I move on, when a few days ago, I was planning on becoming a mother? It feels selfish and wrong. Sometimes it feels like I'm betraying our child by moving on without them. And I never want them to think they're being replaced.

Today is the first time CJ hasn't been with me, catering to my every need, and I miss him terribly. He's the only thing that is keeping me together right now. Without him, I don't know what I'd do.

He's been great and supportive, but I can see the grief in his eyes every time he looks at me. He's trying to act brave, like he's getting through this, but I can see through it all. Deep down he's dying inside, just like me.

He left rather quickly this morning when he got a text message off Cole, and I haven't heard from him since then. He grabbed his bag and laptop, kissed me goodbye, then left.

A light tap on the door shakes me from my thoughts. "Come in," I shout, turning down the volume on my television.

Willow pops her head in first. "Want some company?"

I look around my empty room, feeling alone without CJ, and nod. "You're late back. Is everything okay?"

She looks hesitant as she sits down next to me on the bed. She faces me, inhaling deeply. "Has Jordan told you about her new friend, Emma?"

The hairs on the back of my neck stand on end and I grip my sheets tightly in my fist.

"Yes, why?"

"Jordan and I went to meet up with her. There's been rumours around the university that she reported Mr. Flint when he cornered her in his office and assaulted her."

"What?" I yell, feeling my blood boil at hearing his name and what he has done.

She nods solemnly. "Yeah, my feelings exactly."

"What did she say? Is she okay? What did he do?"

"That's the thing; she wouldn't see us. Her cousin, or brother, or whoever he is, said she didn't want to see anyone at the moment. He did say she has a few bruises, and a broken wrist, but she managed to stop him from going further. The one I think is her boyfriend, he said it could have been a lot worse."

"I've never met her, but I've seen her. She's tiny and looks so fragile," I whisper, staring at my sock-covered feet. "Why do I keep doing this to people, Low?"

I feel her eyes on me, but I can't look at her. Not right now.

"Do what?" she asks, her tone concerned.

I steel myself and turn to her, watching as she flinches away from my expression.

"Cause them pain. Curse them. I had a chance to right a wrong, to avoid further incidents, but I didn't. I just sat back and ignored what my mind and body was telling me to do. I did it because I'm weak, because I'm scared of what the consequences will be if I'm right, and worse, if I'm wrong," I tell her, flicking my eyes away. "If she was attacked by Mr. Flint, then it's because I didn't report him in the first place. And I should have done it the first time he made me uncomfortable. I just kept thinking, what if it's just me, what if I'm reading it wrong and what's happening is harmless? I would have gotten an innocent man fired for nothing. But my intuition was right—I was right, and someone else got hurt because I didn't listen. It's a repeating pattern when it comes to me." I laugh, but there's no humour in it.

She places a hand on my arm, her eyebrows scrunched together when I peer up at her. "Allie, you don't really think like that, do you?"

I glance at her with watery eyes. "Yes. Look at how many people lives I've ruined, Low. Because of my actions, people got seriously hurt. *I lost* my baby because of my stupidity. *My baby.*"

Her expression morphs from stricken to angry. She smacks me sharply on the shoulder and I yelp, narrowing my eyes at her. "Stop talking bullshit, Allie. You didn't cause what has happened here anymore than I did. You think you're the first person who has kept quiet? You're not. And you won't be the last. Abused women keep quiet because they are frightened, because they're afraid of what they'll do next or afraid of tomorrow. Victims of rape don't speak out because they feel ashamed, scared, alone. People who are bullied keep quiet because they are afraid it will make the situation worse, or they've spoken out and learnt it hasn't gotten them anywhere." She pauses, gazing at me closely. "What you did was out of fear, but not because you are weak. You were afraid of what speaking up would do to your family—to your dad and to yourself. You thought it was an isolated incident. But,

Allie, the second you found out what he did to me, you spoke out, damned the consequences. And you would have done that if you had found out what he was doing beforehand. You forget, I know you Allie. You don't have a bad bone in your body. I may not have shown it at the time, but it meant a lot to me that you didn't lie to me."

"But I did," I whisper, looking away.

She grabs my chin, turning me to look at her. "No, you didn't. I heard you talking to CJ, ya know?"

Perplexed, I shake my head at her. "Talking about what?"

"What Logan did to you," she whispers. "I also know why you didn't come between us when you knew what he tried to do. I know your mum threatened you and told you that you'd lose me if you told me. She brainwashed you into thinking I would take his side. You also feared that if I knew, he would do the same to me."

"I remember telling CJ what he did to me, but I've never said the rest," I tell her, utterly confused.

She smiles, bringing my hand into her lap to hold. "No, but you forget, I watched and listened to your mum belittle you. I watched you shrink into yourself every time she put you down. It might not have registered right away when I first found out, but it's slowly sunk in. What happened wasn't your fault. You aren't to blame. And I don't care how many times I've got to tell you that. If you believed, deep down, that Logan would have hurt me or another person, you would have spoken up. If you were one-hundred percent sure Mr. Flint was a predator, you would have reported him. But because of your good heart, you didn't want to risk people losing stuff by speaking up. So please, *please*, stop with this nonsense."

I don't think it's as easy as that but hearing how she sees it has made me pause. I guess to see what she sees will take time. Time I'm willing to give if it stops me from hurting so much.

"I'll try, but it's not easy," I tell her. "I just feel so useless."

She pulls me towards her, so I rest my head on her shoulder. Her body rumbles beneath me when she speaks. "We all feel like that sometimes, even CJ," she teases.

I giggle, wrapping my arm around her waist and hugging her. "I love you, Low. You're the bestest friend a girl could wish for."

"I try," she says, then giggles.

We shift so we're laying with our backs to the pillows, looking up at the ceiling.

"Do you think the world has always been this jaded, or is it from moving here?" I ask quietly.

She squeezes my hand she holds between us. "I think we were just blissfully unaware. Our parents protected us as much as they could. But I truly believe it will not always be like this—always looking over our shoulders wondering what will happen next."

"Let's hope only good things come next. If something else starts happening around here, I'll start thinking it's a conspiracy and will move my arse out of this place so fast you'll never see me go. I'll be like The Flash: now you see me, now you don't."

She giggles lightly. "Just make sure that when it happens, I have my phone with me."

I tilt my head to the side to look at her. "Um, why?"

She turns to glance at me, grinning. "Because if Allie Davis is going to do exercise, I want to document the hell out of that shit."

I kick her leg lightly, giggling. It feels good, like the heaviness on my chest has lightened just a little.

"Maybe the next thing to happen is mobile phones crashing, being wiped from the earth."

She gasps, narrowing her eyes at me. "Bite your tongue. It could be books are destroyed and going digital only. I mean, you did get a break in at the library."

It's my turn to look horrified, and I'm pretty sure I lose all colour in my face. "Take that back," I demand. "We could go back to the stone ages, only wearing dirty rags as clothes." I stick my tongue out, smiling when she inhales sharply. She sits up, looking down at me.

"Sweets might stop being made because they're giving people diabetes."

I sit up, facing her with narrowed eyes. "All the high-heeled shoes are burnt because people are breaking their ankles in them."

We go on for a while, swapping what might happen next theories. Before I know it, my eyes start to close, my entire body feeling exhausted.

I feel Willow leave the bed, but I'm too tired to open my eyes since I'm still recovering from blood loss.

~

I groan when I hear the annoying ringtone coming from my phone. I miss the days when everyone could have songs as their ringtone.

I roll over, noticing the sun has gone down. I grab my phone, reading the time. I've slept for a good few hours—more than I have in days. I'm surprised CJ isn't back; it's eight, past his dinner time.

Tina, one of the supervisors, is calling, so I answer, lifting the phone to my ear with a yawn.

"Hello?"

"Hi, Allie, I'm really sorry to call you like this. I know it's not a really good time, but you're the only one I can think of to call."

I sit up, rubbing my tired eyes. "It's fine. What's up?"

"It's about Alex. He started his shift like normal, but he's been gone for two hours now, and he isn't meant to finish for another two. We have an address and number for him, but his phone is off at the moment."

I swivel around in bed, resting my feet on the carpet. I tuck the phone between my shoulder and ear while slipping on some trainers.

"He said his nan was ill not long ago, maybe something happened?"

"Oh, crap. I forgot about his nan. I hope she's okay. But it's not like him to disappear like this. He's always told us if he's had to leave early."

I pause by my desk where CJ's hoodie lies. "He's left work before?"

"Yeah. Recently, he's left early a lot. He mentioned she had been in hospital."

I shake my head, wondering what he was thinking. "I've told him so many times, I'm here to help. He never even said anything."

224

"Maybe he didn't want to bother you. I heard about your news. I'm sorry."

My heart stops for a second and I rub my chest. "Thank you," I tell her, then clear my throat. "Can you text me his address?"

She sighs. "I wouldn't normally do this, but you're the only friend I've seen him with. If anyone asks, though, I didn't give it to you. I'd go check on him myself but I'm on my own here now."

"It's fine, and I won't. I need some fresh air, anyway. Thank you."

"It's my pleasure. Let me know if he needs us to cover his shift tomorrow."

"I will."

I end the call and finish getting ready. I'm still bleeding, so I've been comfortable in leggings and my graphic T-shirts. I pull CJ's hoodie over my head and grab my phone and keys.

When I find him, I'm going to shake some sense into him. Friends are there to support each other; ours is not a one-sided friendship, and he's been here for me through a lot.

The flat is empty as I walk out, but I send another text to CJ, letting him know I'm popping out and won't be long.

By the time I get to my car, I'm already tired and achy. Tina's message pops up, and it doesn't take me long to enter his details into my satnav.

I guess I'm going to see where Alex lives. Finally.

Let's just hope I'm not intruding when I arrive, and everything is okay with his nan.

Chapter 22

Two Hours Earlier

CJ

When I was younger and found out what my mum went through, and that I was the product of rape, it made me see life in a different way. She showed me every day how to live life, how to move on from those things that can destroy you. Thanks to her, I lived life to the fullest.

She went through something horrific, something most women can't move on from—understandably so—but she did it. She showed me what it meant to be strong, that it doesn't always mean how much weight you can lift, but how much strength you can find inside you. My mum, to me, is the definition of strong.

I fucked around a lot as kid—and not just messing around with my friends. I've fucked a lot of chicks. What can I say; sex is my thing. I'm good at it. And I'm not one of those lads that brag. In fact, I'm the complete opposite. Why? Because I know I get the girl I'm with, off. More than once. I didn't discriminate; I loved all girls: curvy, thin, tall, small—it didn't matter to me. I never once mistreated any of them or promised them something I knew I would never give. I was always upfront and honest. And I liked it that way. I liked not having the commitment of a girlfriend.

All my life I've been worried I'd turn out like my sperm donor, somehow hurting those around me. So, I stayed away from any kind of relationship. I didn't want to taint someone else.

Then I laid eyes on Allie Davis.

My cupcake.

I'd only been a few feet away from her and I could smell the yummy baked goods instantly. I wanted to devour her. She had the most intoxicating scent I'd ever smelled. That's what first drew me to her, had my body moving unconsciously towards her.

She was dressed so out there, funky, her own little style, and she rocked it. She looked fucking hot, but sexy and sweet at the same time. I had a boner every time I thought of her.

But it was her relentless attempt to avoid my advances that made me try harder. It was refreshing. She's been the only person in my life, apart from Cole, who has seen me for me. Everyone else sees the cool guy they want to hang out with or want to be. They see someone who won't amount to anything, other than a fuck up, when in reality, I'm a fucking genius and will go far. They just don't see it.

She did.

She saw past the exterior. It may have taken for me to argue with her over English literature, but she never underestimated me after. She didn't jump at my every whim and cater to me. Having her in my life was like the sun on a rainy day.

What I hadn't expected was that I would fall helplessly in love with her. At first, I wanted to fuck her. Then the days went by, and I saw different parts to her. I found myself enjoying her company. It didn't take long for me to fall head over heels. She has this way about her; you can't help but love her.

I didn't realise loving someone so much would once again change my views on how to live life, though. I viewed almost everything differently. No longer did I want to go out and get so drunk I wouldn't remember anything of the night before the next morning. No. Instead, I wanted to spend every waking moment with her, whether it was to watch her work, read, or sleep.

And I'm man enough to admit I've watched her sleep—to the point it's considered creepy. But when she sleeps, her face is still, her expression peaceful, and I get to see another side to her. When I admired her in that position, it made me realise just how lucky I was to have met her and have her love me back. I never wanted to fuck it up. Ever. She's the best thing to ever happen to me.

However, I didn't need to worry about something I did fucking things up. Just being CJ would do it. My past has put her in danger. She just doesn't know it.

When we woke up this morning, I planned on spending the day with her in bed again. The doctors said she needs at least a week's rest before she does anything too strenuous. Anything other than going to the toilet and watching TV, to me, classes as too strenuous.

After Allie woke me up in the dead of night, crying out in pain, I've barely been able to breathe or think. I'll never get her pleas or cries out of my head. I never want to see her in pain like that ever again.

I really believed we had it all.

Then we didn't.

And that night... I might have lost her, too, not just our baby. I'm not sure I'd be able to ever move on from that. It would be like losing half my heart.

And although my mum has shown me, more times than I count, how strong the human mind can be, I knew mine wouldn't be. When we were in the ambulance and her blood pressure went alarmingly low, it hit me like a ton of bricks. I knew, knew deep in my soul, I'd never be strong enough to live without her.

Becoming a dad was something I never pictured being, until I met Allie. When I look to the future, all I see is her. I want us to get married, to have children and grow old together.

When you know, you know.

Our plans this morning got broken when I received a message from an unknown number, threatening to take my everything from me.

I glance down at the phone, clicking my neck from side to side, trying to ease the ache from looking down at my laptop all day. I hadn't realised how long. My body is stiff, sore. I'm not used to sitting down for as long as I have. I like being on the move, doing something, anything, just as long as I'm doing *something*.

I open the message I received this morning, feeling my jaw crack from clenching my teeth.

UNKNOWN: She didn't deserve to be tied to you for the rest

of her life. I did her a favour by getting rid of that parasite. Tell Allie her time is up. She's next. PS, I'd stop looking for me, if I was you. More will die if you don't.

I must have read the message a million times today, motivating me, angering me. I need to be ready for when I find this wanker.

I should have told Cole to stay at the flat to keep an eye on Allie, but then I would have had to of told him why. And at the minute, I need my head focused, not having him text me every five minutes. And as much as Allie deserves to know, I'm not putting more stress on her shoulders. She needs to rest, and if I had told her this, she would have wanted to help. I couldn't let that happen.

This fucker is the Whithall murderer, killing innocent girls. Someone who shares my DNA. And now I find out he's the one who murdered our baby, our innocent fucking baby.

If he thinks I'm going to give up looking for him, from protecting the woman I love, he's got another thing coming.

I'll die trying.

He's already taken our baby. If he thinks I'm going to sit back and let him take Allie, he's more delusional than I originally thought.

I've been researching Mr. Flint all day, trying to find any connection to the man who raped my mother, but so far, I've not found anything that suggests the two are connected. I'm not going to stop though.

I run my fingers through my hair, feeling the hairs on my neck stand on end. For some reason, my intuition is telling me the answer is right in front of me. I'm just too blind to see it.

I open the next web page, noticing the data I've been downloading for the past hour is nearly finished. The police may have sealed off reports and documents, but there's always a way to get hold of them. You just have to know how. Nothing is gone forever. And today, I got lucky, getting into the online documents by going through the back. It may take longer, but it's my only shot at finding something to point me in the right direction.

When I found the newspaper clippings on Jordan's laptop, I

couldn't help but look into it. The birth certificate they found isn't much help but knowing Claire Forest gave birth to a boy is a start. Which is why I've hacked and committed various felonies.

If I can get the name of the child, I'll be one step closer to finding this fucker and ending him for good.

It's the only way this shit is going to end.

"Come on, motherfucker, I've nearly got you," I mutter, rubbing my tired eyes.

I lift my Styrofoam coffee cup to my mouth, groaning when a drop of cold liquid touches my lips. I look around, finding no one nearby, so I leave my shit and move over to the coffee machine. It's not even good coffee, but it's done the trick nicely, and I haven't got the time to traipse all over Whithall university for it. Having no sleep over the past few days is starting to catch up to me. I'm afraid that if I close my eyes, something else will happen to Allie. It's my duty to protect her, to keep her safe. I understand there was nothing I could have done to prevent the miscarriage—none of us could have predicted someone would do that to her—but it still makes me feel useless, like I've failed her.

The coffee machine takes its sweet-arse time pouring me my fucking coffee, the brown liquid dripping in a slow pour.

I watch it, feeling my vision double.

Come on.

I nearly jump with glee when it's finished, but I'm worried using any more energy will knock me flat on my arse, I'm that exhausted.

Blowing the steam away, I bring the cup to my lips, taking a sip. I hiss, sucking my lips into my mouth when the horrid liquid burns.

This fucking coffee sucks.

It's not bad enough it tastes like shit, now it has to give me third degree burns, too? It's lucky I have other shit on my mind, otherwise I'd destroy that machine.

My laptop dings, letting me know the file I'm downloading is finished, and my heart leaps. I rush over, putting the coffee down next to my laptop, and open the first file.

When I glance at the screen, my eyes widen in horror and shock. NO!

"Motherfucker," I growl.

I reach out to grab my phone to ring Cole, and then Allie. I've been ignoring her calls and texts all day, but she needs to know about this. My fingers brush my screen, but before my call can connect to Cole, something bounces off the side of my head. The pain knocks me to the floor, my hand going to my wound.

What the fuck?

I land on my knees with a sickening thud, my vision blurring from the pain it causes. Warm liquid runs down the side of my face, and when I pull my hand away, it's covered in blood. I fall to my side, looking up at my attacker.

My eyes narrow into dangerous slits, and a murderous rage builds up inside me.

I'm going to kill that sick son of a bitch.

"It's you," I growl.

A creepy smile spreads across his face. I'm so stunned, so angry, that I don't get a chance to move before his foot comes down on the side of my face, knocking me out completely.

Allie!

Chapter 23
Present

ALLIE

The storm is rolling in quickly, the rain already pouring down on my windshield, making it hard to see. I slow down to a stop when my sat nav announces I've reached my destination. It says the house should be here, but I'm driving down a dirt road with banks of trees on either side.

"Where the hell am I?" I whisper. I check my phone, but with the storm and tree coverage, there's no signal.

I check my mirrors before pulling off down the road. Either the address Tina gave me is wrong, or my sat nav needs rebooting. It's not the first time she's given up on me or steered me in the wrong direction.

Whenever Alex talked about his home life, I pictured him living on a busy street. Not in the middle of nowhere nearly an hour away from the university. How the hell does he commute to Whithall every morning? I've never seen him drive, but then again, I've never really asked how he gets from A to B.

I hate driving down roads like this. They're thin and have barely enough room for two cars, which is why they have little dips at the side for you to pull into. I'm always afraid a car will be driving too fast and hit me head on.

Another road splits off to my right, and without thinking, I turn onto it, hoping for the best. I'm driving back on myself now, but as I follow the road for a few minutes, a house comes into view. I relax into my seat, pulling up outside next to an older car.

I pull my hood up over my head and grab my umbrella and phone. My body starts shivering the second I open the car door and get out.

I rush up to the house as fast as I can go without hurting myself. It looks old and could do with a lick of paint and new windows. They've got cracks in, some even covered with plastic.

As I knock on the door, white paint peels off, and I wince, stepping back guiltily. I rub my arm, and bounce on my feet to keep my blood flowing. I should have brought a coat with me, but I wasn't really thinking. I didn't think it would rain, either.

I knock again, louder this time, hoping someone is in.

Maybe his nan was taken to the hospital, which is why no one is answering.

"Come on," I whisper, my teeth chattering.

I'm about to give up when I hear a voice call out, "Coming."

The relief I feel at knowing his nan might be okay, relaxes me. The door opens, revealing an old lady, who I presume is his nan, Jessica. She's bent forward, barely holding herself up.

She looks startled to see me, so I put on my best smile, hoping to ease her worries. Her hair is as white as snow, her face wrinkled and sagging at the cheeks. Her glasses sit on the tip of her nose.

"Hi, I'm Allie, Alex's friend from school. Is he in?"

Her smile lights up her face, making her look a little younger. "Come, get out of the rain, pet. Come on. It's so lovely to meet one of my Alex's friends."

"Thank you. You must be Jessica?"

The second I step inside, I have to hold my breath. The house smells rusty and damp. It hits me in the face like a rubbish tip in the summer. I have to breathe through my mouth it's so strong.

She leads me into a tiny living room, filled with knick-knacks and pictures. There's two, two-seater sofas, the pea green colour looking faded and worn. In the middle of the room is a coffee table with burnt cup rings staining the top. There's a shelving unit in the alcove—my grandparents had one just like it. It's filled with more pictures, ornaments, and other bits and bobs.

I glance around again, taking in the old TV box that would need a crane to move. It's been a long time since I've seen one. The curtains are brown, with embroidered flowers on them.

The house is old, outdated, but you can see she's tried her best to make it a home. It's the cups of tea or coffee left on the coffee table, the newspapers stacked beside the sofa, and the smell of days old food that has surprised me. It looks like no one has cleaned for a few weeks, if not longer. She shouldn't be living in this condition.

I'm so lost in a daze that I nearly miss her stumble. I grab under her elbow, steading her. "Are you okay?"

Her hands are shaking, her knees bent like she's struggling to support herself. "I just need to sit down, pet. I'm not as young as I used to be."

I help her into the nearest seat, one I think is hers, as the remote is on the arm and another cup of tea on the little side table next to it.

"Are you okay? Would you like me to get you something?"

She waves me off, shifting the cushion behind her to get comfortable. "I'm fine, pet. Now, take a seat. My boy has told me all about you. He said you work in the library together?"

I take a seat on the other sofa, cringing at the thought of what I might be sitting on. "We do. It's actually why I'm here. Our supervisor, Tina, called me to say Alex walked out of work. We thought something had happened as he mentioned you've been sick?"

Her eyes seem to glass over for a second, before her attention turns to me. "Hello, pet, are you one of Alex's friends?"

A little puzzled, I nod my head slowly. "Yes, do you know where he is?"

She lifts her cup of tea, drinking it, and I inwardly cringe. It looks hours old. "My Alex isn't here. He's at work. Do you work with him?"

"I do. Our supervisor said he walked out from his shift. We thought he would come home. He said you've been ill?"

She nods her head enthusiastically, and she looks so fragile I'm worried it's not good for her brain. "He's a good boy. Always looking after me. He isn't back from work yet, though."

I grab my phone out of my front pocket, checking to see if I've had any missed calls from Tina, and hoping for one from CJ. I'm worried he still hasn't called.

"Do you know when he'll be back?" I ask.

"He'll be back soon with my medication," she tells me. I sigh, smiling. So that's why he rushed out of work.

"That's good. I'm sorry for interrupting your night."

"It's no bother," she says, before leaning over and coughing. I rush over, bending down to rub her back.

"Is there anything I can get you? A glass of water?"

When she sits up, she's pale, and it's worrying. "Can you be a dear and grab me my pills? I've got a headache coming and they always make me feel better. And a glass of water would be lovely."

"Where are your pills?" I ask softly, getting up.

She looks around the room for a second, like she's searching for something. She frowns. "I'm not sure where I left them."

This woman isn't well, and as much as I admire Alex for looking after her for all these years, she needs real medical care. She needs to be monitored all the time. She needs help.

"Are you okay with me going to look for them?"

"Of course. Are you Allie?"

I smile, glad she remembered my name. "I am."

She pats my hand with her cold ones, making me frown. "Such a good girl."

I give her a soft smile before reaching over the back of the sofa for the red knitted blanket. I cover her, tucking it into her lap to keep her warm.

"I'll back in a few," I tell her, leaving the room.

The hallway is as dim and dull as the front room, the wallpaper peeling from the walls. A yellow patch covers most of one wall and the ceiling.

God, Alex, why didn't you come to me for help?

There are stairs to my left, but I carry on walking down to the kitchen, gagging when the smell hits me.

My god.

Plates covered with leftover food, and piles of dirty washing, fills the sides and sink. The cupboard doors are non-existent, the one still attached barely hanging on.

Not wanting to stay in here a second longer, I grab the cleanest glass I can find and swill it out. I fill it before looking around for her tablets.

I find a basket filled with different bottles and packets of medication, and grab it, taking that and the glass of water with me to the front room.

"Do you know what the medication is called, Jessica?" I ask, setting the water down on the side.

She gets that distant look in her eyes, like she's having trouble remembering. "Naproxen, I think."

"Naproxen, that's good. I think my dad had to take that. He used to get headaches all the time," I tell her, feeling one of my rambles coming on. I'm already feeling the effects of leaving the house too soon. I'm tired, sore, but there's no way I can leave her here on her own like this.

I sort through the medication, reading labels. There's so many of them. She can't possibly be taking all of these.

One of the labels catches my eye, and I bring it up closer to make sure I'm reading it right. *Methotrexate.*

I fall back on my arse, taking the basket of medication with me and spilling the tablets all over the floor.

He wouldn't.

No!

I shake myself out of it, placing all the medication back in the basket and finding the right ones. I quickly read through the instructions, making sure I have the right dosage, and pass them to her. I get up, pacing the floor, when a picture on the mantelpiece stops me. I walk over, picking it up and lifting it closer.

In the picture are a middle-aged couple, so far removed from each other and unhappy, standing in a garden. They're both staring into the camera with no emotion whatsoever. It's supposed to be a family photo. The woman in the picture is holding a crying baby, and two kids are standing side by side, looking skinny and pale. The boy is staring at the girl, but she's looking at the camera, looking as robotic as the parents behind her.

Why would she have this on show?

I put it down gently, ready to leave. I've seen enough, but a picture on the far end has me turning pale. I grab it quickly, nearly knocking the pictures close by off the mantelpiece.

"Jessica, who is the lady in this picture?" I ask, moving over to her.

She opens her eyes, smiling when she sees what I'm holding. "Oh, I've not seen that picture in years. That's my daughter, Claire, and my son, Conrad."

"No, no, no," I chant.

This cannot be happening.

It can't.

But it all makes sense.

Alex is the killer. He's the person we've all been searching for.

"Jessica, I'm just going to find Alex. I'll be back soon, okay?"

She looks up at me in a daze. "Are you Allie?"

I force a smile. "I am."

She takes my hand, and I have to do everything I can not to flinch or let the tears threatening, spill.

"I'm so glad my boy has a girlfriend like you." She inhales, squeezing my hand. "Not like those other girls. They were noisy," she whispers, before closing her eyes once again.

A shiver runs up my spine and I feel the blood drain from my face.

This can't be the Alex I've come to know and love like a brother. It can't be. For once in my life, I want to be wrong about someone.

He's been there for me through a lot. He was there when me and Willow were going through a rough patch. We might have made up after her attack, but that rift was still there. He helped me through that.

When CJ drove me mad, he was there.

When we went to court, he stood by my side and supported me.

He kept me company at work and made me laugh.

He was my best friend.

I move back towards the kitchen, starting there. There has to be something that can prove I'm right or wrong. Something—anything.

I suddenly find it hard to breathe, my chest tightening. The back-door comes into view and I rush over, flinging it open and taking in a breath of fresh air. I lift my face to the sky, letting the rain pelt down on my face whilst panting heavily.

What am I going to do?

What *am* I going to do?

I take my phone out of my pocket, clicking CJ's number. It goes straight to voicemail. "CJ, please call me, it's important. It's about the killer. I know who it is. Well, I think I do. No, I know I do." I stop when I see a building at the bottom of the garden. "Call me. Call the police—something," I tell him, trailing off and ending the call.

Something about that building doesn't feel right. It's like when you watch a horror movie and the house is creepy as hell, yet the morons still walk inside to check it out.

It looks like I'm going to be one of those morons, because before I know it, my feet are taking me down the path. I look around to check no one else is here, keeping my phone tightly clutched in my hand.

As it comes closer, dread works its way through me.

I press my ear against the door, but I can't hear anything out of the ordinary. But that feeling won't go.

I flick through my phone, calling Jordan. She normally has Wednesdays free. Something tells me I'm not going to like what's behind that door.

When I hear it ringing, I put the phone down my hoodie and into my bra, hiding it. The second I put my hand on the door handle, my heart starts racing and my palms turn sweaty.

The click of it opening causes me to flinch and pause, holding my breath.

Oh, god. What am I doing?

I push it open, my shoulders sagging when it only leads into an empty room. It's short-lived when I see another door. I move towards it, nerves raking my body. I shake my hands out, taking long deep breaths.

I twist the handle, pulling the door towards me.

I had prepared for the worst—the worst of the worst. But what I'm seeing in front of me is so far from anything I ever imagined.

"Oh, my God," I breathe out, my shaking hand going to my mouth.

Hearing my voice, the girl's head lifts, her eyes widening. She starts screaming behind her taped mouth, her eyes widening, imploring something I can't read. I take a step forward, needing to help her. She shakes her head, her body furiously trying to get free from her chains.

Chains.

I can't believe what I'm seeing.

I scream when a body steps out in front of me. I reach out for the door frame, feeling faint and sick.

I gasp, struggling to understand what I'm seeing. "It's you."

He smiles, opening the door wider. I stumble back a step, screaming at the top of my lungs. No! I feel like my heart has been ripped from my chest.

I fall to my knees, tears falling and blurring my vision, but I can't take my eyes away from the scene in front of me.

CJ.

Bloody.

His head hanging lifelessly to the side.

It's the last thing I see before I pass out.

Chapter 24

The grief of losing my baby hits me the second I come to, like it has done every time I've woken up since it happened. It's suffocating. There's a split second where I forget. For that split second, I'm a mum-to-be, and I'm happy, blissfully happy. Then it's ripped away from me all over again.

I open my eyes, a little disorientated, and blink, looking around the foreign room.

What the hell? Where am I?

I shoot up in the bed I'm in and everything comes flooding back. I'm drowning in emotions. I can't hear over the sound of buzzing in my ears.

CJ.

I close my eyes, seeing his dead body all over again. All that blood... I rub my chest, breathing heavily. There's a hole in my heart from losing him, from losing my life.

This can't be happening to me. It can't. I can't live my life without him. I won't.

I run my fingers through my hair, opening my eyes and letting tears fall.

There's not much to the room I'm in, but I don't really get a chance to look. My eyes take in CJ sitting tied to a chair. I jump off the bed, and in my haste, I nearly trip over my own feet.

He's awake.

My eyes aren't deceiving me. He's really awake.

"Oh, my God, you're alive."

He struggles against his restraints, the veins in his temples pulsing, his face bright red and covered in blood and sweat. The muscles in his arms bulge, and he growls deep in the back of his throat as he fights to get free. His wrists are red raw from the rope, and my breath gets caught in my throat.

CJ.

"We need to get you out of here. OhmyGod, ohmyGod," I chant.

I kneel on the floor in front of him and immediately fiddle with the rope at his wrists. My hands shake, making it harder for me to grip it. I begin to panic, my vision blurring as I struggle to get him free.

We have to get out of here. We have to get him medical help.

"CJ, I can't get them loose. What do I do?" I cry, pulling on them harder.

He tries to tell me something, but it's muffled behind his gag. I look up through my tears, feeling helpless and panicked. He has a gash on the side of his head, blood still pouring from the wound. The left side of his face is just swollen, covered in a dark, purple and black bruise.

I rise up on my knees, pulling the dirty gag out of his mouth and palming the good side of his face.

"What do I do?" I sob.

He inhales, taking a gasp of breath. "Get out of here, Allie. Get out of here now," he yells.

"I'd stop touching him, if I were you."

I spin around, falling on my arse with my back against CJ's knees. "Alex!"

"I didn't want you to find out like this," he says, a sardonic expression etched on his face.

He looks like my friend—sounds like him. But something inside him has changed, something in his eyes and his body language. No longer is he slouching, looking like the goofy boy I've come to know. Instead, he stands tall, looking confident. He no longer has that shy, timid boy look. Instead, his expression is bored, uncaring and dark. It's like there's an imposter inside my friend's body.

"You touch her, and I'll fucking kill you," CJ growls, still struggling in his chair, making the sores on his wrists worse.

"Stop," I warn him, glancing down at his wrists, but he doesn't seem to care that he's hurting himself. He doesn't look away from Alex. I turn back around, biting my bottom lip and willing my heart to stop racing.

Alex laughs patronisingly, glancing at CJ like he could take him on and win. And in CJ's vulnerable position, he could.

I can't let that happen.

If I want to get us out of this unscathed, then I need to talk to him, calm him down and get him to see reason. If there's a chance of that. The person in front of me is too far gone; I think my efforts might be a waste.

"Why are you doing this, Alex?"

His head turns in my direction, but his eyes stay on CJ a moment longer, before falling on me. "Because he took what wasn't his. It runs in the family, so I shouldn't be surprised."

"She's not yours," CJ snaps.

I reach behind me, putting my hand on his ankle and squeezing.

"What do you mean it runs in the family?"

"My mum's little sister, my auntie, tempted him when she knew he belonged to my mum. She shouldn't have. It got her killed, you know. It got her killed. My mum made sure of it, she did," he rants, pulling at the ends of his hair. "I can't let him take you from me. I can't kill you."

I should be relieved, but I'm not. The fact he's capable of killing is something I can't comprehend.

I wipe at my eyes, trying my hardest to keep eye contact with him without flinching. "We were friends, Alex. Best friends. Why would you do this to me? You killed those girls," I say, my eyes flicking to the side, where a girl, who I presumed is Lilian, is panting in her chair, looking terrified. When I look back to him, my chest tightens in pain. "You killed my baby."

CJ makes a sound in the back of his throat as he pulls on his restraints.

"I couldn't let him ruin your life, Allie. You're too good for that," he says softly, taking a step towards me. I flinch, shuffling back further against CJ. My entire body is shaking to the point it hurts. The blood pumping through me feels like it's on fire, I'm that scared.

When Alex's gaze meets mine, its filled with hurt. "I'd never hurt you, Allie. Never. I did this all for you. I needed to get him out of the way, so we could be alone. I couldn't kill you. Not you."

"You did hurt me. You killed my baby," I scream, feeling tears stream down my face.

CJ struggles again, and I hear the pained sound at the back of his throat. It's probably killing him that he can't comfort me, protect me. But it's my turn to protect him.

"Get me out of these restraints," CJ snaps, and I hear the emotion in the back of his throat.

"I did it for you," Alex screams back.

"And the girls? Why did you hurt all those innocent girls? Why did you pretend to care they were missing when all along you had killed them? Why, Alex? Why?"

I gasp, frozen, when he pulls out a knife from his back pocket, using it to scratch his head, and starts pacing back and forth, his eyes never leaving mine.

I look towards the door, wondering if I can make it before he catches me, or if I'd get help in time before he hurts them.

He chuckles. "I wouldn't bother. It's locked," he admits, and my stomach sinks. "And I'd slit their throats before you made it to the door."

"Why are you doing this? Why did you hurt those girls?"

"Why? Because I needed to get him out of the way. I needed them to be you. I couldn't hurt you, but when they were bad, I could hurt them. I could. They weren't you, so I had to hurt them. I needed you."

I feel sick. What I'm hearing is It's outrageous, unbelievable. He's insane, completely delusional.

"You're fucking sick. You did it because you're a fucking psycho. This has nothing to do with Allie," CJ snaps angrily.

Alex's head snaps to CJ, glaring. He points the knife in his direction, spit flying from his mouth when he shouts, "No! You can't say her name. Don't say her name. You don't know anything."

I interrupt CJ before he can say anything else to anger Alex. Making someone unpredictable angry isn't a wise idea.

"Who are you, Alex?"

"You still don't know?" he asks, seeming genuinely confused.

I shake my head. "No. I don't know who you are. The person I know wouldn't have hurt anybody, not even people who deserved it. How did you end up here? What happened to you?" I ask softly.

He looks around the room before spotting something. I use the opportunity to shift my body, so I can cover CJ's legs. I reach behind me, watching Alex the whole time while trying to loosen the ropes tying his ankles to the chair.

"Allie," CJ warns under his breath, trying to nudge me away with his foot. I hardly hear him, so I know Alex didn't, but it still doesn't stop me from pausing, my heart racing as I watch Alex grab a chair from the corner.

I keep going, using slow movements so he won't know what I'm doing.

"I'm going to tell you two a story," Alex says, sitting down when he finishes dragging the chair to place in front of us.

"Great, a bed time story. Could you be any sadder?" CJ taunts.

Alex just smirks. It's creepy, deadly. He places the knife on his lap, leaning back in the chair casually, like he isn't holding three people hostage.

Hostage.

God, how did we get here? How could he do this? This is Alex. I still can't wrap my mind around it all. I honestly didn't see this coming, not by a mile away.

"Seems we share more than DNA, brother. I don't like bedtime stories, either," Alex taunts back, his eyes hard.

"Brother?" CJ and I say simultaneously. My jaw falls slack, looking between them. They look nothing alike for which I'm thankful for.

Alex laughs, throwing his head back before looking at us, his expression dead, changed completely from the person I know. I don't even recognise him right now. And the more he talks, the more he doesn't even sound like himself at all.

He taps his hand against his leg. "Let's start from the beginning, shall we?"

"Yeah, why don't you share how a family can all turn into a bunch of crazy sickos."

I glance at CJ. "His nan seems pretty stable. She's losing her mind, though," I blurt out. I'm nervous and scared—it happens. I don't even know why I said it.

He looks down at me, his eyes twinkling, but I can see the penetrating fear behind them. He's scared shitless, just like me.

"Cupcake," he says dryly, rolling his eyes. "Like I said before: *crazy*."

"Shut up!" Alex screams, jumping up from his chair and clutching his head.

He pulls the knife up in front of him, aiming it at CJ, and storms towards us. My hands are visibly shaking when I hold them up in front of me.

"Stay away from her," CJ screams.

"No! Please, don't hurt him," I shout, but start screaming when Alex grabs a handful of hair and starts dragging me towards Lilian. I grab onto his wrist, at the same time trying to shuffle on my knees so I can keep up with him, trying to ease the pain in my scalp.

He drops me, and I fall limply against Lilian. I look up, taking her in. She looks dazed, a bruise swelling on her cheek, and I'm wondering what's he's done to her that has kept her quiet all this time.

"Let her fucking go! I'm going to kill you. Do you hear me? I'm going to rip your fucking head off," CJ screams, turning bright red.

"Stay there," Alex yells, pointing the knife at me. I rear back, my heart stopping from shock.

I tense when he walks towards CJ. I panic, freezing on the spot. "Please don't hurt him," I beg. "Alex, if you cared for me as a friend, you wouldn't hurt him."

He holds the knife up to CJ's face, pressing it into his cheek. I gasp in horror when fresh blood starts trickling down his face. "No!"

"Not so fucking cocky now you have a knife pressed against your face, are you?"

CJ smiles, showing a cut on the inside of his lip that hasn't stopped bleeding. "Like you? Get me out of these ropes and we'll see how cocky you are."

I watch in horror as Alex brings the butt of his knife down on CJ's cheek, splitting it open. "Stop! Stop! Please, don't," I scream, wanting to go to CJ, but the look Alex gives me stops me, and I heed the silent warning.

"Now shut the fuck up and listen. Or next time, I'll hurt her," he says to CJ, pointing towards me and Lilian.

CJ grits his teeth. "You're dead, Potter. Fucking dead."

"Yeah, we'll see," Alex mutters before sitting back down in his chair.

"Can you let the girl go? This is Lilian, right? The last girl to go missing? Why don't you let her go? This is between us," I ask softly, hoping he will see reason. Maybe she can call for help from the house.

I'm still hoping Jordan has answered my call and is listening in. She will call for help; I know she will. I have to believe that.

"No, now shut up or I'll stab her," he snaps, rubbing his temple again.

"Okay," I whisper. I rub the girl's leg over the long white nighty she's wearing, looking up at her. "It will be okay."

Tears are running down her face as she nods slowly, looking too petrified to move. I can't imagine what she is going through.

"Family tree time," Alex starts, and I look away from Lilian to him. "My nan, the woman I live with, and her many boyfriends, were responsible. I blame her for everything. She should have protected them better."

"Is that why she isn't in a home and living in filth?" I ask.

He laughs. "Payback's a bitch, that's what you always say. Do you know she let her boyfriend's rape her kids? *My mum,*" he tells me, his voice strangled. "Did you know that when her last husband, my aunt's dad, didn't touch them, my dad took over? It was his job, anyway, not the lowly excuses of men she brought round."

"What the fuck? That doesn't make any sense," CJ snaps, but when I glance over at him, I can see the interest, the need to know what happened, and the disgust at what he's pieced together already.

Alex smiles. "Well, he's your dad, but he's *my* uncle *and* dad."

I'm going to be sick. He can't be serious.

"You're telling me, your mum and uncle—dad, whatever —had sex?"

"All the time," Alex says, smiling like it's the best thing in the world. "My mum didn't like her mum's boyfriends, but she loved our dad. She would tell me how much she loved him all the time. My nan's last husband never understood their relationship, but I don't think he knew just how close they were. She was ill you know—my mum. She didn't know any different. She got worse when he got sent to prison for raping a woman. Your mum," he bites out. "Slut."

CJ loses it, trying to fight his way out of his chair, screaming and yelling. His face is red, enraged. "You don't fucking speak about my mum. He deserved to go to jail. I'm glad he rotted there."

Alex shoots up in his seat, stepping closer. "She needed him, and your slut of a mum tempted him, just like my aunt did. If he had stayed, she wouldn't have been sent away to the psychiatric unit. She was already pregnant with me when he got sent to prison. It's why she married my step-dad so quickly; she needed to keep our bloodline going. She didn't love him, though. But she could have had given me a sister. I could have had Allie. She would have been my sister. I know it. But then dad died in prison ten years later, just when she found out my step-dad was having an affair and got the mistress pregnant. She had been waiting for my dad to come out and give her another baby. One to give to me," he spits, thumping his chest.

What the fuck? This is beyond wrong.

I can't look away from him, trying to see what I missed since I met him. There had to be signs he went through this. There had to be, and I missed them.

CJ, still going mad, glares up at him, spitting in his face. "It doesn't work like that, dickhead. Allie isn't related to you; she isn't a part of you. She never will be. And what happened to your mum, your aunt, was fucking sick. Your nan fucked all her kids up in the head. What they were doing to them was wrong, Alex; what *you* are doing is wrong."

"She would have been mine," Alex screams. "We could have shared what my mum and dad had. We could have been good together. But you had to get in the way. Just like my aunt, just like my step-father's mistress. You got in the way."

"You're fucking sick," CJ spits.

Alex ignores him, turning to me. "Now, you chose. You could have left him after he flirted with that girl on the field, when he was taken in for questioning, or when you got pregnant, but you didn't. I've gave you chances, Allie. I gave you loads of chances, and you let me down. You disappointed me."

CJ scoffs. "Fucking listen to yourself, man. You're fucking mental. You ain't right in the head."

I get up on my knees slowly, my entire body shaking. "Alex, I don't belong to you. I love CJ, that is why I'm with him."

He shakes his head. "Nope. Nope. Nope," he screams, pacing back and forth, his knife still in his hand.

"Alex, you need to stop. It's over. Just let us go."

He stops pacing, turning to me with narrowed eyes. "No, no, no," he chants. He rushes over, and I flinch, thinking he's reaching out for me. When Lilian starts screaming, I open my eyes. He's pulling her chair, pulling her towards his own, and my heart sinks.

I reach out for her, grabbing the leg of her chair and stopping him. "No. Don't hurt her. Please. We can sort this out, Alex, we can. You just need to calm down."

"Let her go, man. You don't need to hurt her," CJ yells, also trying to get him to see reason.

He kicks my hand away from the chair and I cry out in pain. "You never tell me what to do. I'm the big brother. You have to do as I say," he shouts.

I pull my arm close to my chest, feeling the throbbing all the way to my shoulder. Lilian keeps screaming, struggling in her chair, her eyes wide, sweat mixing with tears, matting her hair to her face. Alex wipes it back, looking down at her with so much hatred.

"Please, Alex, don't do this," I plead, wiping my tears away.

He looks to me, then to CJ. "You want me to let her go?"

Relaxing somewhat, I nod. "Yes, Alex. You should let her go. She can wait outside while we talk. Just us three."

He nods, deep in thought. "Okay, okay."

Lilian relaxes, breathing out a sigh of relief and mouthing the words, 'Thank you'.

"Untie her, Alex," I order softly when he doesn't move.

His head snaps up to me, his eyes dilated and filled with darkness. "Choose."

"Choose?"

He nods again, pulling roughly on Lilian to straighten her in the chair. "Yes, choose. You can either save CJ or save her."

The blood drains from my face as I look between Alex and CJ. "You mean to let go?"

He shakes his head, chuckling dryly. "No. To live. Either I kill CJ, or I kill her. Which one? Which one will you save, Allie? Which one means the most to you?"

I feel faint, dizzy, and my throat closes with emotion. "You can't make me choose."

He holds the knife up against her throat. "You don't choose, and I'll slit both their throats."

I sob, clutching my chest. "No, please don't this. Please, Alex."

"Alex, listen to me. It doesn't have to be like this. Just let the girls go. It's me you want out of the way."

I look to CJ in horror, shaking my head. "No. Don't do this. We can all get through this. Alex, you don't need to hurt any more people. Don't do this."

"Too late. Who will you choose, Allie?"

I cry harder, standing now and hold my hand up to Alex. "Please, think about this. You want us to be together, to be brother and sister, but if you do this, I won't."

He pauses, the knife on Lilian's neck loosening.

"Don't kill me. Please, don't kill me. I want to go home," Lilian cries, her eyes locked on mine. "Please don't let him kill me."

"You listen to me!" Alex yells, looking at me.

I scream when he raises the knife, plunging it into her shoulder. My hands cover my mouth, watching in devastation as her eyes roll to the back of her head and a scream so loud it pierces my eardrums erupts from her throat.

"Stop!" I scream, rushing over to them.

"Allie, no!" CJ yells.

I only get so close before he yanks the knife out of her shoulder and points it at me. I stop short, looking him dead in the eye.

"Stop. Please, just stop."

"Choose," he screeches, spit flying everywhere. "CJ's next, Allie, if you don't choose, and it won't be his shoulder I'll be stabbing. I'll be removing a body part."

I make a pained sound, struggling with what to do, how to stall. "I can't," I sob, looking at CJ helplessly.

"Cupcake, you don't have to do this," he tells me, before turning to Alex. "Kill me. If you want to kill someone, kill *me*. Just let them go, Alex. Do the right thing and let them go. There's been too much death."

"No, CJ," I sob, struggling to breathe.

"You don't get to choose, lover-boy. Allie has to choose."

How do I choose one life over someone else's? How can I stand here and let him kill the love of my life? I can't. I also can't stand here and let him kill an innocent girl. I would never forgive myself or survive the guilt.

I glance up at Alex, tears falling silently down my face. "Kill me," I whisper.

Chapter 25

Alex laughs dryly, a crazed look on his face. "No, no, no, Allie. We need you to choose."

Slowly, I take another step closer. "Alex, you need to think about what you're doing here. You can't make me choose, it's selfish and unfair."

The glare he sends me has me taking a step back. "Allie, you've got to choose. You've got to choose."

I shake my head, sobbing so hard my chest hurts. He starts dragging her over to CJ, her screams piercing the air.

"Choose," he yells when he drops her chair next to CJ. "We're the same. We're the same, Allie."

"No, you're batshit fucking crazy; she isn't. You're forcing someone so pure, so good, to do something bad, something against her will. This wouldn't be her decision, it would be yours. Alex, you need help, serious medical help," CJ snaps.

Alex brings the knife up again, and I move forward, but I'm too late. I watch in alarm as he stabs CJ in the shoulder, twisting the knife with a sick look of satisfaction on his face.

CJ howls and I run to him, needing to help him. "CJ," I cry. I'm a breath away, just a breath, but a hand shoving against my chest knocks the wind out of me and pushes me back. I trip over my own two feet, staring wide-eyed up at Alex.

I glance at CJ. His face is white, his hair wet from sweat and sticking to his forehead. He breathes heavily, the rabid animal sounds he was making turn into raspy moans.

He opens his mouth, more than likely to say something sarcastic or threatening, but only a wisp of air escapes him.

"Stop hurting him. Stop it!" I bark, clenching my hands into fists.

Alex circles CJ and Lilian like predators hunt down their prey. When he's done a full circle, he stands in front of CJ, twisting the knife further in his wound before pulling it out. Blood sprays, making me feel queasy.

Lilian screams behind her gag, her body shaking violently as he approaches her. He runs his fingers through her hair, clucking his tongue. He doesn't say anything, just stares down at her blankly, void of any emotion.

I feel helpless, like there's nothing I can do to help either of them. Whenever I get close, he stops me. I could run for the door, try to escape and get help, but how far would I get? How far would I get before he killed one or both of them.

I crawl closer to CJ, looking up at him. His pupils are dilated, and he can barely keep his head up. He notices my movements, though, and his eyes widen a touch. He begins to shake his head.

My hand shakes as I lift my finger to be quiet. I glance at Alex, watching him stroke Lilian's hand, and my blood turns cold. He seems lost in his own mind, his own thoughts, which gives me a moment to discretely try to loosen CJ's legs from the ropes.

Alex's voice startles me, causing me to squeal. "You've got ten seconds to choose, Allie. We don't have time."

I straighten my back, biting my lip as I struggle to even my breathing. "No, Alex. I don't want to do this. I don't want to hurt anyone, and I don't want you to, either."

When he looks at me, his eyes are void of emotion, staring right through me. A cold shiver runs up my spine, and before my eyes can take in what I'm seeing, he's slicing the knife through Lilian's finger. It slides off to the floor, blood spurting everywhere.

I turn to the side, throwing up everything I've eaten today. I clutch my stomach as tremors rake through my body.

This can't be real. It can't be.

"Ten seconds, Allie. Ten seconds, then I kill them both."

I jump at the sound of his voice, getting to my feet. He can't do this. He can't.

I have to stop him.

I hold my palms up to him, trying to hide the panic and fear eating away at me. "No. Don't do this. Don't do this, Alex." He's not hearing me, standing behind the two like they're prized possessions.

"Ten."

"Please, Alex, listen to me," I beg, stepping closer.

"Nine."

"Oh, God," I sob, running my fingers through my hair.

"Eight."

I look to CJ, the love of my life, then to Lilian, who is sobbing uncontrollably, her eyes glazed over.

"Seven."

"I can't do this. I can't do this," I chant, glancing back and forth between them.

"Allie, run. Forget about us and run," CJ screams.

"Six."

"I can't leave you," I tell him, standing there uselessly.

"Five."

"Don't let him kill me," Lilian sobs, her voice weak.

I can't breathe.

"Four."

"Allie, look at me, it's going to be okay," CJ demands, his voice strong but strained.

"Three."

"Alex, please, I'm begging you. I'll do anything, just don't hurt them," I plead, looking around the room for something to help me.

Maybe I can use something to hit him over the head with.

Jordan, where are the police?

"Two," he says slowly, moving closer to CJ.

I cry out, running my fingers through my hair, and step forward. "No, don't kill CJ. Don't kill CJ!" I scream.

He looks up, staring at me straight on. "One."

He lifts the bloodied knife, and I move, not caring if he hurts me in the process. I can't let him hurt either of them.

The knife descends and at first, I think he's aiming for CJ, but at the last minute, he turns to Lilian. I cry out, my legs feeling like jelly as I take the few steps forward to get to him. The knife comes down and I close my eyes, using all my strength to push him away. My hands connect with his shoulders, and I hear him grunt in surprise. My eyes fly open. He falls back, tripping over a coffee table and landing with a thud.

Everything moves in slow motion. I turn my head to the sound of CJ's screams, and watch as tears run down his face as he looks at me in horror.

A gurgle, followed by a choking noise has me glancing down, my mind taking a few moments to register what I'm seeing.

My knees buckle beneath me. "No!" I wail. My hands shake over the knife that's embedded in her stomach. My gaze flickers between the knife and her eyes that are slowly dimming. "I'm so sorry," I sob. "I'm so sorry."

She tries to force a smile, her chest heaving with long shallow breaths. Her good hand moves, her fingers wiggling like they're reaching out for me. I ignore the yells and cursing coming from CJ and place my hand over hers.

"I'm so sorry."

A hand appears on the knife handle, and before I can stop it, Alex is pulling the blade out, slicing through her stomach.

I throw myself backwards, screaming in terror as I watch blood pour from the wound, intestines hanging out.

There's so much blood. I would never have thought someone so small, so skinny, could produce so much.

"Now, who is it going to be, Allie?"

I barely hear him over mine and CJ's screams, but I shake myself out of it, looking up at Alex in a daze, a hitch in my chest.

"What?"

"Who? Who will be next? You and me, or CJ?"

"What?" I repeat, still dazed.

He walks around Lilian's prone body, still wielding the knife in his hand. I watch his every move, too scared to look away, too afraid of what he will do next.

"Me and you, or CJ. I can't let him win. You're mine. We're meant to be together."

"No, Alex, we aren't," I whisper, looking away. Seeing Lilian's body —Lilian's dead body—has numbed me. I can't feel anything.

He tilts his head to the side, his gaze seeing through me. "You said yourself, I was like your brother. I heard you, time and time again."

"That was before she knew what having a sibling meant to you, you fucking sick bastard."

"I'm not choosing," I whisper. "This is unspeakable—what you're doing is unspeakable. I won't do it. You're just going to kill us all, anyway," I tell him, feeling dead inside.

"You belong to me," he screams.

"So you keep saying," I scream back. "But I don't. I belong to CJ— we belong to each other. And you want to know why? Because he loves me. Because I love him. Because he wouldn't hurt a fly, unless it was to protect the ones he loves. You want to know why I don't belong to you?" I ask, then look to CJ, gazing at him through watery eyes. "Because he only has to walk into a room and my heart stops beating and I get butterflies in my stomach." I smile, placing a hand over my stomach. "I could be having a bad day, and the first person I want to speak to is him. He can bright up the darkest of days by just being there."

I look at Alex, really look at him, and with shaky limbs, I get up from the floor, my gaze never faltering. "I'm sorry you didn't have the right upbringing; I'm sorry you were born into this. *I'm sorry.* But it doesn't excuse your behaviour. It doesn't justify your atrocious actions. You need to the put the knife down. You need to stop this and hand yourself in. Give those families you've destroyed, peace. Give them something, because you've taken everything from them. Just stop."

"You don't mean that," Alex whispers, looking so wounded, so like the Alex I know. My heart aches. If someone had noticed what was happening, if someone had helped him, raised him with a real family, then maybe he would have had a chance.

Maybe.

"Yes, Alex, I do," I tell him softly, wiping my cheeks.

"We belong together," he tells me angrily, slamming his fist on the floor. "We do. He deserves to die. He does."

"She doesn't deserve this, Alex. Lilian over there—she didn't fucking deserve this. You won't get away with any of this. The police will catch you and you'll never see her again. Listen to her. Just listen to what she is telling you. You can't be this delusional."

Alex angrily turns his narrowed eyes to him. With shaking limbs, I get ready to stop him, but before I can, he slashes the knife across CJ's chest.

"You did this!" he roars.

I scream out for CJ, something snapping inside me, and the next thing I know, I'm moving. I charge at him, using the move I've watched CJ use a thousand times when he plays rugby, my upper body gunning for his chest.

The second my body hits his, everything around me disappears. I don't hear CJ yelling. I don't smell the metallic, coppery scent of blood. My senses focus on the thumping of my pulse and the feel of my blood rushing through my veins.

We tumble to the floor, and I roll, reaching for the wrist in which Alex holds the knife. A crazed look moves across his expression, his eyes dangerously close to black. There's no soul, no remorse, no guilt for what he's done or is doing. There's nothing.

I'm stunned, frozen for a split second at the sight, which helps him take me by surprise. He kicks out at me, and I fly backwards in the air, landing into the chair CJ is tied to and knocking him over. I cry out, but don't let it stop me. I get up, looking around for a weapon.

The room is mostly empty, but from the corner of my eye, I notice a stool in front of a vanity mirror and rush over.

"I'm going to end this. It's meant to be us. You turned her against me. You brainwashed her," Alex yells.

I whimper, picking the stool up by the legs, surprised by how heavy it is. My hair whips in my face when I spin around, and I find Alex getting up from the floor, his eyes on CJ with so much hatred a shiver runs up my spine.

"Allie, run. Now!" CJ screams from the floor, where he's lying on his side, blood covering his clothes.

I shake my head, my legs moving across the room before I can even think of what I'm about to do.

But it's him or us. And I'm not about to give up. Not now. We've been through too much together.

He bends down in front of CJ, holding the knife in the air. I cry out, feeling my life flash before my eyes.

My chest hurts, aches. A life without CJ isn't a life at all. I push harder, my legs feeling like jelly and my knees threatening to give out.

I reach them, and with a roar so loud, I lift the stool above by head and swing. I swing with all my might, all my strength, and hit Alex across the head. I hit him so hard the vibrations of the impact cause my hand to spasm. I drop the stool to the floor, breathing heavily, and watch with a sick feeling in my gut as Alex's body sways from side to side.

I feel sick. I feel sick at myself for being capable of doing something so brutal. But I can't look away. So, I wait, watching with suspense and shock.

I wait.

I don't even know if he's dead or alive.

I just watch, clutching my chest and trying to even my breathing. It doesn't feel real. It doesn't feel like I've just smacked a stool round someone's head.

Alex's body sways once more before dropping to the floor with a sickening thud. I whimper, sobbing uncontrollably as I move into action, taking the knife out of his hands.

"Allie, it's okay, it's going to be okay."

I nod, my entire body shaking. I cut through the rope, feeling my body about to collapse with relief. I move onto the other, my mind on the task and not on what CJ is saying.

The second his hands are free, he takes the knife from me and pulls me into his arms, his face resting in the crook of my neck. The dam inside me breaks, and I cling to him, sobbing uncontrollably.

"Shh, Cupcake. Shh."

Sirens pierce the air and we pull apart, both turning to the door. "How?" he murmurs, and I glance down at my hoodie, now covered in blood, and thank God for Jordan.

"My phone is tucked into my bra," I whisper, and help him pull the rope from around his ankles, grateful the chair legs had snapped from his fall and I won't have to pick up the knife again.

"I love you, Allie. I love you so fucking much," he tells me fiercely.

I cry harder, and through my sobs, I tell him, "I love you too."

We glance at each other, relief that we're ok pouring out of us. When a look of terror and horror flashes across his face, I pull back, confused.

My hair gets pulled so hard I feel like it's ripping my scalp. I scream out, turning a little to see Alex, crazed and inhuman. Blood cakes his teeth, and half his scalp is missing and dented from where I hit him with the stool.

I freeze, incapable of doing anything but staring on in horror, not knowing what will happen.

Alex opens his mouth, but not one word or breath escapes. His eyes roll to the back of his head, and he slumps over me.

His body is covering mine, and it only takes a second for me to register it and start screaming, pushing him off me.

"Get him off me. Get him off me," I cry out.

He's rolled off me, and above me, CJ breathes heavily, sweat and blood covering him. I roll my head to the side, whimpering at the life-less eyes staring blankly back at me. A knife is sticking out of Alex's back—where his heart is.

He's dead.

He's gone.

"Game over," I whisper, unable to look away.

We don't get a moment to register what just happened, to comfort one another, before police are knocking the door down. CJ helps me sit up, keeping me steady in his arms.

I watch the scene before me, wondering how life got to this point. I think of how one person could destroy and take so many lives, without remorse or guilt, and get away with it for so long. Right under our noses.

A stab of guilt hits me for a split second for feeling like the world is a safer place now Alex is dead. He was my friend, someone I cared deeply for. But I can't seem to care. I'm glad he's dead. I'm glad he can no longer hurt another soul. But look at the cost. Look at how many lives have been ruined in the process.

I feel guilt for thinking about our future; a future where CJ doesn't have the stormy cloud of his past hanging over him or his mum. I should be thinking of Lilian, of the other six girls he murdered.

Justice has been served, their killer has been killed, but in the end, it doesn't bring any of them back. His death doesn't mean anything. Not really.

I lift my head from CJ's shoulder and watch his mouth move as he speaks to the paramedic, forgetting about everything else.

I might be selfish—heartless—but I'm just glad he's alive. Because if it came down to it, really down to a choice of who should have lived or died, I would have happily of died for him.

He's my everything.

My life.

Chapter 26

CJ

Life has a way of changing with a blink of an eye. Whether something incredibly amazing happens to you or something tragic, that moment can change the course of your life.

I always thought I knew how the world worked. There was good, there was bad, and there were good people who did bad things. I thought I understood how the human race worked. Experiencing first-hand the part of the world I didn't fully understand or comprehend has blinded all my senses.

On the news, you hear of horrific events; shootings, bombs, accidents, but you never fully feel what the victims are going through. You care, you're sad, but you never fully know what they went through or what they felt.

The world is a scary place. But until tonight, I never realised just how terrifying it could be.

I knew Alex Cliff. I ate with him, hung out with him, and I never saw the real him. Until tonight. He always came across as a geek, a geeky nerd who stuttered when spoken to, and seemed shy and distant. Never did I suspect he was a killer, that he had it in him to take the life of six people.

Six people we know about.

How could I have missed this?

I look down at Allie, feeling my eyes water. We got lucky tonight, so damn lucky it's hard to breathe.

For a moment, a split second, I truly believed I was going to lose her. When he came at me with that knife, all I could think about was him going after her next, suffering through his drivel and delusions. I pictured her stabbed, no longer a part of this world, and the thought alone is enough to send me crazy. It would tear out my heart. The world would be a darker place without her in it.

"Mr. Everhert, we need to get her into her own bed. You need to rest, to recover," Nurse Louise says, looking softly down at Allie. They've tried to move her since I was placed in this bed, but she's thrown a fit every single time, so to keep her calm, they let her stay—against their wishes. It feels like we've been here longer than an hour.

She's tucked into my side, fast asleep. She hasn't stopped clinging to me since it ended, and I wouldn't have it any other way. I need her next to me as much as she needs me next to her.

"She's not going anywhere."

She sighs. "The police would like to speak with you."

My heart sinks. "Because I killed him?"

She looks away, messing with the machines they've got me hooked up to. "I couldn't say."

I took a life. He might not have been innocent, but he was still a human being. And the sick part? I'd do it all over again to save Allie.

"Where's my son?" I hear my mum scream from down the corridor.

I sit up, glancing at Louise. "That's my mum. Can you tell her where I am?"

She looks up from my charts and nods. Seconds later, my mum comes running into the room, tears streaming down her face.

"Oh, my god, what happened to you?" she cries, eyes round. "They said you were taken and that you suffered knife injuries." She begins to sob, looking me over and wincing at my injuries. She looks down at my right, to Allie tucked into my side, and sniffles, wiping her nose. "Is she okay? What happened? I thought I lost you, CJ. I tried to get here as soon as I could, but I had to get a taxi. I wouldn't have been able to drive back from London without crashing."

"Mum, I'm fine," I croak out, squeezing her hand. I watch her for a minute, wondering how much they told her. "Did they tell you anything else?" I ask carefully.

"They told me you were taken by the maniac who was killing those poor innocent girls, and that her friend called them," she tells me, her eyes flicking to Allie.

Allie stirs in my arms, but she doesn't wake, too exhausted from today's events. I look back up at my mum, the person who has been my rock my whole life, and fill her in on everything, needing her to be strong once more. I tell her about Alex, about his fucked-up family and the delusions he had that Allie was his, that she was his sister. How he related a sibling to a lover.

Mum gasps, her hand covering her mouth. Her other hand hovers over my stab wound that the doctors stitched up not long after we arrived. "And he did this to you? Have they arrested him?"

I look away, unable to meet her eyes. "I killed him," I whisper.

Her hand twitches in mine. "What?"

I look at her, feeling my eyes water, and my throat clogs with emotion. "I killed him. He was going to kill her, Mum. I stabbed him in the back, where his heart is, and I killed him. I killed him," I grit out, feeling frustrated and angry. Frustrated because I felt so useless, felt useless and angry because I should have done something to prevent the whole thing. I should have watched my back in the library, worked harder to find him—something.

"Oh, my darling boy," Mum cries, leaning forward to kiss my forehead. Her lips lightly touch my skin, but I flinch, the sting too much even with all the pain meds they're feeding me.

"I killed him. I don't know how I'm going to come back from that, Mum."

I watch my mum transform from a crying mess to the mum I'm used to. She wipes her eyes, straightens her spine, and looks me dead in the eye.

"You will get back from this because you had no choice. He killed six girls, CJ. Do you think he wouldn't have killed you? Look at you; he tried to. He killed that girl in front of you. You did what you had to do to survive. And you have your friends and family around you—to support you and show you every day that what you did was the only option. And every time you look at Allie, you'll be reminded of what you saved—who you saved. That, my boy, is how you're going to get through this."

"I thought we were going to die, Mum. I kept thinking he'd kill me first, so I wouldn't be able to help her. She would have been all alone, Mum. How did social services or his nan's doctors not pick up on who he was, what he had inside him?"

"Maybe we can answer those questions?" a man standing at the door announces.

I watch as two uniformed police officers walk inside. I look away when Allie begins to stir, whimpering in her sleep.

"Please don't hurt him," she cries, tossing and turning. I wince from the pain, and slowly, with my bad arm, lightly stroke her cheek.

"Allie, Cupcake, you need to wake up. You're having a nightmare."

When her whimpering sounds painful, I shake her awake. She flinches, shooting up in bed. "Kill me, not him!" she screams.

My mum rushes around the bed, coming to her side. "Allie, it's okay. We're here."

"Cupcake, breathe," I instruct, wishing I could move my stiff body to hold her against me.

She looks around the room, disorientated. "We're in the hospital?"

Mum rubs her hand down her back. "You are. Do you remember what happened?"

My mum looks at Allie, and whatever she sees on her face... it fills her eyes with tears. "I remember everything."

"Everything will be okay, Allie. Your dad is on his way, and Willow, Cole, and the rest of them are in the waiting room. You aren't alone."

Allie nods and mum helps her lie back down. I wrap my good arm around her, pulling her against me and gritting through the pain. "I'm here; I've got you," I tell her. She nods absently, resting her head on my shoulder.

I look at the men in the room. "Can we help you?"

"We've just come to inform you no charges will be pressed against you, Mr. Everhert" he tells me gently, talking to me like I'm ten years old. I sag against the bed in relief. I don't regret killing him, but the thought of going to prison scared me.

I'm too fucking pretty.

"Do you know how he got away with this for so long? Allie told me about the state of his house and the condition his nan was in. His past was muddled with files after files—they were there for you to access. Why didn't you know it was him?"

If I'm remembering correctly, the man talking in front of me is Grady.

Guilt flashes across his face. "Name changing. There were so many surnames used it got lost in transaction. Alex changed his name—illegally—to Alex Cliff, his nan's maiden name. He was born Adam Forest, his mum was born Lane, and his uncle—or dad—was born Pearson. All of them changed their names more than once over the course of their lives."

"But how did no one pick up that he was a murderer, that he was messed up? After his mum killed his dad—I mean, step-dad—they should have made a case for him. He should have been seen."

"He was," Grady reveals, taking me aback.

"What?"

He looks to Allie, still in my arms. I look down at her, worried for her mental health. She still seems in shock—out of it.

"Are you sure you want me to discuss this now?"

I grit my teeth, fighting the urge to clench my hands into fists. "I think we have the right to know. He nearly killed us. He killed innocent girls. I think we deserve to know why nothing was done to prevent this, why he was left in the hands of someone incapable of caring for him."

"Now we know his real name, we've looked into it. His first diagnosis was when he was six. They diagnosed him with BPD—borderline personality disorder. It's a long-term pattern of abnormal behaviour, which was picked up and reported by the school he attended. He was never treated for it. In their reports, they stated Adam—I mean, Alex—couldn't, or wouldn't, form relationships with anyone in the school. The doctor who diagnosed him never followed up, but we're still questioning the parties involved."

"That's it?" I ask dryly, clearing my sore throat.

"No." He sighs, looking reluctant to answer. "When he was ten, after his parent's death, he was referred to a child psychologist by his social worker. That doctor also diagnosed him with BPD and noted he had sociopathic tendencies. We've yet to speak with her, but from her notes left in the social worker's case, he had crescent moon-shaped scars on his palms, was caught stabbing himself in the leg—whilst smiling—and had zero social skills. At ten years old he had already mastered the ability to manipulate those around him. He was removed from three children's home before they found his nan. There were incidents where other children were hurt, and his behaviour came up as odd and unusual."

"And none of them kept an eye on him after he went to live with his nan?" Allie asks. I hold her a little tighter, not realising she had been listening.

"He was twelve by the time he got put into the custody of Jessica Cliff. We had her down as a Jessica Lane. They both changed their names and disappeared altogether."

My mum clears her throat. "If he had stayed, received the medical care he needed, would this have turned out differently, would *he* have?"

Grady looks at my mum, shaking his head. "Professionally speaking, I can't say. It's hard to tell with cases like this. But in my personal opinion, I'd say no. I don't think anything would have changed when it came to him. He was diagnosed with BPD at a young age, that and the childhood trauma he was subjected to, the beliefs he had drilled into him... it was always going to be there for him. Sooner or later, he would have snapped."

"So why now? What made him snap now?" Allie asks.

Grady looks to me. "I think you. We found a diary in the house dating from last Halloween. Alex had mentioned Christie, the humiliation she inflicted on him that night and how he felt you mocked him. And from photos I saw in the house, I think Allie reminded him of his mother. That combined, I think he felt something was being taken away from him."

"She drugged him on Halloween, and Christie and her friends made fun of him. Is that why he killed her?" Allie says quietly.

"A lot of anger was written in that section, Allie. We still aren't sure why that night snapped something inside of him, but if I have to guess, from what I already know, I would say he felt vulnerable and bullied. He's not used to feeling emotion, and it brought out anger. We do know from an earlier entry that he found out who CJ was to him. He mentions overhearing you two talking about it."

"He knew who I was all along, then?"

Grady nods. "Yes."

"So, what now? Will you be arresting CJ? Because I hit him, too. I hit him over the head with a stool."

Grady steps forward, squeezing her foot. "Allie, calm down. We aren't arresting CJ. We still have a lot of investigating to do, but from CJ's statement, it's clear it was self-defence."

"You aren't going to take him away from me?" she asks, a sigh of relief escaping her. "He saved me."

"I'm not going anywhere, Cupcake," I whisper, kissing her forehead.

"We'll leave you to get some rest. A uniformed police officer will be by in the morning to get your statements. We just wanted to stop by and keep you updated."

I nod, watching them leave, and glance down at Allie.

Being arrested hadn't even crossed my mind. I've been too worried about Allie and facing the fact I took a life to even think about it.

But knowing I won't be held accountable is a huge relief. Because looking down at Allie, I can't picture my life without her.

It's just after midnight and Allie and I have been put into our own room, thanks to my mum. She wanted to give us privacy, since the doctors admitted the both of us to stay overnight.

Mum walks in with two cups of coffee. She hands Allie one, and I pout. "Where's mine?"

She leans over and kisses my forehead. "None for you. They told you to drink water and to eat something."

"I'm allowed food?" I ask, my mood brightening.

Allie laughs, shaking her head. "The doctor said it's fine, as long as you don't overeat."

I scoff. "I don't overeat."

"You do," Allie and Mum say simultaneously.

"Anyway, your dad is waiting for me outside. We're going to stay next door—in the hotel. Call me if you need anything."

"I will. Can you bring me something to eat in the morning? The food is crap here."

Mum nods. "I will. I promise. They have a McDonald's down the road, and a Greggs. Oh, and your friends are going to come in. They can't stay long, but under the circumstances, the nurse has agreed to let them in."

We both nod and say our goodbyes. It's not long before we hear feet stomping outside the room.

"Do you think they'll hate me?" I ask before they reach the door. "I'm part of the reason those girls were killed."

Allie moves, looking up at me. "I've blamed myself for so much, for so long, CJ. But it hasn't been until tonight that I realise we don't control the actions of others. We can factor in it, but we don't cause it. We aren't the ripple effect that sets something into motion. We didn't do anything to set Alex off. We didn't bully him, we didn't hurt him, and we certainly didn't raise him to be this person. All we did was be his friend."

I look down at her in awe. "When did you start making sense?"

She forces a smile, looking away. "From the moment I realised I'd never be able to live in a world you aren't in."

I lean in and capture her lips with a kiss.

The door pushes open and we pull away, taking in our friends stricken faces. Jordan is the first to enter the room, her face bright red and blotchy.

"I'm so fucking sorry. I butt answered your call and didn't realise until twenty minutes into it that something was wrong. I called the police straight away when I heard what Alex was saying. I'm so fucking sorry," she cries.

Allie sits up, pressing the button to our bed to sit us up higher. "You saved our lives, Jordan. Thank you."

Jordan looks stunned as she pauses at the end of the bed. The others file into the room, Willow, Rosie and Becca heading Allie's side and Cole to mine.

"What?"

"If you hadn't of phoned them, things might have turned out differently. The door in the room we were in was locked. And you gave me hope. I knew the phone call had connected; I knew you would be listening and get help. You saved us."

Jordan wipes under her eyes and Rosie wraps her arm around her waist, comforting her.

"How are you doing?" Cole asks, his eyes not focusing on one thing, but scanning everywhere. I know I look a mess. I have a bandage on my shoulder from my stab wound, and my face looks like Edward Scissorhands attacked it.

"A little banged up, but I'll get some cool scars after," I tell him lightly.

He tries to force a smile, but I can see my friend is worried and concerned for me. "Yeah, but Allie's immune to your ways, so you can't charm her with stories on how you got them," he teases, his jaw tensing.

My chuckle turns into a wince when it jars my shoulder. "She'll listen anyway, 'cause she loves me."

"I do," she whispers.

"Are you okay? How did you figure out it was Alex?" Willow asks.

I've been asking myself that same question. She's told me bits, but I think because she was in so much shock, she muddled everything up. She seems to be doing a lot better now, though, more with it.

"Tina called me from the library to say Alex had walked out of work. I went to check on him because I was worried something had happened to his nan. When I got there, I had to get his nan some tablets. I found a box of the ones the doctor mentioned caused my miscarriage. Then there were the photos; they were the same as the ones me and Jordan found when we were researching the murders and learned about the murder that happened fifteen years ago. That's when it all got too much for me and I went outside to get some fresh air and saw the building at the bottom of the garden. From there, it's all a blur."

"I was so worried. Jordan had stolen her sister's phone to call the police, and because she had to stay on the line with both of you, she ran all the way to ours. I was so scared for you. We heard everything—what he did. I'm so sorry this happened to you," Willow says, wiping her cheeks.

Allie stiffens next me. "It still doesn't feel real. I trusted him. He took so much from so many people, and for nothing."

Willow leans over to hug her. "Ah, where's mine. I'm the one who got stabbed."

When Willow looks up from hugging Allie, her eyes are filled with tears. "Thank you for being there for her."

I rear back, puzzled. "Um, kind of didn't have a choice. He hit me over the back of the head," I tell her dryly.

She chuckles, wiping her eyes. "But you saved her. We might not have been there in person, but we heard you. He attacked her."

She has no idea.

I look down at Allie, my lips pulling into the first real smile since everything happened. "She's the one who saved me," I whisper.

A new nurse walks in with her cart, not looking up from whatever she's reading on it. "Charles-Jay, it's time for your next dose of pain medication."

Everyone in the room stops what they're doing. Even the water-works and sniffles come to an end.

I groan inwardly, wishing they would sedate me so I don't have to subject myself to what is to come.

Slowly, so slowly, everyone's stunned faces turn to me, glancing at me with slack jaws.

Allie is the first to speak. "Your name is Charles-Jay?"

I glare at the nurse as she measures out what dosage to put in my tubes, before turning to answer Allie. "I didn't get a say in what my name would be. My mum was going through a tough time. She'd just delivered the world's most perfect baby."

"Charles?" Willow asks, still open-mouthed.

I close my eyes, groaning. "Yes, now can we move on to how great I am?"

"Charles?" Allie repeats, before bursting into a fit of laughter. The others follow, laughing uproariously.

Cole slaps me on the leg, smiling. "They were gonna find out sooner or later."

"Yeah, when it was printed on my gravestone," I mutter.

He chuckles. "At least they aren't crying now."

I glance at everyone in the room, then back at Cole. "They're crying with laughter—it's the same thing."

"Suck it up," Cole says, then chuckles at my murderous expression.

The pain meds start to kick in and I fight to stay awake. I can't go to sleep without explaining my mum's reasons for giving me such a crappy name.

Allie turns when she sees I'm fighting it. "Go to sleep, Charles, we'll be here when you wake up."

"Don't call me Charles," I croak out groggily.

I feel her lean in, her lips pressing against my ear. "I'm going to love you no matter what, Charles-Jay Everhert."

My head flops to the side, my mouth feeling like sandpaper. "Love you, my… Cupcake," I tell her, feeling myself sink into the darkness.

Epilogue
Six years later

ALLIE

Today's the day I open a new chapter in my life. It's the day I pledge myself to the love of my life. It's the day I've been dreaming about since CJ asked me to marry him six years ago, a few weeks after leaving the hospital.

The day finally is here, and I couldn't be happier.

I glance in the long-length mirror behind the door, running a hand down my white, silk dress.

"You make a beautiful bride," Milly says, leaning over my shoulder to kiss my cheek.

I look at her through the mirror, smiling. "Thank you. Is everything ready?"

"Nearly?"

I panic, turning to face her. "What do you mean, nearly?"

She giggles, taking both my hands in hers. "Calm down," she tells me, before facing the door. "Willow, come in now."

Willow, my maid of honour, walks in wearing her floor-length, dark green bridesmaid dress. She looks beautiful, and my eyes immediately go to her round bump under her dress. At eight months, she looks radiant. Pregnancy suits my best friend.

I glance from Willow to Milly, nervous about what's going on. "Has something happened?"

Willow chuckles. "No, we came to give you these," she tells me, and signals for Milly to go ahead.

I watch her pull a box out of her bag, handing it to me.

"This is something borrowed from me. They belonged to my nan," she tells me.

My eyes begin to water when I open the box, finding a matching pearl earrings and necklace set. "They're beautiful. Thank you," I tell her, feeling choked up.

She helps me put them on before stepping aside, letting Willow through. "This is something blue from me," she tells me, and hands me a tiny gift bag.

I look inside, laughing when I see the baby-blue garter inside. I pull it out and pass it to her. "Can you put it on? In these shoes I'm afraid I'll break an ankle."

She laughs, her eyes glancing to Milly for a second before nodding. "Sure."

I help lift my elegant but simple dress, cursing at the high-heeled shoes they made me wear. I can't walk for shit in them, but they don't seem to care.

I drop the dress when she's finished, and a thought occurs to me. "Wait, shouldn't there be something new, something borrowed, and something blue?"

"We thought we'd save the best till last," Willow answers, glancing at Milly.

I turn her way, grateful she stepped in with Mel to organise the wedding. Without those two, this day would have been impossible.

"This is something new, from CJ." She hands me a box and I sit down in the chair behind me to open it.

I gasp, no longer able to hold back the tears.

"Oh, no, don't cry," Milly panics, rushing to get me a tissue.

I pick up one of the Converse, smiling when I see our initials on the side of each shoe. On the inside is written, 'Our story isn't over'.

"CJ got these?" I ask, smiling wide.

Milly hands me a tissue. "It was a surprise. He knew you'd hate high heels, so he got these made for you."

"I nearly called our wedding off over those bloody high heels," I whisper.

Willow laughs. "We know. Now swap the shoes and let's get going. It's time."

I look up at Milly, smiling so wide my cheeks hurt. "I am going to love him for eternity."

She dabs her eyes with a tissue. "Now you're going to make me cry. Stop it."

"Let's go get me married."

"Let's get you married," Willow says, her smile just as wide as mine.

We change my shoes, and the second I stand in them, I feel relief. We've been together for nearly seven years, and he still never fails to amaze me. He's always thinking of me.

My dad is standing outside the door when we exit. He makes a choked sound in the back of his throat, his eyes filling with tears.

"You are the most beautiful bride I've ever seen."

I blush, running a hand down my dress. "Thank you."

"Are you ready?"

I glance up at him. "I was born ready."

He chuckles, then leads me down the hallway to the hall we're getting married in.

"Once the doors open, it's time," the organiser announces quietly next to me. We nod, and I stare at the door, willing it to open.

"Dad, don't let me fall," I whisper from the side of my mouth.

He looks down at me, happiness and pride shining in his eyes. "Never. And your husband-to-be would never let that happen, either."

Nervous jitters begin in the pit of my stomach when the doors open, the wedding march playing in the background.

I look to my dad, feeling an array of emotions. "I'm really getting married."

He smiles, lifting his arm up for me to take. "You are, and I couldn't be prouder."

"Go then," Willow whispers behind me, and I hear Rosie, Jordan and Becca start giggling.

I roll my eyes and take the first step.

The first step to forever.

The first step to a lifetime of happiness.

The first step of my new chapter.

The moment I lock eyes with CJ, I can't look away. He looks so handsome standing there with our daughter in his arms, rocking her to sleep.

Lena is nine months old and a real daddy's girl. I shouldn't be surprised she's in CJ's arms and not Mel's, who's she's supposed to be with.

His mouth drops open as he watches me. I bite my lip, blushing at the way he's looking at me.

Mel quietly takes Lena from him, but he doesn't seem to notice, his attention solely on me. I keep walking, feeling my legs pick up the pace, wanting to get to him quicker. My dad laughs and lengthens his stride to keep up with me.

When I reach him, I remember my cue and turn to face him. He looks me up and down, his eyes turning misty as he tries to hold back tears.

"You look devastatingly beautiful," he whispers hoarsely, taking my hands in his. The way he looks at me, right down into my soul, soothes me. "I'm going to love you in every lifetime."

I melt, feeling my body sway towards him, unable to say something, I'm that speechless.

There's no one out there who could love me more than CJ, and no one could love him more than I do.

We belong together; we're made for each other.

There's no one else I would want to spend the rest of my life with. No one but him.

And today we make it official.

Today we begin a new journey, one full of love, hope and happiness.

There's no greater joy than that.

THE END

If you enjoyed Game Over, please don't forget to leave a review. I enjoy reading your reviews, and I read ALL of them. They encourage me, motivate me, and help me know where I'm going right or wrong. Many readers choose to read a book recommended to them by a friend rather than from a Facebook post or ad, so if you liked the story, please do tell your friends on social media.

Also, if you wondering what happened to Mr. Flint, then keep an eye out for my next release. Almost Free will be releasing next.

Author's note

To my readers,

Game Over went down a different route to what people expected. A lot of you were prepared for an immature, loyal, alpha male that made a fool of himself every chance he got. With CJ, you get that and more.

I hope you enjoyed CJ and Allie's story, and that it wasn't too far out of your comfort zone.

I feel blessed every time I release a book. Knowing this is my 13th book truly amazes me. I get to do what I love every single day, and it's all thanks to you, my readers. You guys keep me going, keep me motivated and inspired. And for that, I'll be forever thankful.

If you're reading this note, it's you I'm thankful to. It's you who buys my books, who helps me continue writing.

Thank you.

Bloggers,

You guys are a godsend. I want to thank each and every one of you who took part in the cover reveal and release day. You guys are awesome.

Stephanie Farrant,

Without this psycho midget, this book would have taken longer to write. Not only did she edit my novel, but she helped me piece together the darker scenes. For someone so incredibly sweet and kind, she's kind of scary. But I love her for it.

Stephanie, you rock. Never change who you are or what you do because you are incredible at it. Most people excel at gymnastics, medicine, numbers etc., but you… you excel with words. You go above and beyond for me, and I'll be forever grateful.

You're amazing.

(But you're still a psycho midget, to me. And yes, that nickname is here to stay.)

Other Titles by Lisa Helen Gray

FORGIVEN SERIES
Better Left Forgotten

Obsession

Forgiven

CARTER BROTHERS SERIES
Malik

Mason

Myles

Evan

Max

Maverick

A NEXT GENERATION CARTER NOVEL SERIES
Faith

Aiden – Coming 2018

WHITHALL UNIVERSITY SERIES
Foul Play

Game Over ~ Out Now

Almost Free – Available soon

I WISH SERIES
If I Could I'd Wish It All Away

Wishing For A Happily Ever After

Wishing For A Dream Come True ~ Coming Soon

About the Author

Lisa Helen Gray is Amazon's best-selling author of the Forgotten Series and the Carter Brothers series.

She loves hanging out, but most of all, curling up with a good book or watching movies. When she's not being a mum, she's a writer and a blogger.

She loves writing romance novels with a HEA and has a thing for alpha males.

I mean, who doesn't!

Just an ordinary girl surrounded by extraordinary books.

Printed in Great Britain
by Amazon

36544147R00173